"You can take care of yourself, right? Never need any help."

"I wouldn't say that." Frankie opened her door and got out.

Hank swore and, throwing the pickup into Park, got out and went after her. "Frankie, wait."

She stopped and turned back to him.

"I don't know what your story is, but I do know this," he said. "You have closed yourself off for some reason. I recognize the signs because I've done it for the past three years. In your case, I suspect some man's to blame, the one who keeps calling. One question. Is he dangerous?"

She started to step away, but he grabbed her arm and pulled her back around to face him again.

"I'm fine. There is nothing to worry about."

He shook his head but let go of her arm. "You are one stubborn woman."

He couldn't help but smile because there was a strength and independence in her that he admired.

He'd never known a woman quite like her...

B.J. Daniels is a *New York Times* and *USA TODAY* bestselling author. She wrote her first book after a career as an award-winning newspaper journalist and author of thirty-seven published short stories. She lives in Montana with her husband, Parker, and three springer spaniels. When not writing, she quilts, boats and plays tennis. Contact her at bjdaniels.com, on Facebook or on Twitter, @bjdanielsauthor.

Books by B.J. Daniels

Harlequin Intrigue

Cardwell Ranch: Montana Legacy

Steel Resolve
Iron Will

Whitehorse, Montana: The Clementine Sisters

Hard Rustler
Rogue Gunslinger
Rugged Defender

The Montana Cahills

Cowboy's Redemption

Whitehorse, Montana: The McGraw Kidnapping

Dark Horse
Dead Ringer
Rough Rider

HQN Books

Sterling's Montana

Stroke of Luck
Luck of the Draw

Visit the Author Profile page at Harlequin.com.

B.J. DANIELS

NEW YORK TIMES AND USA TODAY
BESTSELLING AUTHOR

IRON WILL
&
JUSTICE AT
CARDWELL RANCH

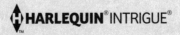
HARLEQUIN® INTRIGUE®

ISBN-13: 978-1-335-01670-6

Iron Will & Justice at Cardwell Ranch

Copyright © 2019 by Harlequin Books S.A.

The publisher acknowledges the copyright holder of the individual works as follows:

Iron Will
Copyright © 2019 by Barbara Heinlein

Justice at Cardwell Ranch
Copyright © 2012 by Barbara Heinlein

Recycling programs for this product may not exist in your area.

Printed in U.S.A.

www.Harlequin.com

This one is for Paula Morrison,
who believes like I do that if one schlep bag is a
great idea, then let's make a dozen. Thanks for
making Quilting by the Border quilt club so fun.

IRON WILL

Chapter One

Hank Savage squinted into the sun glaring off the dirty windshield of his pickup as his family ranch came into view. He slowed the truck to a stop, resting one sun-browned arm over the top of the steering wheel as he took in the Cardwell Ranch.

The ranch with all its log-and-stone structures didn't appear to have changed in the least. Nor had the two-story house where he'd grown up. Memories flooded him of hours spent on the back of a horse, of building forts in the woods around the creek, of the family sitting around the large table in the kitchen in the mornings, the sun pouring in, the sound of laughter. He saw and felt everything he'd given up, everything he'd run from, everything he'd lost.

"Been a while?" asked the sultry, dark-haired woman in the passenger seat.

He nodded despite the lump in his throat, shoved back his Stetson and wondered what the hell he was doing back here. This was a bad idea, probably his worst ever.

"Having second thoughts?" He'd warned her about his big family, but she'd said she could handle it. He wasn't all that sure even he could handle it. He prided

himself on being fearless about most things. Give him
a bull that hadn't been ridden and he wouldn't hesitate
to climb right on. Same with his job as a lineman. He'd
faced gale winds hanging from a pole to get the power
back on, braved getting fried more times than he liked
to remember.

But coming back here, facing the past? He'd never
been more afraid. He knew it was just a matter of time
before he saw Naomi—just as he had in his dreams, in
his nightmares. She was here, right where he'd left her,
waiting for him as she had been for three long years.
Waiting for him to come back and make things right.

He looked over at Frankie. "You sure about this?"

She sat up straighter to gaze at the ranch and him,
took a breath and let it out. "I am if you are. After all,
this was your idea."

Like she had to remind him. "Then I suggest you
slide over here." He patted the seat between them and
she moved over, cuddling against him as he put his free
arm around her. She felt small and fragile, certainly not
ready for what he suspected they would be facing. For
a moment, he almost changed his mind. It wasn't too
late. He didn't have the right to involve her.

"It's going to be okay," she said and nuzzled his neck
where his dark hair curled at his collar. "Trust me."

He pulled her closer and let his foot up off the brake.
The pickup began to roll toward the ranch. It wasn't that
he didn't trust Frankie. He just knew that it was only
a matter of time before Naomi came to him pleading
with him to do what he should have done three years
ago. He felt a shiver even though the summer day was
unseasonably warm.

I'm here.

Chapter Two

"Looking out that window isn't going to make him show up any sooner," Marshal Hud Savage said to his wife.

"I can't help being excited. It's been three years." Dana Cardwell Savage knew she didn't need to tell him how long it had been. Hud had missed his oldest son as much or more than she had. But finally Hank was coming home—and bringing someone with him. "Do you think it's because he's met someone that he's coming back?"

Hud put a large hand on her shoulder. "Let's not jump to any conclusions, okay? We won't know anything until he gets here. I just don't want to see you get your hopes up."

Her hopes were already up, so there was no mitigating that. Family had always been the most important thing to her. Having her sons all fly the nest had been heartbreak, especially Hank, especially under the circumstances.

She told herself not to think about that. Nothing was going to spoil this day. Her oldest son was coming home after all this time. That had to be good news. And he was bringing someone. She hoped that meant Hank was moving on from Naomi.

"Is that his pickup?" she cried as a black truck came into view. She felt goose bumps pop up on her arms. "I think that's him."

"Try not to cry and make a fuss," her husband said even as tears blurred her eyes. "Let them at least get into the yard," he said as she rushed to the front door and threw it open. "Why do I bother?" he mumbled behind her.

FRANKIE KNEW THE sixty-two-year-old woman who rushed out on the porch had to be Dana Cardwell Savage. Hank had told her about his family. She thought about the softness that came into his voice when he talked about his mother. She'd heard about Dana's strength and determination, but she could also see it in the way she stood hugging herself in her excitement and her curiosity.

Hank had warned her that him bringing home a woman would cause a stir. Frankie could see his mother peering inside the pickup, trying to imagine what woman had stolen her son's heart. She felt a small stab of guilt but quickly pushed it away as a man appeared behind Dana.

Marshal Hud Savage. She'd also heard a lot about him. When Hank had mentioned his dad, she'd seen the change not just in his tone, but his entire body. The trouble between the two ran deep. While Dana was excited, holding nothing back, Frankie could see that Hud was reserved. He had to worry that this wouldn't be a happy homecoming considering the way he'd left things with his oldest son.

Hank's arm tensed around her as he parked and cut the engine. She had the feeling that he didn't want to let her go. He finally eased his hold on her, then gave her a gentle squeeze. "We can do this, right? Ready?"

"As I will ever be," she said, and he opened his door. The moment he did, Dana rushed down the steps to throw her arms around her son. Tears streamed down her face unchecked. She hugged him, closing her eyes, breathing him in as if she'd thought she might never see him again.

Frankie felt her love for Hank at heart level. She slowly slid under the steering wheel and stepped down. Hud, she noticed, had descended the stairs, but stopped at the bottom, waiting, unsure of the reception he was going to get. Feeling for him, she walked around mother and son to address him.

"Hi, I'm Frankie. Francesca, but everyone calls me Frankie." She held out her hand, and the marshal accepted it in his large one as his gaze took her measure. She took his as well. Hud Savage was scared that this visit wasn't an olive branch. Scared that his son was still too angry with him. Probably more scared that he was going to let down his wife by spoiling this reunion.

"It's nice to meet you," the marshal said, his voice rough with what she suspected was emotion. A lot was riding on what would happen during this visit, she thought, and Hud didn't know the half of it.

"Frankie," Hank said behind her. His voice broke. "I want you to meet my mom, Dana."

She turned and came face-to-face with the ranch woman. Dana had been a beauty in her day; anyone could see that. But even in her sixties, she was still very attractive with her salt-and-pepper dark hair and soft, gentle features. She was also a force to be reckoned with. Dana eyed her like a mama bear, one who was sizing her up for the position of daughter-in-law.

Whatever Dana saw and thought of her, the next thing Frankie knew, she was being crushed in the woman's arms. "It is so wonderful to meet you," Dana was saying tearfully.

Behind her, Frankie heard Hud say hello to his son.

"Dad," Hank said with little enthusiasm, and then Dana was ushering them all into the house, telling her son that she'd baked his favorite cookies and made his favorite meal.

Frankie felt herself swept up in all of it as she told herself this would work out—even against her better judgment.

"Hank seems good, doesn't he," Dana said later that night when the two of them were in bed. She'd told herself that things had gone well and that once Hank was home for a while, they would get even better. She hadn't been able to ignore the tension between her son and husband. It made her heart ache because she had no idea how to fix the problem.

"He seems fine." Hud didn't look up from the crime novel he was reading.

"Frankie is pretty, isn't she."

"Uh-huh."

"She's not what I expected. Not really Hank's type, don't you think?"

Hud glanced over at her. "It's been three years since we've seen him. We have no idea what his type is. He probably doesn't know either. He's still young. I thought Naomi wasn't his type." He went back to his book.

"He's thirty-three, not all that young if he wants to

have a family," she said. "It's just that Frankie isn't anything like Naomi."

"Maybe that's the attraction."

She heard what he didn't say in his tone. *Maybe that's a blessing.* Hud had never thought Naomi was right for Hank. "I suppose it might be why he's attracted to her. I just never thought he'd get over Naomi."

Hud reached over and, putting down his book, turned out his bedside light. "Good night," he said pointedly.

She took the hint and switched off her own lamp as her husband rolled over, turning his back to her. Within minutes he would be sound asleep, snoring lightly, while she lay awake worrying. The worst part was that she couldn't put her finger on what made her anxious about Hank coming home now and bringing a young woman.

"He wants to move on, put Naomi and all that ugliness behind him, don't you think?" She glanced over at Hud's broad back, but knew he wasn't going to answer because he didn't have the answer any more than she did.

She was just glad that Hank was home for however long he planned to stay and that he wasn't alone anymore. "As long as he's happy…" Hud began to snore softly. She sighed and closed her eyes, silently mouthing her usual nightly prayers that her family all be safe and happy, and thanking God for bringing Hank home.

"It's beautiful here," Frankie said as she stood on the guest cabin deck overlooking the rest of the ranch in the starlight. The cabin was stuck back high against the mountain looking down on the ranch and the Gallatin River as it wound past. "I feel like I can see forever. Are those lights the town?" she asked as Hank joined her.

"Big Sky, Montana," he said with little enthusiasm.

She turned to him. "How do you think it went?"

He shook his head. "I'm just thankful that my mother listened to me and didn't have the whole family over tonight. But maybe it would have been less uncomfortable if they'd all been there. Tomorrow you'll meet my sister, Mary, and her fiancé, Chase."

"There's your uncle Jordan and aunt Stacy."

"And a bunch of my mother's cousins and their families," he said with a sigh.

She couldn't imagine having all that family. Her father had left when she was three. Her mother had married several times, but the marriages didn't last. Her mother had died in a car accident right after she'd graduated from high school, but they'd never been close. The only real family she'd ever felt she had was an uncle who'd become her mentor after college, but he was gone now too.

"You could just tell them the truth," she said quietly after a moment. She envied Hank his family, and felt lying to them was a mistake.

He shook his head. "This is difficult enough." He turned to go back inside. "You can have the first bedroom. I'll take the other one." With that, he went inside and closed the door.

Frankie stood on the deck, the summer night a fragrant blend of pine and water. There was just enough starlight that she caught glimpses of it shining off the surface of the river snaking through the canyon. Steep, rocky cliffs reflected the lights of the town, while the mountains rose up into the midnight-blue star-filled canopy.

She felt in awe of this ranch and his family. How could Hank have ever left it behind? But the answer seemed to be on the breeze as if everything about this place was inhabited by one woman. Naomi. She was what had brought Hank home. She was also why Frankie was here.

Chapter Three

Hank rose before the sun and made his way down the mountainside to the corral. He'd missed the smell of saddle leather and horseflesh. He was breathing it in when he heard someone approaching from behind him.

He'd always been keenly aware of his environment. Growing up in Montana on a ranch, he'd learned at a young age to watch out for things that could hurt you— let alone kill you—in the wild. That instinct had only intensified in the years he'd been gone as if he felt a darkness trailing him, one that he could no longer ignore.

"You're up early," he said to his father without turning around as Hud came up behind him.

"I could say the same about you. I thought you and I should talk."

"Isn't that what we did at dinner last night?" Hank asked sarcastically. His father hadn't said ten words. Instead his mother had filled in the awkward silences.

"I'm glad you came back," Hud said.

He turned finally to look at his father. The sun glowed behind the mountain peaks to the east, rimming them with a bright orange glow. He studied his father in the dim light. They were now both about the same height, both with broad shoulders and slim hips. Both stubborn to a fault. Both never backing down from a fight. He stared at the marshal, still angry with him after all these years.

"I'm not staying long."

Hud nodded. "That's too bad. Your mother will be disappointed. So am I. Son—"

"There really isn't anything to talk about, is there? We said everything we had to say three years ago. What would be the point of rehashing it?"

"I stand by what I did."

Hank laughed. "I'd be shocked if you didn't." He shook his head. "It must be wonderful to know that you're always right."

"I'm not always right. I just do the best I can with the information and evidence I have."

"Well, you're wrong this time," he said and turned back to the horses. One of the mares had come up to have her muzzle rubbed. Behind him, he heard his father head back toward the house and felt some of the tension in his chest release even as he cursed under his breath.

DANA HAD INSISTED on making them breakfast. After a stack of silver-dollar-sized pancakes swimming in butter and huckleberry syrup, a slab of ham, two eggs over easy and a tall glass of orange juice, Frankie sat back smiling. She couldn't remember the last time she'd eaten so much or liked it more.

No matter what happened on this visit to the ranch, she planned to enjoy herself as much as was possible.

"I thought dinner was amazing," she told Dana. Hank's favorite meal turned out to be roast beef, mashed potatoes, carrots and peas and homemade rolls. "But this breakfast… It was so delicious. I never eat like this."

"I can tell by your figure," her host said, beaming. Clearly Dana equated food with love as she looked to her son to see if he'd enjoyed it. He'd cleaned his plate, which seemed to make her even happier. "So, what do you two have planned today?"

"I thought I'd show Frankie around Big Sky," Hank said.

"Well, it's certainly changed since you were here," his mother said. "I think you'll be surprised. Will you two be back for lunch? Your father still comes home every day at twelve."

"I think we'll get something in town, but thanks, Mom. Thanks for everything."

Tears filled her eyes and her voice broke when she spoke. "I'm just glad to have you home. Now, plan on being here for supper. Your dad's doing steaks on the grill and some of the family is stopping by. Not everyone. We don't want to overwhelm Frankie."

"I appreciate that," he said.

Frankie offered to help with the dishes, but Dana shooed them out, telling them to have a fun day.

Fun was the last thing on the agenda, she thought as she left with Hank.

HANK HAD BEEN restless all morning, but he'd known that he couldn't get away from the house without having one of his mother's breakfasts. The last thing he wanted to do was hurt her feelings. It would be bad enough when she learned the truth.

Pushing that thought away, he concentrated on his driving as he headed downriver. He'd grown up with the Gallatin River in his backyard. He hadn't thought much about it until Frankie was doing her research and asked him, "Did you know that the Gallatin River begins in the northwest corner of Yellowstone National Park to travel one hundred and twenty miles through the Gallatin Canyon past Big Sky to join the Jefferson and Madison Rivers to form the Missouri River?"

That she found this so fascinating had surprised him. "I did know that," he told her and found himself studying her with renewed interest. The river had been part of his playground, although he'd been taught to have a healthy respect for it because of the current, the deep holes and the slippery rocks.

Now as he drove along the edge of the Gallatin as it cut through the rocky cliffs of the canyon, he caught glimpses of the clear green water rushing over granite boulders on its way to the Gulf of Mexico and felt a shiver because he'd learned just how deadly it could be.

A few miles up the road, he slowed to turn onto a dirt road that wound through the tall pines. Dust rose behind the pickup. He put down his window and breathed in the familiar scents. They made his heart ache.

Ahead, he could see the cliffs over the top of the pines. He parked in the shade of the trees and sat for a moment, bracing himself.

"This is the place?" Frankie whispered, her gaze on the cliff that could be seen over the top of the pines.

He didn't answer as he climbed out. He heard her exit the pickup but she didn't follow him as he walked down through the thick pines toward the river, knowing he needed a few minutes alone.

An eerie silence filled the air. When he'd first gotten out of the truck, he'd heard a squirrel chatting in a nearby tree, a meadowlark calling from the tall grass, hoppers buzzing as they rose with each step.

But now that he was almost to the spot, there was no sound except the gentle lap of the water on the rocks. As he came out of the pines, he felt her—just as he always had. Naomi. It was as if her soul had been stranded here in this very spot where she'd died.

His knees went weak and he had to sit down on one of the large boulders along the shore. He put his head in his hands, unaware of time passing. Unaware of anything but his pain.

Like coming out of a daze, he lifted his head and looked across the river to the deep pool beneath the cliff. Sunlight glittered off the clear emerald surface. His heart in his throat, he lifted his gaze to the rock ledge high above the water. Lover's Leap. That was what it was called.

His gaze shifted to the trail from the bridge downriver. It was barely visible through the tall summer grass and the pines, but he knew that kids still traveled along it to the ledge over the water. The trick, though, was to jump out far enough. Otherwise…

A shaft of sun cut through the pine boughs that hung out over the water, nearly blinding him. He closed his eyes again as he felt Naomi pleading with him to find out the truth. He could feel her arguing that he knew her. He knew she was terrified of heights. She would never have gone up there. Especially alone. Especially at night. Why would she traverse the treacherous trail to get to the rock ledge to begin with—let alone jump?

It had made no sense.

Not unless she hadn't jumped to her death. Not unless she'd been pushed.

Hank opened his eyes and looked up through the shaft of sunlight to see a figure moving along the narrow trail toward the rock ledge high on the cliff. His throat went dry as shock ricocheted through him. He started to call to her even as he knew it was his mind playing tricks on him. It wasn't Naomi.

He opened his mouth, but no sound came out and he stared frozen in fear as he recognized the slim figure. Frankie. She'd walked downriver to the bridge and, after climbing up the trail, was now headed for the ledge.

HUD HEAVED HIMSELF into his office chair, angry at himself on more levels than he wanted to contemplate. He swore as he unlocked the bottom drawer of his desk and pulled out the file. That he'd kept it for three years in the locked drawer where he could look at it periodically was bad enough. That he was getting it out now and going over it as he'd done so many times over those years made it even worse.

He knew there was nothing new in the file. He could practically recite the report by heart. Nothing had changed. So why was he pulling it out now? What good would it do to go over it again? None.

But he kept thinking about Hank and his stubborn insistence that Naomi hadn't committed suicide. He didn't need a psychiatrist to tell him that suicide was the most perverse of deaths. Those left behind had to deal with the guilt and live with the questions that haunted them. Why hadn't they known? Why hadn't they helped? Why had she killed herself? Was it because of them? It was the why that he knew his son couldn't accept.

Why would a beautiful young woman like Naomi Hill kill herself? It made no sense.

Hud opened the file. Was it possible there was something he'd missed? He knew that wasn't the case and yet he began to go over it, remembering the call he'd gotten that morning from the fisherman who'd found her body in the rocks beneath Lover's Leap.

There had been little doubt about what had happened. Her blouse had caught on a rock on the ledge, leaving a scrap of it fluttering in the wind. The conclusion that she'd either accidentally fallen or jumped was later changed to suicide after more information had come in about Naomi's state of mind in the days before her death.

Add to that the coroner's report. Cause of death: skull crushed when victim struck the rocks below the cliff after either falling or jumping headfirst.

But his son Hank had never accepted it and had never forgiven his father for not investigating her death longer, more thoroughly. Hank had believed that Naomi hadn't fallen or jumped. He was determined that she'd been murdered.

Unfortunately, the evidence said otherwise, and Hud was a lawman who believed in facts—not conjecture or emotion. He still did and that was the problem, wasn't it?

Chapter Four

Hank felt dizzy and sick to his stomach as he watched Frankie make her way out to the edge of the cliff along the narrow ledge. She had her cell phone in her hand. He realized she was taking photos of the trail, the distance to the rocks and water below as well as the jagged rocky ledge's edge.

As she stepped closer to the edge, he heard a chunk of rock break off. It plummeted to the boulders below, and his heart fell with it. The rock shattered into pieces before dropping into the water pooling around the boulders, making ripples that lapped at the shore.

He felt his stomach roil. "Get down from there," he called up to her, his voice breaking. "Please." He couldn't watch. Sitting down again, he hung his head to keep from retching. It took a few minutes before his stomach settled and the need to vomit passed. When he looked up, Frankie was no longer balanced on the ledge.

His gaze shot to the rocks below, his pulse leaping with the horrible fear that filled him. There was no body on the rocks. No sign of Frankie. He put his head back down and took deep breaths. He didn't know how long he stayed like that before he heard the crunch of pine needles behind him.

"I'm sorry," Frankie said. "I should have known that would upset you."

He swore and started to get to his feet unsteadily. She held out a hand and he took it, letting her help him up. "I'm usually not like this."

She smiled. "You think I don't know that?"

"You should have told me you were going up there," he said.

"You would have tried to stop me," she said and pulled out her phone. "I needed to see it." She looked up from her screen. "Have you been up there?"

"Not since Naomi died, no."

She frowned, cocking her head. "You've jumped from there."

"When I was young and stupid."

Nodding, Frankie said, "You have to push off the cliff wall, throw your body out to miss the rocks and to land in the pool. Daring thing to do."

"Helps if you're young, stupid and with other dumb kids who dare you," he said. "And before you ask, yes, Naomi knew I'd jumped off the ledge. She was terrified of heights. She couldn't get three feet off the ground without having vertigo. It's why I know she didn't climb up there on her own. Someone made her."

"Sometimes people do things to try to overcome fears," Frankie said and shrugged.

"Naomi didn't. She was terrified of so many things. Like horses. I tried to teach her to ride." He shook his head. "I'm telling you, she wouldn't have climbed up there unless there was a gun to her head. Even if she'd wanted to kill herself, she wouldn't have chosen that ledge as her swan song."

With that, he turned and started toward the truck,

wishing he'd never come back here. He'd known it would be hard, but he hadn't expected it to nearly incapacitate him. Had he thought Naomi would be gone? Her soul released? Not as long as her death was still a mystery.

Frankie didn't speak again until they were headed back toward Big Sky. "At some point you're going to have to tell me why your father doesn't believe it was murder."

"I'll do one better. I'll get a copy of the case file. In the meantime, I'll show you Big Sky. I'm not ready for my parents to know the truth yet."

She nodded and leaned back as if to enjoy the trip. "I timed how long it took me to walk up the trail from the bridge to the ledge. Eleven minutes. How long do you think it would have taken Naomi?"

"Is this relevant?"

"It might be." She turned to look at him then. "You said the coroner established a time of death because of Naomi's broken wristwatch that was believed to have smashed on the rocks. We need to examine the time sequence. She left you at the ranch, right? The drive to the cliff took us ten minutes. She could have beat that because at that time of the evening in early fall and off season, there wouldn't have been as much traffic, right?"

He nodded.

"So if she left the ranch and went straight to the bridge—"

"She didn't. She met her killer at some point along the way. Maybe she stopped for gas or… I don't know. Picked up a hitchhiker."

Frankie shot him a surprised look. "From what you've told me about Naomi, she wouldn't have stopped for a hitchhiker."

"It would have had to be someone she knew. Can we

stop talking about this for just a little while?" He hated the pleading in his voice. "Let me show you around Big Sky, maybe drive up to Mountain Village."

She nodded and looked toward the town as he slowed for the turn. "So Big Sky was started by Montana native and NBC news co-anchorman Chet Huntley. I read it is the second-largest ski resort in the country by acreage." She gazed at Lone Mountain. "That peak alone stands at over eleven thousand feet."

He glanced over at her and chuckled. "You're like a walking encyclopedia. Do you always learn all these facts when you're…working?"

"Sure," she said, smiling. "I find it interesting. Like this canyon. There is so much history here. I've been trying to imagine this road when it was dirt and Yellowstone Park only accessible from here by horses and wagons or stagecoaches."

"I never took you for a history buff," he said.

She shrugged. "There's a lot you don't know about me."

He didn't doubt that, he thought as he studied her out of the corner of his eye. She continued to surprise him. She was so fearless. So different from Naomi. Just the thought of her up on that ledge— He shoved that thought away as he drove into the lower part of Big Sky known as Meadow Village. His mother was right. Big Sky had changed so much he hardly recognized the small resort town with all its restaurants and fancy shops along with miles of condos. He turned up the road to Mountain Village, where the ski resort was located, enjoying showing Frankie around. It kept his mind off Naomi.

"So you met the woman Hank brought home?"

Dana looked up at her sister, Stacy. They were in the

ranch house kitchen, where Dana was taking cookies out of the oven. "I thought you might have run into them this morning before they took off for some sightseeing."

Her sister shook her head. Older than Dana, Stacy had been the wild one, putting several marriages under her belt at a young age. But she'd settled down after she'd had her daughter, Ella, and had moved back to the ranch to live in one of the new cabins up on the mountainside.

"I stopped over at their cabin this morning to see if they needed anything," Stacy said now, avoiding her gaze.

Dana put her hands on her hips. She knew her sister so well. *"What?"*

Stacy looked up in surprise. "Nothing to get in a tizzy over, just something strange."

"Such as?"

"I don't want to be talking out of turn, but I noticed that they slept in separate bedrooms last night." Her sister snapped her lips shut as if the words had just sneaked out.

Dana frowned as she put another pan of cookie dough into the oven and, closing the door, set the timer. Hadn't she felt something between Hank and Frankie? Something not quite right? "They must have had a disagreement. I'm sure it is difficult for both of them being here after what happened with Naomi. That's bound to cause some tension between them."

"Probably. So, you like her?"

"I do. She's nothing like Naomi."

"What does that mean?" Stacy asked.

"There's nothing timid about her. She's more self-assured, seems more…independent. I was only around her for a little while. It's just an impression I got. You remember how Naomi was."

Her sister's right brow shot up. "You mean scared of everything?"

Dana had been so surprised the first time Hank had brought Naomi home and the young woman had no interest in learning to ride a horse.

I would be terrified to get on one, she'd said.

Naomi isn't...outdoorsy, was the way Hank had described her. That had been putting it mildly. Dana couldn't imagine the woman living here. As it turned out, living at Cardwell Ranch was the last thing Naomi had in mind.

"Frankie looks as if she can handle herself. I saw Hank gazing at her during dinner. He seems intrigued by her."

"I can't wait to meet her," Stacy said now.

"Why don't you come to dinner? Mary's going to be here, and Chase. Jordan and Liza are coming as well. I thought that was enough for one night." Her daughter and fiancé would keep things light. Her brother and his wife would be a good start as far as introducing Frankie to the family.

"Great. I'll come down early and help with the preparations," her sister said. "I'm sorry I mentioned anything about their sleeping arrangements. I'm sure it's nothing."

FRANKIE LOOKED OUT at the mountain ranges as she finished the lunch Hank had bought them up at the mountain resort. This was more like a vacation, something she hadn't had in years. She would have felt guilty except for the fact that technically she *was* working. She looked at the cowboy across the table from her, remembering the day he'd walked into her office in Lost Creek outside of Moscow, Idaho.

"Why now?" Frankie had asked him after he'd wanted to hire her to find out what had really happened to his girlfriend. "It's been three years, right? That makes it a cold case. I can't imagine there is anything to find." She'd seen that her words had upset him and had quickly lifted both hands in surrender. "I'm not saying it's impossible to solve a case that old…" She tried not to say the words *next to impossible*.

She'd talked him into sitting down, calming down and telling her about the crime. Turned out that the marshal—Hank's father—had sided with the coroner that the woman's death had been a suicide. She'd doubted this could get worse because it was clear to her that Hank Savage had been madly in love with the victim. Talk about wearing blinders. Of course he didn't want to believe the woman he loved had taken a nosedive off a cliff.

"I thought I could accept it, get over it," Hank had said. "I can't. I won't. I have to know the truth. I know this is going to sound crazy, but I can feel Naomi pleading with me to find her murderer."

It didn't sound crazy as much as it sounded like wishful thinking. If this woman had killed herself, then he blamed himself.

Her phone had rung. She'd checked to see who was calling and declined the call. But Hank could tell that the call had upset her.

"Look, if you need to take that…" he'd said.

"No." The last thing she wanted to do was take the call. What had her upset was that if she didn't answer one of the calls from the man soon, he would be breaking down her door. "So, what is it you want me to do?"

Hank had spelled it out for her.

She'd stared at him in disbelief. "You want me to go to Big Sky with you."

"I know it's a lot to ask and this might not be a good time for you."

He had no idea how good a time it was for her to leave town. "I can tell this is important for you. I can't make you any promises, but I'll come out and look into the incident." She'd pulled out her standard contract and slid it across the table with a pen.

Hank hadn't even bothered to read it. He'd withdrawn his wallet. "Here's five hundred dollars. I'll pay all your expenses and a five-thousand-dollar bonus if you solve this case—along with your regular fee," he'd said, pushing the signed contract back across the table to her. As the same caller had rung her again, Hank had asked, "When can you leave?"

"Now's good," she'd said.

Chapter Five

Frankie had tried to relax during dinner later that night at the main ranch house, but it was difficult. She now understood at least the problem between Hank and his father. From what she could gather, the marshal was also angry with his son. Hank had refused to accept his father's conclusion about Naomi's death. The same conclusion the coroner had come up with as well.

Hank thought his father had taken the easy way out. But Frankie had been around Hud Savage only a matter of hours and she knew at gut level that he wasn't a man who took the easy way out. He believed clear to his soul that Naomi Hill had killed herself.

During dinner, Hank had said little. Dana's sister, Stacy, had joined them, along with Dana's daughter, Mary, and her fiancé, Chase, and Dana's brother, Jordan, and wife, Liza. Hank had been polite enough to his family, but she could tell he was struggling after going to the spot where Naomi had died.

She'd put a hand on his thigh to try to get him to relax and he'd flinched. The reaction hadn't gone unnoticed by his mother and aunt Stacy. Frankie had smiled and snuggled against him. If he hoped to keep their secret longer, he needed to be more attentive. After all, it was

his idea that they pretend to be involved in a relationship. That way Frankie could look into Naomi's death
without Hank going head-to-head with his father.

When she'd snuggled against him, he'd felt the nudge
and responded, putting an arm around her and pulling
her close. She'd whispered in his ear, "Easy, sweetie."

Nodding, he'd laughed, and she'd leaned toward him
to kiss him on the lips. It had been a quick kiss meant
to alleviate any doubt as to what was going on. The kiss
had taken him by surprise. He'd stared into her eyes for
a long moment, then smiled.

When Frankie had looked up, she'd seen there was
relief on his mother's face. His mother had bought it.
The aunt, not so much. But that was all right. The longer they could keep their ruse going, the better. Otherwise it would be war between father and son. They both
wanted to avoid that since it hadn't done any good three
years ago. Frankie doubted it would now.

"Cake?" Dana asked now, getting to her feet.

"I would love a piece," Frankie said. "Let me help
you." She picked up her plate and Hank's to take them
into the kitchen against his mother's protests. "You out-
did yourself with dinner," she said as she put the dishes
where the woman suggested.

Taking advantage of the two of them being alone with
the door closed, Dana turned to her—just as Frankie
had known she would. "I'm not being nosy, honestly. Is
everything all right between you and Hank?"

She smiled as she leaned into the kitchen counter.
She loved this kitchen with the warm yellow color, the
photographs of family on the walls, the clichéd saying carved in the wood plaque hanging over the door.
There was a feeling of permanency in this kitchen, in

this house, this ranch. As if no matter what happened beyond that door, this place would weather the storm because it had survived other storms.

"It's hard on him being back here because of Naomi," Frankie said.

"Of course it is," Dana said on a relieved breath. "But he has you to help him through it."

She smiled and nodded. "I'm here for him and he knows it. Though it has put him on edge. But not to worry. I'll stand by him."

Tears filled the older woman's eyes as she quickly stepped to Frankie and threw her arms around her. "I can't tell you how happy I am that Hank has you."

She hadn't thought her generic words would cause such a response but she hugged Dana back, enjoying for a moment the warm hug from this genuine, open woman.

Dana stepped back, wiping her tears as Stacy and Jordan's wife, Liza, came in with the rest of the dirty dishes and leftover food. "We best get that cake out there or we'll have a riot on our hands," Dana said. "If you take the cake, I'll take the forks and dessert plates."

"I'M SORRY," HANK SAID when they reached their cabin and were finally alone again. Dinner had been unbearable, but he knew he should have played along better than he had. "You were great."

"Thanks. Your mother was worried we were having trouble. I assured her that coming back here is hard on you because of Naomi. Your family is nice," she said. "They obviously love you."

He groaned. He hated lying to his mother most of all. "That's what makes this so hard. I wanted to burst out with the truth at dinner tonight." He could feel her gaze on him.

"Why didn't you?"

Hank shook his head. He thought about Frankie's kiss, her nuzzling against him. He'd known it would be necessary if they hoped to pass themselves off as a couple, but he hadn't been ready for it. The kiss had taken him by surprise. And an even bigger surprise had been his body's reaction to it, to her.

He turned away, glad it was late so they could go to bed soon. "I think I'm going to take a walk. Will you be all right here by yourself?"

She laughed. "I should think so since I'm trained in self-defense and I have a license to carry a firearm. You've never asked, but I'm an excellent shot."

"You have a gun?" He knew he shouldn't have been surprised and yet he was. She seemed too much like the girl next door to do the job she did. Slim, athletic, obviously in great shape, she just kept surprising him as to how good she was at this.

If anyone could find out the truth about Naomi, he thought it might be her.

AFTER HANK LEFT, Frankie pulled out her phone and looked again at the photographs she'd taken earlier from the ledge along the cliff. Standing up there being buffeted by the wind, her feet on the rocky ledge, she'd tried to imagine what Naomi had been thinking. If she'd had time to think.

Hank was so sure that she'd been murdered. It was such a strange way to murder someone. Also, she suspected there were other reasons his father believed it was suicide. The killer would have had to drag her up that trail from the bridge and then force her across the ledge. Dangerous, since if the woman was that terrified of heights, she would have grabbed on to her killer for dear life.

How had the killer kept her from pulling him down with her? It had been a male killer, hadn't it? That was what Frankie had imagined. Unless the couple hadn't gone up to the ledge with murder in mind.

Frankie rubbed her temples. People often did the thing you least expected them to do. Which brought her back to suicide. What if Hank was wrong? What if suicide was the only conclusion to be reached after this charade with his family? Would he finally be able to accept it?

The door opened and he came in on a warm summer night gust of mountain air. For a moment he was silhouetted, his broad shoulders filling the doorway. Then he stepped into the light, his handsome face twisted in grief. Her heart ached for him. She couldn't imagine the kind of undying love he'd felt for Naomi. Even after three years, he was still grieving. She wondered at the size of Hank's heart.

"I'd like to talk to Naomi's mother in the morning," she said, turning away from such raw pain. "Lillian Brandt, right?"

"Right." His voice sounded hoarse.

"It would help if you told me about the things that were going on with Naomi before her death, the things that made the coroner and your father believe it was a suicide." When he didn't answer, she turned. He was still standing just inside the door, his Stetson in the fingers of his left hand, his head down. She was startled for a moment and almost stepped to him to put her arms around him.

"There's something I haven't told you." He cleared

his throat and looked up at her. "Naomi and I had a fight that night before she left the ranch." He swallowed.

She could see that this was going to take a while and motioned to the chairs as she turned and went into the small kitchen. Opening the refrigerator, she called over her shoulder, "Beer?" She pulled out two bottles even though she hadn't heard his answer and returned to the small living area.

He'd taken a seat, balancing on the edge, nervously turning the brim of his hat in his fingers. When she held out a beer, he took it and tossed his hat aside. Twisting off the cap, Frankie sat in the chair opposite him. She took a sip of the beer. It was icy cold and tasted wonderful. It seemed to soothe her and chase away her earlier thoughts when she'd seen Hank standing in the doorway.

She put her feet up on the well-used wooden coffee table, knowing her boots wouldn't be the first ones that had rested there. She wanted to provide an air of companionship to make it easier for him to tell her the truth. She'd learned this from her former cop uncle who'd been her mentor when she'd first started out.

"What did you fight about?" she asked as Hank picked at the label on his beer bottle with his thumb without taking a drink.

"It was stupid." He let out a bitter laugh as he lifted his head to meet her gaze. "I wasn't ready to get married and Naomi was." His voice broke again as he said, "She told me I was killing her."

Frankie took a drink of her beer before asking, "How long had you been going out?" It gave Hank a moment to collect himself.

He took a sip of his beer. "Since after college. We

met on a blind date. She'd been working as an elementary school teacher, but said she'd rather be a mother and homemaker." He looked away. "I think that's what she wanted more than anything. Even more than me."

She heard something in his voice, in his words. "You didn't question that she loved you, did you?"

"No." He said it too quickly and then shook his head. "I did that night. I questioned a lot of things. She seemed so…so wrong for me. I mean, there was nothing about the ranch that she liked. Not the horses, the dust, the work. I'd majored in ranch management. I'd planned to come home after college and help my folks with the place."

"And that's what you were doing."

He nodded. "But Naomi didn't want to stay here. She didn't like the canyon or living on my folks' place. She wanted a home in a subdivision down in Bozeman. In what she called 'civilization with sidewalks.'" He shook his head. "I had no idea sidewalks meant that much to her before that night. She wanted everything I didn't."

"What did she expect you to do for a living in Bozeman?"

"Her stepfather had offered me a job. He was a Realtor and he said he'd teach me the business." Hank took a long pull on his beer. "But I was a rancher. This is where I'd grown up. This is what I knew how to do and what I…"

"What you loved."

His blue eyes shone as they locked with hers. She saw that his pain was much deeper than even she'd thought. If Naomi had committed suicide, then he blamed himself because of the fight. He'd denied her what she wanted most, a different version of him.

"So she left hurt and angry," Frankie said. "Did she

indicate where she was going? I'm assuming the two of you were living together here at the ranch."

"She said she was going to spend the night at her best friend Carrie White's apartment in Meadow Village here at Big Sky and that she needed time to think about all of this." He swallowed again. "I let her go without trying to fix it."

"It sounds like it wasn't an easy fix," Frankie commented and finished her beer. Getting up, she tilted the bottle in offer. Hank seemed to realize he still had a half-full bottle and quickly downed the rest. She took both empties to the kitchen and came back with two more.

Handing him one, she asked, "You tried to call her that night or the next morning?" As she asked the question, she knew where his parents would have stood on the marriage and Naomi issue. They wouldn't want to tarnish their son's relationship because of their opinions about his choice for a partner, but they also wouldn't want him marrying a woman who was clearly not a good match for him. One who took him off the ranch and the things he loved.

"That night, I was in no mood to discuss it further, so I waited and called her the next morning." He opened his beer and took a long pull. "Maybe if I'd called not long after she left—"

"What had you planned to say?" she asked, simply curious. It was a moot point now. Nor had his plans had anything to do with what happened to Naomi. By then, she was dead.

"I was going to tell her that I'd do whatever she wanted." He let out a long sigh and tipped the beer bottle to his lips. "But when she didn't answer, I changed my mind. I realized it wasn't going to work." His voice broke again. "I loved her, but she wanted to make me over, and I couldn't be the man she wanted me to be." His eyes narrowed. "You can dress me up, but underneath I'm still just a cowboy."

"Did you leave her a message on her phone?"

He nodded and looked away, his blue eyes glittering with tears. "I told her goodbye, but by then it would have been too late." His handsome face twisted in pain.

Frankie sat for a moment, considering everything he'd told her. "Was her cell phone found on her body or in her car?"

He shook his head. "Who knows what she did with it. The phone could have gone into the river. My father had his deputies search for it, but it was never found." His voice broke. "Maybe I did drive her to suicide," he said and took a drink as if to steady himself.

"I'm going to give you my professional opinion, for what it's worth," she said, knowing he wasn't going to like it. "I don't believe she killed herself. She knew that you loved her. She was just blowing off some steam when she headed for her friend's house. Did her friend see her at all?"

He shook his head.

"So she didn't go there. That would explain the discrepancy in the time she left you and when her watch was broken. Is there somewhere else she might have gone? Another friend's place? A male friend's?"

His eyes widened in surprise. "A male friend's? Why would you even ask about—"

"Because I know people. She was counting on you to change and do what she wanted, but after four years?

She would have realized it was a losing battle and had someone else waiting in the wings."

He slammed down his beer bottle and shoved to his feet. "You make her sound like she was—"

"A woman determined to get married, have kids, stay home and raise them while her husband had a good job that allowed all her dreams to come true?"

"She wasn't—she—" He seemed at a loss for words.

"Hey, Hank. Naomi was a beautiful woman who had her own dreams." He had showed her a photograph of Naomi. Blonde, green-eyed, a natural beauty.

Ignoring a strange feeling of jealousy, Frankie got to her feet and finished her beer before she spoke. She realized that she'd probably been too honest with him. But someone needed to be, she told herself. It wasn't just the beer talking. Or that sudden stab of jealousy when she'd thought of Naomi.

In truth, she was annoyed at him because she knew that if he'd reached Naomi on the phone that night, he would have buckled under. He would have done whatever she wanted, including marrying her. On some level, he would have been miserable and resented her the rest of his life, but being the man he was, he would have made the best of it. Naomi dying had saved him and he didn't even realize it.

"We need to find the other man," Frankie said as she took her bottle to the recycling bin before turning toward the bedroom.

Hank let out a curse. "You're wrong. You're dead wrong. I don't know why I—"

She cut off the rest of his words as she closed the bedroom door. She knew he was angry and probably ready to fire her. All she could hope was that he would cool down by the morning and would trust that she knew what she was talking about. Oh, she'd known women like Naomi all her life—including her very own mother, who chewed up men and spit them out one after another as they disappointed her. That was the problem with trying to make over a man.

HANK COULDN'T SLEEP. He lay in the second bedroom, staring up at the ceiling, cursing the fact that he'd brought Frankie here. What had he been thinking? This had to be the stupidest idea he'd ever come up with. Clearly, she didn't get it. She hadn't known Naomi.

Another man?

He thought about storming into her bedroom, telling her to pack her stuff and taking her back to Idaho tonight. Instead, he tossed and turned, getting more angry by the hour. He would fire her. First thing in the morning, he'd do just that.

Who did she think she was, judging Naomi like that? Naomi was sweet, gentle, maybe a little too timid… He rolled over and glared at the bedroom door. Another man in the wings! The thought made him so angry he could snap off nails with his teeth.

As his blood pressure finally began to drop somewhere around midnight, he found himself wondering if Naomi's friend Carrie knew more than she'd originally told him. If there had been another man—

He gave that thought a hard shove away. Naomi had loved him. Only him. She'd wanted the best for him. He rolled over again. She thought she knew what was best for him. He kicked at the blanket tangled around his legs. Maybe if she had lived she would have realized that what was best for him, for them, was staying on the ranch, letting him do what he knew and loved. Sidewalks were overrated.

Staring up at the ceiling, he felt the weight of her death press against his chest so hard that for a moment he couldn't breathe.

You don't want to let yourself believe that she committed suicide because you feel guilty about the argument you had with her before she left the ranch, his father had said. *Son, believe me, it took more than some silly argument for her to do what she did. We often don't know those closest to us or what drives them to do what they do. This wasn't your fault.*

Hank groaned, remembering his father's words three years ago. Could he be wrong about a lot of things? He heard the bedroom door open. He could see Frankie silhouetted in the doorway.

"If there is another man, then it would prove that she didn't commit suicide," the PI said. The bedroom door closed.

He glared at it for a long moment. Even if Frankie had gone back to her bedroom and locked the door, he knew he could kick it down if he wanted to. But as Frankie's words registered, he pulled the blanket up over him and closed his eyes, exhausted from all of this. If there had been another man, then he would be right about her being murdered.

Was that supposed to give him comfort?

Chapter Six

"I told my mother that we were having breakfast in town," Hank said when Frankie came out of the bedroom fully dressed and showered the next morning. He had his jacket on and smelled of the outdoors, which she figured meant he'd walked down to the main house to talk to his mother.

"I'm going to take a shower," he said now. "If you want to talk to Naomi's mother, we need to catch her before she goes to work." With that, he turned and went back into his bedroom.

Frankie smiled after him. He was still angry but he hadn't fired her. Yet.

She went into the kitchen and made herself toast. Hank didn't take long in the shower. He appeared minutes later, dressed in jeans and a Western shirt, his dark, unruly hair still damp at his collar as he stuffed on his Stetson and headed for the door. She followed, smiling to herself. It could be a long day, but she was glad she was still employed for numerous reasons, number one among them, she wanted to know now more than ever what had happened to Naomi Hill.

Lillian Brandt lived in a large condo complex set back against a mountainside overlooking Meadow Village. She'd married a real-estate agent after being a single mother for years, from what Hank had told her. Big Sky was booming and had been for years, so Lillian had apparently risen in economic stature after her marriage compared to the way she'd lived before Naomi died.

From her research, Frankie knew that Big Sky, Montana, once a ranching area, had been nothing more than a sagebrush-filled meadow below Lone Mountain. Then Chet Huntley and some developers had started the resort. Since then, the sagebrush had been plowed up to make a town as the ski resort on the mountain had grown.

But every resort needed workers, and while million-dollar houses had been built, there were few places for moderate-income workers to live that they could afford. The majority commuted from Gallatin Gateway, Four Corners, Belgrade and Bozeman—all towns forty miles or more to the north.

Lillian was younger than Frankie had expected. Naomi had been four years younger than Hank. Frankie estimated that Lillian must have had her daughter while in her late teens.

"Hank?" The woman's pale green eyes widened in surprise. "Are you back?"

"For a while," he said and introduced Frankie. "Do you have a minute? We won't take much of your time."

Lillian looked from him to Frankie and back before she stepped aside to let them enter the condo. It was bright and spacious with no clutter. It could have been one of the models that real-estate agents showed prospective clients. "I was just about to leave to go to the office." She worked for her husband as a secretary.

"I just need to ask you a few questions," he said as she motioned for them to take a seat.

"Questions?" she asked as she moved some of the pillows on the couch to make room for them.

"About Naomi's death."

The woman stopped what she was doing to stare at him. "Hank, it's been three years. Why would you dig all of it back up again?"

"Because he doesn't believe she killed herself," Frankie said and supplied her business card. "I didn't know your daughter, but I've heard a lot about her. I'm sorry for your loss, ma'am." Then she asked if it would be okay if Mrs. Brandt would answer a few questions about her daughter. "She was twenty-six, right? Hank said she was ready to get married."

Lillian slumped into one of the chairs that she'd freed of designer pillows and motioned them onto the couch. "It's all she wanted. Marriage, a family."

"Where was she working at the time of her death?" Frankie asked.

"At the grocery store, but I can't see what that—"

She could feel Hank's gaze on her. "Is that where she met her friend Carrie?"

Lillian nodded. Her gaze went to Hank. "Why are you—"

"I'm curious," Frankie said, drawing the woman's attention back again. "Was there anyone else in her life?"

"You mean friends?"

"Yes, possibly a male friend," Frankie said.

The woman blinked before shooting a look at Hank. "She was in love with Hank."

"But she had to have other friends."

Lillian fiddled with the piping along the edge of the chair arm. "Of course she had other friends. She made friends easily."

"I'm sure she did. She was so beautiful," Frankie said.

The woman nodded, her eyes shiny. "She got asked out a lot all through school."

"Do you remember their names?"

Lillian looked at Hank. "She was faithful to you. If that's what this is about—"

"It's not," Hank assured her.

"We just thought they might be able to fill in some of the blanks so Hank can better understand what happened to Naomi. He's having a very hard time moving on," Frankie said.

The woman looked at Hank, sympathy in her gaze. "Of course. I just remember her mentioning one in particular. His name was—" she seemed to think for a moment "—River." She waved her hand wistfully. "Blame it on Montana, these odd names."

"You probably don't remember River's last name," Frankie said.

"No, but Carrie might. She knew him too." Lillian looked at her watch. "I really have to go. I'm sorry."

"No," Frankie said, getting to her feet. "You've been a great help."

"Yes," Hank agreed with much less enthusiasm. "Thank you for taking the time."

"It's good to see you," the woman said to him and patted his cheek. "I hope you can find some peace."

"Me too," he said as he shared a last hug with Mrs. Brandt before leaving.

HANK CLIMBED BEHIND the wheel, his heart hammering in his chest. "You aren't going to give up on your other man theory, are you?"

"No, and you shouldn't either," Frankie said from the passenger seat.

He finally turned his head to look at her. Gritting his teeth, he said, "You think she was cheating on me? Wouldn't that give me a motive for murder?"

"I don't think she was cheating. I said she had someone waiting in the wings. Big Sky is a small town. I suspect that if she'd been cheating on you, you would have heard."

"Thanks. You just keep making me feel better all the time."

"I didn't realize that my job was to make you feel better. I thought it was to find a killer."

He let out a bark of a laugh. "You are something, you know that?"

"It's been mentioned to me. I'm hungry. Are you going to feed me before or after we visit Naomi's best friend, Carrie?"

"I'm not sure I can do this on an empty stomach, so I guess it's going to be before," he said as he started the pickup's engine.

"Over breakfast, you can tell me about Carrie," she said as she buckled up.

"I don't know what you want me to tell you about her," he grumbled, wishing he'd gone with his instincts last night and stormed into her bedroom and fired her. Even if he'd had to kick down the door.

"Start by telling me why you didn't like her."

He shot her a look as he pulled away from the condo complex. "What makes you think...?" He swore under his breath. "Don't you want to meet her and decide on your own?"

"Oh, I will. But I'm curious about your relationship with her."

Hank let out a curse as he drove toward a local café off the beaten path. The place served Mexican breakfasts, and he had a feeling Frankie liked things hot. She certainly got him hot under his collar.

It wasn't until they were seated and had ordered—he'd been right about her liking spicy food—that he sat back and studied the woman sitting across from him.

"What?" she asked, seeming to squirm a little under his intent gaze.

"Just that you know everything about me—"

"Not everything."

"—and I know nothing about you," he finished.

"That's because this isn't about me," she said and straightened her silverware. He'd never seen her nervous before. But then again, he'd never asked her anything personal about herself.

"You jumped at this case rather fast," he said, still studying her. She wasn't the only one who noticed things about people. "I suspect it was to avoid whoever that was who kept calling you." He saw that he'd hit a nerve. "Angry client? Old boyfriend?" He grinned. "Old boyfriend."

"You're barking up the wrong tree."

"Am I? I don't think so." He took her measure for the first time since he'd hired her. She was a very attractive woman. Right now her long, dark hair was pulled back into a low ponytail. Sans makeup, she'd also played down the violet eyes. And yet there was something sexy and, yes, even sultry about her. Naomi wouldn't leave the house without her makeup on.

That thought reminded him of all the times he'd stood around waiting for her to get ready to go out.

This morning Frankie was more serious, more professional, more hands-off. Definitely low-maintenance in a simple T-shirt and jeans. Nothing too tight. Nothing too revealing.

And yet last night at dinner when she'd snuggled against him, he'd felt her full curves. Nothing could hide her long legs. Right now, he could imagine her contours given that she was slim and her T-shirt did little to hide the curve of her backside.

"Why isn't a woman who looks like you married?" he asked, truly surprised.

"Who says I'm not?"

He glanced at her left hand. "No ring."

She smiled and looked away for a moment. "Isn't it possible I'm just not wearing mine right now?"

Hank considered that as the waitress brought their breakfasts. "*Are* you married?" he asked as the waitress left again.

"No. Now, are you going to tell me why you didn't like Naomi's best friend or are you going to keep stalling?"

Chapter Seven

Johnny Joe "J.J." Whitaker tried the number again. Frankie hadn't been picking up, but now all his calls were going to voice mail. Did she really think he would quit calling? The woman didn't know him very well if she did. That was what made him so angry. She *should* know him by now. He wasn't giving up.

He left another threatening message. "Frankie, you call me or you're going to be sorry. You know I make good on my threats, sweetheart. Call me or you'll wish you had."

He hung up and paced the floor until he couldn't take it anymore. She had to have gotten his messages. She had to know what would happen if she ignored him.

He slammed his fist down on the table, and the empty beer bottles from last night rattled. One toppled over, rolled across the table and would have fallen to the floor if he hadn't caught it.

"Frankie, you bitch!" he screamed, grabbing the neck of the bottle. He brought the bottle down on the edge of the table.

The bottom end of the bottle broke off, leaving a lethal jagged edge below the neck in his hand. He held it up in the light and imagined what the sharp glass could do to a person's flesh. Frankie thought he was dangerous?

He laughed. Maybe it was time to show her just how dangerous he could be.

CARRIE WHITE HAD gotten married not long after Naomi died, Hank told her on the way over to the woman's house. She had been about Naomi's age, and they'd met at the grocery store where Naomi had worked. Carrie had worked at one of the art shops in town. They became friends.

"Was she a bad influence?" Frankie asked.

Hank shrugged. "I don't know."

"How was Carrie with men?"

"She always had one or two she was stringing along, hoping one of them would pop the question."

Frankie laughed. "Is this why you didn't like her?"

"I never said I didn't like her. I just didn't think she was good for Naomi. You have to understand. Naomi was raised by her mother. Her father left when she was six. It devastated her. Lillian had to go to work and raise her alone without any more education than a high school diploma."

"So they didn't have much money?"

"Or anything else. Naomi wanted more and I don't blame her for that."

"Also Naomi didn't want to end up like her," Frankie supposed.

"She wanted a husband, a family, some stability. When her mother started dating the real-estate agent, she wanted that for us."

"Seems pretty stable at the ranch," Frankie said.

"I would have been working for my parents. Naomi

couldn't see how I would ever get ahead since even if they left me the ranch, I still have a sister, Mary, and two younger brothers, Brick and Angus. I could see her point. She wanted her own place, her own life, that wasn't tied up with my family's."

Frankie held her tongue. The more she found out about Naomi, the more she could see how she would not have been in the right place emotionally to be involved in a serious relationship. But she was having these thoughts because the more she learned about Hank, the more she liked him.

"So Carrie encouraged her how?"

Hank seemed to give that some thought as he pulled up in front of a small house in a subdivision in Meadow Village. "Carrie encouraged her to dump me and find someone else, someone more…acceptable. Carrie married a local insurance salesman who wears a three-piece suit most days unless he's selling to out-of-staters, and then he busts out his Stetson and boots."

Frankie got the picture. She opened her door, anxious to meet Carrie White and see what she thought of her for herself. She heard Hank get out but could tell that he wasn't looking forward to this.

At the front door, Frankie rang the bell. She could hear the sound of small running feet, then a shriek of laughter followed by someone young bursting into tears.

"Knock it off!" yelled an adult female voice.

She could hear someone coming to the door. It sounded as if the person was dragging one of the crying children because now there appeared to be at least two in tears just on the other side of the door.

"Naomi's dream life?" she said under her breath to Hank. The woman who opened the door with a toddler on one arm and another hanging off her pants leg looked harried and near tears herself. Carrie was short, dark-haired and still carrying some of her baby weight. She frowned at them and said, "Whatever you're offering, I'm not inter—" Her voice suddenly broke off at the sight of Hank. Her jaw literally dropped.

"Fortunately, we aren't selling anything," Frankie said.

"We'd just like a minute of your time," Hank said as the din died down. The squalling child hanging off Carrie's leg was now staring at them, just like the toddler on her hip. "Mind if we come in?"

The woman shot a look at Frankie, then shrugged and shoved open the screen door. "Let me just put them down for their morning naps. Have a seat," she said over her shoulder as she disappeared down a hallway.

The living room looked like a toy manufacturing company had exploded and most of the toys had landed here in pieces. Against one wall by the door was a row of hooks. Frankie noticed there were a half-dozen sizes of coats hanging there.

They waded through the toys, cleaning off a space on the couch to sit down. In the other room they could hear cajoling and more crying, but pretty soon, Carrie returned.

Frankie could see that she'd brushed her hair and put on a little makeup in a rush and changed her sweatshirt for one that didn't have spit-up on it. The woman was making an effort to look as if everything was fine. Clearly the attempt was for Hank's benefit.

"It's so good to see you," Carrie said to him, still looking surprised that he'd somehow ended up on her couch.

Frankie guessed that things had not been good be-

tween Carrie and Hank after Naomi's death. It seemed
Carrie regretted that.

"How have you been?" she asked as she cleared toys
off a chair and sat down. She looked exhausted and the
day was early.

"All right," he said. "We need to ask you some questions."

The woman stiffened a little. She must have thought
this was a social call. "Questions about what?"

"I understand you didn't see or hear from Naomi
the night she died," Frankie said. Carrie looked at her
and then at Hank.

He said, "This is Frankie, a private investigator. She's
helping me find out what happened that night."

The woman turned again to her, curiosity in her gaze,
but she didn't ask about their relationship. "I've told
you everything I know," she said to Hank before turning back to Frankie. "I didn't hear from her or see her.
I told the marshal the same thing."

"Were you planning to?"

The question seemed to take Carrie off guard. "I
can't…" She frowned.

"Hadn't your best friend told you that she was going
to push marriage that night and if Hank didn't come
around…"

The woman's eyes widened. "I wouldn't say she was
pushing marriage exactly. It had been four years! How
long does it take for a man to make up his mind?" She
slid a look at Hank and flushed a little with embarrassment.

"How long did it take your husband?"

Carrie ran a hand through her short hair. "Six months."

Frankie eyed her, remembering the coats hanging on the hooks by the door. "Were you pregnant?"

The woman shot to her feet, her gaze ricocheting back to Hank. "I don't know what this is about, but—"

"She was your best friend. You knew her better than anyone," Frankie said, also getting to her feet. "She would have told you if there was someone else she was interested in. I'm guessing she planned to come back to your place that night if things didn't go well. Unless you weren't such good friends."

Carrie crossed her arms. "She was my *best* friend."

"Then she would have told you about River."

That caught the woman flat-footed. She blinked, looked at Hank again and back to Frankie. "It was Hank's own fault. He kept dragging his feet."

She nodded. "So Naomi must have called to tell you she was on her way."

Carrie shook her head. "I told you. I didn't see her. I didn't hear from her. When I didn't, I just assumed everything went well. Until I got the call the next morning from her mother."

Frankie thought the woman was telling the truth. But Naomi would have called someone she trusted. Someone she could pour her heart out to since she left the ranch upset. "Where can we find River?"

HANK SWORE AS he climbed into his pickup. "I don't want to go see River Dean," he said as Frankie slid into the passenger seat.

"After Naomi left you, she would have gone to one of two places. Carrie's to cry on her shoulder. Or someone else's shoulder. If the man waiting in the wings was River Dean, then that's where she probably went.

Which means he might have been the last person to see her alive. If he turned her down as well, maybe she did lose all hope and make that fatal leap from the cliff. You ready to accept that and call it a day?"

Without looking at her, Hank jerked off his Stetson to rake a hand through his hair. "You scare me."

"She wanted to get married and have babies and a man who came home at five thirty every weekday night and took off his tie as she gave him a cocktail and a kiss and they laughed about the funny things the kids had done that day. It's a fantasy a lot of people have."

He stared at her. "But not you."

She shrugged.

"Because you know the fantasy doesn't exist," he said, wanting to reach over and brush back a lock of dark hair that had escaped from her ponytail and now curled across her cheek.

"I'm practical, but even I still believe in love and happy-ever-after."

Surprised, he did reach over and push back the lock of hair. His fingertips brushed her cheek. He felt a tingle run up his arm. Frankie caught his hand and held it for a moment before letting it go. He could see that he'd invaded her space and it had surprised her. It hadn't pleased her.

"You said you wanted the truth," she reminded him, as if his touching her had been an attempt to change the subject. "Have you changed your mind?"

RIVER DEAN OWNED a white-water rafting company that operated downriver closer to what was known as the Mad Mile and House Rock, an area known for thrills and spills.

Frankie could still feel where Hank's fingertips had brushed her cheek. She wanted to reach up and rub the spot. But she resisted just as she had the shudder she'd felt at his sudden touch.

Hank got out of the pickup and stopped in front of a makeshift-looking building with a sign that read WHITE-WATER RAFTING.

The door was open, and inside she could see racks of life jackets hanging from the wall. A motorcycle was parked to one side of the building. Someone was definitely here since there was also a huge stack of rafts in the pine trees, only some of them still chained to a tree. It was early in the day, so she figured business picked up later.

All she could think was that Naomi was foolish enough to trade ranch life for this? A seasonal business determined by the weather and tourists passing through? But maybe three years ago, River Dean had appeared to have better options. And if not, there was always Naomi's stepfather and the real-estate business.

Hank stood waiting for her, staring at the river through the pines. She felt the weight of her cell phone and her past. She'd turned off her phone earlier, but now she pulled it out and checked to see that she had a dozen calls from the same number. No big surprise. She didn't even consider checking voice mail since she knew what she'd find. He'd go by the office and her apartment—if he hadn't already. He would know that she'd left town. She told herself he wouldn't be able to find her even if he tried. Unfortunately, he would try, and if he got lucky somehow…

"You ready?" Hank said beside her.

She pocketed her phone. "Ready as *you* are."

He chuckled at that and started toward the open door of the white-water rafting business. She followed.

The moment she walked in she spotted River Dean. She'd known men like him in Idaho. Good-looking ski bums, mountain bikers, river rafters. Big Sky resembled any resort area with its young men who liked to play.

River Dean was tanned and athletically built with shaggy, sexy blond hair and a million-dollar smile. She saw quickly how a woman would have been attracted to him. It wasn't until she approached him that she could tell his age was closer to forty than thirty. There were lines around his eyes from hours on the water in sunshine.

Hank had stopped just inside the door and was staring at River as if he wanted to rip his throat out.

"You must be River," she said, stepping in front of Hank. River appeared to be alone. She got the feeling that he'd just sent some employees out with a couple of rafts full of adventure seekers.

"Wanting a trip down the river?" he asked, grinning at her and then Hank. His grin faded a little as if he recognized the cowboy rancher Naomi had been dating.

"More interested in your relationship with Naomi Hill," Frankie said.

"You a…cop?" he asked, eyeing her up and down.

"Something like that. Naomi came to see you that night, the night she died."

River shook his head. "I don't know who you are, but I'm not answering any more of your questions."

"Would you prefer to talk to the sheriff?" Frankie snapped.

"No, but…"

"We're just trying to find out what happened to her.

I know she came to see you. She was upset. She needed someone to talk to. Someone sympathetic to her problem."

River rubbed the back of his neck for a moment as he looked toward the open door and the highway outside. She could tell he was wishing a customer would stop by right now.

"We know you knew her," Hank said, taking a threatening step forward.

River was shaking his head. "It wasn't like that. I was way too old for her. We were just friends. And I swear I know nothing about what happened to her."

"But she did stop by that night," Frankie repeated.

The river guide groaned. "She stopped by, but I was busy."

"Busy?" Hank said.

"With another woman." Frankie nodded since she'd already guessed that was what must have happened. "Did you two argue?"

"No." He held up his hands. "I told her we could talk the next day. She realized what was going on and left. That was it," River said.

Hank swore. "But you didn't go to the sheriff with that information even though you might have been the last person to see her alive."

"I wasn't why she jumped," River snapped. "If you're looking for someone to blame, look in the mirror, man. You're the one who was making her so unhappy."

Frankie could see that Hank wanted to reach across the counter and thump the man. She stepped between them again. "Tell me what was said that night."

River shook his head. "It was three years ago. I don't

remember word for word. She surprised me. She'd never come by before without calling.".

Behind her, Frankie heard Hank groan. River heard it too and looked worried. Both men were strong and in good shape, but Hank was a big cowboy. In a fight, she had no doubt that the cowboy would win.

"It's like I just told you. She was upset before she saw what was going on. I told her she had to leave and that we'd talk the next day. She was crying, but she seemed okay when she left."

"This was at your place? Where was that?"

"I was staying in those old cabins near Soldiers' Chapel. Most of them have been torn down since then."

"Did you see her leave?" Frankie asked. "Could she have left with anyone?"

River shook his head and looked sheepish. "Like I said. I thought she was all right. I figured she was looking for a shoulder to cry on over her boyfriend and that she'd just find someone else to talk to that night."

"Was there someone you thought she might go to?" she asked.

River hesitated only a moment before he said, "Her friend Carrie maybe? I don't know."

Chapter Eight

"You should have let me hit him," Hank said as he slipped behind the wheel and slammed the door harder than he'd meant to.

"Violence is never the answer."

He shot her a look. "You read that in a fortune cookie?" He couldn't help himself. He couldn't remember the last time he was this angry.

He saw Frankie's expression and swore under his breath. "Yes, I'd prefer to blame River Dean rather than the dead woman I was in love with. You have a problem with that?"

She said nothing, as if waiting for his anger to pass. His father had warned him that digging into Naomi's death would only make him feel worse. He really hated it when his father was right—and Hud didn't even know that was what he was doing.

He drove back to the ranch, his temper cooled as he turned into the place.

"I had no idea about what was going on with Naomi," he said, stating the obvious. "You must think me a fool."

Frankie graced him with a patient smile as he drove down the road to the ranch house. "She loved you, but you both wanted different things. Love doesn't always overcome everything."

"Don't be nice to me," he said gruffly, making her laugh. Her cell phone rang. She checked it as if surprised that she'd left it on and quickly turned it off again.

"You're going to have to talk to him sometime," Hank said, studying her.

"Is there anyone else you want to go see?"

He shook his head, aware that she'd circumvented his comment as he parked at the foot of the trail that led to their cabin on the mountainside. "I need to be alone for a while, Frankie. Is that all right?"

"Don't worry about me."

He smiled at her. "You can take care of yourself, right? Never need any help."

"I wouldn't say that." She opened her door and got out.

He swore and, after throwing the pickup into Park, got out and went after her. "Frankie, wait."

She stopped and turned back to him.

"I don't know what your story is, but I do know this," he said. "You have closed yourself off for some reason. I recognize the signs because I've done it for the past three years. In your case, I suspect some man's to blame, the one who keeps calling. One question. Is he dangerous?"

She started to step away, but he reached for her arm and pulled her back around to face him again. "I'm fine. There is nothing to worry about."

He shook his head but let go of her arm. "You are one stubborn woman." He couldn't help but smile because there was a strength and independence in her that he admired. He'd never known a woman quite like her. She couldn't have been more different from Naomi, who he'd always felt needed taking care of. Just the thought of

Naomi and what he'd learned about her before she died was like a bucket of ice water poured over him. He took a step away, needing space right now, just like he'd told her.

"I'll see you later." With that, he turned to his pickup and drove off, looking back only once to see Frankie standing in the ranch yard, a worried expression on her face.

"Nothing to worry about, huh?" he said under his breath.

As FRANKIE TURNED toward their cabin on the mountain, she saw movement in the main house and knew that their little scene had been witnessed. They didn't appear to be a loving couple. She didn't know how much longer they could continue this ruse before someone brought it up.

But this was the way Hank wanted it. At least for the time being. She felt guilty, especially about his mother. Dana wanted her son to move on from Naomi's death and find some happiness. Frankie wasn't sure that was ever going to happen.

She hated to admit it to herself, but the moment Hank had told her about the problems they'd been having, she'd nailed the kind of young woman Naomi had been.

The weight of her cell phone in her pocket seemed to mock her. She was good at figuring out *other* people, but not so good when it came to her own life.

"Frankie!" She turned at the sound of Dana's voice. The older woman was standing on the ranch house porch, waving at her. "Want a cup of coffee? I have cookies."

She couldn't help but laugh as she started for the main house. Dana wanted to talk and she was using cookies as a bribe. Frankie called her on it the moment she reached the porch.

"You've found me out," Dana said with a laugh. "I'll stoop to just about anything when it comes to my son."

"I understand completely," she said, climbing the steps to the porch. "Hank is a special young man."

"Yes, I think he is," the woman said as she shoved open the screen door. "I thought we could talk."

Frankie chuckled. "I had a feeling." She stepped inside, taking in again the Western-style living room with its stone fireplace, wood floors, and Native American rugs adjacent to the warm and cozy kitchen. She liked it here, actually felt at home, which was unusual for her. She often didn't feel at home at her own place.

"I never asked," Dana said as she filled two mugs with coffee, handed one to Frankie and put a plate of cookies on the table. "How did you two meet?" She motioned her into a chair.

Hank hired me to pretend to be his girlfriend. "At a bar." It was the simplest answer she could come up with. She wondered why she and Hank hadn't covered this part. They should have guessed at least his mother would ask.

"Really? That surprises me. I've never known Hank to be interested in the bar scene and he isn't much of a drinker, is he?" Dana let out an embarrassed laugh. "I have to keep reminding myself that he's been gone three years. Maybe I don't really know my son anymore."

Frankie chuckled and shook her head. "Hank only came into the bar to pick up some dinner. Apparently it had been a long day at work and he'd heard that we served the best burgers in Idaho. I just happened to be working that night, and since it was slow, we got to talking. A few days later, he tracked me down because I was only filling in at the bar. A friend of mine owns it. Anyway, Hank asked me out and the rest is history."

It was pure fiction, but it was what she saw Dana needed to hear. Hank was no bar hound. Still, she felt guilty even making up such a story. It would have been so much easier to tell the truth. But her client had been adamant about them keeping the secret as long as they could.

Dana took a sip of her coffee and then asked, "So when not helping a friend, what do you do?"

"I'm a glorified secretary for a boss who makes me work long hours." That at least felt like the truth a lot of days. "Seriously, I love my job and my boss is okay most of the time. But I spend a lot of time doing paperwork."

"Oh my, well, you must be good at it. I'm terrible at it. That's why it is such a blessing that our Mary stayed around and does all of the accounting for the ranch."

"These cookies are delicious," Frankie said, taking a bite of one. "I would love your recipe." The diversion worked as she'd hoped. Dana hopped up to get her recipe file and began to write down the ingredients and explain that the trick was not to overbake them.

"So you cook," Dana said, kicking the conversation off into their favorite recipes. Frankie had no trouble talking food since she did cook and she had wonderful recipes that her grandmother had left her.

Frustrated and angry at himself and Naomi, Hank drove out of the ranch, not sure where he was going. All he knew was that he wanted to be alone for a while.

But as he turned onto the highway, he knew exactly where he was headed. Back to the river. Back to the cliff and the ledge where she'd jumped. Back to that deep, dark, cold pool and the rocks where her body had been found.

He knew there was nothing to find there and yet he couldn't stay away. It was one of the reasons he'd left after Naomi died. That and his grief, his unhappiness, his anger at his father.

After pulling off the road, he wound back into the pines and parked. For a moment he sat behind the wheel, looking out at the cliff through the trees. What did he hope to find here? Shaking his head, he climbed out and walked through the pines to the rocky shore of the river. Afternoon sunlight poured down through the boughs, making the surface of the river shimmer.

A cool breeze ruffled his hair as he sat down on a large rock. Shadows played on the cliff across from him. When he looked up at the ledge, just for a moment he thought he saw Naomi in her favorite pale yellow dress, the fabric fluttering in the wind as she fell.

He blinked and felt his eyes burn with tears. Frankie was right. He and Naomi had wanted different things. They hadn't been right for each other, but realizing that didn't seem to help. He couldn't shake this feeling he'd had for three years. It was as if she was trying to reach him from the grave, pleading with him that he find her killer.

Hank pulled off his Stetson and raked a hand through his hair. Was it just guilt for not marrying her, not taking the job with her stepfather, not giving up the ranch for her? Or was it true? Had she been murdered?

He reminded himself that this was why he was back here. Why he'd gone to Frankie to begin with and talked her into this charade. He realized, as he put his hat back on to shade his eyes from the summer sun, he trusted

Frankie to find out the truth. Look how much she'd discovered so far. He told himself it was a matter of time. If they could just keep their…relationship secret…

At the sound of a twig breaking behind him, Hank swung around, startled since he'd thought he was alone. Through the pines he saw a flash of color as someone took off at a run.

He jumped to his feet, but had to work his way back through the rocks, so he couldn't move as fast. By the time he reached the pines, whoever it had been was gone. He told himself it was probably just a kid who was as startled as he was to see that there was someone at this spot.

But as he stood, trying to catch his breath, he knew it hadn't been a kid. The person had been wearing a light color. The same pale yellow as Naomi's favorite dress or just his imagination? He'd almost convinced himself that he'd seen a ghost until, in the distance, he heard the sound of a vehicle engine rev and then die away.

Chapter Nine

After her visit with Dana, Frankie realized that she and Hank had to move faster. His mother was no fool. Frankie could tell that she was worried.

"Is there a vehicle I could borrow?" Frankie asked after their coffee and cookies chat.

"Of course." Dana had moved to some hooks near the door and pulled down a set of keys. "These are to that blue pickup out there. You're welcome to use it anytime you like. Hank should have thought of that. Where did he go, anyway?"

"He had some errands to run and I didn't want to go along. I told him I would be fine exploring. I think I'll go into town and run a few errands of my own." She gave the woman what she hoped was a reassuring smile and took the keys and the pickup to head into town.

Frankie felt an urgency to finish this. It wasn't just because their pretense was going to be found out sooner rather than later. Nor was it because she'd left a lot of things unfinished back in Idaho, though true. It was being here, pretending to be in love with Hank, pretending that there was a chance that she could be part of this amazing family at some time in the future.

That, she knew, was the real problem. Hank was the

kind of man who grew on a woman. But with his family, she'd felt instant love and acceptance. She didn't want to hurt these people any longer. That meant solving this case and getting out of here.

At the local grocery store, she found the manager in the back. She'd assumed that after three years, the managers would have changed from when Naomi had worked here. She was wrong.

Roy Danbrook was a tall, skinny man of about fifty with dark hair and eyes. He rose from his chair, looked around his incredibly small office as if surprised how small it really was and then invited her in. She took the plastic chair he offered her, feeling as if being in the cramped place was a little too intimate. But this wouldn't take long.

"I'm inquiring about a former worker of yours, Naomi Hill," she said, ready to lie about her credentials if necessary.

Roy frowned and she realized he probably didn't even remember Naomi after all this time. The turnover in resort towns had to be huge.

"Naomi," he said and nodded. "You mentioned something about an insurance claim?"

She nodded. She'd flashed him her PI credentials, but he'd barely looked at them. "I need to know what kind of employee she was."

He seemed to think for a moment. "Sweet, very polite with customers…" She felt a *but* coming. "But I had no choice but to let her go under the circumstances."

This came as a surprise. Did Hank know Naomi had been fired? "The circumstances?" That could cover a lot of things.

The manager looked away for a moment, clearly uncomfortable with speaking of past employees, or of the dead? "The stealing." He shook his head.

"The stealing?" All she could think of was groceries.

"Unfortunately, she couldn't keep her hand out of the till. Then there was the drinking, coming in still drunk, coming in late or not coming in at all. I liked her mother, so I tried to help the girl." He shook his head. "Finally, I had to let her go, you understand."

Frankie blinked. He couldn't be talking about the same Naomi Hank had been involved with. "We're talking about Naomi Hill, the one who—"

"Jumped off the cliff and killed herself. Yes."

Stealing? Drinking? Partying? Blowing off work? She tried to figure out how that went with the image Hank had painted of Naomi, but the two didn't fit.

A thought struck her. "She wasn't doing all this alone, right? There had to be someone she hung out with that might be able to give me some insight into her character."

He nodded. "Tamara Baker."

"Is she still around?"

"She works at the Silver Spur Bar." She didn't have to ask him what he thought of Tamara. He glanced at the clock on the wall. "She should be coming to work about now. If she is able to." He shook his head. "I hope this has helped you. I find it most disturbing to revisit it."

"You have been a great help, thank you." She got to her feet, feeling unsteady from the shock of what she'd learned. Sweet, timid little Naomi. Frankie couldn't wait to talk to her friend Tamara.

WHEN HUD CAME home for lunch, as he always did, Dana had sandwiches made and a fresh pot of coffee ready.

She hadn't planned to say anything until he'd finished eating.

"What is it?" her husband demanded. "You look as if you're about to pop. Spit it out."

She hurriedly sat down with him and took half of a sandwich onto her plate. Broaching this subject was difficult. They'd discussed Hank on occasion but it never ended well. Sometimes her husband could be so mule-headed stubborn.

"It's Hank."

"Of course it is," Hud said with a curse.

"Something's wrong."

Her husband shook his head as he took a bite of his lunch, clearly just wanting to eat and get out of there.

"This relationship with Frankie, it just doesn't feel... real."

"You have talked about nothing else but your hopes and prayers for Hank to move on, get over Naomi, make a life for himself. Now that he's doing it—"

"I don't believe he's doing it. Maybe coming back here was the worst thing he could do. I can tell it's putting a strain on him and Frankie. Earlier, I saw them... They aren't as loving toward each other as they should be."

Hud groaned as he finished his sandwich and reached for a cookie, which he dunked angrily into his coffee mug. "What would you like *me* to do about it?"

"Why is it we can't talk about Hank without you getting angry?" she demanded. They hardly ever argued, but when it came to the kids, she was like a mama bear, even with Hud. "I want to know more about Frankie." She said the words that had been rolling around in her mind since she'd first met the woman.

"You don't like her."

"No, I do. That's the problem. She seems so right for Hank."

Hud raked a hand through his hair before settling his gaze on her. "What am I missing here?"

"That's just it. I like her so much, I have to be sure this isn't— I mean, that she's not— Can't you just do some checking on her to relieve my mind so I can—"

"No." He stood up so abruptly that the dishes on the table rattled, startling her. "Absolutely not. Have you forgotten that the trouble began between my son and me when I did a background check on Naomi?"

"Because he was so in love with her. It was his first real crush. I asked you to make sure that she was all right for him because he seemed blind to her…"

"Blind to the fact that she didn't want what he wanted more than anything? That she would never have been happy with Hank if he settled here? She wanted marriage so badly that it was all she talked about. That she was pressuring our son and I could see that he felt backed against a wall?" Hud demanded. "Yes. Those were all good reasons. Along with the fact that I sensed a weakness in her. A fragility…"

"You questioned her mental stability, not to mention she'd been arrested for shoplifting."

He nodded, looking sick. "Something I never told our son. As it turned out, maybe I should have. I was right about her, which gives me no satisfaction." He raised his head to meet her gaze. His eyes shone. "I lost my son. I'm not sure I will get him back because of everything that happened. I can't make that mistake again." He reached for his Stetson on the wall hook where he put it each time he entered the kitchen. "Thank you for lunch." With that, he left.

Dana looked after him, fighting tears. She couldn't help the knot of fear inside her. Something was wrong, but she had no idea what to do about it.

TAMARA BAKER WAS indeed behind the bar at the Silver Spur. The place was empty, a janitor was just finishing up in the restroom, and the smell of industrial-strength cleanser permeated the air.

"Tamara Baker?" Frankie asked as she took a bar-stool.

"Who wants to know?" asked the brunette behind the bar. She had a smoker's rough voice and a hard-lived face that belied her real age. Frankie estimated she was in her midthirties, definitely older than Naomi.

"You knew Naomi Hill."

Tamara's eyes narrowed to slits. "You a reporter?"

Frankie laughed. "Not hardly. I heard that you and Naomi used to party together."

"That's no secret." That was what she thought. "But if you aren't with the press, then—"

Frankie gave her the same story she had Roy, only Tamara wasn't quite as gullible. When Frankie flashed her credentials, the bartender grabbed them, taking them over into the light from the back bar to study them.

"You're a PI? No kidding?"

"No kidding. I was hoping you could tell me about Naomi. Other people I've spoken with have painted a completely different picture of her compared to the stories I've heard about the two of you." She was exaggerating, but the fib worked.

Tamara laughed. "Want something to drink?" she asked as she poured herself one.

"I'd take a cola."

"I knew a different side of Naomi," the woman said after taking a pull of her drink. "She let her freak flag fly when she was with me."

"How did you two meet?"

"At the grocery store. She helped me out sometimes when I didn't have enough money to feed my kids." Tamara shrugged. "I tried to pay her back by showing her a good time here at the bar."

Frankie understood perfectly. Naomi would steal out of the till at the grocery store for Tamara, and Tamara would ply her with free drinks here at the bar. "What about men?"

"*Men?* What about them?"

"Did this wild side of her also include men?"

Tamara finished her drink and washed out the glass. "Naomi wasn't interested. She had this rancher she said she was going to marry. She flirted a little, but she was saving herself for marriage. She had this idea that once she was married, everything would come up roses." The bartender laughed.

"You doubted it?"

"I've seen women come through here thinking that marriage was going to cure whatever ailed them," Tamara said. "I've been there. What about you?" she asked, glancing at Frankie's left hand. "You married?"

She shook her head. "You must have been surprised when you heard that Naomi dove off the cliff and killed herself."

The woman snorted. "I figured it was just a matter

of time. She was living a double life. It was bound to catch up with her."

"You mean between the bar and the cowboy?"

Tamara looked away for a moment as if she thought someone might be listening. "Naomi had a lot more going on than anyone knew."

"Such as?"

The front door opened, sending a shaft of bright summer sun streaming across the floor like a laser in their direction. A man entered, the door closing behind him, pitching them back into cool darkness.

"Hey, Darrel," she called to the man as he limped to the bar. "What ya havin'?" The bartender got a beer for the man and hung around talking to him quietly for a few minutes.

Frankie saw the man glance in her direction. He was about her age with sandy-blond hair, not bad-looking, but there was something about him that made her look away. He seemed to be suddenly focusing on her a little too intensely. She wondered what Tamara had told him about her.

When the bartender came back down the bar, Frankie asked, "You didn't happen to see Naomi that night, the night she died, did you?"

"Me?" She shook her head. "I was working until closing. It's my usual shift. You can ask anyone."

Frankie noticed that the woman now seemed nervous and kept glancing down the bar at the man she'd called Darrel.

As she straightened the shirt she was wearing, Tamara asked, "Can I get you anything else?" She didn't sound all that enthusiastic about it.

"You said Naomi was into other things. Like what?"

"I was just shooting my mouth off. You can't pay any attention to me. If I can't get you anything else, I really need to do some stocking up." She tilted her head toward the man at the end of the bar. She lowered her voice. "You know, want to look good in front of the customers."

"Sure." She could tell that was all she was going to get out of Tamara. But she wondered what it was about the man at the end of the bar that made her nervous.

As she left, she found herself still trying to piece together what she'd learned about the woman known as Naomi Hill. The pieces didn't fit. She tried to imagine what Naomi could have been involved in that would get her murdered—if that had been the case.

More and more, though, Frankie believed that the woman had come unhinged when she'd seen her planned life with Hank crumbling, and it had driven her to do the one thing that terrified her more than her so-called double life.

HANK KNEW HE couldn't put it off any longer. He swung by his father's office, knowing the man was a creature of habit. Marshal Hudson Savage went home every day for lunch. And every day, his wife would have a meal ready. Hank used to find it sweet. Then his father went back to his office. If nothing was happening, he would do paperwork for an hour or so before he would go out on patrol.

He found his father sitting behind his desk. The marshal looked up in surprise to see Hank standing in the doorway. "Come on in," he said, as if he knew this wasn't a personal visit. "Close the door."

Hank did just that, but he didn't take the chair his father offered him. "I want a copy of Naomi's file." Hud started to shake his head. "Don't tell me I can't have it. She'd dead. The case is closed. Pretend I'm a reporter and give me a copy."

His father sighed as he leaned back in his chair, gazing at him with an intensity that used to scare him when he was a boy and in trouble. "Your mother and I had hoped—"

"I know what you'd hoped," he interrupted. "Don't read too much into my wanting a copy of the file."

"What am I supposed not to read into it? That you still haven't moved on?"

Hank said nothing.

"What's the deal with you and Frankie?" the marshal asked, no longer sounding like his father. "Are you in love with her?"

"Seriously? Mother put you up to this?"

"We're concerned."

Hank laughed. "Just like you were concerned when I was in love with Naomi."

"Are you in love with Frankie?"

"Who wouldn't be? She's a beautiful, smart, talented woman. Now, if we're through with the interrogation, I still want that file. Let's say I need it to get closure."

"Is that what it is?"

He gave his father an impatient look.

The marshal leaned forward, picked up a manila envelope from his desk and held it out to him.

Hank stared at it without taking the envelope from him for a moment. "What is this?"

"A copy of Naomi's file."

"How—"

"How did I know that you would be asking for it?" His father asked the question for him as he cocked his head. Hank noticed his father's hair more graying than he remembered. "Maybe I know you better than you think."

Hank took the envelope from him. "Is everything in here?"

"Everything, including my notes. Will there be anything else?"

He shook his head, feeling as if there was something more he should say. "Thank you."

His father gave him a nod. His desk phone rang.

Hank opened the door, looking back as his father picked up the phone and said, "Marshal Savage." He let the door close behind him and left.

Chapter Ten

J.J. went by Frankie's apartment and banged on the door until the neighbor opened a window and yelled out.

"I'm going to call the cops."

"Call the cops. Where's Frankie?"

"The woman who lives in that apartment? She packed up and left with some man a few days ago."

"What?" He described Frankie to the man since it was clear the fool didn't know what he was talking about.

"That's her," the man said. "I know my own neighbor. She left with a cowboy—that's all I can tell you. She's not home, so please let me get some sleep."

He thought he might lose his mind. Where could she have gone? He'd been by her office. It was locked up tight. He told himself she was on a case. But why wouldn't she answer her phone? Why wouldn't she call him back? She knew what a mistake that would be once he got his hands on her.

He'd called her number, left more messages, and still she hadn't gotten back to him. What if she'd left for good?

She wouldn't do that. She was just trying to teach him a lesson, playing hard to get. Once he saw her again, he'd teach *her* a lesson she wouldn't soon forget. No one pulled this kind of crap on him. Especially some woman.

He knew there was only one thing to do. Track her down and make her pay.

After all, he had the resources. He just hadn't wanted to use them. He'd hoped that Frankie would have come to her senses and realized she couldn't get away from him. But she had.

And now he was going after her.

FRANKIE FOUND HANK poring over papers on the small table in their cabin.

Hank looked up, surprised as she came in the door, as if he'd forgotten all about her. "Where have *you* been?"

"I've been working. You all right?"

He nodded. "I stopped by the marshal's office and got a copy of Naomi's file."

"Your dad gave it to you?" She couldn't help being surprised.

"He'd already made a copy for me." He grunted. "He says he knows me better than I think he does. You're probably right about them seeing through us. Mom said you took one of the pickups into town. I'm sorry I didn't think to give you keys for a vehicle."

"It was fine," she said, pulling out a chair at the table and sitting down. "I had coffee and cookies with your mother before I left."

He raised a brow. "How did that go?"

"She quizzed me about us, about me. She wanted to know how we met. We should have come up with something beforehand. I had to wing it." She told him the story she'd given to his mother.

Hank nodded. "Sorry about that, but it sounds like you covered it."

"We had a nice visit. I don't like lying to her, though. She's going to be hurt."

"I know." He got to his feet. "You hungry? I haven't had lunch."

"Me either."

"I know a place up the canyon, the Corral. They used to make great burgers. Want to give it a try?"

She smiled as her stomach rumbled loudly.

It was one of those beautiful summer days. Frankie breathed it in as Hank drove them through the canyon. Sunlight glimmered off the pines and the clear green of the river as the road and river wound together through cliffs and meadows.

Frankie sat back and enjoyed the ride. She'd decided she would tell Hank later what she'd learned so as not to spoil his lunch. It could wait, and right now she was enjoying just the two of them on this amazing day. Even Hank seemed more relaxed than she'd seen him. He turned on the radio, and as a country song came on from a local station, they both burst into song. Frankie had grown up on the old country classics, so she knew all the words.

They laughed as the song ended and fell into a companionable silence as the news came on and Hank turned off the radio.

"You said you were working while I was gone—"

"We can talk about it later."

He shot her a look before going back to his driving, as if he knew it wasn't going to be good news. Not far up the road he turned into the Corral. The place had originally been built in 1947. It had changed from

when Hank was a boy, but it still served great burgers
and fries. Now you could also get buffalo as well as
beef and sweet potato fries or regular. The booths had
been replaced with log furniture and yet he still felt as
at home here as he had as a boy when his grandfather
used to play guitar in a band here.

After they ordered, Hank said, "I like your hair." He
reached over and caught a long lock between his thumb
and finger. "Do you ever wear it down?"

She eyed him suspiciously.

"What? I can't compliment you? You said we needed
to act like lovers."

"Lovers?" She broke into a smile. "Something happen I don't know about?"

He let go of her hair and glanced toward the bar.
"Before I went down to my father's office for a copy
of Naomi's file, I stopped by the river again where she
died. There was someone else there. I heard them behind me and when I turned around they ran. I caught
only a glimpse of fabric through the trees and then I
heard a car engine start up and the vehicle leave."

Frankie could see that the incident had spooked him.
She wasn't sure why, though. Nothing about it sounded
sinister. "Who do you think it was?"

He shook his head. "I thought I caught a glimpse of
Naomi up on the ledge, wearing this pale yellow dress
she loved."

"Was anyone up on the ledge?"

He shook his head. "But there was someone behind
me. Someone wearing a light-colored garment running
through the trees."

"You thought it was Naomi?"

"Naomi is dead. She can't step on a twig and break it directly behind me and startle me." He picked up his napkin and rearranged his silverware. "I'm not losing it."

"I know you're not. You saw someone. But that doesn't mean it had anything to do with Naomi. Unless you think you were followed."

He shook his head. "Why would someone follow me?"

She shrugged. Clearly neither of them knew. He realized that she was right. It was just someone who was looking for a spot on the river. He'd probably startled them more than they had him.

"But then again," Frankie said, "if you're right and Naomi was murdered, then her murderer is still out there."

"If you're trying to scare me—"

"What you have to figure out is why anyone would want to kill Naomi in the first place. I have some thoughts that I'll share on the way back to the ranch. But in the meantime—"

"Just a minute. You learned something?"

Fortunately, their burgers and fries came just then. They'd both gone for beef, regular fries and colas. Hank looked down at the food, then at her. She picked up a fry and dragged it through a squirt of ketchup she'd poured onto her plate before taking a bite.

"I can't remember the last time I had a burger and fries," she said with enthusiasm. Picking up the burger, she took a juicy hot bite and made a *hmmm* sound that had him smiling.

He could see that she didn't want to talk about what she'd found out. Not now. He decided to let it go until after their lunch because it was a beautiful day and he was sitting here with a beautiful woman. "Did I just see you put mayo on your burger?"

"You have a problem with that?" she joked.

He reached for the side of mayo she'd ordered. "Not if you share. I guess it's just one more thing we have in common."

"We have something in common?"

Hank met her gaze. "Maybe more than you realize." He took a bite of his burger and they ate as if it might be their last meal.

HANK COULDN'T REMEMBER the last time he'd enjoyed a meal more—or his dining companion. Frankie was funnier than he'd expected her to be. The more time he spent around her, the more he liked her. She'd definitely been the right choice when he'd gone looking for a private investigator.

He'd asked around and was told he couldn't beat Frankie Brewster. At that point, he'd thought Frankie was male. It wasn't until he saw her that he knew how to come back to the ranch without drawing attention to his reason for returning. So far, it seemed to be working, even if his parents were suspicious of their relationship. Let them worry about that instead of his real reason for bringing her home.

"Okay, let's hear it," he said as they left the Corral and headed the five miles back toward Big Sky and the ranch.

She started to say something when she glanced in her side mirror. "Do you know the driver of that truck behind us?"

He glanced in his rearview mirror and saw a large

gold older-model truck behind them. As he watched, he saw that the truck was gaining speed on them. "No, why?"

"I saw it behind us earlier on the way to the Corral."

"You think whoever is driving it is following us?" The idea sounded ludicrous until he reminded himself of the person he'd seen by the river earlier—and the reason he was home. She was right. If Naomi had been murdered, then her killer was still out there.

Looking in the rearview again, he saw that the truck was coming up way too fast. The canyon road was winding with tight curves and few straightaways, and yet the driver of the truck acted as if he planned to pass—and soon—given the speed he was traveling.

"Hank, I have a bad feeling," Frankie said as the driver of the truck closed the distance.

He had the same bad feeling. Earlier there'd been more traffic, especially close to Big Sky, but other than a few semis passing by, they seemed to be the only two vehicles on this stretch of the highway right now.

Hank looked for a place to pull off and let the truck pass. Maybe it was a driver who didn't know this canyon and how dangerous it could be. Or maybe— The front of the truck filled his rearview mirror.

"He's going to ram us," he cried. "Brace yourself."

The driver of the truck slammed into the back of them. Hank fought to keep the pickup on the road. This section of highway was bordered on one side by cliffs and the river on the other. Fortunately, there was a guardrail along the river, but up ahead there was a spot where the guardrail was broken apart from a previous accident and hadn't been replaced yet.

All thoughts of the driver of the truck behind them

being new to the area dissolved. Whoever was at that wheel knew exactly what he was doing. Hank knew going faster wasn't going to help. He couldn't outrun the truck.

"He's going to try to knock us into the river at this next curve," he told Frankie as the bumper of the truck banged into them again and he had to fight the wheel to keep from wrecking. "There is nothing I can do, so I have a bad feeling we will be swimming soon."

As he came around the curve, the trucker did exactly what he'd anticipated he would do. Hank tried to stay on the highway, but the truck was too large, the driver going too fast. The large truck smashed into the side of his pickup, forcing them off the road. Fortunately, Hank saw that the riverbank wasn't steep. Rather than let the trucker roll the pickup off into the river, he turned the wheel sharply toward the water and yelled, "Hang on!" and hoped for the best as the pickup left the highway and plunged into the Gallatin River.

Chapter Eleven

"I was just at the grocery store," Dana said without preamble when her husband answered his phone at the marshal's office. "I overheard the manager talking to one of his employees about Naomi."

"Dana, I'm right in the middle of—"

"Roy said that a woman named Francesca Brewster with some insurance company had come in and was asking questions about Naomi and her death. Why would Frankie be asking about Naomi's death?"

"Maybe she's curious," her husband said after a moment. "After all, Naomi was Hank's former girlfriend. Frankie probably wants to know what happened to her and I doubt Hank is very forthcoming. Hell, he still thinks she was murdered."

"I'm worried. You know how I felt about Naomi and I'm afraid Hank did too. Now it's like he doesn't trust me. I have no idea how he feels about Frankie."

"He brought her home with him. That should tell you something."

"It would if they were getting along. Stacy said they aren't sleeping in the same bed and earlier I saw them having another argument. If she's asking people questions about Naomi—"

"I think you're making too much out of this."

"We don't know anything about her."

"Dana—"

"He's our son, Hud. I don't want to see him make a terrible—"

"There is nothing we can do about it. If either of us says anything…" He swore. "Honey, we have to let him make his own mistakes. We both tried to warn him about Naomi and look where that left us."

"It's just that I don't think he can take another woman breaking his heart." She hated how close to tears she sounded.

"He's a grown man. He can take care of himself. Give him a little credit. Maybe Frankie is exactly what he needs."

IT HAPPENED SO FAST, Frankie didn't have time to react. One minute they were on the highway, the next in the river. The pickup plunged into the water, the front smashing into the rocks. Water rushed around them and began to come in through the cracks, building up quickly at her side window.

"We have to get out of here," Hank yelled over the roar of the river and the sound of water as it began to fill the cab.

She saw him try to open his door and fail against the weight of water. Her door was facing upstream, so she knew there was no opening it. She unhooked her seat belt, only then aware of her deflated airbag in her lap. Water was rising quickly. Hank was right. They had to brave the river because if they stayed in the pickup much longer—

Next to her, Hank had unsnapped his seat belt and

was trying to get his side window to slide down, but it didn't appear to be working. He moved over and leaned back against her. "Get ready," he said. "Once I kick out the window…" He didn't need to tell her what would happen. She could see the water rushing over the cab of the pickup and forming an eddy on his side of the truck.

Hank reared back and kicked. The glass turned into a white spiderweb. He kicked again and the window disappeared out into the river. Cold water rushed in. Hank grabbed her hand. "Hang on," he said as the cab filled faster.

She held on as if her life depended on it. It did. For a moment, the force of the water rushing in wouldn't let them escape. But Hank kicked off the side of the pickup, dragging her with him. For a few moments, which felt like an eternity, she saw and felt nothing but water all around her. Her chest ached from holding her breath. She needed air, would have done anything for one small intake of oxygen. Hank never let go of her hand, or her his, even as the river tried to pull them apart.

And then, gloriously, they surfaced, and she gasped for breath. Nothing had ever felt so good as she took air into her lungs. As Hank pulled her toward shore, she looked back, surprised by how far downriver they'd surfaced. The truck cab was completely submerged in the water. She coughed and gasped for air as she stumbled up onto the rocks.

Hank pulled her to him, rubbing her arms as if to take away the chill. She hadn't realized how hard she was trembling until his strong body wrapped around her. She leaned into him, taking comfort in his warmth as what had just happened finally hit her. Someone had tried to kill them—and she'd lost her purse as well as her gun.

On the highway, vehicles had stopped. People were calling to them. Someone said they'd phoned for help and that the marshal was on his way.

DRENCHED TO THE skin and still shivering from the cold water and the close call, Hank climbed into the back of his father's patrol SUV with Frankie. His father had given them blankets, which they'd wrapped up in. Still he put his arm around her, holding her close to share his body heat. He still couldn't believe what had happened and was just thankful they were both alive.

He'd gotten her into this. So of course he felt responsible for her. But he knew it was more than that as he pulled her closer. He wasn't sure when it had happened but they felt like friends. Almost dying did that to a person, he thought.

He became aware of how her wet clothes clung to her, revealing curves he'd always known were there but hadn't seen before. The fact that he could think about that now told him that he was definitely alive—and typically male.

"Why would someone want to force you off the road?" his father asked after he'd told him what had happened.

He heard the disbelief in his father's tone. He'd been here before. Hud hadn't believed that Naomi was murdered. He didn't believe that someone had just tried to kill them. "Believe whatever you like," he snapped. "But this was no accident. The truck crashed into us twice before it forced me off the road. It wasn't a case of road rage. Frankie had seen it behind us on the way to the Corral. The driver must have followed us and waited until we came out."

"Okay, son. I've called for a wrecker. I'll have your truck taken to the lab. Hopefully there will be some paint from the other truck on it that will help us track down the make and model, along with the description you've already given me of the driver. Even if the driver wasn't trying to kill the two of you, he left the scene of an accident. I've put a BOLO out. Later, after the two of you get a shower and warm clothes on, I'll take your statements."

Hank rested his head on the top of Frankie's as she leaned into his chest and tried not to let his father get to him. The man always had to be Marshal Hudson Savage, all business. The show-me-the-evidence lawman. Just for once, Hank would have liked him to believe his own son.

He drew Frankie closer and closed his eyes, just thankful to be alive. Thankful he hadn't gotten her killed. And more aware than ever of the woman in his arms.

FRANKIE FELT AS if she was in shock. After they were dropped off at their cabin, Hank led her into the bathroom and turned on the shower. *It's probably hypothermia*, she thought, since she'd felt fine in Hank's arms, but the moment he'd let her go, she'd begun to shake again.

The mirror in the bathroom quickly steamed over. "Get in with your clothes on." She looked at him as if he'd lost his mind. "Seriously," he said and, opening the glass shower door, pushed her toward the warm water streaming down from the showerhead. "Just toss your wet clothes on the floor of the shower. I'll take care of them later. I'll use the other shower. You need to get warm and dry as quickly as possible. Trust me."

Trust him? She looked into his handsome face and had to smile. Surprising herself, she did as he suggested and stepped into the walk-in shower, clothes and all. She did trust him. More than he knew. The warm water felt so good as it soaked her clothing and took away the cold. With trembling fingers, she began to peel off the wet garments to let the warm water get to her bare skin.

She felt something heavy in her jeans pocket. Her cell phone. She pulled it out and reached out to lay it next to the sink. At least she wouldn't have to worry about getting any more calls she didn't want to take since she could see that the screen was fogged over, the phone no doubt dead.

Worse, earlier, she'd put her gun into her purse. She could only hope that her purse had stayed in the pickup. Otherwise, it had washed downriver.

A shiver moved through her and she stepped back into the shower. But she knew that it would take more than warm water to stop her from shaking. Someone had tried to kill them. She thought about the truck that had forced them off the highway and into the river. She'd only glimpsed the driver. A man. A large angry man.

It wasn't him, she told herself. It couldn't have been. Where would he have gotten a truck like that and how would he—

Unless he had somehow tracked her to Big Sky. She glanced at her phone and felt her heart drop. Tracking her phone would have been child's play for anyone who knew how. Especially for a cop.

She leaned against the shower wall, suddenly weak

with fear. The last thing she wanted was her past catching up with her here. She told herself that she was only running scared. He hadn't found her. The man in the truck hadn't been him. All of this was about Naomi—not about her.

Refusing to give in to her fears that she might have been responsible for almost getting Hank killed, she concentrated on the feel of the warm water cascading down her body. As she turned her face up to the spray, she assured herself that she was fine. Hank was fine. Better than fine. She thought of how he'd held on to her until they were both safe on shore and then hugged her in his arms, sharing his warmth, protecting her, taking care of her even when he had to be as cold as she was.

She felt her nipples pucker to aching tips at the memory of his hard body against hers. It had been so long since she'd felt desire for a man. It spiked through her, turning her molten at her center at just the thought of Hank in the other shower, warm water running down his naked body.

Frankie shut off the water and, stepping over her wet clothes, reached for a towel. Hank was her employer. Nothing more. She was reacting to him like this only because they'd just shared a near-death experience.

But even as she thought it, Frankie knew it was much more than that. She'd never met anyone like Hank. His capacity to love astounded her. Look how he'd mourned Naomi's death for three long years and still refused to give up on finding out the truth. Frankie couldn't imagine a man loving her like that.

She toweled herself dry and pulled on the robe she saw that Hank had left for her. After drawing it around her, she pulled up the collar and smelled the freshly washed scent. Hugging herself, she realized she was crying softly. She'd never been so happy to be alive.

Frankie quickly wiped her tears and busied herself wringing out her clothes and hanging them in the shower to dry. Then, bracing herself, she tied the robe tightly around her and stepped out of the bathroom.

HUD RETURNED TO his office. He quickly checked to make sure that a deputy and a highway patrol officer were taking care of traffic while the wrecker retrieved Hank's pickup from the river.

He realized he was still shaken. He didn't want to believe that the driver of the truck who'd run them off the road had been trying to kill them. But the driver had forced them off the road where the guardrail was missing—as if he knew exactly where to dump them into the river. That made the driver a local and that was what worried Hud.

Hank believed this had something to do with Naomi's death. But Hud had seen Frankie's face in the rearview mirror. She'd just been through a terrifying experience, no doubt about it. Yet he'd seen a fear in her eyes long after she'd been safe and warm in the back of his patrol SUV.

Swearing under his breath, he turned on his computer, his fingers hovering over the keys for a moment as he considered what he was about to do. He ticked off the reasons he had to do this. Hank's unexpected return. His son bringing a woman home after three years. Francesca "Frankie" Brewster, someone they'd never heard about before. The two were allegedly a couple, but their behavior was in question by Dana, who was good at these things. Add to that, Frankie had been asking around about Naomi's death. Throw in the "accident" that ended up with them in the river and what did it give you?

With a curse, he put his fingertips on the computer keys and typed Francesca "Frankie" Brewster, Lost Creek, Idaho.

What popped up on the screen made him release the breath he'd been holding. He sat back, staring at the screen. What the hell? Frankie Brewster Investigations?

It took him only another minute to find out that she was a licensed private investigator in the state of Idaho and had been in business for four years. Her name came up in articles in the local paper. She'd actually solved a few cases that had made the news.

He sat back again, berating himself for looking and, at the same time, wondering what he was going to do now with the information. Just because she was a PI didn't mean that she and Hank weren't really a couple. In fact, Hud thought that might be what attracted his son to her to begin with. So why make waves?

If he said anything to Hank, his son would be furious. He would know that his father did it again, checked up on Frankie—just as he had with Naomi. Only with Frankie there was no sign that she'd ever been arrested or put under mental evaluation, at least.

"That's a plus," he said to himself and turned off the computer to rub the back of his neck and mentally kick himself. "Frankie's investigating Naomi's death," he said to himself, realizing that was what was going on. His son thought he could pull a fast one, bring Frankie home, pretend to be an item, and all the time the two were digging into Naomi's death.

He swore under his breath. Was it possible that someone was getting nervous? Was that why that truck had forced them off the road? To warn them to stop? But if that was the case…

Hud picked up the phone and called the lab. "I want information on the vehicle that forced that pickup off the road ASAP. Call me at home when you get it."

In all his years in law enforcement, he'd never felt this unsettled. What if Hank had been right all along and Naomi had been murdered? Enter Frankie, and the next thing he knew, his son and the PI were run off the highway and into the river. A little too coincidental to suit him.

With a sigh, he knew what he had to do. He had to stop them from investigating even if it meant making his son mad at him again. Hank had to let him look into it. Even as he thought it, Hud knew hell would freeze over before his son would trust him to do that. There would be no stopping Frankie and Hank if they were doing what he suspected they were.

He thought of all the mistakes he'd made with his oldest son. As he got to his feet, he just prayed that he wasn't about to make an even bigger one. But he had to stop the two of them before they ended up dead.

HANK CAME OUT of the bathroom only moments after Frankie. He'd stood under the warm spray for a long time. His emotions were all over the place. The trucker running them off the road proved what he'd been saying all along, didn't it?

So why didn't he feel more satisfaction? He'd been right. But as he stood letting the water cascade over his body, all he'd been able to think about was Frankie. He kept picturing her soaking wet, her clothes clinging to every curve. The memory had him aching.

He had turned the shower to cold and tried to get a handle on his feelings. Shivering again, he'd turned off the shower and had stood for a moment, still flooded with a desire like none he'd ever felt. He'd loved Naomi but she hadn't stirred this kind of passion in him. Was that another reason he hadn't wanted to rush into marriage?

Shaking his head, he'd stepped out of the shower and grabbed a towel to roughly dry himself off. He didn't want to be feeling these yearnings toward Frankie, not when he'd come home to set things right with Naomi. He told himself that he would keep her at a distance. But try as he might, he still felt an aching need at even the memory of her in his arms in the back of the patrol SUV.

He'd hung up his wet clothes and pulled on one of the guest robes that his mother supplied to the cabins. He promised himself that he would keep his mind on the investigation. If he was right, then they had rattled Naomi's killer. They were getting close. Maybe too close, he'd thought as he'd stepped out of the bedroom.

At the sight of Frankie standing there, his bare feet faltered on the wood floor. Her long, dark hair was down, hanging below her shoulders to the tips of her breasts beneath the robe. Her face was flushed, as was her neck and throat. Water droplets still clung to her eyelashes, making her eyes appear even larger, the violet a darker purple.

She looked stunning. When their gazes met, he saw a need in her that matched his own and felt all his resolve to keep her at arm's length evaporate before his eyes. He closed the distance between them without a word, without a thought. She didn't move, her gaze locked with his, a vein in her slim neck throbbing as he approached.

He took a lock of her long hair in his fingers. It felt silken even wet. She still hadn't moved. Still hadn't broken eye contact. His heart pounded as he brushed her hair back on one side before leaning in to kiss that spot on her neck where her blood pulsed. The throbbing beat quickened beneath his lips and it was as if he could feel his own heart drumming wildly to the same beat.

It had been so long since he'd felt like this. As his lips traveled down her neck into the hollow at her shoulder, she leaned back, giving him access. He heard her sharp intake of breath as he stroked her tender flesh with the tip of his tongue. From the hollow at her shoulder, it would have been too easy to dip down to the opening of her robe and swell of her breasts he could see rising and falling with each of her breaths.

He lifted his head again to look into her eyes before he cupped the back of her neck and drew her into a kiss, dragging her body against his. Desire raced along his veins to the riotous pounding of his heart. She looped her arms around his neck as he deepened the kiss and pulled her even closer until their bodies were molded together, almost as one. He could feel her breasts straining against the robe. He wanted desperately to lay open her robe and press his skin to hers. He wanted her naked body beneath his more than he wanted his next breath.

Reaching down, he pulled the sash of her robe. It fell away. He untied his own. As their robes opened, he pushed the fabric aside. He heard a gasp escape her lips as their warm, naked bodies came together. He felt her hard nipples press against his chest. Desire shot through him.

The knock at the door startled them both. "Hank? Frankie? I need to talk to you." Another knock and then the knob turned slowly.

They burst apart, both frantically retying their robes as the marshal stuck his head in the door. "Sorry. I…" He started to close the door.

"It's all right," Hank said. His voice sounded hoarse with emotion and need even to his ears. He shot a look at Frankie and saw that she was as shaken as he was. If only he had thought to lock the door. If only his father had picked any time but now to stop by.

And yet, now that he'd cooled down some, he knew it was for the best. He had enough problems without jumping into bed with Frankie—as much as he would have loved to do just that. But life was complicated enough as it was. A part of him was still in love with Naomi. He wasn't sure he'd ever get over her—and he had a feeling that Frankie knew that.

"Did you find out something about the truck that ran us off the road?" Frankie asked, her voice breaking.

They shared a look. Both of them struggling not to laugh at the irony of the situation. He wondered if she felt as disappointed as he did—and maybe just as relieved. Their relationship was complicated enough without this. And, he reminded himself, there was that man who kept calling her, the one Frankie didn't want to talk to. The one he suspected was her lover, past or present. Whoever the man was, Frankie hadn't dealt with him, he thought as his father stepped into the cabin, Stetson in hand and a sheepish, amused and yet curious look on his face.

HUD LOOKED FROM his son to Frankie. Both were flushed and not just from their showers. He hadn't known what he was going to say, but after walking in on what he'd just seen, he surprised himself.

"I've decided to reopen Naomi's case," he said as the two hurriedly moved away from each other like teenagers caught necking on the couch. Dana had thought they weren't lovers. If he hadn't come along when he did, they would have been. Maybe his wife was wrong about the two of them. Maybe he was too.

"Why would you reopen the case?" Hank asked as Frankie straightened her robe.

"I'm going to get dressed," she said. "If you'll excuse me." She hurried off toward the bedroom.

"I'm sorry," Hud said. "Clearly I interrupted something."

His son waved a hand through the air. "I thought you didn't believe that Naomi was murdered?"

"I'm still not sure I do. But after what happened today, I want to take another look."

Hank shook his head, mumbling under his breath as he turned toward the kitchen. "I'm going to get dressed and have a beer. You want one?"

He glanced at his watch. He was off the clock. Normally he would pass because he wasn't in the habit of drinking before dinner, but today he'd make an exception. "I would love one." That apparently had taken Hank by surprise, because he felt his son studying him as Hank returned in jeans and a Western shirt with two bottles of beer.

As Hank handed him one and twisted off the top on his own, he said, "Thank Mom for stocking our refrigerator."

"You know your mother. She wanted you and Frankie to be…comfortable up here." Earlier, he'd come up to the cabin, planning to bust them, exposing Frankie as a PI and their relationship as a fraud. But seeing them together, he'd changed his mind and was glad of it. He could eat a little crow with his son.

Anyway, what would it hurt to reopen the case unofficially? He still had misgivings about Hank's accident earlier today. Maybe all it had been was road rage. Either way, he was determined to track down the truck—and driver.

Frankie came out of the bedroom dressed in a baggy shirt and jeans, her feet still bare. Without asking her, Hank handed her his untouched beer and went into the kitchen to get another one.

Hud stood for a moment, he and Frankie somewhat uneasy in each other's presence. He was sure that his son had given the PI an earful about him. He'd lost Hank's respect because of Naomi's case. He'd thought he wouldn't get another chance to redeem himself. Maybe this would be it.

Hud took a chair while Frankie curled up on the couch, leaving the chair opposite him open. Hank, though, appeared too restless or stubborn to sit. He stood sipping his beer.

"Any word on the truck that put us in the river?" Frankie asked into the dead silence that followed.

"Not yet. I've asked that it be moved to priority one," he said. "I also have law enforcement in the canyon watching for the truck. It will turn up." He sounded more confident than he felt. He needed that truck and its driver. He needed to find out what had happened earlier and why—and not just to show his son that he knew what he was doing. If Hank was right and the driver of that truck was somehow connected to Naomi's death… well, then he needed to find Naomi's killer—before his son and Frankie did.

"If I was wrong, I'll make it right," he told his son, who nodded, though grudgingly. As he finished his beer, his cell phone rang. "That will be your mother. Don't tell her about this," he said, holding up his empty bottle. "We'll both be in trouble," he joked, then sobered. "Dinner isn't for a while. But I also would play down what happened earlier in the river during the meal. You know your mother."

Hank smiled. "I certainly do." Hud saw him glance at Frankie. A look passed between them, one he couldn't read, but he could feel the heat of it. He really wished his timing had been better earlier.

FRANKIE WAS STILL shaken from those moments with Hank before the marshal had arrived. She'd come so close to opening herself up to him, to baring not just her naked body, but her soul. She couldn't let that happen again. She reminded herself that their relationship was fake. He was her employer. He was still in love with the memory of Naomi.

That last part especially, she couldn't let herself forget. Not to mention the fact that she had her own baggage he knew nothing about. With luck, he never would. Once she was finished with this job, she would return to Idaho. Who knew what Hank would do.

Clearly, he loved the ranch and wanted to be part of the family's ranching operation. Would what they discovered free him from the past? Free him from Naomi enough that he could return?

"We have time for a horseback ride," Hank said out of the blue as the marshal left. "It's time you saw the ranch. You do ride, don't you?"

"I grew up in Montana before I moved to Idaho," she said. "It's been years since I've ridden, but I do know the front of the horse from the back."

"Good enough," Hank said. "Come on."

Frankie got the feeling that he didn't want to be alone with her in their cabin for fear of what would happen between them. She felt relieved but also a little disappointed, which made her angry with herself. Had she learned nothing when it came to men?

They walked down to the barn, where Hank saddled them a couple of horses. She stood in the sunlight that hung over Lone Mountain and watched him. She liked the way he used his hands and how gentle he was with the horses. There were many sides to this handsome cowboy, she thought as he patted her horse's neck and said, "Buttercup, you be nice to Frankie, now."

He handed her the reins. "Buttercup said she'll be nice. You need to do the same. No cursing her if she tries to brush you off under a pine tree." He turned to take the reins of the other horse.

"Wait," Frankie cried. "Will she do that?"

He shrugged as he swung up into the saddle and laughed. "Let's hope not." He looked good up there, so self-assured, so at home. He spurred his horse forward. "Also, Buttercup's got a crush on Romeo here, so she'll probably just follow him and behave. But you never know with a female." He trotted out of the barn, then reined in to wait for her.

She started to give Buttercup a nudge, but the mare was already moving after Romeo and Hank.

They rode up into the mountains through towering pines. The last of the summer air was warm on her back. She settled into the saddle, feeling more comfortable than she'd expected to be. Part of that was knowing that she was in good hands with both Buttercup and Hank.

Frankie stole a glance at him, seeing him really relax for the first time since she'd met him. He had his head tilted back, his gaze on the tops of the mountains as if soaking them into his memory for safekeeping. Was he sorry he'd left? It didn't really matter, she realized. He couldn't come back here—not with Naomi's ghost running rampant in his heart and mind. Until he knew what had happened to her, Frankie doubted he would ever find peace.

In that moment, she resolved to find out the truth no matter what it was. She wanted to free this man from his obvious torment. But even as she thought it, she wondered if he would ever really be free of Naomi and his feelings for the dead woman.

"Wait until you see this," Hank said and rode on a little ahead to where the pines opened into a large meadow. She could see aspens, their leaves already starting to turn gold and rust and red even though summer wasn't technically over. This part of Montana didn't pay much attention to the calendar.

As she rode out into the meadow, she was hit with the smells of drying leaves and grasses. It made her feel a little melancholy. Seasons ended like everything else, but she hated to feel time passing. It wouldn't be long before they would be returning to Idaho and their lives there. That thought brought back the darkness that had been plaguing her for the past few months.

She was going to have to deal with her past. She only wished she knew how.

Hank had ridden ahead across the meadow. She saw that he'd reined in his horse and was waiting for her at the edge. Buttercup broke into a trot across the meadow and then a gallop. Frankie surprised herself by feeling as if she wasn't going to fall off.

She reined in next to Hank. He was grinning at her and she realized she had a broad smile on her face. "I like Buttercup."

"I thought you might. She's a sweetheart. Except for when she tries to brush you off under a pine tree." His grin broadened.

"You really are an awful tease," she said as he came over to help her off her horse.

"You think so?" he said as he grabbed her by her waist and lifted her down to stand within inches of him. Their gazes met.

Frankie felt desire shoot like a rocket through her. She'd thought she'd put the fire out, but it had only been smoldering just below the surface. She wanted the kiss as much as her next breath.

He drew her closer. "What is it about you that is driving me crazy?" he asked in a hoarse whisper.

She shook her head, never breaking her gaze with his. "I could ask you the same thing."

He chuckled. "I want to kiss you."

She cocked her head at him. "So what's stopping you?"

"I've already had my heart broken once. I'm not sure I'm up to having it stomped on just yet," he said, but he didn't let her go. Nor did he break eye contact.

"You think I'm a heartbreaker?" she said, surprised

how breathy she sounded. It was as if the high altitude of the mountaintop had stolen all her oxygen.

He grinned. "I know you are and yet…" He pulled her to him so quickly that she gasped before his mouth dropped to hers.

The kiss was a stunner, all heat. His tongue teased hers as he deepened it, holding her so tightly against him that she felt as if their bodies had fused in the heat.

He let her go just as quickly and stepped away, shaking his head. "We should get back, but first you should see the view. My mother is bound to ask you at dinner what you thought of it."

She was still looking at the handsome cowboy as she swayed under the onslaught of emotions she didn't believe she'd ever felt before. "The view?" she said on a ragged breath.

Hank laughed and took her hand. "It's this way." He led her to the edge of the mountaintop, still holding her hand in his large warm one. "What do you think?"

She thought that, for a while, they'd both forgotten Naomi. "I've never enjoyed a horseback ride more in my life," she said, her gaze on the amazing view of mountains that seemed to go on forever.

He gently squeezed her hand. "It is pretty amazing, isn't it?"

Chapter Twelve

Dinner was a blur of people and laughter and talk as more relatives and friends gathered around the large dining room table, including Dana's best friend, Hilde, and her family. Fortunately, most of it was going on around Frankie, and all she had to do was smile and laugh at the appropriate times. She avoided looking at Hank, but in the middle of the meal, she felt his thigh brush against hers. She felt his gaze on her. When he placed his hand on her thigh, she wasn't able to control the shiver of desire that rocketed through her. She moved her leg and tried to still her galloping pulse. Getting her body to unrespond to his touch wasn't as easy.

Once the meal was over, she and Hank walked back up to their cabin. For a long way, neither said a word. It was still plenty light out.

"Are you all right?" Hank asked over the evening sounds around them. She could hear the hum of the river as it flowed past, the chatter of a squirrel in the distance and the cry of a hawk as it caught a thermal and soared above them.

"Fine. You?"

He stopped walking. "Damn it, Frankie. You can't

pretend that the kiss didn't happen. That things haven't changed."

She stopped walking as well and turned to face him. Was he serious? They were pretending to be in a relationship and had almost consummated it. Worse, it was all she could think about. And maybe even worse than that, she wanted it desperately. "It hasn't changed anything."

He made a disbelieving face. She wanted to touch the rough stubble on his jaw, remembering the feel of it earlier when he'd kissed her. Not to mention the memory of their naked bodies molded together for those few moments was so sharp that it cut her to the core. "Don't get me wrong. I wanted you more than my next breath. I still do. But—"

"But?" he demanded.

"But you're my employer and this is a job. For a moment we let ourselves forget that."

"So that's the way we're going to play it?" he asked, sounding upset and as disappointed as she felt.

"Let's not forget why we're here. You're still in love with the memory of Naomi after three years of mourning her death. Let's find out who killed her—if she really was murdered—and then…" She didn't know what came after.

"Do you doubt Naomi was murdered after what happened when we left the Corral?" he demanded.

She thought there could be another explanation, though not one she felt she could share with him until she knew for sure. She still wanted to believe that no one knew where she was, especially the man who'd left her dozens of threatening messages on her phone.

Choosing her words carefully, she said, "Based on

that and what I've learned about Naomi, I think there is a very good chance that she was murdered."

He stared at her for a moment. "That's right. You haven't told me what you learned about her today." He started walking again as if bracing himself for the worst. "So let's hear it."

HANK LISTENED, GETTING angrier by the moment. They'd reached the cabin by the time she'd finished. "This woman, Tamara Baker, is lying. Naomi hated the taste of booze."

"Tamara insinuated that Naomi was into something more than booze. Not men. But something more dangerous."

"Like what? Money laundering? Drugs? Prostitution?" He swore. "Stop looking at me like that. Go ahead, roll your eyes. You think I didn't know my own girlfriend?"

"Why would Tamara lie?"

"I have no idea. But she's wrong and so is Roy at the grocery store. Naomi wouldn't steal. He's thinking of the wrong girl. Naomi sure as heck didn't get fired. She was one of his best workers. She showed me the bonus she got for…" His voice trailed off. "I can't remember what it was for, but I saw the money."

Frankie said nothing, which only made him even angrier. He shoved open the door to the cabin, let her go in first and stormed in behind her. "What if it's all a lie to cover up something else?" He knew he was reaching. He couldn't imagine why these people would make up stories about Naomi.

She shrugged. "I only told you what I'd learned. Maybe she had another life when she wasn't with you."

He shook his head and began pacing, angry and frustrated. "You didn't know her. She was afraid of everything. She was…innocent."

"All right, maybe that's how she got involved in something she didn't know how to get out of."

He stopped pacing. "Like what?"

"She had a boyfriend before you, right?"

"Butch Clark. Randall 'Butch' Clark. But she hadn't seen him in years."

"I want to talk to him. Alone," she added before he could say he was going with her.

"Why? I just told you that she hadn't seen him in years."

She said nothing for a moment, making him swear again. "Just let me follow this lead. I'll go in the morning. Any idea where I can find him?"

"His father owns the hardware store. He'd probably know." He felt sick in the pit of his stomach as he recalled something. "He was at Naomi's funeral. I recognized him."

"So you knew him?"

He shook his head. "Naomi pointed him out once when we first started dating. He didn't seem like her type. I asked her about him, but she didn't want to talk about him, saying he was her past."

Frankie nodded knowingly and he caught a familiar glint in her eye.

"I don't even want to know what you're thinking right now," he said with a groan.

She shrugged. "Naomi had a past. That's all."

He cocked his head at her, waiting.

"That she didn't want to talk about," she added. "Happy?"

"You are so sure she had some deep dark secret. I might remind you that you have a past you don't want to talk about."

"True, but you and I aren't dating."

"We're supposed to be," he said, stepping toward her. "I don't see that as being so unbelievable given what almost happened earlier. How about I fire you, end this employer-employee relationship, and we quit pretending this isn't real?"

FRANKIE LOOKED INTO Hank's blue eyes and felt a shiver of desire ripple through her. It would have been so easy to take this to the next level—and quickly, given the sparks that arced between them. Common sense warned her not to let this happen. But the wild side of her had wanted him almost from the first time he'd walked into her office. The chemistry had been there as if undercover, sizzling just below the surface.

Any woman in her right mind would have wanted this handsome, strong, sexy cowboy. She doubted Hank even knew just how appealing he was. Naomi had held his sensuality at arm's length, using herself as a weapon to get him to the altar. Frankie could see that the wild side of Hank wanted out as badly as she wanted to unleash it.

He stopped directly in front of her, so close she could smell the musky outdoor male scent of him. She felt her pulse leap, her heart pounding as she waited for him to take her in his arms.

Instead, he touched her cheek with the rough tips of his fingers, making her moan as she closed her eyes and leaned into the heavenly feel of his flesh against hers.

At a tap on the door, Hank groaned. "If that's my father—"

"Hello?" Dana called. "Are you guys decent?"

Hank swore softly under his breath and then, locking his gaze with Frankie's, grinned. "Come on in, Mom," he said as he grabbed Frankie, pulled her to him and kissed her hard on the mouth. Breaking off the kiss only after the door had opened, he said, "We are now, Mom."

Chapter Thirteen

It was late by the time Dana left. She'd seemed in a talk-ative mood, and it was clear that she wanted to spend more time with her son. Frankie excused herself to go to bed. She hadn't been able to sleep, though. Her body ached with a need that surprised her. She hadn't felt this kind of desire in a very long time and definitely not this strong.

Trying to concentrate on something, anything else, she considered what she'd learned about Naomi Hill. Sweet, quiet, timid, scared of everything, a nondrinker who was honest as the day was long with only one de-sire in life—to get married and settle down.

Frankie frowned. Was her reason for giving Hank an ultimatum that night only because of that desire? Or was she running from something?

The thought wouldn't go away. Hours later, she heard Dana leave. She lay on her back, staring up at the ceil-ing, hardly breathing, wondering if Hank would come to her bed.

He didn't. She heard the creak of the bed in the other bedroom as he threw himself onto it. She smiled to her-self hearing how restless he was. Like her, he was hav-ing trouble sleeping.

Frankie didn't remember dozing off until she awakened to daylight and the sound of rain pinging off the panes in her window. By the time she'd showered and dressed, determined to do what she had been hired to do, the rain had stopped and the sun had come out. Droplets hung from the pines, shimmering in the sunlight.

When she came out of the bedroom, she found that Hank was also up and dressed.

"I'm going to go talk to Tamara and then maybe go by the grocery store and talk to Roy," he said, not sounding happy about either prospect.

She nodded. He'd shaved and she missed the stubble from last night, but he was still drop-dead handsome. "I'd call you when I get back from seeing Butch Clark, but my phone…"

"Mine too. Why don't we meet back here and have lunch together and share whatever information we come up with? Be careful. I'm sure you haven't forgotten yesterday."

Not hardly. "See you before lunch." She could feel his gaze on her and knew their conversation wasn't over yet.

"About last night—"

"Did you have a nice visit with your mother?"

He grinned, acknowledging that he'd caught her attempt to steer the subject away from the two of them. "I did, but I wasn't referring to yet another interruption just when things were getting interesting. I was going to say, I didn't come to your bed last night not because I didn't want to. Just in case you were wondering. You say you want to keep this strictly professional, but should you change your mind…all you have to do is give me a sign."

She tried to swallow the lump in her throat. He was throwing this into her court. If she wanted him, she'd have to make the next move. Her skin tingled at the thought. "That's good to know," she said and headed for the door.

"No breakfast?" he said behind her. There was humor in his tone, as if he knew she needed to get away from him right now or she might cross that line.

"I'll get something down the road," she said over her shoulder without looking at him because he was right. The thought of stepping into his arms, kissing those lips, letting him take her places she could only imagine, was just too powerful. She turned up the hood on her jacket against the rain and ignored the cold as she kept walking.

HANK SWORE AS he watched Frankie leave. He would have loved to have spent this day in bed—with her. He almost wished he had gone to her bed last night.

As much as he wanted Frankie, he hadn't forgotten why they'd come back to the ranch, back to Big Sky, back to where Naomi had died. He would always love Naomi, he told himself. But for the first time in years, he felt ready to move on. Maybe he could once they'd found out the truth.

He saw his cell phone sitting in the bowl where he'd put it this morning and went to look for Frankie's. He found it beside the sink. It was still wet. He tried to open it. Nothing. Well, at least now she couldn't get those calls that she'd been ignoring.

Who was so insistent? Someone she didn't want to talk to. He'd seen her reaction each time she'd recognized the caller. She'd tensed up as if...as if afraid of the person on the other end of the line? Definitely a man, he thought, and wondered if anyone had ever tried to kill her before yesterday.

He could almost hear her say it went with the job.

But he'd felt her trembling in the water next to him after their escape from his pickup. She'd been as scared as he had been, so he doubted nearly dying went with the job. Although he had a bad feeling that someone *had* tried to kill her. Maybe the person who kept calling.

"Well, now he can't find you, just in case he's been tracking your phone," he said to the empty room.

Hank couldn't put it off any longer. He needed to get to the truth about Naomi. Confronting Tamara and Roy were at least places to start. He wasn't looking forward to it. He doubted they would change their stories, which would mean that he hadn't known Naomi.

He sighed, wishing he was curled up in bed with Frankie, but since that wasn't an option, he grabbed his jacket and headed out into the cool, damp summer morning.

RANDALL "BUTCH" CLARK was easy to find—in the back of his father's hardware store, signing in the most recent order. As the delivery driver pulled away, Butch turned and stopped as if surprised to see that he had company. He was short, average-looking with curly sandy-blond hair and light brown eyes.

"Frankie," she said, holding out her hand as she closed the distance between them.

Butch hesitated. "If this is about a job, my dad does the hiring. I'm just—" He waved a hand as if he wasn't sure exactly what his title was.

"I'm not looking for a job. I'm here about Naomi."

"Naomi?" he repeated, both startled and suddenly

nervous as he fiddled with the clipboard in his hands. "Is there something new with her that I don't know about?"

Frankie decided to cut to the chase. "I'm a private investigator looking into her death." If he asked for her credentials, she was screwed. Fortunately, he didn't.

His eyes widened in surprise. Or alarm? She couldn't be sure. "Why? It's been three years. I thought her death was ruled a suicide?" His voice broke.

She closed the distance between them, watching the man's eyes, seeing how badly he wanted to run. "You and I know it wasn't suicide, don't we, Butch?"

"I don't have any idea what you're talking about."

Frankie went on instinct based on Butch's reaction thus far. He was scared and he was hiding something. "You and Naomi were close." She saw him swallow as if he feared where she was headed. "So if anyone knew what was going on with her, it was you."

Butch didn't deny it. "Why are you asking about this now?"

"The marshal has reopened the case."

He took a step back, put down the clipboard on one of the boxes stacked along the delivery ramp and wiped his palms on the thighs of his dirty work pants. "Look, I don't want to get involved."

"You're already involved, Butch. But I might be able to help you. No one needs to know about your... part in all this if—" he started to object but she rushed on "—you tell me what you know. The marshal didn't question you the first time, right?" She saw the answer. Hud hadn't known about the old boyfriend. "So there is no reason for your name to come up now, right?"

His eyes widened in alarm. "I didn't do *anything.*"

"But Naomi did."

He looked down at his scuffed sneakers.

"Could we sit down?" she asked and didn't wait for an answer. There were three chairs around a folding card table that appeared to be used as a break room. Probably for the smokers since there was a full ashtray in the middle of the table along with several empty soda cans.

"Just tell me what you know and let me help you," she said. "I'm your best bet."

He pulled out a chair, turned it around and straddled it, leaning his chin on his arms as he looked at her with moist brown eyes. "I don't even know who you are or who you work for."

"Probably better that you don't if you want me to keep your name out of it, but—" She reached for her shoulder bag.

He quickly waved it off. "You're right. I don't want to know. But if you work for them, I had nothing to do with this. I told her not to keep the money. It was like she'd never seen a movie and known that they always come after the money."

Frankie did her best not to let her surprise show as she quickly asked, "Where did she find it?"

"She told me on the highway." His tone said he didn't believe her.

"Did she tell you how much money was in it?"

He looked away. "I told her not to count it. Not to touch it. To put it back where she found it and keep her mouth shut. But she saw there was a small fortune in the bag. She'd never seen that much money."

"What did she plan to do with it?"

Butch let out a bark of a laugh. "Buy a big house,

marry that rancher she was dating, move down here in the valley, raise kids, go to soccer practice. She had it all worked out except…" He shook his head.

"Except?"

He looked at her as if she hadn't been listening. "The rancher didn't want to marry her, she thought someone was following her and she ended up dead."

Frankie caught on two things he'd said. Butch knew that the night of Naomi's death, Hank said he wasn't ready to get married. Someone was following her that night. "Did she tell the rancher about the money?"

"No way. She said he was too straitlaced. He'd want to turn it in to his father. He'd be too scared to keep it."

But timid little Naomi apparently wasn't. "You said someone was following her?" He glanced down, obviously just realizing what he'd said. "The night she died. That's when you talked to her."

He looked up but she shook her head in warning for him not to lie. "She called the bar where I was having a drink with friends and told me that she thought she was being followed."

"What did you tell her to do?"

He rubbed a hand over his face. "I didn't know what to tell her. She sounded hysterical. I said give it back. Stop your car, give it to them. She said she couldn't, that she'd put some of the money down on a house and couldn't get it back."

"So then what did you tell her to do?"

"I thought that maybe if she explained the situation…"

Frankie groaned inside. If the money Naomi had found was what she thought it was, negotiating was out of the question. "So she pulled over and tried to bargain?"

He shrugged, his voice breaking when he spoke. "I don't know. The line went dead. I tried to call her back but there was no answer."

"Did she know who she'd taken the money from?" Frankie asked.

"If she did, she never said anything to me. I swear it." He rose from the chair. "Please, I thought this was over. I thought your people… Whoever you're working for. I thought they got most of their money back. At least, what was left." He frowned. "I thought it was over," he repeated.

Frankie got up from her chair. "As far as I'm concerned, it is over."

Relief made him slump and have to steady himself on the back of the chair he'd abandoned. He let out a ragged breath and straightened. "So we're good?"

She nodded as a loud male voice called from inside the store.

"That's my father. I have to—" He was gone, running through the swinging doors and disappearing from sight.

Frankie went out the back way and walked around to the pickup Dana Savage had lent her. Climbing behind the wheel, she wished she had a cell phone so she could call Hank. Up the block she spotted the time on one of the banks. It was about forty minutes back to Big Sky. She'd tell Hank when she saw him. But at least now she knew the truth.

Naomi Hill had been murdered—just as he'd suspected. It didn't put them any closer, though, to knowing who'd killed her, but at least now they knew why.

HANK DROVE INTO Meadow Village after he left the ranch. Frankie had told him that Tamara worked at the

Silver Spur Bar. But when he parked and went inside, he was told that it was her day off. He asked for her address and wrangled for a moment with the bartender before the man gave it over. Hank dropped a twenty-dollar bill on the bar as he left.

He knew the old cabins the bartender had told him about. But as he neared the row of four cabins, he spotted marshal office vehicles parked out front. Crime scene tape flapped in the wind.

Swearing, he pulled in and, getting out, started past the deputy stationed outside.

"Hold up," the deputy said. "No one goes inside. Marshal's orders."

"Tell him I need to see him," Hank said. He held up his hands. "Tell him his son is out here, Hank. Hank Savage. I'll stand right here until you get back and won't let anyone else get past. I promise."

The deputy disappeared inside and almost at once returned with Hud.

"What's going on?" Hank asked in a hushed voice as the two of them stepped over to the ranch pickup he'd driven into town.

"What are you doing here?"

"I came by to see Tamara Baker. Frankie had spoken to her about Naomi. I wanted to talk to her." Immediately he realized his mistake as he saw his father's eyes narrow. "Tamara said some things about Naomi that didn't seem right."

"Like what?"

He didn't really want to discuss this out here, let alone voice them at all, especially to his father. Also, the marshal hadn't answered his question. He pointed out both.

"Tamara's dead."

"Dead? Not—" He didn't have to say "murdered." He saw the answer in his father's expression.

"When I get through here, I think we'd better talk." With that, his father turned and went back inside as the coroner's van pulled up.

Chapter Fourteen

Back at the ranch, Frankie went straight to the cabin to wait for Hank. She felt anxious. What she'd learned was more than disturbing. Naomi had apparently found the answer to her prayers—or so she thought. Where had she picked up the bag of money? It seemed doubtful that it had been tossed out beside the road.

At the sound of the door opening, she spun around and saw Hank's face. "What's happened?" she asked, feeling her pulse jump and her stomach drop.

"I went over to talk to Tamara Baker. She wasn't at the bar. I got directions to her cabin. My father was there along with a crime team and the coroner." He met her gaze. "She'd been murdered."

The news floored her. Stumbling back, she sat down hard on the sofa. The ramifications rocketed through her. She'd talked to Tamara and now she was dead. Swallowing down the lump in her throat, she said, "There's more. I'm pretty sure I know why Naomi was murdered."

Hank moved to a chair and sat down as if suddenly too weak to stand. "You talked to Butch."

"He said she found a bag of money."

"What?" he asked in disbelief.

"Drug money, I would imagine. Enough money that she put some of it down on a house in Bozeman for when the two of you got married."

He dropped his head into his hands. "This can't be true," he mumbled through his fingers.

"She called Butch that night at the bar where he was meeting his friends—"

"So this bastard knew about this the whole time?" Hank demanded as his head came up, his blue eyes flaring.

"She told him she was being followed. She was afraid it was them, whoever the money belonged to. She debated stopping and giving back what she had left with a promise to pay back the rest."

He groaned. "She was going to make a deal with a bunch of drug dealers?"

"Her phone went dead. He tried to call her back but there was no answer."

Hank shook his head. "She told him all of this? So he knew she was in trouble and he didn't do anything?"

Frankie knew that the tough part for Hank was that Naomi hadn't trusted him with her secret. It wasn't just that she'd been living a lie, the bonus at work, not telling him about getting fired, the drinking with Tamara, the close connection with her old boyfriend when she felt she was in trouble, and River Dean, the backup if things didn't work out with Hank.

It was a lot for the cowboy to take. She wondered how Naomi had planned to explain all this money she'd come into, including the house she was in the process of buying. Maybe an inheritance? Maybe Hank would have bought the explanation, except that he hadn't wanted to get married and move to Bozeman.

Naomi had been so naive that she'd thought the drug dealers wouldn't find out who'd taken their money? Especially if it had been a lot. A small fortune to Naomi might not have been that much to some people in the wealthy part of Big Sky. But the drug dealers would have wanted it back.

"I suspect, given what you just told me," Frankie said, "that Naomi also confided in Tamara."

Hank pushed to his feet, a hand raking through his hair as he walked to the window, his back to her. "I didn't know her at all." He sounded shocked. "I loved her so much and I had no idea who she really was."

"You loved the idea of her. You fell in love with what she wanted you to see. Eventually, you would have seen behind the facade. Hopefully, before it was too late to walk away unscathed."

HANK HEARD SOMETHING in her voice. Regret. He turned to study Frankie. "Is that what happened with this man who keeps calling you?" He didn't expect an answer. He thought of Naomi. "I'm not sure it was love—at least on her part. With love comes trust. She didn't trust me enough to tell me about the money."

"Your father is the marshal."

He let out a snort. "She really thought I'd go to my father with this?"

"Wouldn't you have?"

Hank laughed and shook his head. "I would have made her turn the money over to my father." He nodded. "It would have been the only smart thing to do and she would have hated me for it."

Frankie gave him a that's-why-she-didn't-tell-you shrug.

"Well, he has to know about all of this now. He probably has people he suspects are dealing drugs in the area. What are the chances that they killed Naomi and now Tamara?" His gaze came up to meet hers and his quickly softened. "You can't blame yourself."

"I talked to her and now she's dead. Who should I blame?"

"The man you said was sitting down the bar. He was the only witness when the two of you were talking, right?"

She nodded. "But she could have told someone after that."

He shook his head as all the ramifications began to pile up. "I knew she'd been murdered. I damn well knew it. But I would never have guessed…" He sighed. "When I saw my father at Tamara's cabin, I told him that you'd talked to Tamara about Naomi. I'm sorry. I slipped up."

"Don't you think it's time we tell your parents the truth? It's pretty obvious that we're investigating Naomi's death."

"Come on. Let's go." He headed for the door.

"Just like that?"

He shook his head. "My father could be here any moment. Let's go get some lunch. I don't want to be interrogated on an empty stomach."

They left the ranch with him driving the ranch pickup he'd borrowed that morning. "I know this out-of-the-way place." He turned onto the highway and headed south toward Yellowstone Park.

Lost in thought, he said little on the drive. He could see that Frankie was battling her own ghosts. He wondered again about the man in her life who kept calling. All his instincts told him that the man was dangerous.

As he neared the spot they would have lunch, he

dragged himself out of his negative thoughts, determined to enjoy lunch with Frankie and put everything behind them for a while.

"My father and grandfather used to tell stories about driving down here in the dead of winter to get a piece of banana cream pie," he said as they turned into a place called the Cinnamon Lodge. "It used to be called Almart. Alma and Art owned it and she would save pieces of banana cream pie for them."

"That's a wonderful story," Frankie said, as if seeing that he wanted to talk about anything but Naomi. "Something smells good," she said as they got out and approached the log structure.

Hank figured she wasn't any more hungry than he was. But he'd needed to get out of the cabin, away from all of it, just for a little while. It wasn't until after they'd had lunch and were in the pickup again that he told her what he'd been thinking from the moment he saw the crime scene tape around Tamara's cabin.

"It's time for you to go back to Idaho. You can take one of the pickups and—"

"I'm not leaving," she said as he started the pickup's engine, backed out and pulled onto the highway.

"You don't understand. You're fired. I have no more use for your services."

Frankie laughed and dug her heels in. "You think you can get rid of me that easily?"

"I'll pay you the bonus I promised you as well as your per diem and—"

"Stop! You think I don't know what you're doing?"

He glanced over at her, worry knitting his brows. "It's too dangerous. I should have realized that after what happened yesterday with that truck. But now that we know what we're dealing with—"

"Exactly. What *we're* dealing with. I want to see this through. With you." Her last words broke with emotion.

Hank sighed and reached for her, pulling her over against him on the bench seat of the older-model pickup. She cuddled against him, finding herself close to tears. She couldn't quit this now. She couldn't quit Hank. "Frankie—"

She touched a finger to his lip. "I'm not leaving."

"Yesterday was a warning," he said. "I see that now. If we don't quit looking into Naomi's death—"

"Her *murder*," she said, drawing back enough to look at him. "Are you telling me that you can walk away now that you know the truth?" She could see that he hadn't thought about what he would do.

"We have no idea who they are. Unless my father can track down that truck and find the driver…"

"So you think that makes us safe? You think they won't be worried about what we know, what we found out?"

"I don't want to think about it right now." He pulled her close again, resting his head against the top of hers for a moment as he drove.

She could hear the steady, strong thump of his heart as she rested her head against his chest. This man made her feel things she'd never felt before. Together there was a strength to them that made her feel safe and strong…and brazen.

"Then let's go back to the cabin and not think at all," she said, taking that unabashed step into the unknown as if she was invincible in his arms.

HANK MEET HER gaze and grinned as he slowed for the turnoff to the ranch. "Are you making a move on me, Miss Brewster?"

She sat up and started to answer when she looked out the windshield at the road ahead and suddenly froze. Following her gaze, he could see a large dark sedan parked on the edge of the road into the ranch. He looked over at Frankie as she moved out from under his arm to her side of the pickup. All the color had drained from her face.

"Frankie?" he asked as he made the turn into the ranch and drove slowly by the car. He could see a man sitting behind the wheel. Frankie, he noticed, hadn't looked. Because, he realized, she knew who it was.

"Frankie?" Her gaze was still locked straight ahead, her body coiled like a rattler about to strike.

"Stop," she said and reached for her door handle.

He kept going. "No way am I letting you face whatever that is back there alone."

She shot him a desperate look that scared him. "Damn it, Hank, this has nothing to do with you. Stop the pickup and let me out. *Now!*"

Frankie was right. He'd opened up his life to her, but hers had been off-limits to him from the get-go. Nothing had changed.

He gritted his teeth as he brought the pickup to a stop. Her door opened at once and she jumped out, slamming the door behind her as she started to walk back to where the car and driver waited.

Watching in the side mirror, he cursed under his breath as he remembered her frightened expression every time her cell phone had rung with a call from whoever the man had been. Hank would put his money on that same man now sitting in that car, waiting for her.

All his instincts told him that whoever this man was, he was trouble. Frankie could pretend he wasn't, but Hank knew better. Except that she'd made it abundantly clear she wanted to handle this herself.

With a curse, he shifted into gear and headed the pickup down the road toward the ranch. She didn't need his help. Didn't want it. The PI thought she could handle this herself. She probably could.

After only a few yards up the road, he slammed on the brakes. Like hell he was going to let her handle this on her own, whether she liked it or not.

Throwing the pickup in Reverse, he sped back up the road, coming to a dust-boiling stop in front of the car.

Frankie had almost reached the vehicle. He saw that the driver had leaned over to throw the passenger-side door open for her to get in. The jackass wasn't even going to get out.

He could hear the man yelling at her to get in. Grabbing the tire iron from under the seat, Hank jumped out.

"She's not getting into that car with you," he said as he walked toward the driver's-side window. He could feel Frankie's angry gaze on him and heard her yell something at him, but it didn't stop him. "You have a problem with Frankie? I want to hear about it," he said, lifting the tire iron.

Chapter Fifteen

The man behind the wheel of the car threw open his door and climbed out. He was as tall as Hank and just as broad across the shoulders. The man had bully written all over him from his belligerent attitude to the bulging muscles of his arms from hours spent at the gym. Hank heard Frankie cry, "J.J., don't!"

"Who the hell are you and what are you doing with my fiancée?" the man she'd called J.J. demanded.

Hank shot a look at Frankie across the hood of the man's car.

"She didn't mention that she's engaged to me?" J.J. said with obvious delight. "I see she's not wearing her ring either. But you haven't answered me. Who the hell are—" His words were drowned out by the sudden *whop* of a police siren as the marshal pulled in on the other side of Hank's pickup.

J.J. swore. "You bitch," he yelled, turning to glare at her. Frankie had stopped on the other side of his car. She looked small and vulnerable, but even from where he stood, Hank could see that she would still fight like a wild woman if it came to that. "You called the law on me?"

The man swung his big head in Hank's direction.

"Or did you call the cops, you son of a..." He started to take a step toward Hank, who slapped the iron into his palm, almost daring him to attack.

J.J.'s gaze swung past him. Out of the corner of his eye, he saw his father standing in front of his patrol SUV. J.J. saw the marshal uniform as well, swore and hurriedly leaped back into his car. The engine revved and Hank had to step back as J.J. took off, tires throwing gravel before he hit the highway and sped away.

"What was that about?" Hud asked after he reached in to turn off the siren before walking over to his son.

Hank looked at Frankie, who was hugging herself and shaking her head. "It was nothing," he said. "Just some tourist passing through who wanted to give us a hard time."

His father grunted, clearly not believing a word of it. "I need to talk to the two of you. Your cabin. Now."

Hank nodded, his gaze still on Frankie. "We'll be right there."

J.J. DROVE AWAY, fuming. *She called the cops on me?* Had she lost her mind? And that cowboy... Hank Savage had no idea what he'd stepped into, but he was about to find out.

"The cowboy's name is Hank Savage. His father's the marshal of the resort town of Big Sky, Montana," his friend at the station told him after he'd managed to get the license plate number off one of the business surveillance cameras near Frankie's office. The camera had picked up not just the man's truck but a pretty good image of the cowboy himself going into Frankie's office and coming out again—with her. She'd gone down the block, gotten into her SUV and then followed the pickup.

"You recognize the cowboy?" his friend had asked.

"No. It must be a job." But she'd left her rig in her garage.

"Well, if it is a job, she went with him, from what you told me her neighbor said."

That was the part that floored him. Why would she take off with a man she didn't know? Unless she did know him. He thought of how the man had defended her. Hell, had she been seeing this cowboy behind his back?

He drove down the highway, checking his rearview mirror. The marshal hadn't come after him. That was something, anyway. But how dare his cowboy son threaten him with a tire iron. That cowboy was lucky his father came along when he did. He swore, wanting a piece of that man—and Frankie. He'd teach them both not to screw around with him.

He pulled into the movie theater parking lot and called his friend back in Lost Creek. After quickly filling him in, he said, "I'm going to kill her."

"Maybe you should come on back and let this cool down until—"

"No way. I don't know what's going on, but she's my fiancée."

Silence. Then, "J.J., she broke off the engagement. You can't force her to marry you."

"The hell I can't. Look, she's mad at me. I screwed up, got a little rough with her, but once we sit down and hash this out, she'll put the ring back on. I just can't have some cowboy get in the middle of this."

"Where'd she meet this guy?"

"That's just it. I have no idea. Why would she just leave with him unless she knew him before? The neighbor said she packed a small bag and left. If she'd been seeing this cowboy behind my back, I would have heard, wouldn't I?"

"It's probably just what you originally thought. A job."

He shook his head. "She was sitting all snuggled up next to him in the pickup. It's not a job. The bitch is—"

"Come back and let yourself cool down. If you don't, you might do something you're going to regret. You already have a couple strikes against you at work. You get in trouble down there—"

"Not yet. Don't worry. I'll be fine." He disconnected. Fine once he got his hands on Frankie. He sat for a moment until he came up with a plan. He'd stake out the ranch. The next time she left it, he'd follow her. But first he had to get rid of this car. He needed a nondescript rental, something she or the cowboy wouldn't suspect.

"I DIDN'T WANT you involved," Frankie said with rancor the moment they were in his pickup, headed back to the ranch. The marshal had waited and now followed them into the ranch property.

"You made that clear. None of my business, right?" He looked over at her, his eyes hard as ice chips. "It isn't like you and I mean anything to each other. Still just employer and employee. Why mention a fiancé?"

"I told you, I broke it off."

He continued as if he hadn't heard her. "It isn't like we were just heading up to our cabin to… What was it we were going to do, Frankie?"

She sighed and looked away. "J.J. and I were engaged. I called it off two months ago. He didn't take it well."

"So I gathered. Now he's still harassing you. Why haven't you gone to the authorities?"

"It's complicated. I don't have the best relationship with the local cops in Lost Creek."

"Because you're a private investigator?"

"Because J.J. is one of them. He's a cop."

"A cop?" Hank shook his head. He was driving so slowly, he knew it was probably making his father crazy. It was his own fault for insisting he follow them into the ranch. As if he thought they might make a run for it?

"How long did you date him?"

"Six months. He seemed like a nice guy. The engagement was too quick but he asked me at this awards banquet in front of all his friends and fellow officers. I...I foolishly said yes even though I wasn't ready. Even though I had reservations."

"He doesn't seem like the kind of guy who takes no for an answer." When she said nothing, he added, "So he put a ring on your finger and then he wasn't a nice guy anymore. Nor does he seem like a guy who gives up easily." Hank met her gaze.

She dragged hers away. "It's his male pride. All his buddies down at the force have been giving him a hard time about the broken engagement. It isn't as if his being unable to accept it has anything to do with love, trust me. He just refuses to let this go. I gave him back his ring and he broke into my house and left it on my dining room table. But this isn't your problem, okay? I'll handle it."

He shook his head. "He comes back, *I'll* handle it," he said. "I can see how terrified you are of him and for good reason. I asked you if he was dangerous. I know now that he is. That man's hurt you and next time he just might kill you. I'm not going to let that happen as long as you're—" their gazes met "—in my employ," he finished.

After parking next to his father's patrol SUV, he sat for a moment as if trying to calm down. He'd been afraid for her. She understood he'd been worried that she would have stupidly gotten into that car.

Through the windshield, she could see the marshal was standing next to his patrol SUV, arms crossed, a scowl on his face as he waited.

Beside her in the pickup cab, she could feel Hank's anger. "Right now I don't even know what to say to you. Would you have been foolish enough to climb into that car with that man?" He glanced over at her. "You make me want to shake some sense into you until your teeth rattle. Worse, you stubbornly thought you could handle a man like J.J. and didn't need or want my help."

She wanted to tell him that she'd been on her own for a long time. She wasn't used to asking for help, but he didn't give her a chance.

"I thought you trusted me," he said, his voice breaking with emotion as he parked in front of the house and climbed out.

FOR A MOMENT, Frankie leaned back against the seat, fighting tears. Hank had shot her a parting look before getting out and slamming the door behind him. It was filled with disappointment that wrenched at her heart. He'd thought she was smart. Smart wasn't getting involved with J.J. Whitaker. Worse was thinking she could handle this situation on her own. Hank was right. J.J. was dangerous. If he got her alone again, he would do more than hurt her, as angry as he was.

Wiping her eyes, she opened her door and followed the two men up the mountain to the cabin. She ached with a need to be in Hank's arms. J.J. had found her at the worst possible time. Had he been delayed a few hours, she would have been curled up in bed with Hank. Instead, Hank was furious at her, and with good reason.

She should have told him the truth way before this. J.J. was a loose cannon. What would have happened if the marshal hadn't come along when he did? She just hadn't thought the crazed cop would find her. Why hadn't she realized he would use any and every re-source he had at his disposal to get to her? Especially if her nosy neighbor had told him that she'd left with some cowboy.

J.J. would have been jealous even if her relationship with Hank were strictly business because he thought every man wanted what he had. With Hank acting the way he did…well, J.J. would be convinced she and Hank were lovers. They would have been, she thought as a sob bubbled up in her chest and made her ache.

Not that it would have solved anything. In fact, it would have complicated an already difficult situation. But now she was drowning in regret.

Chapter Sixteen

The marshal and Hank were both waiting for her when she topped the hill at the cabin. Hank held the door open for her and his father. She walked past him, feeling his anger and his fear. She'd told him to let her handle it and yet he'd come back to save her. She loved him and wanted to smack him for it.

"Anyone else want a beer besides me?" Hank asked as he went straight to the kitchen. His father declined as he took a seat in the living area. Frankie could have used something stronger, but she declined a beer as well. She felt as if she needed to keep her wits about her as she sat down on the couch.

"You want to tell me what that was about on the highway?" Hud said quietly to Frankie since he'd already heard Hank's version.

"An old boyfriend who won't take no for an answer," she said. "He's a cop in Lost Creek, where I live. He tracked me here."

The marshal nodded. "He going to be a problem?"

She swallowed. "I hope not."

Hank came back into the room carrying a bottle of beer, half of it already gone. "If he comes back here—"

"You call me," Hud interrupted. "You call me and let me handle it. I mean it."

Hank said nothing, his face a mask of stubborn determination mixed with anger. She couldn't tell how much of it was anger at her for not telling him or wanting to handle it herself or being frustrated by the J.J. situation as well as the two of them and where they'd been headed earlier.

The marshal cleared his voice. "We found the truck that ran you off the road. It's an old one that's been parked up at an abandoned cabin. Lab techs are checking for prints, but they're not hopeful. Anyone who knew about the truck could have used it. I'm surprised the thing still runs. Anyway, the paint matched as well as the damage to the right side."

"So it was someone local," Hank said. He looked at Frankie and saw her relief that it hadn't had anything to do with her and J.J. The woman had so many secrets. He thought of Naomi and cursed under his breath. Except Naomi had been needy. Frankie was determined to handle everything herself. He shook his head at her and turned back to his father.

"That makes sense given what we've learned about Naomi's death," he said and looked to Frankie again to see if she wanted to be the one to tell him. She gave him a slight nod to continue.

She was on the couch, her legs curled under her with one of Hank's grandmother's quilts wrapped around her. He could tell that her run-in with her former fiancé had rattled her more than she'd wanted him to see.

He was still angry and had a bad feeling that J.J. might come to the ranch next time looking for her. He'd obviously tracked her as far as the main entrance. How crazy was the cop? Wasn't it enough that they had drug dealers wanting to kill them?

"Naomi found a bag of money," Hank began and told his father what Frankie had found out about Naomi's final phone call to an old boyfriend saying she was being followed and asking him what she should do. Give what money she had left back? "And then apparently her phone went dead or she turned it off."

Hud swore under his breath. "Drug money?"

"That's the assumption."

"Did this old boyfriend, whose name I'm going to need, did he say where she'd found it?" He looked to Frankie. She shook her head. "And you knew nothing about this?" he said, turning back to Hank.

"Nothing." He chewed at his cheek for a moment, trying to hold back his hurt and anger, realizing that he was more angry at Naomi than Frankie, though both had kept things from him. He was aware of the distinction between the two. Naomi was his girlfriend, the woman he'd planned to marry. Frankie… He looked over at her. She was a hell of a lot more than his employee—that much he knew. "Apparently Naomi didn't trust me. Must be something about me that women don't trust."

Frankie groaned and shook her head. "Let's leave you and me out of this."

He saw his father following the conversation between them with interest for a moment before getting back to Naomi and the drug money.

"If she had told you, I hope you would have been smart enough to come to me. Wouldn't you?"

Hank nodded. "I certainly wouldn't have let her keep the money, which I'm sure is why she didn't tell me."

"So the two of you have been digging around in

Naomi's death," Hud said after a moment. Hank glanced over at Frankie and considered telling his father about his arrangement with the PI. But he had a feeling his father already knew. Anyway, their arrangement was beside the point.

"Tamara must have at least suspected who the drug dealers were," Hank said.

"And contacted them to let them know that we were asking questions," the marshal said.

"Would explain how we ended up in the river."

"I'm pretty sure she was involved." They both looked over at Frankie, surprised that she'd spoken.

"You talked to Tamara," Hud said. "Did you get the feeling she knew more than she was telling you?"

"She hinted that Naomi was wilder than anyone knew, that she had secrets and lived a double life. But from what Hank had told me about her," Frankie continued, "I had the feeling Tamara was talking about herself."

"Well, whatever she knew, she is no longer talking," the marshal said. "And the two of you…" He took a breath and let it out. "I wish you'd been honest with me about what you were doing."

"You didn't believe that Naomi had been murdered," Hank pointed out, feeling his hackles rise a little.

"I know, and I'm sorry about that. You were right. I was wrong. But now you have to let me handle this. I need you both to promise that you're done investigating."

"I promise," Hank said, looking at Frankie.

"Fine," she said. "If that's what you want," she said to him, rather than the marshal.

"Do you have some suspects?" Hank asked.

"I hear things," his father said. "The problem is getting evidence to convict them. Are there drugs being distributed in Big Sky? Maybe even more than in other places in Montana just because of the amount of money here." He rose to leave. "I'm expecting you both to keep your promise. Otherwise, I'm going to lock you up. I'm tempted to anyway, just to keep you both safe. As much as I hate to say this, it might be a good idea for the two of you to go back home to Idaho. At least for a while."

Hank looked at Frankie. "We'll leave in the morning."

"After breakfast. Your mother will be upset enough, but at least have one more meal with her before you take off," Hud said and met Hank's gaze. "You might want to tell your mother the truth. I don't want her planning a wedding just yet."

Hank walked his father out. "Dad, that car earlier? It was Frankie's former fiancé. She broke up with him two months ago but he's continued to stalk her. He's a cop from Lost Creek."

"I'll keep an eye out for him."

"Thanks." He felt his father's gaze on him and seemed about to say something but must have changed his mind.

"See you at breakfast," Hud said, turned and left.

FRANKIE FELT AS if her heart would break. She felt ashamed. She should have known better with J.J. She'd ignored all the red flags. It made her more ashamed when she remembered how she'd given Hank grief for ignoring the obvious signs with Naomi. She prided herself on reading people, on seeing behind their masks, on using those skills to do her job.

But when it came to her own personal life? She'd

failed miserably. It didn't matter that J.J. had hidden his real self from her. She still should have seen behind the facade. Now she couldn't get away from him. He must have tracked her phone. How else could he have found her? At least he hadn't tried to kill them in that old truck that forced them into the river. She could be thankful for that.

Throwing off the quilt, she headed for the shower, feeling dirty and sick to her stomach. She'd never wanted Hank to know about J.J., let alone have the two meet. After turning on the shower, she stepped under the warm spray and reached for the body gel to scrub away her shame and embarrassment.

Tomorrow she and Hank would go back to Idaho. She hated leaving anything unfinished. She'd at least found out why Naomi Hill had died. But she had no idea who might be behind the murder. As she tilted her face up to the water, she remembered the man sitting at the end of the bar the day she went to talk to Tamara. He'd been acting like he wasn't paying them any attention, but he'd probably been listening to their conversation. Also, Tamara had gone down the bar and the two had been whispering. What if he was—

The shower door opened, making her spin around in surprise, all thoughts suddenly gone as she looked into Hank's baby-blue eyes. "Mind if I join you?"

She stepped back and watched as he climbed in still dressed in everything but his boots. "You don't want to take off your clothes?"

"Not yet," he said as he closed the shower door behind them and turned to take her in. "Damn, woman, you are so beautiful."

"I'm so sorry that you had to find out about J.J.," she

said, close to tears. "He's the big mistake of my life and I'm so ashamed for getting involved with such a loser."

He touched his finger to her lips and shook his head. "We all make mistakes. Look at me and Naomi. But you don't have to worry. I'm not going to let J.J. hurt you ever again. I promise."

"I don't want you—"

"Involved? Once I take off my clothes and get naked with you? We'll be in this together, you understand?"

She swallowed the lump in her throat, but could only nod.

He slowly began to unsnap his Western shirt.

"I think you'd better let me help you with that," she said, grabbing each side of the shirt and pulling. As the shirt fabric parted, revealing his muscled, tanned chest, she ached to touch him. As he drew her to him, she pushed her palms against the warmth of his flesh and leaned back for his kiss.

"Last chance," Hank said as he ended the kiss and reached for the buttons of his jeans. "There won't be any going back once these babies come off."

She laughed and pushed his hands away to unbutton his jeans and let them drop to the floor of the shower along with his underwear and his socks. She looked at his amazing body—and his obvious desire—and returned her gaze to his handsome face. "No going back," she said as she stepped into his arms again and molded her warm, wet body to his.

HANK KISSED HER passionately as he backed her up against the tiled wall of the shower, before his mouth dropped to her round, full breasts. Her nipples were dark and hard, the spray dripping off the tips temptingly. He bent his head to lick off a droplet before taking the erect nipple into his mouth and sucking it.

Frankie leaned her head back, arching her body against his mouth, a groan of pleasure escaping her lips. He took the other nipple in his mouth as his hand dropped down her belly and between her legs. He felt her go weak as his fingers found the spot that made her tremble. She clung to him as he made slow circles until she cried out and fell into his arms again.

He reached around to turn off the water and opened the shower door. After grabbing several large white bath towels from the hooks, he tied one around his waist and wrapped Frankie in the other. Sweeping her into his arms, he carried her toward his bedroom. His heart pounded. He meant what he'd told her. They were now in this together. No more secrets.

She looped her arms around his neck and leaned her face into the hollow of his shoulder as he kicked open the door to the bedroom, stalked in and, still holding her, kissed her, teasing her lips open with his tongue. The tip of her tongue met his and he moaned as he laid her on the bed.

She grabbed him and pulled him down with her. "I want you, Hank Savage," she said, the words like a blaze she'd just lit in his veins. "Oh, how I want you."

MUCH LATER THEY lay in each other's arms, Frankie feeling as if she was floating on a cloud. She couldn't remember ever feeling this happy, this content. But there was another emotion floating on the surface with her. She had trouble recognizing it for a moment because it was so new to her. Joy.

It made her feel as if everything was going to be all

right. She usually wasn't so optimistic. She was too ra-
tional for that. But in Hank's arms, she believed in all
the fairy tales. She even believed in true love, although
she knew it was too early to be thinking this way. Look
at the mistake she'd made with J.J. Six months hadn't
been long enough to date him before getting engaged.

She looked over at Hank. And here she was curled
up in bed with a man she'd only known for days.

"Are you all right?" he asked as she sat up to sit on
the edge of the bed.

The reality of it had hit her hard. "I was just thinking this might be too fast."

He caressed her bare back. "I can understand why
you're scared, but is that what your heart tells you?"

Gripping the sheet to her chest, she turned to look at
him. She knew only too well what her heart was telling
her. She just wasn't sure she could trust it right now.

Finding safer ground, she said, "I remembered something when I was in the shower—before you joined me.
The man sitting at the bar. He was more than a regular.
He and Tamara…they had a connection. I'm sure of it
and it wasn't romantic. He had to overhear our conversation, which could mean…that if he was involved in
the drug distribution and Tamara knew about it or was
involved, he could have ordered the driver of that truck
to either scare us or kill us."

"You're purposely avoiding the question."

Frankie gave him an impatient look. "Sandy blond,
about your height, a little chunkier." That made him
raise a brow. "You know what I mean."

Hank stopped her. "I know who you're talking about.
I know exactly who you're talking about. I went to school
with him. Darrel Sanders. He has a snow removal busi-

ness in the winter. I have no idea what he does in the summer." He reached for his phone and realized the late hour. "I'd better wait and tell Dad at breakfast."

He drew her back onto the bed, turning her to spoon against her. "We can take all the time you want," he whispered into her ear, sending a shiver through her. "I'll wait."

She pressed her body against his in answer and felt his desire stir again. Chuckling, she turned in his arms to kiss him. He deepened the kiss and rolled her over until she was on top of him.

Frankie looked into his blue eyes and felt so much emotion that it hurt. Too fast or not, she was falling hard for this cowboy.

Chapter Seventeen

Dana noticed right away that there was something differ-ent about her son and Frankie. She shot a look at Hud. He shrugged, but as he took his seat at the breakfast table, she saw him hide a knowing grin. She knew that grin.

"So, how are you two this morning?" she asked, look-ing first at her son, then Frankie.

"Great," they both said in unison and laughed.

She noticed that they were sitting closer together, and if she wasn't wrong, her son's hand was on Frankie's thigh. Whatever problems they'd been having, she was relieved to see that they'd moved on from them. At least for the time being. She feared that the ghost of Naomi was still hanging around.

"I made a special breakfast," she said. "Waffles, eggs, ham and bacon, orange juice and fresh fruit."

"Mom, you shouldn't have gone to all this trou-ble," Hank said, "but we appreciate it. I'm starved." He picked up the plate of waffles, pulled three onto his plate and passed the plate to Frankie.

"I can't remember the last time I had waffles," Frankie said and helped herself.

"Try the huckleberry syrup," he suggested. "It's my grandmother's recipe. Or there is chokecherry syrup, also my grandmother Mary's recipe." Dana had named her daughter after her.

She loved seeing her son and Frankie in such a good mood. She watched with a light heart as they helped themselves to everything she'd prepared. They both did have healthy appetites. She smiled over at Hud, remembering how he'd appreciated hers, back when she was that young.

She looked at the two lovebirds and wondered, though, if she'd really ever been that young. Nothing could spoil this moment, she thought, right before the phone rang.

Hud excused himself to answer it since it was probably marshal business.

Hank got up too, to follow his father into the other room.

Dana pushed the butter over to Frankie. "You look beautiful this morning. I love that shirt." It wasn't one of those baggy ones like she wore most of the time.

"Thank you." Frankie looked down at the shirt as if just realizing that she'd put it on that morning. When she looked up, her eyes clouded over.

"I'm sorry—was it something I said?"

"No, it's just that I love being here and—"

Hank came back into the room, followed by his father. Dana saw their expressions and said, "What's happened?"

Hud put a hand on his wife's shoulder. "It's just work, but Hank and Frankie are going back to Idaho today. They're leaving right after breakfast."

Dana shook her head as she felt her eyes burn with tears. "So soon?" she asked her son. "It feels like you just got here."

"It's for the best right now," Hank said. "We both

have jobs to get back to, but don't worry. I'll be home again before you know it."

Her gaze went to Frankie as she recalled how close the young woman had been to tears just moments ago. Because she knew they were leaving? Or because she wouldn't be coming back?

"She'll be coming back too," Hank said quickly as if reading her expression. Her son sat back down at the table to finish his breakfast and gave Frankie a look that was so filled with love, Dana felt choked up.

"I certainly hope you'll both be back," she said, fighting tears.

"I have to go," her husband said as he leaned down to give her a kiss on the cheek. She reached back to grab his hand and squeeze it. She wished he would retire. There were days he left the house when she wasn't sure he would make it home alive again. It was a thought that filled her with fear. She couldn't wait for the days when the two of them would be here together on the ranch with their grandchildren and the phone wouldn't ring with marshal business.

"You TOLD YOUR dad about the man I saw at the bar?" Frankie asked as they left the ranch house.

"Darrel Sanders." He nodded as they walked up to the cabin to get their things.

She could tell that leaving here was hard on Hank. Probably because it was so hard on his mother. "Your mom is so sweet."

"Yeah, she is. Frankie, I know all this is new between us, but I have to be honest with you. Being here, it makes me wish I'd never left. I miss it."

She nodded. "I can see that."

"Not because of Naomi. Maybe in spite of her. I miss my family. I miss ranch work."

"There's no reason you shouldn't come back. This is your family legacy." Frankie could feel his gaze on her.

"You have to know that if, down the road, once you've had enough time to accept that we belong together…"

"What are you saying?" she asked, stopping on the trail to face him.

"That if my coming back here was a deal breaker with us, I would stay in Idaho and I would be fine at my job."

She shook her head. "I would never keep you from what you love or your family. But we still need to slow down. This is way too fast."

"Not for me, but I can see it is for you. Plus we still have to deal with your ex-fiancé. I get it. Like I told you, I'll wait." He leaned toward her, took her face in his big hands and kissed her. "Umm, you taste like huckleberries."

She saw the look in his eye and laughed. Why not? It wasn't as if they were in a hurry to get back to Idaho.

As HANK DROVE out of the ranch, he couldn't help looking back. Frankie noticed and reached over to put her hand on his thigh.

"You'll be back."

He nodded. "*We'll* be back."

She smiled and looked out her window. He realized she was looking in her side mirror.

His gaze went quickly to his rearview mirror. No sign of J.J. "Let's hope he gave up and went back to Idaho."

"I doubt it. But since that's where we're headed…"

"What are we going to do about him when we get back?"

"I've hesitated to get a restraining order because, one, I know it won't do any good, and, two, it will only infuriate him and make things worse."

He stole a look at her as he drove. He still couldn't believe this. He was crazy about her. She was all he'd thought about. But the J.J. situation scared him. They weren't out of the woods yet. Until J.J. was no longer a problem, he and Frankie couldn't move forward. "What other option is there?"

"Short of shooting him?" She brushed her hair back. This morning she'd tied back her long mane. Tendrils had escaped and hung in a frame around her face. She couldn't have looked more beautiful.

"I understand why he doesn't want to lose you. I feel the same way. But his methods are so desperate, so…"

"Insane?" She nodded. "Also his reasons. He wants me back to save face. If he loved me he wouldn't—" Her voice broke.

"I'm guessing he's been violent with you," he said as he drove away from Big Sky headed north.

She nodded without looking at him. "Please, I don't want to talk about him. It's a beautiful day and I don't want to spoil it."

It was. A crisp blue cloudless sky hung over the tall pines and rocky cliffs of the canyon. Beside them, the river flowed, a sun-kissed clear green. He felt her gaze on him.

"Are you all right with leaving? I mean, we came here to—"

"Because I was convinced Naomi was murdered. We have good reason now to believe it's true. It's up to my father now to find out the truth."

She nodded. "It feels unfinished."

He glanced over at her. "Once we knew what Naomi had gotten involved with, it was too dangerous to stay because I know you. You wouldn't stop looking. I couldn't let you do that. It was getting too dangerous. Not to mention my father would have locked us up if we continued to investigate it."

FRANKIE STARED AT him in surprise. "But you wouldn't have stayed and kept looking if I wasn't with you."

"I just told you. My father would have probably thrown me in jail is what would have happened."

"Hank—"

"There is no way I'm putting you in that kind of danger."

"That isn't your choice. This is what I do for a living."

"I've been meaning to ask you how you came to be a private eye."

She could see that he was changing the subject, but she answered anyway. "I had an uncle who was a private investigator. I started out working for him in his office. He took me on a few cases. I was pretty good at it. When he moved to Arizona and closed his office, I opened mine." She shrugged. "I kind of fell into it. Would I do it over? I don't know." She looked at him. "That day we went on the horseback ride up into the mountains?" He nodded. "I felt the kind of freedom I've always felt with my job. It was…exhilarating. If I could find a job that let me ride a horse every day…"

"As a rancher's wife, you could ride every day."

She'd been joking, wanting to change the subject. But now she stared at him and saw that he was completely serious. They hadn't even said that they loved each other and he was suggesting she become his wife.

But as she looked at him, she knew it in her heart. She did love him. She'd fallen for him, for his lifestyle, for his family. She'd fallen for the whole ball of wax and now he was offering it to her?

Frankie looked away. As she did, she saw the man stagger out into the highway. "Hank, look out!"

HANK HIT THE BRAKES. The pickup fishtailed wildly, but he got it stopped before he hit the man who'd dropped to his hands and knees in the middle of the highway.

He threw open his door, jumped out and rushed to the man gasping for breath, whose face was smeared with blood.

"Help me," the man said. "My car went off the road back in the mountains."

Hank reached down to help him up. Traffic had been light. What few drivers passed slowed down to look, but didn't stop.

"Here, let me help you to my pickup," he said as he half lifted the man to his feet. As they approached the passenger side, Frankie moved over to give him room to climb in with Hank's help.

After closing the door, Hank hurried around to slide behind the wheel. "I can take you to the hospital in Bozeman."

"That won't be necessary," the man said, no longer wheezing.

Hank shot a look at the man and felt his eyes widen as he saw the gun now pressed to Frankie's temple.

"Drive up the road," the man ordered. "I don't want to kill her, but I will."

Chapter Eighteen

J.J. had parked down the road from the ranch turnoff. He'd been able to see anyone coming or going. Stakeouts were something he was good at because he required so little sleep. He was usually wired. Catching bad guys was his drug of choice.

Catching Frankie and straightening her up was enough motivation to keep him awake for days. His dedication paid off in spades this morning when he saw the pickup coming out of the ranch with both the cowboy and Frankie.

The pickup turned north and J.J. followed in the SUV he'd rented. It cost him a pretty penny to rent, but he would spare no expense to get Frankie back. As he drove, he admitted to himself that he'd made mistakes when it came to her. He'd put off the actual wedding, stringing her along for a while because while he liked the idea of having her all to himself, he wasn't ready to tie himself down.

He'd been happy knowing that no other man could have her as long as she was wearing his ring. So when she'd wanted to break up, he'd been caught flat-footed. He'd thought it was because he hadn't mentioned setting a date for the wedding. But in that case, he would have expected her to start talking about making wedding plans or leaving bride magazines around or dropping hints and crying and giving him ultimatums.

Instead, she'd said she didn't want to marry him, that the engagement had been a mistake and that she wanted out. She'd handed him his ring. Hadn't even flung it at him in anger.

That was when he'd gotten scared that she was serious. No recriminations, no tears, just a simple "I don't want to marry you. I'm sorry."

It had hit him harder than he'd expected. He'd been relieved, and yet the thought of her just tossing him back like a fish that didn't quite meet her standards really pissed him off. He'd thought, *Like hell you're going to walk away from me.*

He'd gotten physical. But what guy wouldn't have under those conditions? That was when she stopped answering his calls, refused to see him, basically cut him off entirely. At first, he thought it was just a ploy to get him to the altar. Of course she wanted to marry him. He was a good-looking guy with a cool job. Didn't all women go for a man in uniform?

Since then he'd been trying to get her back every way he could think of. But it became clear quickly that she was serious. She wanted nothing more to do with him. That was when he got mad.

Now, as he followed the pickup north out of town, he considered what to do next. He had no idea where they were headed. But wherever they were going, they didn't seem to be in a hurry.

It was early enough that traffic was light, so he stayed back, figuring he couldn't miss them if they stopped anywhere in the canyon. Once out of it, he'd have to stay closer. After his all-night stakeout, he wasn't about to lose them now.

They were almost out of the canyon when he saw the pickup's brake lights come on. He quickly pulled over to see what was going on. There was no place for them to turn off, so what the—

That was when he saw the cowboy jump out and rush up the road. A few moments later, the cowboy returned and helped a man into the passenger side of the truck. The man appeared to be injured.

As the pickup pulled back onto the highway, so did J.J. This put a new wrinkle in things, he thought. When not far out of the canyon, the cowboy turned off before the town of Gallatin Gateway. Maybe they were taking the man to his house on what appeared to be the old road along the river. Still, it seemed strange.

J.J. followed at a distance, telling himself this might work out perfectly for him. When they dropped the man off, maybe that was when he'd make his move.

"WHAT IS THIS ABOUT?" Hank asked, afraid he knew only too well.

"You'll find out soon enough," the man said. "Right up here around the next corner, take the road to the left toward the mountains."

Hank couldn't believe he'd fallen for this. But in Montana, you stopped to help people on the road. He hadn't given it a second thought, though he regretted that kindness now.

He shot a look at Frankie. She appeared calm, not in the least bit worried, while his heart was racing. The man had a gun to her head! He couldn't imagine anything worse, and then realized he could. At least Frankie wasn't standing on a ledge over the river, looking down at the rocks, knowing she was about to die.

He saw the turn ahead and slowed to take it, glancing into his rearview mirror. There was a vehicle way back on the road. No way to signal that they needed help.

They were on their own. He knew they would have to play it by ear. He would do whatever it took to keep Frankie safe—even if it meant taking a bullet himself.

He turned onto the road. As it wound back into the mountains, he told himself that it made no sense for the drug dealers to kidnap them, let alone kill them. They'd gotten away with murder for three years. If he and Frankie had uncovered evidence against them, they would have been behind bars by now.

So why take them? That was the part that made no sense. Running them off the road had been a warning to back off, but this…this terrified him. Maybe they were cleaning up loose ends, like with Tamara, since she obviously had known more than she'd told Frankie.

THE FIRST THING the marshal did when he left the ranch after breakfast was drive over to Darrel Sanders's house. He'd hoped to catch him before he got up. He remembered the boy Darrel had been as a classmate of Hank's. A nice-looking kid with a definite chip on his shoulder.

Darrel had moved into his mother's house after she died. It was a small house in a subdivision of other small houses away from Meadow Village.

But when he pulled up, he saw that Darrel's vehicle, an old panel van, was gone. He tried his number, let it ring until voice mail picked up before hanging up.

It made him nervous that Darrel wasn't around. The man worked in the winter but, as far as Hud could tell, did nothing in the summer to earn a living. The supposition was that he made so much with his snow removal business that he had summers off.

Hud sat for a moment, letting his patrol SUV idle in front of the house before he shut off the engine, got out and crossed the yard. He'd always gone by the book. But there was no way he could get a warrant based on what he had, which was simply suspicion.

At the house, he knocked and then tried the door. Locked. Going around the small house, he tried to look in the windows, but the curtains were pulled.

At the back, he stepped up onto the small porch. A row of firewood was stacked head high all along the back side of the house and down the fence, cutting off any view of most of the neighbors.

Hud tried the back door and, finding it locked, he put his shoulder into it. He wasn't as young as when he used to do this. The door held and his shoulder hurt like hell, but he tried again.

The lock gave and he opened the door and quickly stepped in, telling himself that he smelled smoke and thought he'd better check to make sure nothing was on fire inside. A lie, but one he would stand behind. The inside of the house wasn't as messy as he'd expected it to be. He'd wondered if Darrel had gone on the lam after Tamara's death, but if he'd packed up and taken off, there was no sign of it.

A pizza box sat in the middle of the table. He opened it and saw that several pieces were still inside. There were dishes in the sink and beer in the refrigerator. He had the feeling that Darrel hadn't gone far.

He thought about waiting for him, but after looking around and finding nothing of interest, he left by the way he'd come in, feeling guilty and at the same time vindicated.

He'd insisted before Hank left that he get a new cell phone before he left town. He tried his number now.

FRANKIE STARTED AS Hank's cell phone rang. She hadn't replaced her own, saying she'd take care of it once she got home. She wanted a new number, one that J.J. probably wouldn't have any trouble getting, though. That thought had come out of nowhere. A foolish thought to be worrying about J.J. when a stranger had a gun to her head.

Hank's cell rang again.

"Don't touch it," the man ordered, pressing the barrel of the gun harder against her temple and making her wince.

"It's probably my father, and if I don't answer it, he'll be worried and put a BOLO out on us."

The man swore. "Give me your phone." Hank dug it out and handed it over. The man stared down at it for a moment and said, "Answer it. Tell him you're fine but can't talk because of the traffic and will call him later. Say anything more and the last thing your father will hear is this woman's brains being splattered all over you. Got it?"

"Got it." He took the phone back and did just as the man had told him before being ordered to hand the phone back.

Frankie watched the man pocket the phone. She hadn't been able to hear the other side of the conversation. But it appeared the marshal had accepted that Hank couldn't talk right now.

She took even breaths, letting herself be lulled by

the rocking of the pickup as Hank drove deeper into the foothills. She knew better than to try to take the gun away from the man in these close quarters. She would wait and bide her time. She hoped Hank was on the same page. He appeared to be since he hadn't tried to get a message to his father.

They came over a rise and she saw a small cabin set back against rocks and pines. Several rigs were parked in front of it, including a panel van that she'd seen before. It took her a moment to remember where. In front of the Silver Spur Bar in Big Sky. Darrel Sanders's rig. So this was just as they suspected, about the drug money and Naomi's death.

"Park over there and then we're going to get out very carefully," the man said. "This gun has a hair trigger. If you try anything—"

"I get the picture," Hank said impatiently. "But now this. If you shoot her, you'd better shoot me as quickly as possible because if you don't—"

"I get the picture," the man interrupted, and she saw him smile out of the corner of her eye.

Even knowing what this was about, she couldn't understand why they were being brought here. She didn't think it was to kill them, but she knew she could be wrong about that. The thought made her breath catch and her mouth go dry. She and Hank had just found each other. She had hardly let herself believe in this relationship. She didn't want it to be over so soon—and so tragically.

She'd said she needed time, but even after her bad experience with J.J., she knew in her heart that Hank was nothing like the cop. He was the kind of man who made a woman feel loved and protected. The kind of man who loved horses and wanted to make babies and raise a family.

Frankie felt tears burn her eyes as she let herself admit that she wanted that as well. Wanted to come back here to the ranch and raise their kids here. She wanted Hank.

The man opened his door and grabbed her with his free hand to pull her out of the pickup, the gun still pointed at her head. Hank had gotten out on the other side of the pickup and stood waiting, his gaze on the man as if hoping for an opportunity to get the gun away from him.

She willed Hank to look at her, and when he shifted his gaze, she smiled, hoping to reassure him that they were going to get through this. They had to. She'd seen their future and she wasn't ready to give that up. If it meant a fight…well, she was ready.

"WHAT A CHUMP," J.J. said as he looked after Hank and Frankie. He couldn't believe how accommodating the fool was. First he picked up a complete stranger from the middle of the road and then what? Offered to drive him home? And his home ended up being way down a dirt road, back in the foothills?

J.J. had gone on past the turnoff when he'd seen the pickup begin working its way back into the foothills. After turning around, he'd found a place to park, pulled his gun out of the glove box, checked to make sure it was fully loaded, then stuck it in the waistband of his jeans as he got out of the rental car.

It might be a hike back in to wherever the cowboy had taken the man, but J.J. thought the area couldn't be more perfect for what he had in mind. Even if they dropped the man off and were headed back this way before he reached the man's house on foot, he could work with it.

Feeling as if Lady Luck had smiled on him, he couldn't imagine a more perfect place to end this. Once he explained things to the cowboy, he hoped that was the end of any problem from him.

Frankie was his. Period. End of discussion. True, right now she was giving him some trouble, but he would try humbling himself, sweet-talking her, spoiling her, and if that didn't work then he'd have to get physical. It wasn't something he wanted to do, but she had to understand how things were going to be. She couldn't embarrass him in front of his friends and his coworkers. She had to behave. No one respected a man who couldn't keep his woman under control.

Once they established the rules, hell, maybe he'd suggest they pick a wedding date. Marrying her might be the only way to keep her in line. If that was what he had to do, then he'd bite the bullet and get it over with. It wasn't like he had someone else he wanted to marry. There were some he wanted to get into bed, but he could do that easily enough after he was married to Frankie. She had to understand that he had his needs. Real men did.

J.J. was feeling good as he headed up the road. He'd gone a quarter mile when he realized that he couldn't hear the sound of a vehicle engine anymore. He came over a rise and saw why.

In the distance was a small cabin with four rigs parked in front of it, including the cowboy's pickup. What he didn't see was any sign of Frankie or the cowboy, though. Maybe the man they'd rescued had invited

them in for something. A drink to pay them back for
saving him?

Fine with J.J. He was in no hurry. He kept to the trees
along the edge of the foothills until he was close enough
to the cabin that he would see them when they came out.

Maybe he'd just hitch a ride with them when they
left, he thought, feeling the weight of the gun pressing
against his stomach. He pulled it out and sat down on a
rock to wait, thinking about the future he and Frankie
would have. Everything was going to be fine now. Like
his boss had warned him, he just needed to get his life
under control or he could be in trouble at work.

The memory made him grit his teeth. This was all
Frankie's fault. But he would get the bitch in line—one
way or the other.

THE MAN LED them into the cabin at gunpoint. Hank
stepped through the door, Frankie and the man behind
him, the gun still to Frankie's head. The cabin appeared
larger on the inside than it had from outside. At a glance
he took it all in as his mind raced for a way out of this
that didn't get them both killed.

He saw a small kitchen against one wall, a bed and
a half-dozen mismatched chairs around a table. Darrel
was sitting in one of the chairs. A large man he didn't
recognize was standing against the wall, looking tough.
Hank didn't miss the holstered gun visible under the
man's jacket.

He went on the defensive, determined not to let him
see how worried he actually was. "What the hell, Darrel?"

His former classmate smiled. "Sit down, Hank. There's
no reason to get all worked up. Les," he said to the man
they'd picked up in the middle of the highway, "why don't

you and Frankie sit over there." He pointed to the bed. "That way we can all see each other."

Hank hadn't moved. Darrel kicked out one of the chairs across the table from him. "Take a load off and let's talk."

"I can't imagine what we might have to talk about."

"Hank, we've known each other for too long to lie to each other. So let's cut the bull. You know perfectly well why you're here. Sit."

Hank took the chair, turning it around to straddle the seat and rest his arms on the back. He'd be able to move faster this way—if he got the chance.

Darrel smiled, seeing what Hank was up to, but said, "Your father was by my house this morning looking for me and snooping around, I heard. I suspect it's your doing. Yours and your—" his gaze shifted to Frankie "—your lady friend's." He eyed Frankie with interest for a moment before turning back to Hank. "Picked yourself up a private eye, did you? Why would you do that?"

He considered several answers before he said, "I never believed that Naomi killed herself."

Darrel nodded with a grimace. "No, you never did."

"So I hired Ms. Brewster to help prove I was right."

"And did you?" He could feel the man's intense gaze on him.

"No. Suspecting is one thing. Proving is another. It's why Frankie… Ms. Brewster and I were leaving town." He didn't want Darrel thinking there was anything more between him and Frankie than employer and employee. He knew the man well enough to know he would use it against them.

Darrel raised a brow in obvious surprise. "Leaving? Giving up that easy? Just doesn't sound like you, Hank.

Remember how you were when it came to competitive sports? You couldn't stand to let me win. So why give up now?" His former classmate seemed to consider it for a moment before his gaze swung to Frankie. "Things get a little too complicated for you?"

He saw no reason to lie. "They did. So we decided to put all of this behind us and go back to our lives in Idaho."

Darrel shifted his weight to lean across the table toward him. "I'm happy for you. Personally, I thought you were never going to get over Naomi, but apparently you've now found a woman who's made you forget her. Under normal circumstances, I'd wish you well. But here is the problem. I still want my money that your former girlfriend stole. I thought it was lost forever, but then you came back to the canyon and I figured, 'Hank's come back to pick up the money. He was in on it the whole time.' I actually admire you for waiting three years. I kept track of you and knew you hadn't spent it. For a while, I thought maybe Naomi hadn't even told you about it. So where is it? In your pickup? Trent, go take a look."

"Wait a minute," Frankie said, making them all turn to look at her. "Naomi didn't have the money on her that night, the night you killed her?"

Chapter Nineteen

As J.J. had approached the cabin, he considered climbing in the back of the cowboy's pickup. From the hill where he sat, he could see that there appeared to be some old tarps in the back. He could hide, and when the time was right, he could pop up. *Surprise!*

The idea had its appeal. He just wasn't sure he could reach the pickup before they came out, and given the number of vehicles parked outside the cabin, he couldn't be sure how many people were inside.

The rock where he sat was far enough away that he could see the cowboy and Frankie when they came out, but they probably wouldn't notice him. It wouldn't take much for him to trot down to the road and stop them once they were out of sight of the cabin.

They seemed to have been in there for a while now, he thought, frowning. Maybe the man was more injured than he'd thought. What if they'd sent for an ambulance? Worse, the cops?

But as time passed with no sign of either, he was beginning to wonder what could be going on inside that cabin. Maybe he should get a little closer. The rock he was sitting on wasn't that comfortable anyway, he thought as he began to work his way down the hillside through the pines.

The front door of the cabin opened. He jumped back behind a pine, thinking it was about time they came out. But the man who emerged wasn't the cowboy. He was a big, tough-looking dude. Sunlight caught on the gun in the man's holster.

What the hell?

J.J. watched as the man went straight to the cowboy's pickup. It didn't take long to understand what was going on. The man was searching the truck. He obviously didn't find what he was looking for—even after going through their bags behind the seat. When he slammed the pickup door, he glanced at the tarps in the back and quickly climbed in to search there as well.

"Glad I wasn't under one of those tarps," J.J. said to himself as he watched the man finish his search and go back inside the cabin.

Something was definitely wrong and Frankie was in there. He considered what to do. No way was he busting in there, gun blazing. The way he saw it, all he could do was wait. Maybe if he heard screams from Frankie, he might have to change his mind.

Since the man had searched the pickup, it made sense that he wouldn't be looking in the back again. He continued down the hill, keeping his gun ready and his eyes focused on the cabin door.

Staying low, he made his way through the vehicles to the cowboy's pickup and leaped into the back, covering himself with the tarps to wait.

TRENT RETURNED MINUTES later from searching the truck. "Not there."

Frankie watched Darrel's jaw muscle bunch as the

tension in the room became thick as smoke. But beside her, Les had released her arm and now merely sat with the gun pressed into the side of her head.

"I thought we were going to be straight with each other," Darrel said, clearly trying to contain his anger.

Frankie could see that Hank was getting angrier by the moment. "That was you the day at the river," Hank said. "That was you I saw running through the trees."

"I followed you thinking you were going for the money. Instead, you were doing what you always did, sitting and staring at that cliff. Three years, I've waited. When you came back after all this time, I thought it was finally to get the money."

Hank shook his head. "You had us forced off the road and into the river. You could have killed us."

"I doubted you would die, but at that point, you hadn't gone for the money and I was losing patience."

"When are you going to get it through your head?" Hank demanded. "We don't have your money. Now let us go."

"I don't think you realize your circumstances," Darrel shot back as he got to his feet and limped over to where Les had his gun to Frankie's head. He grabbed a handful of Frankie's dark hair in his fist as a switchblade suddenly appeared in his other hand. Frankie cried out in pain as he jerked hard on her hair, exposing her throat to the knife.

"I could cut her throat right now, and I will if you don't stop lying to me."

Hank leaped to his feet and took a step toward him. Behind him, Trent moved too quickly. She felt Darrel release her hair and turn.

"Don't!" Darrel yelled at Trent, but his command

wasn't quick enough. The man had pulled his gun and now brought the barrel down hard on Hank's head.

Frankie screamed and jumped to her feet, only to be pulled back down by Les.

Darrel swore as Hank toppled to the floor. From where Les held her, she could see that his head was bleeding.

"Help him!" she cried.

Darrel, still swearing, limped over to him and checked for a pulse. "He's not dead." Hank moaned and struggled to sit up. "Get a towel for his head," he ordered. "Now!" Trent disappeared into the bathroom. "Everyone just calm down. I don't like things to get violent but I'm tired of being lied to. I want my money." He said the last through gritted teeth.

"Hank doesn't know where your money is," Frankie said, her voice breaking. She could see that he was dazed and bleeding, but alive. At least for now.

"Tie him up," Darrel ordered when Trent returned with the towel. He tossed the towel to Hank, who put it against the side of his head and flinched.

"Is that necessary?" Frankie demanded. "He's injured. He needs to go to the hospital, not be tied up." She got a warning side look from Darrel.

"You both brought this on yourselves," he said. "Maybe you didn't know about the money, but obviously you do now. So stop lying. Since Hank and Naomi were going to get married and she had put money down on a house, don't tell me he doesn't know where she hid the rest of it."

Trent pulled out duct tape and, after helping Hank into a chair, bound him to it.

"I told you, I don't know," Hank mumbled and seemed to be fighting unconsciousness.

"I know who has your money," she said.

Hank's head came up. He shot her a pleading look. "Frankie—"

She turned her gaze on Darrel, who slowly swiveled around to look at her. "If you're lying, something much worse is going to happen to you. Do you understand?"

"Perfectly. But there's something I need to know first."

"You don't seem to be in a position to be making ultimatums," Darrel said, sounding almost amused.

"You're wrong. I'm the only person in this room who can get you your money." Darrel glanced at Hank. "He doesn't know," she said. "So if you didn't find the money on Naomi that night, then you're right—she hid it somewhere. But what I don't get is why you killed her before she told you where."

He seemed to consider whether to answer or not, and then swore. "One of my associates was handling it and made an error in judgment."

"That's what you call killing her?" Hank said through clenched teeth. She could see he was in pain from the head wound. "An error in judgment?"

"Tamara didn't kill her," Darrel said. "She took her up on the ledge to scare her since she knew Naomi was afraid of heights. All Naomi had to do was tell her where the money was. It wasn't in her vehicle. Nor her apartment, which had already been searched. We suspected it was hidden on the ranch, but we needed the location. Naomi refused to give it to her. Tamara argued with her. Naomi tried to push past her on the ledge to leave, making it clear that she was never going to tell. She took a misstep and fell to her death. Killing her was the last thing we wanted to do."

"Until you got the money," Frankie said. She could see that Hank was struggling to stay conscious, struggling with the news about Naomi.

"You both misjudge me," Darrel said. "Dead bodies complicate things. I prefer not to shed blood unless I have to. Unfortunately, some of my other associates are less reasonable." He rose unsteadily from his chair, and Frankie was reminded of his limp when he'd come into the bar.

Stepping back, he lifted his pant leg to expose a mass of red and purple scar tissue. When he spoke, there was fury in his voice. "You have no idea how much your former girlfriend has cost me, and not just in money and pain. I came close to getting my throat cut—and that would have been the faster and least painful in the long run, I realize now. My associates had much worse plans for me. I've been busting my ass for three years to pay them back. I've been waiting for you to return to town to collect the money after that foolish, stubborn woman took it and refused to tell us where she'd hidden it. Now," he said as he covered his injured leg again and slowly lowered himself into his chair.

He turned his attention to Frankie. "You say you know who has my money?"

She nodded. "One more question first, though," she said, making him groan. She knew she was trying his patience, but she also knew that she had leverage and she planned to use it. She had to use whatever she could to get them out of this. "How was Naomi able to steal the bag of money that she referred to as a small fortune? I would have thought you'd be watching it closer than that. Unless she was one of your associates."

Darrel laughed at that. "Hardly. She and Tamara had

become friends. Naomi gave Tamara free groceries and even money out of the till sometimes when she came in and no one else was around." He swung his gaze back to Hank. "Your girlfriend was a shoplifter. Did you know that? She got her kicks by stealing. Tamara failed to mention that until later when my money went missing."

"So you didn't know who took it at first," Frankie said.

"No," Darrel admitted. "I waited to see who started spending."

Frankie thought of the house that Naomi had put a down payment on, hoping Hank would marry her. "How much money are we talking?" she asked.

Darrel shook his head.

"So you knew that Naomi had a larcenous streak and yet you left it lying around?"

Darrel gave her a warning look and then said, "I didn't leave it lying around. I'd brought the money to the bar that afternoon to meet someone. The person was running late and some men came into the bar. I didn't like their looks. I sensed trouble, so I hightailed it into the office. Unfortunately, I didn't have time to put the money into the safe. So I stuck it behind some liquor boxes. Two men jumped me as I walked out of the office. They didn't get far in their plan, but in the confusion of throwing them out of the place with some help from a couple of friends…the money disappeared."

"How did you know Naomi took it?"

He sighed. "It took a little while to figure it out. I had to go through a few possibilities first. In the end, Tamara and I both remembered Naomi being in the bar and disappearing when the trouble started. Tamara thought Naomi might have gone to the restroom before the fight broke out. My office is right across from the women's bathroom. When I heard she'd put money down on a house in Bozeman… Now, no more questions. Who has my money?"

Frankie thought of Randall "Butch" Clark. It hadn't taken much to get the truth out of him and that had worried her at the time. He'd seemed scared enough, but he had wanted her to believe that Naomi had the money on her that night. That she was thinking about stopping and giving the drug dealers what she had left.

But it seemed he'd lied about that. Still, she didn't want to get him killed. "I'm going to take you at your word that you're not into bloodshed," Frankie said, getting to her feet. Les leaped up as well as he tried to keep the gun on her and get a better grip on her. She didn't think he would shoot and knew she was taking a chance, but she'd bluffed her way this far. "Tell him to get that gun out of my face."

Darrel looked from her to Les. "Sit down, Les. I have a gun under the table. I can kill them both if necessary. You can put your piece away." He turned his gaze on her. "You have a lot of guts. He could have killed you just then before I could stop him."

She had a feeling that Les wasn't that quick-thinking, but kept it to herself. "Let me get this straight. Naomi didn't have the money on her that night, right?"

"I believe we already covered that."

"Tamara was following her that night, right? So what if she had the money and Tamara lied? She killed Naomi and kept the—"

"Tamara didn't have the money," Darrel said, talking over her. "Trust me, some of my more bloodthirsty associates talked to her about this at length before she… expired. She stuck to her story. Tamara took her up on the ledge to force her to tell what she did with it, but Naomi refused. Then the stupid woman slipped and fell."

HANK FELT AS if he was in a nightmare, one of his own devising. If he hadn't come back here, if he hadn't brought Frankie, if he'd just let Naomi go. His head ached and his vision blurred.

Frankie was scaring him, but he didn't know how to stop her—especially injured and bound to a chair.

"But if Naomi was being followed, how could she have dumped the money before she stopped or was pulled over?" Frankie asked.

Darrel shrugged. "You tell me."

"She'd already hidden the money," Frankie said, nodding as if to herself. "She called someone to tell the person where the money was in case something happened to her."

Frankie was right. Naomi had hidden the money and called the person she trusted—her old boyfriend, Butch. It was the only thing that made any sense. Naomi thought the money was safe. She didn't think the drug dealers would really kill her until they had it. If she hadn't slipped—

He felt Darrel's gaze on him. "That's exactly how I saw it. She hid the money and made a call to tell her lover where he could find it. How about it, Hank? Isn't that the way you see it?"

"Naomi didn't call Hank," Frankie said.

But Hank knew who Naomi had called—and so did Frankie. He looked at her and felt his heart drop. He could see what she was thinking, but wasn't sure how to head her off.

"Why wouldn't Naomi tell on that cliff?" Hank demanded, stalling for time, afraid that Frankie was only about to get herself in deeper. "That makes no sense." And yet he knew. He didn't even have to look at Frankie and see that she knew too. He felt his stomach drop.

"She wasn't giving up the money," Frankie said, sounding sad for the woman she'd been investigating and sad for him. "It meant that much to her."

He shook his head, unable to accept that he'd never really known Naomi. He knew that she'd always felt deprived and wanted desperately to have the life she dreamed of having. Still, he didn't want to believe that she would put money before her own life.

"That's crazy. She's standing on the edge of the ledge over the river and she'd rather die than give up the money?" he said.

No one said anything, but he saw that Darrel was staring at Frankie.

Hank felt as if he was on a runaway train with no way to stop it. No way to jump off either.

"I can get you your money," Frankie said to Darrel. "But you're going to have to let me leave."

"Frankie, no," Hank said, feeling dizzy. "You can't trust him." He let out a curse, feeling helpless and scared. "You can't expect him to stick by any deal, Frankie. He used to cheat at every sport I ever played with him."

Darrel shook his head at Hank but he was smiling. "I had to cheat. You were too good for me. But right now, I think I have the upper hand."

"Frankie—"

"Put some tape over his mouth," Darrel ordered, and Trent sprang to it.

Hank tried to put up a fight but it was useless. He felt weak even though he hadn't lost that much blood. He wondered if he had a concussion. Right now his only concern, though, was Frankie. He'd foolishly gotten to his feet, knowing that Trent was behind him. He hadn't expected the man to hit him. Neither had Darrel. Now he found himself duct-taped to a chair and gagged. And Frankie was about to make a deal that could get her killed.

SHE'D KNOWN HANK wasn't going to like this and would have tried to stop her if he could have. "Let me go get your money," she said again to Darrel.

"Do I look stupid? If I let you go, you'll hightail it straight to the authorities, and the next thing I know, there'll be a SWAT team outside my door."

"You have another option?" Frankie asked. "We can't tell you where the money is because we don't know. We didn't even know about it until recently. If you kill us, you'll never get the money and Hank's father will never stop looking for you. Stupid would be making your situation worse. Can't you see we're trying to help you figure this out?"

Darrel shook his head. "You make it sound like if you hand over the money, we all just walk away as if nothing ever happened. I just kidnapped the two of you."

"You are merely detaining us," Frankie said. "Until you get your money. Then you'll let us go. No harm, so to speak," she said, looking pointedly at Trent, "no foul. That's the deal."

"Trent goes with you."

She shook her head. "Not a chance. I go alone. It's the only way I have a chance of getting the person who took your money to admit the truth."

"How do I know you'll come back?"

"I'll come back. You have Hank."

"Good point," Darrel said. "I just wasn't sure you were that invested in him. If you don't come back, he dies. You call in the cops—"

"Save your breath. I'm not going to the authorities, but I need your word that he'll be safe until I get back," she said. "No more tough-guy stuff. The thing is, I don't know how long it will take me."

"You'd better not be playing me."

Frankie met Darrel's gaze. "You want your money. Hank and I want to get on with our lives." Her gaze went to Hank. He gave a small shake of his head and looked pointedly at Trent leaning against the wall again. Frankie knew this was dangerous, but she could see only one way out. Hank was already injured. She could imagine all of this going south quickly if she didn't do something. But what she was suggesting was a gamble, one she had no choice but to take.

"I'll give you until sundown."

Frankie shook her head. "I might need longer. Like I said, this could take a while."

Darrel shook his head. "Sundown or he's dead."

She wanted to argue but she could see she'd pushed the man as much as he was going to take. "Sundown, but promise me that I won't be followed. You need to trust me to handle this."

Darrel wagged his head. "You're asking a lot, sweet-heart."

"It's Frankie. And I have a lot to lose," she said and looked at Hank. "There's one more thing that I need," she said to Darrel. "A gun."

Chapter Twenty

All of her bravado gone, Frankie's hands were shaking as she climbed into the pickup. She laid the unloaded gun on the seat next to her. Darrel said he wasn't about to hand her a loaded gun.

"I'm taking one hell of a chance on you as it is," he'd said. "I give you a loaded gun…" He'd smiled as he'd shaken his head. "I'm betting a whole lot on you as it is, lady."

It was mutual, she thought now. She'd just gambled Hank's life on her suspicion of what had happened to the stolen drug money. What if she was wrong? Even if she was right, the money could be gone. Or Butch might refuse to give it to her. For all she knew, he could have gone on the lam after she'd talked to him at his father's hardware store.

Hank was depending on her. She drove toward Bozeman, checking behind her for a tail, trying not to speed for fear of being pulled over. She considered calling the marshal, but couldn't risk it. Not yet, anyway.

After parking behind the hardware store, she tucked the gun into her jeans and covered it with the shirt and jacket she'd put on earlier that morning. Taking a breath, she climbed out and entered the hardware store at the back through the delivery entrance. In the dim light of the empty area, she did her best to pull it together. Butch wouldn't be excited to see her to begin with. If he sensed how desperate she was, she feared he would run.

He wasn't in the office at the back. She started through the store, keeping an eye out for him. She was almost to the front when an employee asked if she needed help.

"I'm looking for Butch," she said, surprised that her voice sounded almost normal.

"He's on vacation and not expected back for a couple of weeks," the young man said.

Vacation? "It's urgent that I contact him. When did he leave?"

"I believe he planned to leave today."

"Could you give me his address? Maybe I can catch him if he hasn't left yet."

The young employee hesitated.

"Please. It's urgent."

"Well, I suppose it will be all right." He rattled off the address, and Frankie raced back the way she'd come.

Butch lived in a small house on the north side of town that, like most of Bozeman, had been completely remodeled. She wondered when and how much money it had cost. She prayed that he hadn't left yet and that he had been too scared to dip into the money.

As she parked on the street and got out, she noticed that the house looked deserted. The garage door was closed and there was a newspaper lying on the front step, unread. Her heart dropped to her feet as she walked toward the house, wondering what to do next.

That was when she heard a noise inside the house. As she approached the garage, she glanced into one of the small windows high on the door. Butch Clark was hurriedly packing for what looked like more than a two-week vacation.

HANK WATCHED DARREL, seeing him become more anxious and irritated with each passing hour. It hadn't been a surprise when the man had broken his word immediately, sending Trent after Frankie.

"Stay back. Don't let her spot you tailing her," Darrel had ordered. "She takes you to the money, you know what to do."

He'd felt his heart drop, afraid he knew exactly what Trent would do. All he could hope was that Frankie was as good at her job as he knew her to be and would spot the tail or be able to deal with Trent if she had to.

Darrel began pacing again. His pacing the cabin floor had turned out to be a godsend. He'd paid little attention to Hank as if he'd forgotten about him. Les had lain down on the bed and quickly gone to sleep.

Meanwhile, Hank had been working on the duct tape Trent had used to bind his wrists behind him to the chair. He'd found a rough spot on the wood where a screw was sticking out. He could feel the tape weakening as he sawed through layer after layer. It was tedious, but he had time, he kept telling himself. He had to be free when Frankie returned.

His head ached, but if he had a concussion it wasn't a bad one. The dizziness had passed and he was feeling stronger by the moment.

When Darrel's cell phone rang, the man practically jumped out of his thin skin. Hank stopped what he was doing for a moment. He could hear the entire conversation at both ends since Trent was talking so loudly.

"What do you mean you lost her?" Darrel demanded.

"She was headed toward the north end of town but then suddenly veered off on a street. I stayed back like you said but then she was headed toward Main Street and she was gone."

Darrel swore. "You say she was headed toward the north side of town?"

"Yeah. I don't know why she suddenly—"

"She spotted a tail," he snapped. "Go back to the north side of town, where she was originally headed. Drive the streets until you find her. *Find her.*"

"Okay, I'll try, but—"

"Either you find her or you'd better keep going and hope I never find *you*. That clear enough for you?"

"I'll find her. I won't give up until I do."

J.J. WAS GETTING sick of lying in the back of the moving pickup under the tarps. He wasn't sure how much more of this he could take. But he had to know what Frankie was up to.

When she'd stopped the pickup the first time, she'd gotten out. He'd waited for a few moments and then taken a peek. He'd watched her go into the back of a hardware store before quickly covering up again. What was this about? None of it made any sense. She'd left the cowboy and gone shopping? Was it possible Hank Savage had known the man he'd picked up in the road? If so, then…

She'd come back sooner than he'd anticipated, the pickup door opening, closing, the engine starting and the truck moving again. Maybe she'd had to pick up something. An ax? A shovel? He'd shuddered at the thought.

The truck didn't go far before he felt something change. Frankie had been driving at a normal pace when suddenly she took off, turning this way and that. He had to hang on now or be tossed around the back of the pickup like a rag doll. What was going on?

When she finally slowed down and quit turning, she seemed to be backtracking. He'd been listening to the sounds around him. They'd been in traffic but now it had grown quieter. She brought the pickup to a stop. He heard her exit the truck. He listened, afraid to take a peek yet. He definitely had the feeling that they were in a residential part of town. He could hear the sound of someone using a leaf blower some distance away.

When he couldn't take the suspense any longer, he carefully rose and pushed back the edge of the tarp aside to peer out. What he saw shocked him. Frankie had pulled a gun and was now about to open someone's garage door. But before she could, the door suddenly began to rise with the sound of the mechanical engine pulling it up.

He heard an engine start up in the garage and saw Frankie step in front of the idling car, the gun raised to windshield level. "Stop, Butch!"

The car engine revved. Whoever was behind the wheel had backed the vehicle into the garage. For a fast getaway? The fool either had a death wish or was playing his luck. Either way, J.J. could see that Frankie was in trouble. The driver didn't seem afraid of the gun she was holding.

He threw back the tarp and jumped down to run at her, shoving her out of the way as the car came screaming out of the garage. He had drawn his own gun, but when he saw that the fool behind the wheel wasn't going

Chapter Twenty-One

Butch rattled the handcuffs holding him restrained to the passenger-side door of his car. "How do I know you aren't going to kill me?" His voice squeaked—just as it had when she'd jumped into the car as he was trying to get away. She'd shoved the barrel of the gun into the side of his head and told him she was going to kill him if he didn't stop. He'd stopped.

"You don't." She'd grabbed the keys and forced him at gunpoint into the passenger seat to handcuff him to the door.

"Who was that back there?" Butch asked now as they drove away from his house.

"A cop." She glanced in the rearview mirror over the top of all Butch's belongings he'd loaded. So far no tail. Also no J.J. She'd checked for a pulse. He had still been breathing but wasn't conscious. She'd taken his cop gun. At least now she had real bullets and a vehicle that whoever Darrel had sent to follow her wouldn't know. Her tail would find the pickup at the house—if he found the house at all.

"*A cop?* You said you wouldn't go to the cops."

Frankie shook her head, keeping her attention on her driving. "I wanted to keep you out of it, Butch. Unfortunately, I had no idea just how deep you really were in all this. You lied to me, but for your sake and mine, you'd better not be lying to me now."

"I'm not." He sounded whiny. She could see why Naomi had dumped him. But he must have been the closest thing she had to a friend she could confide in.

"Why didn't you tell Naomi to give the money back right away?" she asked.

"I did. She wouldn't listen. She really thought she could get away with it."

Frankie shot him a look. "Kind of like you."

"Hey, what could I have done? They didn't know about me. I didn't know them. Naomi was dead. I knew where the money was hidden. So I waited to see what happened. Nothing happened. Until you showed up."

"You could have gone to the cops," she snapped. And then none of this would be happening. Hank wouldn't be in serious trouble back at the cabin and she wouldn't be racing out of town with two guns, one actually loaded, with a man handcuffed to the car and only a hope and a prayer that he wasn't lying to her.

She glanced over at Butch. He looked scared. That, she decided, was good. "I have to ask. Why did you wait to get the money?"

He turned to look out his side window. They'd passed Gallatin Gateway and were almost to Big Sky and Cardwell Ranch, where he swore Naomi had buried the money. "I had this crazy idea that they were watching the place where she buried it, you know, just waiting for me to show up so they could kill me like they did her."

Frankie thought about telling him what Darrel had said about Naomi's death. That was if he was telling the truth. Either way, Butch might have been able to save her—if he'd gone to the cops right away.

Nor did she point out that there was little chance Darrel would be watching the ranch 24/7 even if he knew where the money was buried.

She turned onto the dirt road into the ranch, her mind racing. What would she do when she found the money? Hank had been right. She couldn't trust Darrel to keep his word. He said she wouldn't be followed. A lie. Once she handed over the money…

As she drove into the ranch yard, Butch pointed in the direction of a stand of trees. The land dropped to a small creek. Frankie groaned inwardly. She just hoped that Naomi was smart enough to bury the money where the rising water didn't send it into the Gallatin River. It could be in the Gulf of Mexico by now otherwise.

"Tell me exactly where it is," she said as she brought the car to a stop at the edge of the incline to the creek.

"There's a statue or something, she said, near the water."

Frankie frowned. "A statue?" she asked as she looked down the hill and saw pine trees and a babbling brook but no statue.

"Maybe not a statue, but—"

"A birdbath," she said, spotting it in a stand of trees. She quickly put the keys in her pocket, opened the door and, grabbing the shovel she'd taken from his garage, got out. As she did, she glanced toward the house and saw no one. Maybe she would get lucky. She needed some luck right now.

It was a short walk down to a stand of trees on a rise above the creek. Someone had put a birdbath down here. Near it were two benches as if someone in the family came down here to watch the birds beside the river. Dana? She couldn't see the marshal sitting here patiently.

The birdbath, apparently made of solid concrete, proved to be heavier than it looked. She could have used Butch, but she didn't trust the man. She tried dislodging it and inching it over out of the way, wasting valuable minutes.

Finally, she just knocked it over, which took all her strength as it was. Then she began to dig. She wondered how Naomi had managed moving the birdbath and realized it had probably been her idea, the benches and the birdbath—after she'd buried the rest of the money.

The bag wasn't buried deep. Frankie pulled it out, sweating with the effort and the constant fear of what might be happening back at the cabin. The bag looked like one used by banks. It was large and heavy. She opened it just enough to see that it was stuffed with money, lots of money in large bills, and quickly closed it.

Leaving the shovel, she climbed back up the incline. As she topped it, she saw Dana standing by the side of the car.

WHEN J.J. CAME TO, he was lying on the grass with a monstrous headache. His gun was gone. So was Frankie and the car and its driver. All she'd left behind was the cowboy's pickup.

J.J. limped into the house through the open garage door. The house felt deserted. He was moving painfully through the living room when he thought he heard a car door slam. Was it possible Frankie had come back? He couldn't believe she'd left him passed out on the concrete and hadn't even called an ambulance. But she'd managed to take his gun.

He pressed himself against a wall out of sight of the hallway as he heard footfalls in the garage. One person moving slowly, no doubt looking for him. Why had Frankie come back now? It didn't matter. He was ready for her.

He smiled to himself as he waited to pounce. She wouldn't know what hit her.

As a figure came around the corner, he lunged. He didn't realize his mistake until it was too late. The figure spun as if sensing him coming and caught him square in the face with his fist. As he took the blow, he realized that the figure was way too large to be Frankie, way too powerful and way too male.

"Who the hell are you?" he heard the man say as he crashed on the floor at the man's feet. Before he could answer, he heard the man pump a bullet into his gun. He rolled over, struggling to pull out his badge, when he heard the first shot echo through the room. The burn of the bullet searing through his flesh came an instant later.

He tried to get up, tried to get his badge out. The second shot hit him in the chest and knocked him back to the floor. As the big man moved closer, J.J. saw that it was the tough guy who'd searched the pickup earlier at the cabin.

"You've really screwed up now," J.J. managed to say as he felt his life's blood seeping from him. "You just killed a cop."

"I'D LIKE TO tell you that this isn't what it looks like," Frankie said as she approached Dana. She saw that the woman had her cell phone clutched in her hand and knew at once that she'd already called the marshal.

"I thought you and Hank had gone back to Idaho," Dana said. Her voice trembled as her gaze took in the weapon Frankie had stuck in the waist of her jeans. Her shirt and jacket had come up during her battle with the birdbath.

"How long before Hud gets here?" Frankie asked.

"Where's Hank?" the older woman asked. She sounded as scared as Frankie felt.

"He's in trouble. I need to get back to him, Dana. I'm a private investigator. It's too long a story to get into right now. I need to leave before Hud gets here."

Dana shook her head, tears in her eyes. "I knew something was wrong. But I hoped…" Inside the car, Butch began to yell for Dana to help him. "That man is handcuffed and you have a…gun."

Frankie knew she couldn't stand here arguing. She started past Dana when she heard the sound of a siren. Moments later she saw the flashing lights as the SUV topped a rise and came blaring into the ranch yard.

She let out a shaky breath and felt tears burn her eyes. There was still time before sundown. But that would mean talking her way out of this, and right now, covered in mud, holding a bag of even dirtier drug money, she wasn't sure she had the words. All she knew was that she had to convince the marshal before sundown.

HUD SHUT OFF the siren. As he climbed out, he took in the scene. The man handcuffed in the car tried to slide down out of sight. Dana stepped to Hud, and he put his arm around her before he turned his attention to the young woman his son had fallen in love with. "Frankie?"

She held out the bag. "It's the drug money. They have Hank. If I don't give the money to them by sundown…" Her voice broke.

He nodded and stepped to her to take the money. "And that?" he asked, tilting his head toward the man in the car.

"It's Butch Clark, Naomi's old boyfriend. He's known where the money was buried all these years."

Hud nodded and glanced at his watch. "We have a little time. Whatever's happened, we will deal with it. You say they have Hank." She nodded. "Tell me everything," he said as he walked her toward the house.

"What about him?" Dana asked behind them.

"He's fine where he is for the time being," Hud said without a backward glance. Inside the house, Frankie quickly cleaned up at the kitchen sink as she told him about the man stumbling out onto the highway, being taken to the cabin, the demand for the money and Hank being injured.

Dana gasped at that point, her eyes filling with tears, but she held it together. Hud had to hand it to her—she was a strong woman and always had been. Her son was injured and being held by drug dealers. It scared the hell out of him, but Dana fortunately wasn't one to panic in a crisis. He appreciated that right now.

"Okay," he said when Frankie finished. "You say Darrel gave you an unloaded gun." He picked up the Glock he'd taken from her. "This one is loaded."

She nodded. "J.J. must have followed us. He was hiding in the back of the pickup. He tried to stop Butch when Butch was attempting to flee. He was hit by the car, but he was alive the last time I saw him."

Hud studied the woman, amazed by her resilience as well as her bravery. "You don't think Darrel will let the two of you go when you take him the money, right?"

She shook her head. "He doesn't want to kill us, but…"

"What will you do?" Dana asked her husband.

"The first thing is read Butch Clark his rights and get him locked up in my jail so he's not a problem." Hud pulled out his phone and called a deputy to come handle it. As he hung up, he looked at Frankie. "I need to take you back to Hank's pickup. There's time before sundown. Then you drive back to the cabin with the bag of money."

"Where will you be?" Dana asked.

"In the back of the pickup. I'll need to grab a few things and have Bozeman backup standing by." He got to his feet. "Let's go get Hank."

HANK WATCHED DARREL pace the cabin floor and worked surreptitiously at the thick tape binding his wrists behind him to the chair. He'd made a point of acting like he was still dizzy and weak from the blow, mumbling to himself incoherently until Darrel had removed the duct tape.

"Water," Hank had mouthed. "Please."

Darrel had gotten him some, holding it to his lips so he could take a few gulps. "She'll be back," Hank said when he took the water away. "With the money." And that was the part that terrified him the most, because he had no doubt that his former classmate would go back on his word. No way were he and Frankie walking out of here alive. "She does what she says she's going to do."

Darrel had started pacing again. Hank saw him looking out the window where the sun was dropping toward the horizon at a pace that had them both worried. Now the man turned to look at him and laughed. "You sure about that? If I were her, I'd take the money and go as far away from here as I possibly could."

"That's you. Frankie isn't like that." But right now, he wished she was. At least she would be safe. He'd gotten her into this. He deserved what he got. But Frankie… He couldn't bear to think of her being hurt, let alone—

"You'd better be right." Darrel sounded sad, as if he would be sorry for killing him. "I hate the way this whole thing spiraled out of control, and all because of that girlfriend of yours."

Hank couldn't argue with that. "I fell in love with a woman I didn't know. She hid so much from me, including stealing your money."

"And you think you know this one?" Darrel scoffed at that. "All women are alike. You really haven't learned anything since high school, have you. They will double-cross you every time. I knew this one—" He stopped talking to turn and look out the window again. He'd heard what Hank had.

The sound of his pickup's engine could be heard as the truck approached the cabin. Frankie had come back with the money. And before sundown.

"I've got to hand it to you, Hank. This woman really is something. If she's got the money, then I'd say this one is a keeper."

"Keep your promise. Let us go. We want nothing to do with any of this and you know it."

"Yeah, I hear you," Darrel said, actually sounding as if he regretted what was going to happen next. "We're going to have to talk about that." He stepped over to the bed and kicked the end of it. Les stirred from a deep sleep. "Wake up. We've got company. Go out and make sure she's alone."

"Me? Why do I have to—"

Darrel cuffed the man on the head. "Go!"

Les stumbled from the bed, clearly still half-asleep, and headed for the door. Darrel stood at the window, his back to him. Hank worked feverishly at the tape. Just a little more. He felt it give.

FRANKIE DID AS Hud had told her and parked next to the panel van, out of sight of the cabin. She stayed in the pickup, sitting behind the wheel, after she'd turned off the engine, waiting.

She desperately wanted to see Hank. She had to know that he was all right. But the marshal had assured her—Hank was safer if they did things his way.

She wasn't going to argue. She was thankful that she wasn't facing this completely alone. Because she had a bad feeling that once she got out of the pickup with the money, both she and Hank were as good as dead.

Les frowned as he saw where she was parking. He walked around the front of the vehicles to stop in front of the pickup. "Get out!" he ordered, still frowning. He looked as if he'd just woken up, which made her heart race. What had Darrel done with Hank after she'd left that he'd let Les sleep?

When she didn't get out, he stepped up to try the door and, finding it locked, glanced back at the cabin before he began to fumble for his gun. That was when Hud rose and coldcocked him with the butt end of a shot-gun. The man dropped between the pickup and panel van without a sound.

As the marshal hopped down out of sight of the cabin windows, Frankie opened her door.

"Leave the bag with the money here," Hud said as he cuffed and gagged Les before rolling his body under the pickup. "Go into the cabin to check on Hank. When Darrel asks, tell him that Les took it from you. I need to know how many men are in there."

She nodded and whispered, "Trent was following me. I don't see his vehicle, so I don't think he's back yet. It should just be Darrel."

"Let's hope," Hud said and motioned for her to go before Darrel got suspicious.

Frankie headed for the cabin, praying with each step that Hank was all right. As she pushed open the door, the first thing she saw was Darrel. He had a gun in his hand, pointed at her heart. Her gaze leaped past him to Hank. She saw pleasure flash in his blue eyes at see-ing her, then concern. He was still in the chair, but he seemed to feel better than the last time she'd seen him.

"Where's my money?" Darrel demanded, already sounding furious as if he'd worked himself up in the time she'd been gone. The door was open behind her, but he was blocking her from going to Hank.

"Les has it. He took it from me." She could see that he didn't believe her. She described the bag. "I didn't touch the money, but the bag is heavy, and when I looked inside… I think all but the five grand she used for a down payment on the house is in there. Or at least enough to get you out of hot water. Now let us go."

Darrel shook his head, still blocking her from going

to Hank, and yelled, "Les!" Not hearing an answer, he yelled again. "Bring the money in here."

She looked past him and saw Hank slowly pull his wrists free from behind him. He shook them out as if he'd lost all feeling in his arms after all this time of being taped to the chair. She gave a small shake of her head for him not to move.

"Les is probably out there counting the money," Frankie said, hoping the man would step outside, where the marshal was waiting. "Or has already taken off with the bag."

"On foot?" Darrel demanded and grabbed her as they both heard the scrape of chair legs on the floor.

HANK MOVED QUICKLY. Darrel was right about one thing. He'd always been better at sports than his classmate. Fortunately, that athletic prowess benefited him now when he needed it the most.

As Darrel turned, there was a moment of surprise, a hesitation that cost him. He was about to put the barrel of the gun to Frankie's head when Hank hit him in the side of his head with his fist and grabbed the gun. Darrel staggered from the blow but didn't go down. His grip on Frankie seemed to be the only thing holding him up.

Hank twisted the gun from the man's hand. The two grappled with it for a moment before Darrel let out a cry of pain. Frankie shoved him off her and pulled the Glock from behind her to point it at the drug dealer as he went down. She looked over at Hank, who stood beside her, the gun in his hand pointed at Darrel's heart as well.

Behind them Frankie heard the marshal say, "Well,

look at the two of you. It appears you didn't even need my help." There was a smile in his voice as well as relief as he reached for his phone to let the cops know that he'd take that backup now. "I have two perps who need to be taken to jail. Also going to need a medic as well," he said, looking at the dried blood on his son's temple. "And I'm going to need a ride back to Big Sky."

"We could have given you a ride," Hank said after his father cuffed Darrel and read him his rights. Frankie could hear sirens in the distance. She leaned against Hank, his arm around her. She told herself that all she needed was a hot shower and she'd stop shaking.

"I thought you two might like some time together. But I guess you know this means you can't leave for Idaho for a while," the marshal said.

Hank glanced at her. "I think we're good with that."

FRANKIE HELPED HERSELF to another stack of silver-dollar-sized pancakes, slathered on butter and then drowned them in chokecherry syrup. She couldn't remember ever being this hungry.

So much had happened and in such a short time. She would have worried about that before Hank. She was no longer worried about it happening too fast. Instead, she was ready for the future in a way she'd never been before. She felt free, everything looking brighter, even before she'd heard the news about J.J.

Trent had been arrested and confessed everything, including killing the cop. He'd said it was self-defense, that J.J. had been reaching for his gun. But the Glock hadn't been found on the cop—or at the scene—because Frankie had taken it.

After hearing what all the cops had against him, including assaulting Hank and dealing drugs, along with killing an unarmed cop, Trent decided to make a deal for a lesser sentence for what he knew about the drug ring and Darrel's part in it.

Frankie could feel Dana watching her eat and smiling. "So you're a private investigator," she said. "Sounds dangerous. I was thinking that if you were to get married and have babies…"

Swallowing the bite in her mouth, Frankie grinned at her. "Hank hasn't asked me to marry him and you're talking babies."

"He'll ask. I've never seen my son happier."

Frankie thought about the hot shower she'd stepped into last night after they'd returned to their cabin. Hank had joined her, sans his clothes this time. Their lovemaking had been so passionate under the warm spray that she felt her cheeks heat at the memory even now.

"He makes me happy too," she said and took another bite of pancake.

"I can tell," Dana said with a secret smile. "You're glowing this morning. If it wasn't too early, I'd think you were pregnant."

Frankie almost choked on her bite of pancake. True, last night in the shower they hadn't used protection, but pregnant? She swallowed.

"Would that be so awful?" Dana asked.

She thought about it for one whole instant and smiled. "Not at all." The thought of her child growing up on this ranch made her happy. She and Hank had talked about the future last night after their shower. He'd asked how she'd feel about living on the ranch, if she would still want to work as a private investigator, if she wanted children, how she felt about dogs and cats and horses.

She'd laughed as she'd listened to his questions and grinned. "I'd love living on this ranch, I'd probably want to be involved in ranching with you rather than continue working as an investigator, I do want children, and I love dogs, cats and horses. After that horseback ride with you, I'm hooked."

"Was it the horseback ride or me that got you hooked?" he'd asked with a grin.

"By the way, where *is* my son?" Dana asked, interrupting her thoughts.

Frankie helped herself to a slice of ham and just a couple more pancakes. "He went to say goodbye to Naomi."

HANK PARKED IN the pines beside the Gallatin River as he'd done so many times before. This time he was anxious to reach the water. He climbed out and wound his way through the tall pines. A breeze swayed the tops of the boughs, whispering. The sound of the river grew louder. He could feel the sun as it fingered its way through the pines. He breathed in the scent of pine and water as if smelling it for the first time.

Ahead, he got his first glimpse of the cliff. It was dark and ominous-looking, shadowed this morning until the sun rose high enough to turn it a golden hue.

It seemed strange to make this trek after everything that had happened. He wasn't sure he could ever forgive Naomi for what she did. He and Frankie had almost gotten killed because of a bag full of money. He still couldn't believe that she'd died protecting it.

He broke out of the pines and stood for a moment at the edge of the trees. The breeze was stronger here. It rippled the moving surface of the river and ruffled his hair at his neck. He took off his Stetson and turned his face up to the breeze, letting it do what it would with his normally tousled dark hair. He couldn't help but think of Frankie's fingers in the wet strands last night as she pulled him down to her mouth. The memory of the two of them laughing and making love in the shower made him smile for a moment before he dropped down to the edge of the river.

He listened to the gentle roar of the water as it rushed over the rocks and pooled at his feet. The breeze lifted his hair as he looked up. The ledge was a dark line cut across the rock surface. For three years it had lured him back here, looking for answers. Now he knew it all.

He thought of Naomi standing on that ledge that night with Tamara. He'd always thought of her as helpless, defenseless, fragile and delicate. He'd always felt he had to protect her—even her memory. He could almost see her teetering on that ledge. Would they have let her live if she'd given them the money? They would never know. But he knew now that she was willing to die rather than give it up.

Hank hated what that said about her. He thought of her mother working all those years to support herself and her daughter. Was that what had made Naomi think she had to steal? Or was it a sickness that had started with shoplifting and had gotten away from her?

Naomi's mother had made a life for herself with a man who loved her. Lillian would survive this since he suspected she knew her daughter much better than he ever had.

He waited to feel Naomi's spirit, to see a ghostly flash of her. He expected to feel her presence as he had so many times before. He'd always thought she was waiting here for him, pleading with him to find her killer.

Now he felt nothing but the summer breeze coming off the cool surface of the river. He stared at the ledge through the sunlight, but felt nothing. Naomi was gone—if she'd ever really been here.

As he settled his Stetson back on his head, he realized it was true. Naomi's ghost had been banished for good. He felt lighter. Freer. The cliff no longer held him prisoner. Neither did Naomi.

"Goodbye," he said, glancing once more at the cliff before he started back to the pickup. He realized that he could walk away without ever looking back, without ever coming back. It felt good. *He* felt good. He couldn't wait to get to Frankie. They were leaving today, but they would return.

He drove toward the ranch, excited about life for the first time in three years. He couldn't wait to see Frankie. But first there was something he had to do.

HUD LOOKED UP to find his son standing in the doorway of his office. "Is everything all right?" he asked, immediately concerned. Hank had an odd look on his face.

"I need to ask a favor."

He and Hank hadn't talked much since everything had happened. His son's statement about what had transpired at the cabin had filled in a lot of the blanks. He'd wondered how Hank had taken the news about Naomi and if he would finally be able to put the past behind him—with Frankie's help.

"Name it. If there's something I can do…"

Hank came into his office and closed the door behind him. His son seemed nervous. That, he realized, was what he'd been picking up on the moment he saw him standing in the doorway. He'd never seen him nervous. Angry, yes. But not like this. He realized that whatever his son had to ask him, it was serious.

"When I asked you for Grandmother's ring—"

Hud swore. He'd forgotten the day that his son had come to him and asked for his grandmother's ring. Since he was a little boy, Hank had been told that his grandmother Cardwell's ring would go to Mary, but that his grandmother Savage's ring was his for the day that he met the love of his life and asked her to marry him.

But when Hank had asked for it, saying he was going to marry Naomi no matter what anyone thought because they were all wrong about her, Hud had turned him down.

"I'm sorry, son. I can't let you give Naomi the ring." He and Dana had discussed it numerous times in the days before Hank had come to him. They'd seen that Naomi was pushing marriage and could tell that their son wasn't ready. Add to that Naomi's...problems, as Dana referred to them.

"She's a thief," Hud had said. "Not just that. You know she's pressing Hank to leave the ranch to work for her stepfather."

"Maybe it's what he wants."

Hud remembered being so angry with his wife that he'd gotten out of bed and pulled on his jeans, had left. He and Dana seldom argued. But that night he hadn't been able to take any more. He'd driven up to Hebgen Lake to see his father, Brick, an old-time lawman. Hud had named one of his twin son's after his father; the other one after Dana's father, Angus.

He and his father had often been at odds, and yet that

night, the old lawman was who he'd gone to for help. It was the same year that Brick had passed away. He remembered waking him up that night. Why he chose his father was a mystery since the two of them had spent years at odds.

But Brick had given him good advice. "Stick to your guns. He's your son. You know him. He won't love you for it. Quite the contrary." He'd seen the gleam in his old man's eyes and known that he was talking about the two of them and the years they'd spent knocking heads. "You're doing him a real disservice if you just give in to keep the peace."

He'd stayed the night, driven back the next morning and told Dana that he wasn't giving Hank the ring if he asked for it again. She'd been furious with him, but he'd stuck to his guns, even though it had cost him dearly both with his wife and his son. He'd never known if Hank would have married Naomi anyway if she'd lived.

"When you'd asked for my mother's ring, I thought you were making a mistake," Hud said now. "I didn't want you giving the ring to the wrong woman and later regretting it when you met the love of your life."

Hank shook his head. "It was your decision since my grandmother apparently put you in charge of it."

"Actually, it was your grandpa Brick," he said.

"Did he also advise you to not give it to me?" Hank asked.

Hud wanted to be as honest with him as possible. "Your mother and I argued about it. I had to leave, so I drove up to your grandfather's place and asked him what I should do."

Hank's eyes widened. "You actually asked your father for advice?"

"It happens," Hud said and smiled. "Admittedly, it took years before I found myself doing that."

With a grin, his son said, "It's hard for me to admit that you were right."

"I understand."

"But I'm back. I want to give Grandmother's ring to Frankie, and I'm not taking no for an answer this time. Rightfully, it's my ring to do—"

"I totally agree." Hud reached into the drawer where he'd put the ring after meeting Frankie.

"You have it here?"

"I had a feeling you'd want it," he said.

Hank shook his head as he took the small velvet box. "I will never understand you."

"Probably not." He watched his son lift the tiny lid and saw Hank's eyes light up as he stared down at the diamond engagement ring.

"Do you think she'll like it?" The nervousness was back.

"She'll love it because she loves you."

Fall was in the air that late day in August. The seasons changed at will in Montana and even more so in the canyon so close to the mountains. One day would feel like summer, the next fall, and in the blink of an eye snow would begin.

Dried leaves rustled on the aspens as Frankie rode her horse out of the pines and into the wide meadow. She breathed in the crisp, clean air, reined in her horse and dismounted at the edge of the mountain to wait for Hank. He'd been acting strange all day. She knew it had to be because they would be leaving here—at least temporarily.

Last night they'd lain in bed, wrapped up in each other after making love, and talked about the future.

"Are you sure you'd be happy at the ranch? Because if not, we could—"

She'd kissed him to stop the words. "Hank, I love the ranch. I can't imagine living anywhere more…magical."

He'd eyed her suspiciously. "You aren't just saying that because you're crazy in love with me."

"I am crazy in love with you, but no, I wouldn't lie to you." He'd told her that the ghost of Naomi was gone, but she wondered. He still thought that because Naomi could never be happy at the ranch, neither could any other woman. She knew it would take time for him to realize that she was nothing like Naomi.

"Look at your mother, Hank. She loves this ranch just like her mother did. Isn't that why your grandmother left it to her, passing on the legacy? And all the women your uncles are married to. They're all happy living here," she continued. "Isn't it possible I'm more like your mother than…?" She wouldn't say "Naomi." "Than some other woman might be?"

He'd nodded and smiled as he kissed her. "I feel so lucky. I keep wanting to pinch myself. I guess that's why it's so hard for me to believe this is real. I never dreamed…" He kissed her again. "That I could be this happy."

Now, as he rode up beside her, his Stetson hiding much of his handsome face, she felt almost afraid. He'd been so quiet all morning and it wasn't like him to hang back on his horse the way he had. As she watched him slowly ride toward her, her heart fluttered. She was crazy in love with this man, just as she had told him. And yet maybe this was too fast for both of them.

She thought of J.J. and quickly pushed it away. Hank wasn't J.J. Whatever was going on with Hank—

At a sound in the pines, she looked past Hank to see Hud and Dana come riding out of the trees. Behind them were Mary and Chase, and behind them were Stacy and the rest of the family.

Frankie blinked. "What?"

Hank looked up and grinned. "I am terrible at keeping secrets, and this one was killing me this morning," he said as he dismounted and took her in his arms. "I hope you don't mind."

Mind that he'd invited his entire family on their horseback ride? She felt confused, and yet as everyone rode toward them, they were all smiling. One of the uncles brought up the rear with a huge bunch of helium balloons.

"Hank?" she asked. He only hugged her tightly. She could see the emotion in his face and felt her heart take off like a wild horse in a thunderstorm. "Hank?" she repeated as they all began to dismount. His uncle was handing out the balloons. "I think you'd better tell me what's going on."

The family had formed a circle around them and seemed to be waiting, just like Frankie. Hank turned to her, taking both of her hands in his.

"I know this is fast, but if I've learned anything, it's that when things are right, they're right," Hank said and cleared his voice. "You are the most amazing woman I've ever met. You're smart, talented, independent to a fault, stubborn as the day is long, courageous—way too courageous, I might add—determined and…beautiful and loving and everything I could want in one unique woman."

She tried to swallow around the lump in her throat. "Thank you, I think."

A murmur of laughter rose from the group gathered.

"You saved my life in so many ways," Hank continued. "I can never thank you enough for that. And you've brought just joy to my life when I never thought I'd ever feel again. Frankie..." He seemed at a loss for words.

"Come on. Get on with it," someone yelled at the back of the group, followed by another burst of laughter.

Hank laughed with them. "They all know that I'm like my father, a man of few words." Yet another burst of laughter. "But if I forget to tell you all of these things in the future, I wanted to be sure and say them today. I love you, Francesca 'Frankie' Brewster, with all my heart."

She watched him drop to one knee to the applause of the group.

He looked up at her, his blue eyes filled with love. She felt her own eyes fill with tears as he asked, "Will you do me the honor of marrying me?"

The tears overflowed and cascaded down her cheeks as she nodded, overwhelmed by all of this.

He reached into his pocket and pulled out a small velvet box. "This ring was my grandmother Savage's." He took it out, held her left hand and slipped it on her finger.

She gazed down at it. "It's beautiful," she said as he got to his feet. Looking into his handsome face, she whispered, "I love you," and threw her arms around him.

As the two of them turned, his family let out a cheer and released the balloons. Frankie looked up toward the heavens as dozens of colorful balloons took flight up into Montana's big sky. She'd never seen a more beautiful sight because of what they all represented.

Hank hugged her and then everyone else was hugging her, the meadow full of love and congratulations. "This is only the beginning," he said with a laugh. "You always wanted a big family. Well, you're going to have one now."

"I never dreamed…" she said and couldn't finish. How could she have dreamed that one day she'd meet a cowboy and he'd take her home and give her a family?

* * * * *

Cardwell Ranch: Montana Legacy continues in 2020
with a brand-new trilogy!

Until then, look for more great books from
New York Times *bestselling author B.J. Daniels.*
Here's a peek at Just His Luck,
from the Sterling's Montana series.

Chapter One

Another scream rose in her throat as the icy water rushed in around her. She fought to free herself, but the ropes that bound her wrists to the steering wheel held tight, chafing her skin until it tore and bled. Her throat was raw from screaming while outside the car the wind kicked up whitecaps on the pond. The waves sloshed against the windows. Inside the car, water rose around her feet before climbing up her legs to lap at her waist.

She pleaded for help as the water began to rise up her chest. As it touched her throat, she screamed even though she knew there wasn't anyone out there who would be coming to her rescue. Certainly not the person standing on the shore watching.

The pond was outside of town, away from everything. She knew now that was why her killer had chosen it. Worse, no one would be looking for her after all the bridges she'd burned tonight at her high school graduation party.

"You're big on torturing people," her killer had said. "Not so much fun when the shoe is on the other foot, huh."

More than half-drunk, the bitter taste of betrayal

in her mouth, she'd wanted to beg for her life. But her pride wouldn't have let her—even if the drug coursing through her veins would have. As her hands were bound to the steering wheel, she was sure that the only reason this was happening was to scare her. But she thought this had gone far enough. No one would actually kill her. Not even someone she'd bullied at school.

She was Ariel Matheson. Everyone wanted to be her friend. Everyone wanted to be her, the sexy, spoiled rich girl. No one hated her enough to go through with this. Even when the car had been pushed into the pond, she'd told herself that her new baby-blue SUV wouldn't sink. Or if it did, the water wouldn't be deep enough that she'd drown.

The dank water splashed into her face. Frantic, she tried to sit up higher, but the seat belt and the rope on her wrists held her down. The car lurched under her as it wallowed half-full of water on the rough surface of the pond. Waves splashed over the windshield, obscuring the lights of Whitefish, Montana, as the SUV slowly sank and she felt the last few minutes of her life slipping away.

She spit out a mouthful of water and told herself that this wasn't happening. Things like this didn't happen to her. This was not the way her life would end. It couldn't be.

Panic made her suck in another mouthful of awful-tasting water. She tried to hold her breath as she told herself that she was destined for so much more. The Girl Most Likely to End Up with Everything She Wanted, it said in her yearbook.

Bubbles rose around her as the car filled to the headliner, forcing her to let out the breath she'd been holding. This was real. This wasn't just to scare her.

The last thing she saw before the SUV sank the rest of the way was her killer standing on the bank in the dark night, watching her die. Would anyone miss her? Mourn her? She'd made so many enemies. Would anyone even come looking for her in the days ahead? Her parents would think that she'd run away. Her friends…

Fury replaced her fear. They thought she was a bitch before? As water filled her lungs, she swore revenge. If she could do it over? She'd make them pay.

Available September 2019 wherever
HQN Books are sold.

JUSTICE AT
CARDWELL RANCH

This book is dedicated to my amazing husband.
He makes all this possible along with inspiring me
each and every day. Thank you, Parker.
Without your love, I couldn't do this.

Prologue

Nothing moved in the darkness. At the corner of the house she stopped to catch her breath. She could hear music playing somewhere down the street. Closer, a dog barked.

As she waited in the deep shadow at the edge of the house, she measured the distance and the light she would have to pass through to reach the second window.

When she'd sneaked into the house earlier, she'd left the window unlocked. But she had no way of knowing if someone had discovered it. If so, they might not have merely relocked it—they could be waiting for her.

Fear had her heart pounding and her breath coming out in painful bursts. If she got caught— She couldn't let herself think about that.

The dog stopped barking for a moment. All she could hear was the faint music drifting on the night breeze. She fought to keep her breathing in check as she inched along the side of the house to the first window.

A light burned inside, but the drapes were closed. Still, she waited to make sure she couldn't hear anyone on the other side of the glass before she moved.

Ducking, she slipped quickly through a shaft of illumination from a streetlamp and stopped at the second bedroom window.

There, she waited for a few moments. No light burned inside the room. Still she listened before she pulled the screwdriver from her jacket pocket and began to pry up the window.

At first the old casement window didn't move and she feared she'd been right about someone discovering what she'd done and locking the window again.

When it finally gave, it did so with a pop that sounded like an explosion to her ears. She froze. No sound came from within the room. Her hands shook as she pried the window up enough that she could get her fingers under it.

Feeling as if there was no turning back now, she lifted the window enough to climb in. Heart in her throat, she drew back the curtain. She'd half expected to find someone standing on the other side lying in wait for her.

The room, painted pink, was empty except for a few pieces of mismatched furniture: a dresser, a rocking chair, a changing table and a crib.

She looked to the crib, fearing that she'd come this far only to fail. But from the faint light coming from the streetlamp, she could see the small lump beneath the tiny quilt.

Her heart beat faster at the thought that in a few minutes she would have the baby in her arms.

She heard the car coming down the street just seconds before the headlights washed over her. Halfway in the window, there was nothing she could do but hurry. She wasn't leaving here without the baby.

Chapter One

The breeze rustled through the aspens, sending golden leaves whirling around him as Jordan Cardwell walked up the hill to the cemetery. He wore a straw Western hat he'd found on a peg by the back door of the ranch house.

He hadn't worn a cowboy hat since he'd left Montana twenty years ago, but this one kept his face from burning. It was so much easier to get sunburned at this high altitude than it was in New York City.

It was hot out and yet he could feel the promise of winter hiding at the edge of the fall day. Only the memory of summer remained in the Gallatin River Canyon. Cold nightly temperatures had turned the aspens to glittering shades of gold and orange against the dark green of the pines.

Below him he could hear the rushing water of the Gallatin as the river cut a deep winding course through the canyon. Across the river, sheer granite cliffs rose up to where the sun hung in a faded blue big Montana sky.

As he walked, the scent of crushed dry leaves beneath his soles sent up the remembered smell of other autumns. He knew this land. As hard as he'd tried to escape it, this place was branded on him, this life as familiar as his own heartbeat—even after all these years.

He thought of all the winters he'd spent in this canyon listening to the ice crack on the river, feeling the bite of snow as it blew off a pine bough to sting his face, breathing in a bone-deep cold that made his head ache.

He'd done his time here, he thought as he turned his face up to the last of the day's warmth before the sun disappeared behind the cliffs. Soon the aspens would be bare, the limbs dark against a winter-washed pale frosty sky. The water in the horse troughs would begin to freeze and so would the pooling eddies along the edge of the river. The cold air in the shade of the pines was a warning of what was to come, he thought as he reached the wrought-iron cemetery gate.

The gate groaned as he shoved it open. He hesitated. What was he doing here? Nearby the breeze sighed in the tops of the towering pines, drawing his attention to the dense stand. He didn't remember them being so tall. Or so dark and thick. As he watched the boughs sway, he told himself to make this quick. He didn't want to get caught here.

Even though it was a family cemetery, he didn't feel welcome here anymore. His own fault, but still, it could get messy if anyone from his family caught him on the ranch. He didn't plan to stick around long enough to see any of them. It was best that way, he told himself as he stepped through the gate into the small cemetery.

He'd never liked graveyards. Nor did it give him any comfort to know that more than a dozen remains of their relatives were interred here. He took no satisfaction in the long lineage of the Justice family, let alone the Cardwell one, in this canyon—unlike his sister.

Dana found strength in knowing that their ancestors had been mule-headed ranchers who'd weathered everything Montana had thrown at them to stay on this ranch. They'd settled this land along a stretch of the Gallatin, a crystal clear trout stream that ran over a hundred miles from Yellowstone Park to the Missouri River.

The narrow canyon got little sunlight each day. In the winter it was an icebox of frost and snow. Getting up to feed the animals had been pure hell. He'd never understood why any of them had stayed.

But they had, he thought as he surveyed the tombstones. They'd fought this land to remain here and now they would spend eternity in soil that had given them little in return for their labors.

A gust of wind rattled through the colorful aspen leaves and moaned in the high branches of the pines. Dead foliage floated like gold coins around him, showering the weather-bleached gravestones. He was reminded why he'd never liked coming up to this windblown hill. He found no peace among the dead. Nor had he come here today looking for it.

He moved quickly through the gravestones until he found the one stone that was newer than the others, only six years in the ground. The name on the tombstone read Mary Justice Cardwell.

"Hello, Mother," he said removing his hat as he felt all the conflicting emotions he'd had when she was alive. All the arguments came rushing back, making him sick at the memory. He hadn't been able to change her mind and now she was gone, leaving them all behind to struggle as a family without her.

He could almost hear their last argument whispered on the wind. "There is nothing keeping you here, let alone me," he'd argued. "Why are you fighting so hard to keep this place going? Can't you see that ranching is going to kill you?"

He recalled her smile, that gentle gleam in her eyes that infuriated him. "This land is what makes me happy, son. Someday you will realize that ranching is in our blood. You can fight it, but this isn't just your home. A part of your heart is here, as well."

"Like hell," he'd said. "Sell the ranch, Mother, before it's too late. If not for yourself and the rest of us, then for Dana. She's too much like you. She will spend her life fighting to keep this place. Don't do that to her."

"She'll keep this ranch for the day when you come back to help her run it."

"That's never going to happen, Mother."

Mary Justice Cardwell had smiled that knowing smile of hers. "Only time will tell, won't it?"

Jordan turned the hat brim nervously in his fingers as he looked down at his mother's grave and searched for the words to tell her how much he hated what she'd done to him. To all of them. But to his surprise he felt tears well in his eyes, his throat constricting on a gulf of emotion he hadn't anticipated.

A gust of wind bent the pine boughs and blew down to scatter dried leaves across the landscape. His skin rippled with goosebumps as he suddenly sensed someone watching him. His head came up, his gaze going to the darkness of the pines.

She was only a few yards away. He hadn't heard the woman on horseback approach and realized she must have been there the whole time, watching him.

She sat astride a large buckskin horse. Shadows played across her face from the swaying pine boughs. The breeze lifted the long dark hair that flowed like molten obsidian over her shoulders and halfway down her back.

There was something vaguely familiar about her. But if he'd known her years before when this was home, he couldn't place her now. He'd been gone too long from Montana.

And yet a memory tugged at him. His gaze settled on her face again, the wide-set green eyes, that piercing look that seemed to cut right to his soul.

With a curse, he knew where he'd seen her before— and why she was looking at him the way she was. A shudder moved through him as if someone had just walked over *his* grave.

LIZA TURNER HAD WATCHED the man slog up the hill, his footsteps slow, his head down, as if he were going to a funeral. So she hadn't been surprised when he'd pushed open the gate to the cemetery and stepped in.

At first, after reining her horse in under the pines, she'd been mildly curious. She loved this spot, loved looking across the canyon as she rode through the groves of aspens and pines. It was always cool in the trees. She liked listening to the river flowing emerald-green below her on the hillside and taking a moment to search the granite cliffs on the other side for mountain sheep.

She hadn't expected to see anyone on her ride this morning. When she'd driven into the ranch for her usual trek, she'd seen the Cardwell Ranch pickup leaving and remembered that Hud was taking Dana into Bozeman today for her doctor's appointment. They were leaving the kids with Dana's best friend and former business partner, Hilde at Needles and Pins, the local fabric store.

The only other person on the ranch was the aging ranch manager, Warren Fitzpatrick. Warren would be watching *Let's Make a Deal* at his cabin this time of the morning.

So Liza had been curious and a bit leery when she'd first laid eyes on the stranger in the Western straw hat. As far as she knew, no one else should have been on the ranch today. So who was this tall, broad-shouldered cowboy?

Dana had often talked about hiring some help since Warren was getting up in years and she had her hands full with a four- and five-year-old, not to mention now being pregnant with twins.

But if this man was the new hired hand, why would he be interested in the Justice-Cardwell family cemetery? She felt the skin on the back of her neck prickle. There was something about this cowboy… His face had been in shadow from the brim of his hat. When he'd stopped at one of the graves and had taken his hat off, head bowed, she still hadn't been able to see more than his profile from where she sat astride her horse.

Shifting in the saddle, she'd tried to get a better look. He must have heard the creak of leather or sensed her presence. His head came up, his gaze darting right to the spot where she sat. He looked startled at first, then confused as if he was trying to place her.

She blinked, not sure she could trust her eyes. *Jordan Cardwell?*

He looked completely different from the arrogant man in the expensive three-piece suit she'd crossed paths with six years ago. He wore jeans, a button-up shirt and work boots. He looked tanned and stronger as if he'd been doing manual labor. There was only a hint of the earlier arrogance in his expression, making him more handsome than she remembered.

She saw the exact moment when he recognized her. Bitterness burned in his dark gaze as a small resentful smile tugged at his lips.

Oh, yes, it was Jordan Cardwell all right, she thought, wondering what had made her think he was handsome just moments before or—even harder to believe, that he might have changed.

Six years ago he'd been the number one suspect in a murder as well as a suspect in an attempted murder. Liza had been the deputy who'd taken his fingerprints.

She wondered now what he was doing not only back in the canyon, but also on the ranch he and his siblings had fought so hard to take from their sister Dana.

DANA SAVAGE LAY back on the examining table, nervously picking at a fingernail. "I can't remember the last time I saw my feet," she said with a groan.

Dr. Pamela Burr laughed. "This might feel a little cold."

Dana tried not to flinch as the doctor applied clear jelly to her huge stomach. She closed her eyes and waited until she heard the heartbeats before she opened them again. "So everything is okay?"

"Your babies appear to be doing fine. Don't you want to look?"

Dana didn't look at the monitor. "You know Hud. He's determined to be surprised. Just like the last two. So I don't dare look." She shot a glance at her husband. He stood next to her, his gaze on her, not the screen. He smiled, but she could see he was worried.

The doctor shut off the machine. "As for the spotting…"

Dana felt her heart drop as she saw the concern in Dr. Burr's expression.

"I'm going to have to insist on bed rest for these last weeks," she said. "Let's give these babies the best start we can by leaving them where they are for now." She looked to Hud.

"You can count on me," he said. "It's Dana you need to convince."

Dana sat up and laid her hands over her extended stomach. She felt the twins moving around in the cramped space. Poor babies. "Okay."

"You understand what bed rest means?" the doctor asked. "No ranch business, no getting up except to shower and use the bathroom. You're going to need help with Hank and Mary."

That was putting it mildly when you had a four- and five-year-old who were wild as the canyon where they lived.

"I'm sure Hud—"

"You'll need more than his help." The doctor pressed a piece of paper into her hand. "These are several women you might call that I've used before."

Dana didn't like the idea of bringing in a stranger to take care of Hud and the kids, but the babies kicked and she nodded.

"Doc said I was going to have to watch you like a hawk," Hud told her on the way home. Apparently while she was getting dressed, Dr. Burr had been bending his ear, down the hall in her office. "You always try to do too much. With the kids, the ranch, me—"

"I'll be good."

He gave her a disbelieving look.

"Marshal, would you like a sworn affidavit?"

He grinned over at her. "Actually, I'm thinking about handcuffing you to the bed. I reckon it will be the only way I can keep you down for a day let alone weeks."

Dana groaned as she realized how hard it was going to be to stay in bed. "What about Hank and Mary? They won't understand why their mommy can't be up and around, let alone outside with them and their animals." Both of them had their own horses and loved to ride.

"I've already put in for a leave. Liza can handle things. Anyway, it's in between resort seasons so it's quiet."

September through the middle of November was slow around Big Sky with the summer tourists gone and ski season still at least a month away.

Dana knew October was probably a better time than any other for her husband to be off work. That wasn't the problem. "Hud, I hate to see you have to babysit me and the kids."

"It's not babysitting when it's *your* wife and kids, Dana."

"You know what I mean. There are the kids and the ranch—"

"Honey, you've been trying to do it all for too long."

She *had* been juggling a lot of balls for some time now, but Hud always helped on the weekends. Their ranch manager, Warren Fitzpatrick, was getting up in years so he had really slowed down. But Warren was a fixture around the ranch, one she couldn't afford to replace. More than anything, she loved the hands-on part of ranching so she spent as much time as she could working the land.

When she'd found out she was pregnant this time she'd been delighted, but a little worried how she was going to handle another child right now.

Then the doctor had told her she was having twins. *Twins?* Seriously?

"Are you all right?" Hud asked as he placed his hand over hers and squeezed.

She smiled and nodded. "I'm always all right when I'm with you."

He gave her hand another squeeze before he went back to driving. "I'm taking you home. Then I'll go by the shop and pick up the kids." Her friend Hilde had the kids in Big Sky. "But I'd better not find out you were up and about while I was gone."

Dana shook her head and made a cross with her finger over her heart. She lay back and closed her eyes, praying as she had since the spotting had begun that the babies she was carrying would be all right. Mary and Hank were so excited about the prospect of two little brothers or sisters. She couldn't disappoint them.

She couldn't disappoint anyone, especially her mother, she thought. While Mary Justice Cardwell had been gone six years now, she was as much a part of the ranch as the old, two-story house where Dana lived with Hud and the kids. Her mother had trusted her to keep Cardwell Ranch going. Against all odds she was doing her darnedest to keep that promise.

So why did she feel so scared, as if waiting for the other shoe to drop?

Chapter Two

Jordan watched Deputy Liza Turner ride her horse out of the pines. The past six years had been good to her. She'd been pretty back then. Now there was a confidence as if she'd grown into the woman she was supposed to become. He recalled how self-assured and efficient she'd been at her job. She was also clearly at home on the back of a horse.

The trees cast long shadows over the stark landscape. Wind whirled the dried leaves that now floated in the air like snowflakes.

"Jordan Cardwell," she said as she reined in her horse at the edge of the cemetery.

He came out through the gate, stopping to look up at her. "Deputy." She had one of those faces that was almost startling in its uniqueness. The green eyes wide, captivating and always filled with curiosity. He thought she was more interesting than he remembered. That, he realized, was probably because she was out of uniform.

She wore jeans and a red-checked Western shirt that made her dark hair appear as rich as mahogany. She narrowed those green eyes at him. Curiosity and suspicion, he thought.

"I'm surprised to see you here," she said, a soft lilt

to her voice. She had a small gap between her two front teeth, an imperfection, that he found charming.

"I don't know why you'd be surprised. My sister might have inherited the ranch but I'm still family."

She smiled at that and he figured she knew all about what had happened after his mother had died—and her new will had gone missing.

"I didn't think you'd ever come back to the ranch," she said.

He chuckled. "Neither did I. But people change."

"Do they?" She was studying him in a way that said she doubted he had. He didn't need to read her expression to know she was also wondering what kind of trouble he'd brought back to the canyon with him. The horse moved under her, no doubt anxious to get going.

"Your horse seems impatient," he said. "Don't let me keep you from your ride." With a tip of his hat, he headed down the mountain to the ranch house where he'd been raised.

It seemed a lifetime ago. He could barely remember the man he'd been then. But he would be glad to get off the property before his sister and her husband returned. He planned to put off seeing them if at all possible. So much for family, he thought.

WHEN DANA OPENED her eyes, she saw that they'd left the wide valley and were now driving through the Gallatin Canyon. The "canyon" as it was known, ran from the mouth just south of Gallatin Gateway almost to West Yellowstone, fifty miles of winding road that trailed the river in a deep cut through the mountains.

The drive along the Gallatin River had always been breathtaking, a winding strip of highway that followed the blue-ribbon trout stream up over the continental divide. This time of year the Gallatin ran crystal clear over green-tinted boulders. Pine trees grew dark and thick along its edge and against the steep mountains. Aspens, their leaves rust-reds and glittering golds, grew among the pines.

Sheer rock cliffs overlooked the highway and river, with small areas of open land, the canyon not opening up until it reached Big Sky. The canyon had been mostly cattle and dude ranches, a few summer cabins and homes—that was until Big Sky resort and the small town that followed at the foot of Lone Mountain.

Luxury houses had sprouted up all around the resort. Fortunately, some of the original cabins still remained and the majority of the canyon was national forest so it would always remain undeveloped. The "canyon" was also still its own little community, for which Dana was grateful. This was the only home she'd known and, like her stubborn ancestors, she had no intention of ever leaving it.

Both she and Hud had grown up here. They'd been in love since junior high, but hit a rocky spot some years ago thanks to her sister. Dana didn't like to think about the five years she and Hud had spent apart as they passed the lower mountain resort area and, a few miles farther, turned down the road to Cardwell Ranch.

Across the river and a half mile back up a wide valley, the Cardwell Ranch house sat against a backdrop of granite cliffs, towering dark pines and glittering aspens. The house was a big, two-story rambling affair with a wide front porch and a brick-red metal roof. Behind it stood a huge weathered barn and some outbuildings and corrals.

Dana never felt truly at home until they reached the ranch she'd fought tooth and nail to save. When Mary Justice Cardwell had been bucked off a horse and died six years ago, Dana had thought all was lost. Her mother's original will when her children were young left the ranch to all of them.

Mary hadn't realized until her children were grown that only Dana would keep the ranch. The others would sell it, take the profits and never look back until the day they regretted what they'd done. By then it would be too late. So her mother had made a new will, leaving the ranch to her. But her mother had hidden it where she hoped her daughter would find it. Fortunately, Dana had found it in time to save the ranch.

The will had put an end to her siblings' struggle to force her to sell the land and split the profits with them. Now her three siblings were paid part of the ranch's profit each quarter. Not surprisingly, she hadn't heard from any of them since the will had settled things six years before.

As Hud pulled into the ranch yard, Dana spotted a car parked in front of the old house and frowned. The car was an older model with California plates.

"You didn't already hire someone—"

"No," Hud said before she could finish. "I wouldn't do that without talking to you first. Do you think the doctor called one of the women she told you about?"

Before Dana could answer, she saw that someone was waiting out on the broad front porch. As Hud pulled in beside the car, the woman stepped from out of the shadows.

"Stacy?" She felt her heart drop. After six years of

silence and all the bad feelings from the past, what was her older sister doing here?

"SURPRISE," STACY SAID with a shrug and a worried smile. Like Dana, Stacy had gotten the Justice-Cardwell dark good looks, but she'd always been the cute one who capitalized on her appearance, cashing in as she traded her way up through three marriages that Dana knew of and possibly more since.

Just the sight of her sister made Dana instantly wary. She couldn't help but be mistrustful given their past.

Her sister's gaze went to Dana's stomach. "Oh, my. You're *pregnant*."

"We need to get Dana in the house," Hud said, giving his sister-in-law a nod of greeting. Stacy opened the door and let them enter before she followed them in.

Dana found herself looking around the living room, uncomfortable that her sister had been inside the house even though it had once been Stacy's home, as well.

The house was as it had been when her mother was alive. Original Western furnishings, a lot of stone and wood and a bright big airy kitchen. Dana, like her mother, chose comfort over style trends. She loved her big, homey house. It often smelled of something good bubbling on the stove, thanks to the fact that Hud loved to cook.

Dana preferred to spend her time with her children outside, teaching them to ride or watching a new foal being born or picking fresh strawberries out of the large garden she grew—just as her own mother had done with her.

As she looked at her sister, she was reminded of some of her mother's last words to her. "Families stick together. It isn't always easy. Everyone makes mistakes. Dana, you have to find forgiveness in your heart. If not for them, then for yourself."

Her mother had known then that if anything happened to her, Jordan, Stacy and Clay would fight her for the ranch. That's why she'd made the new will.

But she must also have known that the will would divide them.

"It's been a long time," Dana said, waiting, knowing her sister wanted something or she wouldn't be here.

"I know I should have kept in touch more," Stacy said. "I move around a lot." But she'd always managed to get her check each quarter as part of her inheritance from the ranch profits. Dana instantly hated the uncharitable thought. She didn't want to feel that way about her sister. But Stacy had done some things in the past that had left the two of them at odds. Like breaking Dana and Hud up eleven years ago. Dana still had trouble forgiving her sister for that.

Stacy shifted uncomfortably in the silence. "I should have let you know I was coming, huh."

"Now isn't the best time for company," Hud said. "Dana's doctor has advised her to get off her feet for the rest of her pregnancy."

"But I'm not *company,*" Stacy said. "I'm family. I can help."

Hud looked to his wife. "Why don't you go. It's fine," Dana said and removed her coat.

"So you're pregnant," her sister said.

"Twins," Dana said, sinking into a chair.

Stacy nodded.

Dana realized Hud was still in his coat, waiting,

afraid to leave her alone with Stacy. "Are you going to pick up the kids?"

He gave her a questioning look.

"I thought you probably had more kids," her sister said. "The toys and stuff around."

Dana was still looking at her husband. She knew he didn't trust Stacy, hated she'd been alone in their house while they were gone and worse, he didn't want to leave the two of them alone. "Stacy and I will be fine."

Still he hesitated. He knew better than anyone what her siblings were like.

"Stacy, would you mind getting me a drink of water?" The moment her sister left the room, Dana turned to her husband. "I'll be *fine*," she said lowering her voice. "Go pick up the kids. I promise I won't move until you get back." She could tell that wasn't what had him concerned.

He glanced toward the kitchen and the sound of running water. "I won't be long."

She motioned him over and smiled as he leaned down to kiss her. At the same time, he placed a large hand on her swollen stomach. The babies moved and he smiled.

"You have your cell phone if you need me?"

Dana nodded. "The marshal's office is also on speed dial. I'll be fine. Really."

Stacy came back in with a glass full of water as Hud left. "I'm glad things have turned out good for you. Hud is so protective."

"Thank you," she said as she took the glass and studied her sister over the rim as she took a drink.

"I would have called," Stacy said, "but I wanted to surprise you."

"I'm surprised." She watched her sister move around

the room, touching one object after another, seeming nervous. Her first thought when she'd seen her sister was that she'd come here because she was in trouble.

That initial observation hadn't changed. Now though, Dana was betting it had something to do with money. It usually did with Stacy, unfortunately.

Years ago Dana had found out just how low her sister would stoop if the price was right. She had good reason not to trust her sister.

"The place hasn't changed at all," Stacy was saying now. "Except for the pile of toys in the sunroom. I heard Hud say he was going to pick up the kids?"

"Hank and Mary, five and four."

"You named your daughter after mother, that's nice," Stacy said. "I thought you probably would." She seemed to hear what she'd said. "I want you to know I'm not upset about mother leaving you the ranch. You know me, I would have just blown the money." She flashed a self-deprecating smile. "And you're pregnant with twins! When are you due?"

"Eight weeks." When she finally couldn't take it anymore, Dana asked, "Stacy, what are you doing here?"

"It's kind of a strange story," her sister said, looking even more nervous.

Dana braced herself. If Stacy thought it was a strange story, then it could be anything. Her sister opened her mouth to say something, but was interrupted.

From upstairs a baby began to cry.

"What is that?" Dana demanded.

"I haven't had a chance to tell you," Stacy said as she started for the stairs. "That's Ella. That's my other surprise. I have a baby."

LIZA PARKED HER PICKUP across the road from Trail's End and settled in to wait. She had a clear view of the small cabin Jordan had rented. Like a lot of Big Sky, the string of cabins were new. But it being off-season and the cabins' only view being Highway 191, she figured they weren't too pricey. She wondered how Jordan was fixed for money and if that's what had brought him back here.

Pulling out her phone, she called Hud's cell. He answered on the third ring. She could hear the kids in the background and a woman's voice. Hilde, Dana's best friend. He must be at Needles and Pins.

"How's Dana, boss?" she asked.

"Stubborn."

She laughed. "So the doctor *did* prescribe bed rest."

"Yes. Fortunately, I know you can run things just fine without me."

"Probably more smoothly without you around," she joked.

He must have heard something in her voice. "But?"

"Nothing I can't handle," she assured him. "But you might want to give Dana a heads-up."

"Dana already knows. Stacy's at the house right now."

"Stacy?"

"Who were *you* talking about?" Hud asked.

"Jordan."

She heard Hud swear under his breath.

"I saw him earlier on the ranch, actually at the family cemetery," Liza said.

"What's he doing in the canyon?"

"He didn't say, but I found out where he's staying. He's rented a cabin past Buck's T-4." Buck's T-4 was a local landmark bar and hotel. "I'm hanging out, watching to see what he's up to."

"Probably not the best way to spend taxpayers' dollars, but I appreciate it. As far as I know, he hasn't contacted Dana."

"Let me know if he does. In the meantime, I'll stick around here for a while."

"You really need to get a life, deputy," Hud said. "Thanks. Let me know if you need help."

"So Stacy's here, too?"

"We haven't heard from any of them in six years and now two of them are in the canyon? This doesn't bode well."

That had been her thought exactly.

"I don't want them upsetting Dana," he said. "All we need is for Clay to show up next. This couldn't come at a worse time. I'm worried enough about Dana and the babies. I have a bad feeling this could have something to do with that developer who's been after Dana to sell some of the ranch."

"The timing does make you wonder," Liza said.

"I'm going back to the ranch now."

"You stick close to Dana. I'll let you know if Jordan heads for the ranch." Hanging up, Liza settled in again. She knew it could be a while. Jordan might be in for the night.

The canyon got dark quickly this time of year. With the dark that settled over it like a cloak came a drop in temperature. She could hear the river, smell the rich scent of fall. A breeze stirred the nearby pines, making the branches sway and sigh. A couple of stars popped out above the canyon walls.

The door of the cabin opened. Jordan stepped out

and headed for his rented SUV parked outside. He was dressed in a warm coat, gloves and a hat, all in a dark color. He definitely didn't look like a man going out for dinner—or even to visit his sister. He glanced around as if he thought someone might be watching him before climbing into his rental.

Liza felt her heart kick up a beat as she slunk down in the pickup seat and waited. A few moments later she heard the SUV pull out. She started the truck, and sitting up, followed at a distance.

To her relief, he didn't turn down Highway 191 in the direction of the Cardwell Ranch—and his sister's house. Instead, he headed north toward Big Sky proper, making her think she might be wrong. Maybe he was merely going out to find a place to have dinner.

He drove on past the lighted buildings that made up the Meadow Village, heading west toward Mountain Village. There was little traffic this time of year. She let another vehicle get between them, all the time keeping Jordan's taillights in sight.

Just when she started speculating on where he might be headed, he turned off on the road to Ousel Falls. They passed a few commercial buildings, a small housing complex and then the road cut through the pines as it climbed toward the falls.

Liza pulled over, letting him get farther ahead. Had he spotted the tail? She waited as long as she dared before she drove on up the road. Her headlights cut a gold swath through the darkness. Dense pines lined both sides of the mountain road. There was no traffic at all up this way. She worried he had spotted her following him and was now leading her on a wild-goose chase.

She hadn't gone far when her headlights picked up

the parking lot for the falls. Jordan's rental was parked in the empty lot. She couldn't tell if he was still in the vehicle. Grabbing her baseball cap off the seat, she covered her dark hair as she drove on past.

Out of the corner of her eye she saw that the SUV was empty. Past it near the trailhead, she glimpsed the beam of a flashlight bobbing as it headed down the trail.

A few hundred yards up the road Liza found a place to pull over. She grabbed her own flashlight from under the seat, checked to make sure the batteries were still working and got out of the truck.

It was a short hike back to the trailhead. From there the path dropped to the creek before rising again as it twisted its way through the thick forest.

The trail was wide and paved and she found, once her eyes adjusted, that she didn't need to use her flashlight if she was careful. Enough starlight bled down through the pine boughs that she could see far enough ahead—and she knew the trail well.

There was no sign of Jordan, though. She'd reached the creek and bridge, quickly crossed it, and had started up the winding track when she caught a glimpse of light above her on the footpath.

She stopped to listen, afraid he might have heard her behind him. But there was only the sound of the creek and moan of the pines in the breeze. Somewhere in the distance an owl hooted. She moved again, hurrying now.

Once the pathway topped out, she should be able to see Jordan's light ahead of her, though she couldn't imagine what he was doing hiking to the falls tonight.

There was always a good chance of running into a

moose or a wolf or worse this time of a year, a hungry grizzly foraging for food before hibernation.

The trail topped out. She stopped to catch her breath and listen for Jordan. Ahead she could make out the solid rock area at the base of the waterfall. A few more steps and she could feel the mist coming off the cascading water. From here, the walkway carved a crooked path up through the pines to the top of the falls.

There was no sign of any light ahead and the only thing she could hear was rushing water. Where was Jordan? She moved on, convinced he was still ahead of her. Something rustled in the trees off to her right. A limb cracked somewhere ahead in the pines.

She stopped and drew her weapon. Someone was out there.

The report of the rifle shot felt so close it made the hair stand up on her neck. The sound ricocheted off the rock cliff and reverberated through her. Liza dove to the ground. A second shot echoed through the trees.

Weapon drawn, she scrambled up the hill and almost tripped over the body Jordan Cardwell was standing over.

Chapter Three

"You have a *baby?*" Dana said, still shocked when Stacy came back downstairs carrying a pink bundle. "I'm just having a hard time imagining you as a mother."

"You think you're the only one with a maternal instinct?" Stacy sounded hurt.

"I guess I never thought you *wanted* a baby."

Stacy gave a little shrug. "People change."

Did they? Dana wondered as she studied her sister.

"Want to see her?" Stacy asked.

Dana nodded and her sister carefully transferred the bundle into her arms. Dana saw that it wasn't a blanket at all that the baby was wrapped in, but a cute pink quilt. Parting the edges, she peered in at the baby. A green-eyed knockout stared back at her.

"Isn't she *beautiful?*"

"She's breathtaking. What's her name?"

"Ella."

Dana looked up at her sister, her gaze going to Stacy's bare left-hand ring finger. "Is there a father?"

"Of course," her sister said with an embarrassed laugh. "He's in the military. We're getting married when he comes home in a few weeks."

Stacy had gone through men like tissues during a sad

movie. In the past she'd married for money. Maybe this time she had found something more important, Dana hoped, glancing down at the baby in her arms.

"Hello, Ella," she said to the baby. The bow-shaped lips turned up at the corners, the green eyes sparkling. "How old is she?"

"Six months."

As the baby began to fuss, Stacy dug in a diaper bag Dana hadn't seen at the end of the couch. She pulled out a bottle before going into the kitchen to warm it.

Dana stared at the precious baby, her heart in her throat. She couldn't imagine her sister with a baby. In the past Stacy couldn't even keep a houseplant alive.

As her sister came out of the kitchen, Dana started to hand back the baby.

"You can feed her if you want."

Dana took the bottle and watched the baby suck enthusiastically at the warm formula. "She's adorable." Her sister didn't seem to be listening though.

Stacy had walked over to the window and was looking out. "I forgot how quiet it is here." She hugged herself as a gust of wind rattled the old window. "Or how cold it is this time of year."

"Where *have* you been living?"

"Southern California," she said, turning away from the window.

"Is that where you met the father?"

Stacy nodded. "It's getting late. Ella and I should go."

"Where are you *going?*" Dana asked, alarmed, realizing that she'd been cross-examining her sister as if Stacy was one of Hud's suspects. She couldn't bear the thought of this baby being loaded into that old car outside with Stacy at the wheel.

"I planned to get a motel for the night. Kurt's got some relatives up by Great Falls. They've offered me a place to stay until he gets leave and we can find a place of our own."

Dana shook her head, still holding tight to the baby. "You're staying here. You and Ella can have Mary's room. I don't want you driving at night."

LIZA SWUNG THE BARREL of her gun and snapped on her flashlight, aiming both at Jordan. "Put your hands up," she ordered.

He didn't move. He stood stock-still, staring down at the body at his feet. He appeared to be in shock.

"I said put your hands up," she ordered again. He blinked and slowly raised his gaze to her, then lifted his hands. Keeping the gun trained on him, she quickly frisked him. "Where is the weapon?" She nudged him with the point of her gun barrel.

He shook his head. "*I* didn't shoot him."

Liza took a step back from him and shone the flashlight beam into the pines. The light didn't go far in the dense trees and darkness. "Who shot him?"

"I don't know."

She squatted down to check for a pulse. None. Pulling out her phone, she called for backup and the coroner. When she'd finished, she turned the beam on Jordan again. "You can start by telling me what you're doing out here."

He looked down at the body, then up at her. "You know I didn't kill him."

"How do I know that?"

True, she hadn't seen him carrying a rifle, but he could have hidden one in the woods earlier today. But how did he get rid of it so quickly? She would have heard him throw it into the trees.

"What are you doing here at the falls in the middle of the night?"

He looked away.

She began to read him his rights.

"All right," he said with a sigh. "You aren't going to believe me. I was meeting him here."

"To buy drugs?"

"No." He looked insulted. "It's a long story."

"We seem to have time." She motioned to a downed tree not far from the body but deep enough in the trees that if the killer was still out there, he wouldn't have a clear shot.

Jordan sighed as he sat down, dropping his head in his hands for a few moments. "When I was in high school my best friend hung himself. At least that's what everyone thought, anyway. I didn't believe he would do that, but there was no evidence of foul play. Actually, no one believed me when I argued there was no way Tanner would have taken his own life."

"People often say that about suicide victims."

"Yeah. Well, a few weeks ago, I got a call from…" He looked in the direction of the body, but quickly turned away. "Alex Winslow."

"Is that the victim?"

He nodded. "Alex asked if I was coming back for our twenty-year high-school reunion."

"You *were?*" She couldn't help her surprise.

He gave her an are-you-kidding look. "I told him no. That's when he mentioned Tanner."

"Alex Winslow told you he was looking into Tanner's death?"

"Not in so many words. He said something like, 'Do you ever think about Tanner?' He sounded like he'd been drinking. At first I just thought it was the booze talking."

He told her about the rest of the conversation, apparently quoting Alex as best as he could remember.

"Man, it would take something to hang yourself," Alex had said. "Put that noose around your neck and stand there balancing on nothing more than a log stump. One little move... Who would do that unless they were forced to? You know, like at gunpoint or... I don't know, maybe get tricked into standing up there?"

"What are you saying?"

"Just...what if he didn't do it? What if they killed him?"

"They? Who?"

"Don't listen to me. I've had a few too many beers tonight. So, are you sure I can't talk you into coming to the reunion? Even if I told you I have a theory about Tanner's death."

"What theory?"

"Come to the reunion. Call me when you get into town and I'll tell you. Don't mention this to anyone else. Seriously. I don't want to end up like poor old Tanner."

"That could have just been the alcohol talking," Liza said when he finished.

"That's what I thought, too, until he wanted to meet at the falls after dark. Something had him running scared."

"With good reason, apparently. Alex Winslow is a former friend?"

Jordan nodded.

"You weren't just a little suspicious, meeting in the dark at a waterfall?"

"I thought he was being paranoid, but I played along."

"You didn't consider it might be dangerous?"

"No, I thought Alex was overreacting. He was like that. Or at least he had been in high school. I haven't seen him in twenty years."

"Why, if he knew something, did he wait all these years?"

Jordan shrugged. "I just know that Tanner wouldn't have killed himself. He was a smart guy. If anything he was too smart for his own good. I figured if there was even a small chance that Alex knew something…" He glanced over at her. "Apparently, Alex had reason to be paranoid. This proves that there is more to Tanner's suicide."

She heard the determination in his voice and groaned inwardly. "This proves nothing except that Alex Winslow is dead." But Jordan wasn't listening.

"Also it proves I wasn't such a fool to believe Alex really did know something about Tanner's death."

She studied Jordan for a moment. "Did he say something to you before he was shot?"

His gaze shifted away. "I can't even be sure I heard him right."

"What did he say?"

"Shelby."

"Shelby?"

He nodded. "We went to school with a girl named Shelby Durran. She and Tanner were a couple. At least until Christmas our senior year."

HUD HAD JUST RETURNED with the kids when he got the call about the shooting.

"Go," Dana said. "I'll be fine. Stacy is here. She said she'd have the kids help her make dinner for all of us."

He mugged a face and lowered his voice. "Your sister *cooking?* Now that's frightening."

"Go," his wife ordered, giving him a warning look. "We can manage without you for a while."

"Are you sure?" He took her hand and squeezed it. "You promise to stay right where you are?"

"Promise."

Still, he hesitated. He'd been shocked to walk into the house and see Dana holding a baby. For a few moments, he'd been confused as to where she'd gotten it.

"Has Stacy said anything about where she's been?" he asked, glancing toward the kitchen. He could hear the voices of his children and sister-in-law. They all sounded excited about whatever they were making for dinner.

"Southern California. She's headed for Great Falls. There's a military base located there so that makes sense since she says the baby's father is in the military."

"If Stacy can be believed," he said quietly.

Dana mugged a face at him. But telling the truth wasn't one of her sister's strong suits. It bothered him that Dana was defending her sister. He figured the baby had something to do with it. Dana was a sucker for kids.

"Stacy seems different now," she said. "I think it's the baby. It seems to have grounded her some, maybe."

"Maybe," he said doubtfully.

"Go on, you have a murder investigation to worry about instead of me."

"You sound way too happy about that."

LIZA ALREADY HAD the crime scene cordoned off when Hud arrived. He waved to the deputy on guard at the falls parking lot as he got out of his patrol SUV. The coroner's van was parked next to the two police vehicles.

"The coroner just went in," the deputy told him.

He turned on his flashlight and started down the trail. Hud couldn't help thinking about his wife's siblings trying to force her to sell the family ranch. They'd been like vultures, none of them having any interest in Cardwell Ranch. All they'd wanted was the money.

Jordan had been the worst because of his New York lifestyle—and his out-of-work model wife. But Stacy and Clay had had their hands out, as well. Hud hated to think what would have happened if Dana hadn't found the new will her mother had made leaving her the ranch.

He smiled at the memory of where she'd found it. Mary Justice Cardwell had put it in her favorite old recipe book next to "Double Chocolate Brownies." The brownies had been Hud's favorite. Dana hadn't made them in all the time the two of them had been apart. When they'd gotten back together six years ago, Dana had opened the cookbook planning to surprise him with the brownies, only to be surprised herself.

Two of her siblings were back in the canyon? That had him worried even before the call from his deputy marshal that there'd been a murder. And oh, yeah, Liza had told him, Jordan Cardwell was somehow involved.

Now as he hiked into the falls, he tried to keep his temper in check. If Dana's family thought they were going to come back here and upset her—

Ahead he saw the crowd gathered at the top of the falls. He headed for the coroner.

Coroner Rupert Milligan was hugging seventy, but you'd never know it the way he acted. Six years ago, Hud had thought the man older than God and more powerful in this county. Tall, white-haired, with a head like a buffalo, he had a gruff voice and little patience for stupidity. He'd retired as a country doctor to work as a coroner.

None of that had changed in the past six years. Just as Rupert's love for murder mysteries and forensics hadn't.

"So what do we have?" Hud asked over the roar of the falls as he joined him.

Rupert answered without even bothering to look up. "Single gunshot through the heart. Another through the lungs. High-powered rifle."

"Distance?"

"I'd say fifty yards."

"That far," he said, surprised. The killer would have needed the victim to be out in the open with no trees in the way to make such a shot. Like at the top of a waterfall. "Any idea where the shot came from?"

Rupert had been crouched beside the body. Now he finally looked up. "In case you haven't noticed, it's dark out. Once it gets daylight you can look for tracks and possibly a shell casing. And once I get the body to Bozeman for an autopsy I might be able to tell you more about the trajectory of the bullet. Offhand, I'd say the shot came from the other side of the creek, probably on the side of the mountain."

"So either it was a lucky shot or the killer had been set up and waiting," Liza said, joining them. "The killer either picked the meeting spot or was told where the victim would be."

Rupert shifted his gaze to her and frowned. Being from the old school, the coroner made no secret of the fact that he didn't hold much appreciation for women law enforcement. If he'd had his way, he would have put them all behind a desk.

Hud liked that Liza didn't seem to let him bother her. His deputy marshal's good looks could be deceiving. Small in stature, too cute for her own good and easygoing, Liza often gave criminals the idea that she was a pushover. They, however, quickly learned differently. He wondered if Jordan Cardwell thought the same thing about the deputy marshal. If so, he was in for a surprise.

"Which could mean either that the victim was expecting to meet not only Jordan Cardwell up here, but also someone he trusted," she continued. "Or—"

"Or Jordan told the killer about the meeting," Hud interjected.

Liza nodded and glanced over to the stump where Jordan was waiting. "That is always another possibility."

"One I suggest you don't forget," Hud said under his breath. "If it's all right with you, I'll take our suspect down to the office."

She nodded. "I want to wait for the crime scene techs to arrive."

Hud hadn't seen Jordan for six years. As he walked toward him, he was thinking he could have easily gone another six and not been in the least bit sorry.

"You just happen to come back to the canyon and a man dies," he said.

"Good to see you again, too, brother-in-law. I guess my invitation to the wedding must have gotten lost in the mail, huh?"

"What are you doing here, Jordan?"

"I already told your deputy marshal."

"Well, you're going to have to tell me, too. Let's get

out of the woods and go to my office. You have a rifle you need to pick up before we go?"

Jordan gave him a grim, disappointed look. "No, I'm good."

THE DOOR OPENED A CRACK. "Oh, good, you're awake," Stacy said as she peered in at Dana. "I brought you some still-warm chocolate chip cookies and some milk."

"That was very thoughtful of you," Dana said, sitting up in the bed and putting her crossword puzzle aside. Earlier, before her doctor's appointment, Hud had made her a bed in the sunroom so she wouldn't have to go up the stairs—and would be where she could see most of what was going on. She patted the bed, and her sister sat down on the edge and placed the tray next to them.

"I'm just glad you let me stay and help out. It was fun baking with Hank and Mary. They are so cute. Hank looks just like a small version of Hud and Mary is the spitting image of you. Do you know..." She motioned to Dana's big belly.

"No," she said, taking a bite of cookie. "We want to be surprised. Did you find out ahead of time?"

Stacy had cautiously placed a hand on Dana's abdomen and now waited with expectation. The babies had been restless all day, kicking up a storm. She watched her sister's face light up as one of the twins gave her hand a swift kick.

Stacy laughed and pulled her hand back. "Isn't that the coolest thing ever?"

Dana nodded, studying her older sister. Stacy had changed little in appearance. She was still the pretty one. Her dark hair was chin-length, making her brown eyes the focus of her face. She'd always had that innocent look. That was probably, Dana realized with a start, why she'd been able to get away with as much as she had.

"So did you know ahead of time you were having a girl?" she asked again.

Stacy shook her head and helped herself to a cookie. "It was a surprise."

"Speaking of surprises…" She watched her sister's face. "Jordan is in town."

"Jordan?" Had Stacy known? "What is *he* doing here?"

"I thought you might know."

Stacy shook her head and looked worried. "I haven't heard from him since we were all here six years ago." She made a face. "I still feel bad about trying to force you to sell the ranch."

Dana waved that away. "It's history. The ranch is still in the family and it makes enough money that you and our brothers get to share in the profits. You know I think my lawyer did mention that he'd received notice that Jordan was divorced."

"I wonder how much of his ranch profits he has to give to Jill? That woman was such a gold digger." Stacy laughed as she realized the irony. "I should know, huh? Back then I figured if I was going to get married, I might as well get paid for it." She shook her head as if amazed by the woman she'd been. "Have you heard from Clay?"

"No." She helped herself to another cookie and sipped some of the milk. "He hasn't been cashing his checks lately. My attorney is checking into it."

"That's odd," Stacy agreed. "Well, I need to clean up the kitchen."

"Thanks so much for giving the kids their baths and getting them to bed." Mary and Hank had come in earlier to say good-night and have Dana read a book to them before bed. They'd been wearing their footie pajamas, their sweet faces scrubbed clean and shiny. They'd been excited about helping their aunt Stacy cook.

"Thank you so much for all your help," Dana said, touched by everything Stacy had done.

"I'm just glad I was here so I could." She smiled. "I didn't know how fun kids could be."

"Wait until Ella is that age. Mary loves to have tea parties and help her daddy cook."

Stacy nodded thoughtfully. "Let me know if you need anything. Knowing you, I can guess how hard it is for you to stay down like this."

Dana groaned in response. She couldn't stand the thought of another day let alone weeks like this. "Thanks for the cookies and milk. The cookies were delicious."

Stacy looked pleased as she left the room.

Chapter Four

Hud walked out with Jordan to the road, then followed him to the marshal's office. Once in the office he got his first good look at his brother-in-law. Jordan had been only two years ahead of Hud in school, three years ahead of his sister Dana. His brother-in-law had aged, but it hadn't hurt Jordan's looks. If anything the years seemed to have given him character, or at least the appearance of it.

"Why don't you have a seat and start at the beginning?" Hud said dropping into his chair behind his desk.

"I thought Liza was handling this case?"

"*Liza?* You mean Deputy Marshal Turner?" He shouldn't have been surprised Jordan was on a first-name basis with the deputy. He, of all people, understood the charm of the Justice-Cardwell genes. Dana could wrap him around her little finger and did.

"Don't think just because she's a woman that she isn't a damned good marshal," Hud said to his brother-in-law. "She's sharp and she'll nail you to the wall if you're guilty."

"If you have so much confidence in her abilities, then why are you here?"

Hud gritted his teeth. Jordan had always been difficult. At least that hadn't changed. "Several reasons. None of which I have to explain to you. But—" He held up a hand before Jordan could speak. "I will because I want us to have an understanding." He ticked them off on his fingers. "One, I'm still the marshal here. Two, Liza has her hands full up at the site. Three, I want to know what happened on that mountain. And four, your sister is my wife. I don't want her hurt."

With a smile and a nod, Jordan ambled over to a chair and sat. "Dana doesn't have anything to worry about. Neither she nor the ranch is why I'm back in the canyon."

"Why *are* you here?" Hud asked, snapping on the recording machine.

"It doesn't have anything to do with family."

"But it does have something to do with Alex Winslow."

"Alex was a good friend from high school. I didn't kill him." Jordan sighed and looked at the ceiling for a moment.

Hud noticed that he was no longer wearing a wedding ring. He vaguely remembered Dana mentioning that she'd heard Jordan was divorced from his ex-model wife, Jill. The marriage had probably ended when Jordan didn't get the proceeds from the sale of the ranch.

"If Alex was your friend, I would think you'd be interested in helping us find his killer," Hud said. "Not to mention you're neck deep in this. Right now, you're the number one suspect."

Jordan laughed. "Does that work on most of your suspects?" He shook his head. "I came back because Alex called me. He hinted that he might know something about Tanner's suicide but it was clear he didn't want to talk about it on the phone. He said he'd share his theory with me if I came to our twenty-year high school reunion. The next time I talked to him, he sounded scared and wanted to meet at the falls. That's it."

That was a lot. Hud wasn't sure how much of it he believed. But at least he had some idea of what might have brought Jordan back to town—and it wasn't family.

"Tanner Cole committed suicide when the two of you were seniors in high school. Why would that bring you back here after all these years?"

"When your best friend commits suicide, you never stop thinking you could have done something to stop him. You need to know *why* he did it."

"Unless that person leaves a note, you never know. Tanner didn't leave a note, as I recall."

Jordan shook his head.

"Did you talk to Alex before he was shot?"

"As I told your deputy, I heard the shot, he stumbled toward me, there was another shot and he went down. All he said was the word *Shelby.* At least that's what I thought he said." Jordan shrugged. "That was it."

Hud studied him openly for a moment. "Maybe the bullets were meant for you and the killer missed."

Jordan sighed. "What are you insinuating?"

"That maybe Tanner didn't commit suicide. Weren't you the one who found his body?"

Anger fired Jordan's gaze. "He was my *best* friend. I would have taken a bullet *for* him."

"Instead, another friend of yours took the bullet tonight," Hud said. "You're telling me you came all this way, hiked into the falls in the dark, just for answers?"

"Why is that so hard for you to understand?"

"What about Alex Winslow? Don't I remember some falling-out the two of you had before you graduated?"

"It was high school. Who remembers?"

Hud nodded. "Is Stacy in the canyon for the same reason?" Stacy had been in the grade between the two of them.

"Stacy?" Jordan looked genuinely surprised. "I haven't seen or talked to her in years."

"Then you didn't know that not only is she back in the canyon, she also has a baby."

Jordan laughed. "Stacy has a *baby?* That's got to be good. Look, if that's all, I need to get some sleep."

"Once Liza allows you to, I'm sure you'll be leaving. I'd appreciate it if you didn't upset Dana before then. She's pregnant with twins and having a rough go of it."

"I'm sorry to hear that," Jordan said, sounding as if he meant it. "Don't worry, I won't be bothering my sister. Either of my sisters," he added.

"Then I guess we're done here."

A WHILE LATER, Dana heard Hud come in. She heard him go upstairs to check on the kids, before coming back down to her room. He smiled when he saw her still awake and came over to her side of the bed to give her a kiss.

"So everything's all right?" he asked.

"I'm the one who should be asking you that. You said there'd been a shooting?"

He nodded. "Liza's got everything under control. The crime techs are on their way from Missoula." He sounded tired.

"Stacy kept a plate of dinner for you. She made chicken, baked potatoes and corn," Dana said. "Then she and kids baked chocolate chip cookies." She motioned to the cookies on the tray next to the bed.

Hud gave her a who-knew-she-could-cook look and took one of the cookies.

Who knew indeed? Dana couldn't believe the change in her sister. She felt horribly guilty for not trusting it. But even Stacy was capable of changing, right? Having a baby did that to a person. But Stacy?

Unfortunately, the jury was still out—given her sister's past.

"Did she mention how long she's staying?" Hud asked, not meeting her gaze.

"She was planning to leave earlier, but I asked her to stay. I'm sure she'll be leaving in the morning."

Hud nodded. She could tell he would be glad when Stacy was gone. Dana couldn't blame him. Her sister had hurt them both. But she desperately wanted to believe Stacy had changed. For Ella's sake.

Unfortunately, like her husband, Dana had a niggling feeling that Stacy wasn't being completely honest about the real reason she'd come to the ranch.

EXHAUSTED, JORDAN WENT back to his cabin, locked the door and fell into bed with the intention of sleeping the rest of the day.

Unfortunately, Deputy Marshal Liza Turner had other plans for him.

"What do you want?" he said when he opened the cabin door a little after eleven o'clock that morning to find her standing outside. He leaned a hip into the doorjamb and crossed his arms as he took her in.

"What do I want? Sleep, more money, better hours, breakfast."

"I can't help you with most of that, but I could use food. I'll buy."

She smiled. "I know a place that serves breakfast all day. We can eat and talk."

"No murder talk until I've had coffee."

"Agreed."

Liza drove them to the upper mountain. The huge unpaved parking lots sat empty. None of the lifts moved on the mountain except for the gondolas that rocked gently in the breeze.

"It's like a ghost town up here," he commented as they got out of her patrol SUV.

"I like the quiet. Good place to talk. Most everything is closed still. Fortunately, there are enough locals that a few places stay open."

The café was small and nearly empty. Liza led him outside to a table under an umbrella. The sun was low to the south, but still warm enough it was comfortable outside. A waitress brought them coffee while they looked at the menu.

Jordan ordered ham and eggs, hashbrowns and whole wheat toast.

"I'll have the same," Liza said and handed back the menu. As soon as the waitress was out of earshot, she said, "You didn't mention last night that you and the victim were no longer friends at the end of your high school years."

"So you spoke with Hud." He looked toward the mountains where snow dusted the peaks, making them gleam blinding bright. "It was a stupid disagreement over a woman, all right? Just high school stuff."

She nodded, not buying it. "What girl?"

"I don't even remember."

Liza's look called him a liar, but she let it go. "I'm

still confused why he contacted *you*. He must have had other friends locally he would have talked to."

"Obviously he must have talked to someone locally. One of them knew where he was going last night and killed him." Jordan said nothing as the waitress served their breakfasts. He picked up his fork. "Look, do we have to talk about this while we eat? I feel like I got him killed."

"You can't blame yourself, or worse, try to take the law into your own hands." She eyed him for a long moment. "Why would I suspect that's what you're planning to do?"

He chuckled. "If you talked to my brother-in-law he would have told you that I'm not that ambitious. Anyway, you're the deputy marshal. I'm sure you'll find his killer."

She took a bite of toast, chewed and swallowed before she said, "You contacted Tanner's girlfriend from his senior year in high school."

Jordan took her measure. "Why, Liza, you've been checking up on me. I contacted Shelby before I went up to the falls last night. She said she had nothing to say to me about Tanner. That was high school and so far back, she barely remembers."

"You didn't believe her?" Liza asked between bites.

Jordan laughed. "High school was Shelby's glory days. Just check out our yearbook. She is on every page either as president or queen of something. Not to mention she was dating Tanner Cole, the most popular guy in school. She was in her element. I'd bet those were the best days of her life and that nothing she has done since will ever compare."

Liza considered that for a long moment before she asked, "So you talked to Shelby before last night. Before the only word Alex got out after he was shot was her name?"

"Like I said, she and Tanner dated."

"When you talked to Shelby, did you mention Alex or where you were meeting him?"

He gave her an exasperated look. "Do you really think I'm that stupid? Alex was acting terrified. I wasn't about to say anything until I talked to him."

"And yet you called Shelby."

"Yeah. I just told her I was in the area as if I was here for the twenty-year reunion and worked Tanner into the conversation. I didn't realize then that anything I might do could put anyone in danger, including her."

"That's so noble. But I thought you didn't like her. In fact, I thought you were instrumental in breaking up her and Tanner."

He shook his head and took a bite of his breakfast. "You're determined to ruin my appetite, aren't you?"

"Is it true?"

"I couldn't stand Shelby and that bunch she ran with. But you're wrong. I had nothing to do with breaking her and Tanner up, no matter what Hud thinks, as I'm sure that's where you got your information."

Liza lifted a brow. "You weren't the one who snitched on her?"

"Wasn't me." He met her gaze. "Why keep questioning me if you aren't going to believe anything I say?"

"I don't want you involved in my investigation," she said. "That includes asking about Tanner among your old friends—and enemies."

He smiled. "What makes you think I have enemies?"

She smiled in answer as she smeared huckleberry jam on a piece of her toast.

He watched her eat for a few moments. He liked a woman who ate well and said as much.

"Does that line work on women?" she asked.

He laughed. "Every time."

They finished their breakfast in the quiet of the upper mountain. She was right about it being peaceful up here. He liked it. But once winter came, all that would change. The parking lots would be packed, all the lifts would be running as well as the gondola. The mountain would be dotted with skiers and boarders, the restaurants and resorts full. He recalled the sounds of people, the clank of machinery, the array of bright-colored skiwear like a rainbow across Lone Mountain.

Tanner had loved it when Big Sky took on its winter wonderland persona. He'd loved to ski, had started at the age of three like a lot of the kids who grew up in the shadow of Lone Mountain.

With a start, Jordan found himself looking high up on the peak, remembering one of the last days he and Tanner had skied the winter of their senior year. Tanner had always been gutsy, but that day he'd talked Alex and him into going into an out-of-bounds area.

They hadn't gone far when Tanner had gone off a cornice. The cornice had collapsed, causing a small avalanche that had almost killed him.

"Hey, man. You have a death wish?" Alex had asked Tanner when they'd skied down to find him half-buried in the snow.

Tanner had laughed it off. "Takes more than that to kill me."

"I THOUGHT YOU'D BE HAPPIER down here," Hud said as he opened the curtains in the sunroom. "You can leave the door open so you can see everything that is going on."

Dana shot him a look. Seeing everything that was going on was his not-so-subtle way of saying he wanted her to keep an eye on her sister.

They'd all gathered around her bed after breakfast. Stacy hadn't made any attempt to leave. Just the opposite, she seemed to be finding more things she wanted to do before she and Ella packed for the rest of their trip.

"Is there any chance you could stay another day or so?" Dana asked her now as Stacy picked up her breakfast tray to take to the kitchen.

Her sister stopped and looked up in surprise. Her face softened as if she was touched by Dana's offer. "I'd love to. I can cook and help with the kids. Hud has this murder investigation—"

"My deputy marshal is handling all of that," Hud interrupted, shooting Dana a what-could-you-be-thinking? look. "Plus the crime techs are down from Missoula. I am more than capable of taking care of Dana and the kids and—"

Dana had been holding Ella since finishing her breakfast. She quickly interrupted him. "Stacy, that would be great if you can. I know Hud won't mind the help and I love having you and Ella here."

Her husband sent her a withering look. She ignored it and looked instead into Ella's adorable face.

"Is Auntie Stacy going to stay, Mommy?" Mary asked excitedly.

"Yes, for a few more days. Would you like that?" Both children cheered.

"Auntie Stacy is going to show us how to make clay," Hank said. "You have to put it in the oven and then paint it."

Stacy shrugged when Dana looked at her. "I found a recipe on the internet. I thought they'd like that."

"That was very thoughtful," she said and shot her husband a see?-everything-is-fine look. "I know Hud will want to check in with the murder investigation, and there are animals to feed."

He tried to stare her down, but Dana had grown up with three siblings. Having to fight for what she wanted had made her a strong, determined woman.

"Fine," Hud said as he left the room. "Stacy, if you need me, Dana has my number. I have animals to feed."

"He'll check in with Liza," Dana said. "He can pretend otherwise, but he won't be able to stay away from this case."

"Are you sure it's all right if I stay?" Stacy asked. "Hud doesn't seem—"

"He's just being territorial," she said. "He can't stand the idea that anyone might think he can't take care of his family." Dana reached for her sister's hand and squeezed it. "I'm glad you and Ella are here."

LIZA FIGURED JORDAN CARDWELL had lied to her at least twice during breakfast.

"I need to know everything you can remember that led up to Tanner's death," she said when they'd finished their breakfast and the waitress had cleared away their plates and refilled their coffee cups.

The scent of pine blew down on the breeze from the mountain peaks. She breathed in the fall day and pulled out her notebook. They still had the café deck to themselves and the sun felt heavenly after so little sleep last night.

"We were seniors." Jordan shrugged. "Not much was going on."

"Who did Tanner date after his breakup with Shelby?"

"A couple of different girls."

"Who was he dating in the weeks or days before he died?" she asked.

"Brittany Cooke." The way he said it gave him away.

"You liked her?" she asked with interest.

His shrug didn't fool her.

"You used to date her?"

He laughed, meeting her gaze. "You got all that out of a shrug?"

"Who were *you* dating at the time?" she asked.

"I don't see what—"

"Humor me."

"I can't remember."

She laughed and leaned back in her chair to eye him. "You don't remember who you were dating the spring of your senior year? Give me a break."

"I wasn't dating anyone, really. It's a small community, cliques. There weren't a lot of options unless you dated someone from Bozeman. I was just anxious to graduate and get out of here."

"Shelby and Brittany were in one of these cliques?"

"Not Brittany. Brittany and Shelby got along, but she was never really one of them. But Shelby, yeah. She was the leader of the mean girls—you know the type. Too much money, too much everything."

Liza knew the type only too well. "So what happened when Brittany went out with Tanner?"

"I'm sure Shelby would deny it, but her and her group of friends closed Brittany out."

"What did Tanner think about that?"

"He thought it was funny. Believe me, that wasn't why he killed himself. Don't get me wrong, Tanner liked Shelby. He went with her a lot longer than any other girl. But once he found out she'd been trying to get pregnant to trap him, it was all over. He wasn't ready to settle down. He'd worked two jobs all through high school while getting good grades so he could do some of the things he'd always wanted to do. Both of us couldn't wait to travel."

"And get out of the canyon," Liza said.

"Tanner not as much as me. He would have come back to the family ranch. He was a cowboy."

"He wasn't from Big Sky resort money?"

"Naw, his folks have a ranch down the canyon. They do okay, just like everyone else who still ranches around here. As my sister is fond of saying, it's a lifestyle more than a paying career. Tanner *loved* that lifestyle, was happiest in a saddle and not afraid of hard work."

"He sounds like a nice, sensible young man."

"He was." Jordan looked away toward the mountains for a long moment. "He worked a lot of odd jobs throughout high school. That's how he ended up at that cabin on the mountain. He talked his folks into letting him stay there because it was closer to school. He traded watching the landowner's construction equipment for the small cabin where he lived that spring."

"He didn't want to live at home?"

Jordan grinned. "Not his senior year. His parents were strict, like all parents when you're that age. Tanner wanted to be on his own and his folks were okay with it."

"So who were the mean girls?"

"Shelby, the leader. Tessa, her closest ally. Whitney. Ashley. They were the inner circle."

"And Brittany?"

"She was always on the fringe. Last I heard Brittany had married Lee Peterson and they have a bunch of kids. I think I heard they live in Meadow Village. Shelby married Wyatt Iverson. She'd started dating him after she and Tanner broke up. Wyatt's father was a contractor who built a lot of the huge vacation homes. It was his maintenance cabin where Tanner stayed with his equipment." He stopped, a faraway look coming to his gaze. "Shelby has a yoga studio near the Gallatin River."

For a life he'd put behind him, Jordan certainly knew a lot about the players, Liza thought as she closed her notebook.

Chapter Five

Yogamotion was in a narrow complex built of log and stone, Western-style. Liza pushed open the door to find the inside brightly painted around walls of shiny mirrors.

According to the schedule she'd seen on the door, the next class wasn't for a couple of hours. A lithe young woman sat behind a large desk in a room off to the side. She was talking on a cell phone, but looked up as the door closed behind Liza.

"You should be getting the check any day. I'm sorry, but I have to go," she said into the phone and slowly snapped it shut, never taking her eyes off the deputy marshal.

"Shelby Iverson?"

As the woman got to her feet she took in Liza's attire, the boots, jeans and tan uniform shirt with the silver star on it. "I'm Shelby *Durran-Iverson*."

"Liza Turner, deputy marshal." Big Sky was small enough that Liza had seen Shelby around. The canyon resort was situated such that there were pockets of development, some pricier than others depending on where you lived.

Shelby lived in a large single-family home on the

north side of the mountain on the way to Mountain Village, while Liza lived in a condo in Meadow Village. She and Shelby didn't cross paths a lot.

"I'd like to ask you a few questions," the deputy said.

"Me?" The catch in her throat was merely for effect. Shelby Durran-Iverson had been expecting a visit from the marshal's office. Everyone within fifty miles would have heard about Alex Winslow's murder at the falls last night. Word would have spread through Big Sky like a fast-moving avalanche.

Liza had to wonder though, why Shelby thought *she* would be questioned. "It's about the shooting last night."

"I don't know anything about it," she said.

"But you knew Alex."

"Sure. Everyone from around here knew him."

"You went to high school with him?" Liza asked pulling her notebook and pen from her pocket.

"Do I need a lawyer?"

"You tell me. Did you shoot Alex?"

"No." Shelby sounded shocked that Liza would even suggest such a thing.

"Then I guess you don't need a lawyer. I just need to ask you a few questions so I can find the person who did shoot him."

"I still can't see how *I* can help." But she motioned Liza to a chair and took her own behind the desk again. Liza could tell that Shelby was hoping to learn more about the murder, getting more information out of her than she provided.

Settling into a chair across the desk from her, Liza studied Shelby. She was a shapely blonde who looked as if she just stepped out of a magazine ad. Her hair was pulled up in a sleek ponytail. Everything about her seemed planned for maximum effect from her makeup to her jewelry and the clothes on her back. She wore a flattering coral velvet designer sweatsuit that brought out the blue of her eyes and accentuated her well-toned body.

"I understand you used to date Tanner Cole," Liza said.

"*Tanner?* I thought you were here about Alex?"

"Did you date Alex, too?"

"No." She shook her head, the ponytail sweeping back and forth. "You're confusing me." She flashed a perfect-toothed smile, clearly a girl who'd had braces.

"I don't want to confuse you. So you dated Tanner how long?"

She frowned, still confused apparently. "Till just before Christmas of our senior year, I guess."

"But the two of you broke up?"

"I can't understand how that—"

Liza gave her one of her less-than-perfect-toothed smiles. She'd been born with a slight gap between her front teeth that her parents had found cute and she had never gotten around to changing. "Humor me. I actually know what I'm doing."

Shelby sighed, making it clear she had her doubts about that. "Fine. Yes, I dated Tanner, I don't remember when we broke up."

"Or why?"

The yoga instructor's eyes narrowed in challenge. "No."

"Here's the thing, I'm trying to understand why Tanner killed himself and why now one of his friends has been murdered."

"I'm sure there is no possible connection," Shelby

said with a mocking laugh as if now she knew Liza didn't know what she was doing.

"So Tanner didn't kill himself over you?"

"No!"

"So you weren't that serious?"

Shelby fumbled for words for a moment. "It was high school. It seemed serious at the time."

"To you. Or Tanner?"

"To both of us." She sounded defensive and realizing it, gave a small laugh. "Like I said, it was *high school.*"

Liza looked down at her notebook. "Let's see, by that spring, Tanner was dating Brittany Cooke? Wasn't she a friend of yours?"

Shelby's mouth tightened. "Tanner was sowing his oats before graduation. I can assure you he wasn't serious about Brittany."

"Oh? Did she tell you that?"

"She didn't have to. She wasn't Tanner's type." Shelby straightened several things on her desk that didn't need straightening. "If that's all, I really need to get back to work."

"I forgot what you said. *Did* you date Alex?"

"No, and I'd lost track of him since high school."

"That's right, he'd moved down to Bozeman and had only recently returned to Big Sky for the class reunion?"

"I assume that's why he came back."

"You didn't talk to him?" Liza asked.

Shelby thought for a moment. More than likely she was carefully considering her next answer. If Liza had Alex's cell phone in her possession, she would know who he called right before his death—and who'd called him.

"I might have talked to him since I'm the reunion

chairwoman. I talked to a lot of people. I really can't remember."

"That's strange since you talked to Alex five times in two days, the last three of those calls just hours before he was killed."

Shelby didn't look quite so put-together. "I told you, it was about the reunion. I talked to a lot of people."

"Are you telling me he didn't ask you about Tanner's alleged suicide?" Liza said.

"*Alleged* suicide?"

"Apparently, Alex had some questions about Tanner's death."

Shelby shook her head. "I might have heard that, but I wouldn't have taken anything Alex said seriously." She leaned forward and lowered her voice even though they were the only two people there. "I heard he had some sort of breakdown." She leaned back and lifted a brow as if to say that covered it.

"Hmmm. I hadn't heard that." Liza jotted down a note. "Whom did you hear this from?"

"I don't—"

"Recall. Maybe one of your friends?"

Shelby shook her head. "I really can't remember. I'm sure you can find out if there was any truth to it."

Liza smiled. "Yes, I can. What about Brittany?"

"What about her?" Shelby asked stiffly.

"Do you still see her?"

"Big Sky is a small community. You're bound to see everyone at some point," Shelby answered noncommittally. "She and her husband, Lee Peterson, own a ski shop up on the mountain. Now I really do need to get to work," she said, rising to her feet.

"Did you see Tanner the night he died?"

"No. As you are apparently aware, we had broken up. He was dating Brittany. If anyone knows why he killed himself, she would, don't you think?"

"Even though she and Tanner weren't that serious about each other?"

Shelby's jaw muscle bunched and her blue eyes fired with irritation. "If she doesn't know, then who would?"

"Good question. Maybe Alex Winslow. But then he isn't talking, is he?" Liza said as she closed her notebook and got to her feet. "One more question. Why would the last word Alex Winslow would say be your name?"

All the color washed from her face. She sat back down, leaning heavily on her desk. "I have no idea."

AFTER BREAKFAST, JORDAN went back to his cabin and crashed for a while. He figured Liza would be keeping an eye on him. Not that he knew what to do next. He couldn't just hang out in this cabin, that was for sure. But he'd been serious about not wanting to put anyone else in danger.

When he woke up, he realized he was hungry again. It was still early since the sun hadn't sunk behind Lone Mountain. According to his cell phone, it was a quarter past three in the afternoon.

He found a small sandwich shop in Meadow Village, ordered a turkey and cheese and took a seat by the window overlooking the golf course. Lone Mountain gleamed in the background, a sight that brought back too many memories. There'd been a time when he'd told himself he'd left here because he didn't want to be a rancher. But coming back here now, he realized a lot of his need to leave and stay gone had to do with Tanner's suicide.

When the waitress brought out his sandwich, he asked if he could get it to go. He followed her to the counter and was waiting when he heard a bell tinkle over the door and turned to see someone he recognized coming through.

With a silent curse, he put a name to the face. Tessa Ryerson. She had already spotted him and something about her expression gave him the crazy idea that she didn't just happen in here. She'd come looking for him.

Before he could react, the waitress brought out his sandwich in a brown paper bag and handed it to him. He dug out the cost of the sandwich and a generous tip and handed it to the server, before turning to Tessa.

She had stopped just a couple of feet from him, waiting while he paid. When he turned to her, he saw that she looked much like she had twenty years ago when the two of them had dated. She wore her light brown hair as she had in high school, shoulder length and wavy, no bangs. A hair band held it back from her face.

She seemed thinner, a little more gaunt in the face, than she had the last time he'd seen her. He recalled that she'd always struggled to keep her weight down. Apparently, she'd mastered the problem.

He couldn't help noticing that her ring finger was bare. Hadn't he heard that she'd gone through a bad divorce from Danny Spring? Two years ahead of them in school, the guy had been a jerk. Jordan recalled being surprised when he'd heard that she'd married him.

"Jordan," Tessa said a little too brightly. "Imagine running into you here."

"Imagine that," he said, now sure the only reason

she'd come in here, crazy or not, was to see him. So did that mean she'd followed him? Or had she just been looking for him?

"Oh, are you getting your sandwich to go?" she asked, sounding disappointed as she glanced at the bag in his hand as if just now noticing it. "I missed lunch and I hate eating alone. Would you mind staying?"

How could he say no even if he'd wanted to? Anyway, he was curious about what she wanted. "Sure, go ahead and order. I'll get us a table."

"Great."

He took a seat away from the girl working behind the counter, positioning himself so he could watch Tessa while she ordered. She dug nervously in her purse, paid for a small salad and a bottled water, then joined him at the table.

"So you came for the reunion," she said, smiling as she unscrewed the lid on her water bottle.

He smiled at that and dug his sandwich out of the bag and took a bite.

"Wow, it's been so long."

"Twenty years," he said between bites.

"I guess you heard about Danny and me." She sighed. "But I've put it behind me."

Too bad the look in her eyes said otherwise. He suspected the slightest thing could set her off if asked about her marriage. Unfortunately, he could remember how he was right after Jill had left him. He didn't want to go there again.

"So wasn't that awful about Alex?" she said. "Were you really there?"

He gave her points for getting right to what she really

wanted to talk to him about. He nodded and took another bite of his sandwich. She hadn't touched her salad.

"When I heard, I just couldn't believe it. How horrible. Do they know who shot him?" she asked when he didn't answer. "I heard it could have been a stray bullet from a hunter."

"Really?" he said. "I heard it was murder. Someone wanted to shut Alex up."

"Who told you that?" she cried.

He said nothing for a moment, letting her squirm. "The state crime lab trucks have been up at the falls since last night looking for evidence to track them to the killer. I thought you would have heard."

Tessa fiddled with her water bottle, looking worried. "Why would anyone want to kill Alex?"

He shrugged. "Probably because he'd been asking a lot of questions about Tanner's suicide. But you'd know better about that than I would."

"Me?"

"I'm sure Alex talked to you." He wasn't sure of anything except that he was rattling her. "If you know something, I'd suggest you talk to Deputy Marshal Liza Turner. Alex was murdered and there is an investigation into Tanner's death, as well. It's all going to come out."

"I don't know *anything*." She squeezed her plastic water bottle so hard it crackled loudly and water shot up and out over the table. She jumped up and grabbed for a stack of napkins.

He watched her nervously wipe up the spilled water, almost feeling guilty for upsetting her. "Then I guess you have nothing to worry about. But I wonder if Alex said the same thing."

"This is all so upsetting." She sounded close to tears.

He reached across the table and put a hand on hers. "Tessa—"

"Please, don't," she said, snatching back her hand. "I told you. I don't know anything."

He put down his sandwich to study her. Why had she come looking for him? Why was she so scared? "You and Shelby have always been thick as thieves. What don't I know about Alex's death? Or Tanner's, for that matter."

She shook her head. "How would I know? Shelby wasn't even dating Tanner then."

"No, but she'd conned you into breaking up with Alex to go out with me. I thought you were just playing hard to get when you wanted to always double date with Brittany and Tanner. I should have known Shelby put you up to spying on him."

"I don't know what you're talking about," she said. "But I do remember you didn't mind double dating. It was Brittany you wanted to be with. Not me." She got to her feet, hitting the table and spilling some of her salad.

"Brittany," he said under his breath. "Thanks for reminding me of that prank you and your friend Shelby pulled on her." It was straight out of a Stephen King novel.

Tessa crossed her toned arms over her flat chest, her expression defiant. He'd expected her to stomp off, but she didn't. Whatever the reason that she'd wanted to see him, she hadn't got what she'd come for apparently.

That spring of their senior year was coming back to him after years of fighting to forget it. Hadn't he had a bad feeling he couldn't shake even before Alex had called him? "Did Shelby send you to find me?" He let out a laugh. "Just like in high school. What is it she wants to know, Tessa?"

"I have no idea what you mean."

He laughed. "Still doing her dirty work even after all these years."

Tessa snatched up her water bottle from the table with one hand, the untouched salad with the other. "I know what you think of me."

"I think you're too smart to keep letting Shelby run your life."

She laughed at that. "Run my life? Don't you mean *ruin* my life? She practically forced me to marry Danny Spring. It wasn't until later that I found out her husband was trying to buy some land Danny owned and thought my marriage would get it for Wyatt." She smiled. "It did."

"Then what are you doing still being friends with her?" he demanded.

"*Seriously?* Because it's much worse to be Shelby's enemy, haven't you realized that yet? My life isn't the only one she's destroyed. Clearly, you have forgotten what she's like."

"No, I don't think so. I know what she did to Tanner."

"Do you?" she challenged.

"She got pregnant to trap him into marrying her. If she hadn't miscarried, he probably would have married her for the kid's sake." Something in Tessa's expression stopped him. "She did have a miscarriage, didn't she? Or did she lie about that, as well?"

Tessa looked away for a moment.

Jordan felt his heart drop. *My life isn't the only one she's destroyed.* The thought came at him with such force, he knew it had been in the back of his mind for a long time.

"She didn't do something to that baby to get back at Tanner, did she?" he asked, voicing his fear.

"I have to go," Tessa said, glancing toward the parking lot.

He followed her gaze, seeing her fear as a white SUV cruised slowly past. He recognized Shelby Durran-Iverson behind the wheel. She sped up when she saw Tessa hurry out of the sandwich shop, barely missing her as she drove away.

Jordan stared after both of them for a moment before he wrapped up his sandwich. He'd lost his appetite. Worse, he wasn't sure what his best friend would have done if he'd found out Shelby hadn't miscarried early in the pregnancy, but waited as long as she could, then aborted his baby to hurt him.

He realized it was possible Tanner really had killed himself.

Chapter Six

The ski shop Brittany Cooke Peterson and her husband Lee owned on the mountain was still closed for the season.

But Liza found her at the couple's condo in Meadow Village. Brittany answered the door wearing a black-and-white polka-dot apron over a T-shirt and jeans. Her feet were bare and her dark hair in disarray. She brushed a long curly lock back from her face, leaving a dusting of flour on her cheekbone. In the background a 1960s hit played loudly. As Brittany's brown eyes widened to see the deputy sheriff at her door, Liza caught the warm, wonderful scent of freshly-baked cookies.

"Don't touch that pan, it's hot," Brittany said over her shoulder after opening the door.

"Did I catch you in the middle of something?" Liza asked facetiously.

Brittany laughed. "Not at all."

"Mommy, Jake stuck his finger in the icing," called a young female voice from the back of the large two-story condo.

Brittany wiped her hands on her apron. "Come on in. We're baking iced pumpkin cookies."

Liza followed the young woman through a toy-cluttered living room and into a kitchen smelling of cinnamon and pumpkin.

Three small children balanced on chairs around a kitchen island covered in flour and dirty baking bowls and utensils. One of the children, the only boy, had icing smudged on the side of his cheek. Brittany licked her thumb pad and wiped the icing from the boy's face, took an icing-dripping spoon from one girl and snatched a half-eaten cookie from the other girl as if it was all in a day's work.

The two girls who Liza realized were identical twins appeared to be about five and were wearing aprons that matched their mother's. The boy had a dish towel wrapped around his neck like a bandana. He was a year or so younger than the girls.

"You'd better have a cookie," Brittany said as she finished slipping warm ones from a cookie sheet onto a cooling rack.

Liza took one of the tall stools at the counter, but declined a cookie.

"Just a little icing on them, Courtney," her mother said to the girl who had the spoon again and was dribbling thin white icing over each cookie as if making a masterpiece. The other girl watched, practically drooling as her sister slowly iced the warm cookies. "Okay, enough sugar for one day. Go get cleaned up." They jumped down and raced toward the stairs. "And don't argue!" she called after them.

With a sigh, Brittany glanced around the messy kitchen, then plopped down on a stool at the counter and took one of the cookies before turning her attention on Liza. "Sure you don't want one?" she asked between bites. "They aren't bad."

"They smell delicious, but I'm fine."

"You didn't come by for cookies," Brittany said. "This is about Alex, isn't it?" She shook her head, her expression one of sadness. "I heard it was a hunter."

"A hunter?"

"You know, someone poaching at night, a stray bullet. It had to be. No one would want to hurt Alex. He was a sweetheart. Everyone liked him."

"Not everyone," Liza said.

Brittany turned solemn. "So it *was* murder. That's the other rumor circulating this morning." She shook her head.

"Any idea who didn't think he was a sweetheart?"

"No one I can think of."

"What about Tanner Cole?"

Brittany blinked. "Even if he came back from the dead, he wouldn't have hurt Alex. They were friends."

Liza smiled. She liked the woman's sense of humor. "Do you know why Tanner killed himself?"

"No. I suppose someone told you that Tanner and I were dating at the time." Brittany chuckled as she realized whom. "Shelby. Of course."

"She did mention that if anyone knew, it would be you. Did Tanner seem depressed?"

"Far from it. He was excited about graduating. He had all these plans for what he was going to do. I think he already had his bags packed."

"He was planning to leave Big Sky?"

"Oh, yeah. He'd been saving his money for years. He wanted to backpack around Europe before college. He had a scholarship to some big college back east."

"What about you?"

"I was headed for Montana State University."

"Weren't you upset that he was leaving?"

She shook her head as she helped herself to another cookie. Upstairs, Liza could hear the kids squabbling over the water and towels. "It wasn't like that between me and Tanner. I liked him. A lot. But I knew from the get-go that it wasn't serious."

"Had it been serious between him and Shelby?"

Brittany stopped chewing for a moment. She sighed and let out a chuckle. "If you talk to Shelby it was. She was planning to marry him, apparently. She loved his parents' ranch and used to talk about when she and Tanner lived on the place, what their lives were going to be like."

"She must have been upset when he broke it off and started dating you."

Brittany laughed. "Livid. But Tanner told me he'd just gone through a scare with her. She'd apparently gotten pregnant."

"On purpose?"

"Tanner thought so. He said he'd dodged a bullet when she miscarried…" Brittany seemed to realize what she'd said. "So to speak. Anyway, he didn't trust her after that, said he didn't want anything to do with her. They broke up right before Christmas. She'd been so sure he would be putting an engagement ring under the tree for her."

"How could Shelby have thought that was going to happen?" Liza asked. "Surely she knew what Tanner was planning to do once they graduated."

"Sure, she knew, but Shelby was so used to getting what she wanted, I think she'd just convinced herself it was going to happen."

"Maybe she thought a baby would be the tipping point," Liza suggested.

"And it probably would have been. Tanner loved kids. He wanted a bunch when he settled down. If she had been pregnant, I still don't think he would have married her, but he would have stuck around to help raise his child. He was that kind of guy. But he was over Shelby. Nothing could have made him go back to her."

"Did she know that?" Liza asked.

Brittany broke a cookie in half and played in the icing for a moment. "I think she did. She really was heartbroken. She cried hysterically at the funeral. I'd never seen her like that. I actually felt sorry for her."

"But you didn't feel sorry enough not to go out with Tanner."

Brittany shrugged. "It was high school. Tanner asked me out. He was a nice guy and a lot of fun. Shelby knew it wasn't serious. She didn't blame me."

"But she did Tanner?"

Brittany smiled. "Let me put it this way. If Shelby was the kind to make voodoo dolls and stick pins in them, she would have had one with Tanner's name on it. But she moved on quick enough. Tanner was barely in the ground before she was dating Wyatt Iverson. One thing about Shelby, she seems to bounce back pretty fast."

"Wyatt Iverson of Iverson Construction?" Liza said. "Isn't that the same construction company that Tanner was working for at the time of his death?"

Brittany nodded and got up to go to the bottom of the stairs to yell up at the kids to quit fighting. When she came back she began to clean up the kitchen. "Wyatt was four years ahead of us in school, so I didn't really know him. But later that summer his father went bankrupt, shot Harris Lancaster and went to prison. Malcolm was never the same after that, I guess. He died in a boating accident. At least that's what they called it. He drowned up on Canyon Ferry. Everyone suspected he killed himself. I've gotten to know Wyatt a little since then. He never got over what happened with his father. That's one reason he's worked so hard to get the construction company going again." She looked up. "Sorry, that's probably a whole lot more than you wanted to hear."

"You like Wyatt."

Brittany smiled at that. "*Like* might be a little strong. He and Shelby are cut from the same cloth. Both go after what they want and the rest be damned." She frowned. "Why all the questions about Tanner?"

"Tanner was Alex's friend."

"And now they're both dead," Brittany said with a nod.

"With all Tanner's plans, he doesn't sound like someone who would commit suicide before graduation. Was anything else going on in his life that you knew of? Maybe with his parents, his friends?"

Brittany shook her head. "His parents are still happily married and still live on the ranch. His friends were fine—well, that is, they were until last night." She sighed. "There was the vandalism, though."

"Vandalism?" Liza asked.

"Tanner was staying in the cabin at the construction site in payment for watching over Malcolm Iverson's equipment. There was a party at the cabin one night. The next morning, Malcolm discovered his equipment had been vandalized. Tanner blamed himself."

"Enough to kill himself?"

"I didn't think so at the time. Wyatt didn't even blame Tanner. The party hadn't been his idea in the first place. Tanner was really responsible, but everyone showed up with beer and things must have gotten out of hand. But who knows. Maybe Tanner was taking it harder than any of us knew. Wyatt talked his father into letting Tanner stay at the cabin even after the vandalism. So I really don't think that had anything to do with Tanner's death."

"Well, thank you for the information," Liza said.

"It's kind of strange though. I heard Jordan Cardwell was back in the canyon—and that he was at the falls when Alex was shot?"

"Why is that strange if they were friends?"

"Because he and Alex had a huge falling-out the night of the party."

Liza felt her pulse quicken. "Over what?"

"I never knew. I just remember Tanner refused to take sides. He said they'd work it out."

"Did they?"

"Not that I know of. Jordan left right after graduation and seldom came back. I'm not sure he and Alex ever spoke again."

"Could it have been over a girl?"

Brittany laughed. "Isn't it always?"

"So who would that girl have been?"

"If I had to guess, I'd say Tessa Ryerson. Shelby's BFF."

Liza laughed. "Best friend forever? Is that still true?"

Brittany nodded and crossed her fingers. "Shelby and Tessa, they're like this and always have been. I was surprised when Jordan went out with Tessa since he never could stand Shelby."

DANA HAD DOZED off for a while, she realized. She woke to find Hud lying on the bed next to her. Listening, she could hear the sound of their children's voices coming from the kitchen along with that of her sister's. She placed a hand on her stomach, felt her two babies and tried to relax. Nothing seemed to be amiss and yet, when she'd awakened...

"What's wrong?" she asked, turning her head to look at her husband.

Hud was staring at the ceiling. "You're going to think I'm crazy."

"I've never thought you were anything but completely sane in all instances," she joked.

"I'm serious," he said, rolling over on his side to look at her.

She saw the worry etched in his handsome face. "What?"

"You aren't going to want to hear this."

"Hud!"

"Something's wrong," he said. "I feel it."

She sighed. "Your marshal intuition again?" She felt her eyes widen, her heartbeat kicking up a notch. "About the murder investigation?"

"It's your sister."

She groaned and, shaking her head, turned to look at the ceiling. "What are you saying?"

"Have you noticed the way she is with the baby?" he demanded, keeping his voice down even though the bedroom door was closed.

Dana hadn't noticed. Usually when her sister brought the baby in, she would hand Ella to her to hold.

"It's as if she has never changed a diaper," Hud was saying.

"She's probably nervous because you're watching her. She's new at this."

He shook his head. "She stares at Ella, I swear, as if she's never seen her before. Not just that," he rushed on. "She arrived with hardly any clothes for the baby and when she came back from buying baby food, I asked her what Ella's favorite was and she said carrots. You should have seen her trying to feed Ella carrots—"

"Stop. Do you realize how ridiculous you sound?" She'd turned to look at him again. "I repeat, what are you *saying?*"

Hud clamped his mouth shut for a moment, his eyes dark. "Okay, I'll just say it. I don't think that baby is hers. In fact, I don't even think the baby's name is Ella. That baby quilt has the name Katie stitched on it."

"Okay, you are *crazy,*" Dana said. "The quilt is probably one she picked up at a secondhand store or a friend lent it to her."

"A friend? Has she received even one phone call since she's been here?" He shook his head. "No, that's because your sister doesn't have friends. She never has."

"You don't know that she hasn't made friends the past six years."

"How could she? She moves around all the time. At least that's her story. And what does she do for money, huh?"

"She didn't go to college or learn a trade so of course she has a hard time supporting herself." Dana knew she was grasping at any explanation, but she couldn't stop herself. "One look at Stacy and you can see she doesn't have much. It's probably the best she can do right now. And you know babies can change their food likes and dislikes in an afternoon. As for diapering…"

Hud shook his head stubbornly.

"Is she helping with the kids?"

"Sure, she seems right at home with a four- and five-year-old." He sighed. "I still have a hard time trusting Stacy."

"I know. She stole five years from us, breaking us up with one of her lies so I understand why you would question everything about her now." Dana didn't want to admit that she had felt the same way around her sister. But when she saw her sister with Ella—

"Okay," Hud said. "After dinner I might check in with Liza and see how the investigation is going." He placed a large hand on her belly and waited for their twins to move as if needing reassurance.

She could see that it was hell for him having a murder investigation going on while he was home playing Candy Land and Old Maid. But she saw something else in his expression, as well. "You're going to your office to do more than check in, aren't you? You're going to investigate my sister."

"I just want to do some checking on her. Just to relieve my mind."

She knew there would be no stopping him no matter what she said. "I want to get to know my niece. After everything that has happened between us and Stacy, it wouldn't take much for us to never see her or Ella again."

"If Ella isn't her baby—"

"You're wrong. So go ahead and see what you can find out."

He bent down to kiss her before getting to his feet. "You're probably right about everything."

Dana nodded as he left the room. But she hated that she didn't feel sure about anything right now. To make matters worse she was trapped in bed, her children were out making clay with a woman who her husband thought might be a kidnapper and meanwhile, her brother Jordan was involved in a murder case.

All she needed right now was for her younger brother, Clay, to show up.

Her babies moved. She splayed her fingers over them, whispered that she loved them and did her best not to cry.

Chapter Seven

Jordan hadn't been back to the cabin long when he heard a knock at his door. He put his unfinished sandwich in the small kitchenette refrigerator, then peeked out the window. He was in no mood for company.

"You've been holding out on me," Liza said when he finally opened the door.

He'd let her knock for a while, then had given up that she wasn't going to take the hint and leave him alone. He was in no mood after his run-in with Tessa and no longer sure about Tanner's death any more than he was Alex's.

"I beg your pardon?" he said.

"Tessa Ryerson Spring. You dated her at the same time Tanner was dating Brittany."

He sighed and stepped back to let Liza in, not wanting to discuss this on the cabin stoop. "I'd forgotten I dated her."

"Uh-huh." The deputy marshal came into the small cabin and looked around. "Why did you and Alex fight over her?"

Jordan shook his head and laughed. "I don't recall."

She smiled. "Try again. It sounds as if it was quite the fight. Didn't speak to each other for years. Does that refresh your memory?" She sat down on the end of his bed and crossed her legs, leaning back on her hands, her gaze on him.

"Make yourself comfortable," he said sarcastically.

"I thought this might take a while."

He sighed and pulled out a chair from the small table that constituted the dining room. He straddled it and leaned his arms on the back as he looked at her. The woman was like a badger burrowing into a hole.

"Fine. It isn't something I like to talk about but since you're determined… Shelby talked Tessa into breaking up with Alex and going out with me so we could double date with Tanner and Brittany."

"Tessa was a spy?"

He nodded.

"But it doesn't explain why you dated Tessa. Or does it?" She grinned. "Brittany. You wanted to be close to her. Wow, what a tangled web we weave."

"Happy? When I found out what Shelby had done, I told Tessa off." He shrugged.

"Which explains why you and Alex got into a fight over her how exactly?"

"I might have called her some names. Alex took offense. When I told him how far Tessa would go to do Shelby's dirty work, he took a swing at me. I swung back. We were in high school. Stuff like that happened."

"Alex had forgotten all about it when he called to talk to you about Tanner?"

Jordan shrugged. "I assume so."

Liza got to her feet and walked around the cabin for a moment. "You all talk about high school as if it was kid stuff." She let out a chuckle. "You forget. *I* went to high school."

"That doesn't surprise me," Jordan quipped.

"Then this probably won't, either. I let mean things happen to other students. No, worse than that, sometimes I was part of those things. I ran into one of the girls who was terrorized recently. She told me that she still has scars from the way she was treated."

He said nothing, afraid she'd been that girl. Liza would have been just different enough that he suspected she hadn't been in a group like Shelby's. He'd sensed a rebellious spirit just under her surface, a fire that the girls who followed Shelby didn't have.

She suddenly turned to face him, her expression angry and defiant. "Don't tell me that what happened in high school didn't matter. It mattered to Tanner and now I believe it has something to do with Alex Winslow's death, as well. What I'm trying to understand is what *happened*."

"You and me both," he said, feeling guilty because he'd been one of the popular kids. In his teens he hadn't given much thought to those who weren't. "If it helps, I saw Tessa today." He held up a hand before she could berate him for getting involved in her investigation. "*She* sought me out. I went to get a sandwich and she came in. She either followed me or had been looking for me."

"What did she want?"

"I don't know. Maybe just information about Alex's death. I thought at first Shelby had sent her. But then Shelby drove past and Tessa got all scared and left."

"What did you tell her?"

"She asked why anyone would want Alex dead. I said it could have something to do with him asking around about Tanner's death."

The deputy sheriff let out an unladylike curse.

"I wanted to see her reaction."

"And?"

"It spooked the hell out of her. She knows something. When I was talking to her I had a thought. If Tanner *did* kill himself, it would have had to be over something big. What if Shelby didn't have a miscarriage? What if she lied about that, maybe as a test to see if Tanner loved her, who knows?"

"What are you suggesting, that she was never pregnant?"

"No, that she aborted the baby," he said. "That she did it out of meanness to get back at him. To hurt him in a way that would haunt him to his grave."

Liza said nothing for a few moments. "You think that little of Shelby?"

He met her gaze and held it. "Tessa is her best friend. She knows the truth. I also think she's scared of that truth coming out."

"Wait, even if you're right and Shelby did do something to get back at Tanner, that wouldn't be something that she'd kill Alex to keep secret."

"Couldn't it? Shelby is all about getting what she wants, whatever it takes, and Tessa and her other minions have always followed her blindly."

"You don't think they'd draw the line when it came to out-and-out murder?" Liza demanded.

"Not if they had something to do with Tanner's death. What's another body if Alex was getting too close to the truth?"

Liza nodded. "So your graduating class from Big Sky was small, right?"

Jordan reached behind him to pick up the crumpled

piece of paper he'd left on the table. "This is the list of people who RSVP'd that they would be attending the reunion this weekend," he said, handing it to her. "I marked the other two girls who ran with Shelby in high school. Ashley and Whitney."

Liza considered the wrinkled-up paper in her hand, then looked at him quizzically.

"I had to dig it out of the trash before I flew out here. I wasn't planning to attend—until Alex called. Then I was curious about who was coming."

"Let me guess," Liza said. "You're planning on going to the reunion now?"

He smiled. "Not without a date. What do you say? Come on, this way you can get to see all the players in their natural habitat."

Liza actually seemed at a loss for words for a moment. "I feel like you're asking me to the prom."

"If you're expecting a corsage, a rented limo, champagne and a fancy hotel room afterwards…" He saw her expression and stopped. "You didn't go to prom?"

"I'm not wearing a prom dress," she said, ignoring his question.

"Just don't wear your silver star or your gun," he joked, hating that he'd been right. She was one of the girls who'd been tormented by girls like Shelby and Tessa.

LIZA STOOD IN front of her closet. She hated to admit how few dresses she owned—and what she did have were old and out of style, though hardly worn. Worse, she hated that she cared what she wore to the reunion.

She'd been a tomboy, so dresses had never really appealed to her. Add to that her profession, she'd had little need of anything besides jeans and boots.

"I don't know what I'm going to wear," she said when Dana answered the phone. "I know it doesn't matter. It's not like it's a date."

"No, going out with a suspect probably couldn't be called a date," her boss's wife agreed with a chuckle. "Come over. You're welcome to dig through my closet. I'll call Hilde. She's more girlie than either of us. She'll help."

"Thanks," Liza said, relieved. She definitely needed help.

"How is the investigation going?" Dana asked.

Liza knew Dana must be bored to tears now that she was being forced to stay in bed. "Slowly." She didn't want to admit that it brought up a lot of high school memories, ones she thought she'd left behind when she'd graduated.

"And Jordan?" Dana asked.

She didn't know how to answer that. "He's fine. Actually, I get the feeling he's changed. Don't worry," she said quickly. "If he hasn't, I'll be the first to know. He's still a suspect."

"But you don't think he killed Alex Winslow."

"No. I think he really did come back to find out what happened to his friend Tanner. It's looking like he had reason to be concerned."

Dana was silent for a moment. "Tell him to stop by, if he wants to."

"I will. I'll drop by later this afternoon for the clothing search." In the meantime, she thought, closing her closet door, she wanted to pay Tessa Ryerson Spring a visit.

DANA COULDN'T HELP thinking of Jordan and half wishing she hadn't told Liza to have him stop by. Feeling the babies kick, she willed herself not to worry about Stacy or her brother. Instead, she put in a quick call to Hilde, who, of course, was delighted to help with Liza's clothing dilemma.

"I'll gather up some dresses and bring them over later," her best friend said. "Can I bring you anything?"

"Maybe some needlepoint from the store?" Dana suggested, cringing since the mere thought had always given her hives.

"Oh, girl, you really are bored to tears!" She laughed as she hung up.

After she'd found her mother's will and got to go back to ranching, Dana had become a silent partner in Needles and Pins, the small sewing shop she and Hilde had started in Meadow Village. She'd never been the one who sewed. That had been Hilde. But Dana had always loved working with her best friend in the shop.

She missed it sometimes. Not that she and the kids didn't often stop in to visit. Mary and Hank loved all the colorful bolts of fabric and Hilde always had some fun craft for them to do.

"Look what we made, Mommy!" Mary and Hank cried in unison now as they came running into the bedroom. They held up the clay figures, and Dana praised them for their imagination and their choice of multiple bright colors.

Behind them, Stacy stood in the doorway looking on with what appeared to be contentment. Dana had been watching her sister all day. She hated letting Hud's suspicions cloud her forgiving thoughts about Stacy. She'd missed having a sister all these years. Not that she and Stacy had been close like some sisters. There were no tea parties, doll playing or dressing up for pretend weddings.

Stacy had done all those things, but Dana had been an outside kid. She loved riding her horse, climbing trees, building forts. Two years older, Stacy had turned up her nose at most things Dana thought were fun and vice versa.

"Okay, let's clean up our mess," her sister told the kids. "I think that's your daddy who just drove up."

As they scampered out of the room, leaving a couple clay figures beside her bed to keep her company, Dana waited expectantly for Hud. She knew where he'd gone and what he'd been up to—running a check on her sister. A part of her feared what he might have discovered.

She listened. The moment he came in the house, Mary and Hank were all over him. He played with them for a moment, and, like her, praised everything they'd made before coming into the bedroom. When he closed the door, she knew the news wasn't going to be good.

LIZA COULDN'T SHAKE the feeling that Jordan was right about the two deaths being connected. While anxious to talk to Tessa Ryerson Spring, she went to the office and pulled out the Tanner Cole investigation file. There wasn't much in it since the coroner had ruled the death a suicide.

The incident had happened back up the North Fork where the victim had been staying in a cabin. His body had been found hanging from a tree limb in sight of the cabin, a rope noose around the victim's neck. There was evidence of a log stump having been dragged over under the limb of the tree. When the body was found, the stump was on its side, a good foot from the dead man's dangling boots. Cause of death was strangulation.

The victim was found by Jordan Cardwell, who'd gone looking for Tanner when he hadn't shown up for school.

Attached were a half dozen black-and-white photographs taken at the scene. She flipped through them, noticing that the tree where Tanner was found hanging was next to a fire ring. She could see that there were dozens of footprints around the scene, no doubt because the area had been used for a party. Other stumps had been dragged up around the campfire area. Numerous discarded beer cans could be seen charred black in the firepit.

As she started to put the file back, something caught her eye. The investigating officer had been Brick Savage—Hud's father.

HUD SMILED SHEEPISHLY at his wife after closing the door. She was watching him expectantly. He wished she didn't know him so well sometimes. Walking over to the bed, he bent down and, touching her cheek, kissed her. "You get more beautiful every day."

She swatted his hand playfully as he drew back. "If you think you can charm me—"

He laughed as she moved over to let him sit on the edge of the bed next to her. "Just speaking the truth." She *was* beautiful. The pregnancy had put a glow in her cheeks and her eyes. Not that she wasn't a stunner anytime. Dana had always smelled of summer, an indefinable scent that filled his heart like helium. He counted his blessings every day he woke up next to her.

"Okay, charmer, let's hear it," she said. "With you being so sweet, I'm guessing it's bad news."

He shook his head. "Am I that transparent?"

"Hud," she said impatiently.

"I didn't find out much. There wasn't much to find out. Apparently, she doesn't have credit cards or even a checking account."

"She's in the process of moving and not having credit cards is a good thing."

He sighed, seeing that she was determined to think the best. But then, that was Dana. But with her family, their history proved out that he definitely had reason to be suspicious. He knew she wanted to believe that Stacy had changed. He did, too. He was just a whole lot more skeptical than Dana.

"A tiger doesn't change its spots," he said.

"Isn't it 'a zebra doesn't change its stripes' and what does that even mean?" she demanded.

"I had a look in her car last night after everyone went to bed. If she's moving to Great Falls, she sure didn't pack much." He held up his hand. "I know. She apparently doesn't have any money. But she gets the check from the ranch profits."

"You know that isn't enough to live on."

"Well, you'd think she would have had a job for the past six years."

"Stacy didn't go to college so more than likely she can't make much more than minimum wage."

He shook his head. "I could find no employment in her past."

"So she worked off the books somewhere. Or maybe the baby's father has been taking care of her and now she can't work because she has a baby to raise."

Yeah, Hud thought. That's what had Dana so desperate to believe Stacy had changed. That baby. Ella was cute as a bug's ear. No doubt about that. Just the thought of Stacy raising the child, though, terrified him.

"So that's all you found," Dana said.

He nodded. "No warrants or outstanding violations." No missing kids on Amber Alert who matched either the name Katie—or Ella's description.

"So there is nothing to worry about."

"Right." He just wished he could shake his uneasy feeling.

"And don't you go interrogating her," Dana said. "Give her the benefit of the doubt. She is in absolute awe of that baby. She couldn't be prouder of Ella. It's the first time I've seen my sister like this."

He nodded, not wanting to argue with her. He needed to keep Dana in this bed for their twins' sake. Placing a hand on her stomach, he felt their babies move. It had a calming affect on him. Just as being here with his family did.

But in the other room he could hear Stacy with the kids. Something wasn't right with her story. Call it his marshal intuition. But Stacy wasn't telling them the truth. And as much as he hated to think it, whatever she was lying about, it had something to do with that precious baby.

Tessa Ryerson Spring didn't answer her phone so Liza drove over to the house. Getting out of the patrol SUV, she walked past the garage, noting that at least one vehicle was inside, before she rang the doorbell.

She had to ring it four times and knock hard before Tessa appeared. She'd wrapped a towel around her head and pulled a robe on, no doubt hoping Liza would think she'd been in the shower.

"I'm sorry," she said, looking more than a little flustered. "Have you been standing here long?"

Long enough. "Mind if I come in for a moment? Or you can come down to the office? Which works better for you?"

"Actually, I was just…" Tessa gave up and said, "I suppose I have a few minutes." She stepped aside to let Liza in. "I should make some coffee."

"No, thanks. Why don't we sit down for a minute." She could tell that Tessa wanted something to occupy herself. Jordan was right about one thing. Tessa was nervous and clearly afraid.

"This won't take long," Liza assured her.

The woman finally perched on the edge of the couch. Liza took a chair across from her. Like many of the residences at Big Sky, the decor was made to look like the Old West from the leather furniture to the antler lamps. The floor was hardwood, the rugs Native American, the fireplace local granite.

Tessa straightened the hem of her robe to cover whatever she was wearing beneath it, then fiddled with the sash.

"I'm here about Alex Winslow's death."

"Oh?" Her smile was tentative. "Why would you want to talk to *me?*"

"You were a friend of his in high school."

"Yes, but that was twenty years ago."

"But you talked to him recently. The calls were on his cell phone," Liza said.

Tessa's eyes widened with alarm. Her hand went to her forehead as if suddenly struck with a migraine.

Clearly she hadn't expected anyone to know about the calls.

"I'm curious what you talked about," Liza said.

After a moment the woman pulled herself together. "I'm sorry. I'm just upset. I heard he was murdered?"

"So what did you talk about?"

"The reunion. Shelby must have told him to call me. I'm in charge of the picnic on Sunday. It's going to be at the top of the gondola. Weather permitting, of course." Her smile was weak, nervous. She worked at the robe sash with her fingers, toying with the edges.

"You and Alex dated in high school."

She nodded. "For a short while."

"But you were close?"

"I'm not sure what you mean."

"I mean Alex trusted you. He would have confided in you."

"I don't know what you're asking."

"He would have told you if he had some reason to suspect that Tanner Cole didn't kill himself." The statement had the effect Liza had hoped for.

Fear shone in the woman's eyes. Her hand went to her throat. Jordan was right. She knew *something*.

"Had you ever been up to the cabin where Tanner was staying that spring before high school graduation?" Liza asked.

"I might have."

"With Alex?"

"Maybe. I really can't remember."

"Do you knit?" Liza asked.

"What?"

"I wondered if you knitted because this case started like a loose thread in a sweater. At first it was just a small problem, but once it started unraveling…" She shook her head. "Alex started it unraveling. Now it's going to come apart. No doubt about it."

Tessa managed a smile. "That's an odd simile."

"Metaphor," Liza said. "It's a metaphor for murder. Alex was just the beginning. As this unravels, more people are going to die. Because even though you believe you can keep this secret, whoever killed Alex is afraid you can't. You see how this works? You just can't trust each other anymore and when push comes to shove…"

"I'm sorry, deputy," Tessa said, getting to her feet. "I have no idea what you're talking about and I'm running late for an appointment. She held her head in a regal manner. Liza got a glimpse of the girl Tessa had been when she and Shelby and the others had been on the pinnacle of popularity and thought nothing could bring them down. But as they all seemed fond of saying, "that was high school." This was real life.

"Think about it, Tessa. If they think you're the weak link, they'll attack you like rabid dogs." Liza rose. "I'll see myself out."

Chapter Eight

Jordan hadn't seen his father since the last time he was in Montana. They talked once in a while by phone, but they really didn't have much to say to each other.

For a long time Jordan blamed his mother for the divorce, believing she cared more about the ranch than she did her husband. There was probably some truth in that. But the divorce wasn't all her fault. She hadn't driven his father away. Angus Cardwell was more than capable of doing that himself.

He found his father at Angus's favorite watering hole, the Corral, down the canyon from Big Sky. Angus had been one handsome cowboy in his day. It was easy to see even now why Mary Justice had fallen in love with him.

Unfortunately, Jordan's mother had loved ranching and her husband had loved bars and booze. The two hadn't mixed well. Angus had taken the healthy settlement Mary had offered him and had left amicably enough. He'd made the money last by working an odd job here and there, including cash he and his brother made playing in a Country-Western band.

Most of the time though, Angus could be found on a bar stool—just as he was now. And most of the time his brother Harlan would be with him—just as he was now.

"Well, look what the cat dragged in," Angus said as Jordan made his way down the bar toward them. Like all out-of-the-way Montana bars, everyone had looked up to see who'd come through the door. Angus and Harlan were no exceptions.

"Hey, Bob," his father called to the owner as he slid off his stool to shake Jordan's hand and pound him on the back. "You remember my eldest."

Bob nodded, said hello and dropped a bar napkin in front of an empty stool next to Angus. Uncle Harlan nodded his hello and Angus patted the stool next to him and said, "What would you like to drink, son?"

Jordan wasn't in the mood for a drink, but he knew better than to say so. Angus took it personally when anyone wouldn't drink with him—especially his son. "I'll take a beer. Whatever's on tap."

Bob poured him a cold one and set it on the napkin, taking the money out of the twenty Angus had beside his own beer.

"What are you doing in Montana?" Uncle Harlan asked.

"I was just asking myself that same thing," Jordan said and took a sip of his beer. He could feel his father's gaze on him. News traveled fast in the canyon. Angus and Harlan would have heard about the shooting night before last.

He braced himself for their questions. To his surprise, that wasn't the first thing his father wanted to know.

"Been to see your sister yet?" Angus asked.

"Not yet. I wasn't sure Dana would want to see me."

"You know better than that." He took a drink of his beer. "That is, unless you're going to try to hit her up for money. No one will want to see you in that case."

Jordan shook his head. "I'm not here looking for money."

"In that case," his father said with a laugh, "you can buy the next round."

Two beers later Jordan asked his father if he remembered when Tanner Cole died.

Angus nodded solemnly. "He hung himself up by that construction site. I remember he was staying up there because there'd been some vandalism."

"There'd been some before Tanner moved into the cabin?" Jordan asked in surprise.

Angus nodded. "Couldn't prove who did it, but Malcolm Iverson was pretty sure it was his competitor, Harris Lancaster, trying to put him out of business. So he hired the kid to keep an eye on things."

Jordan hadn't known about the earlier vandalism or that Iverson had suspected Harris Lancaster.

"Malcolm probably couldn't have survived financially the way things were going even if his equipment hadn't been vandalized a second time," Uncle Harlan said. "Your friend must have taken it hard, though, since everyone blamed it for forcing Iverson into bankruptcy. Apparently, he'd let his equipment insurance lapse."

"How did I never hear this?" Jordan said.

"You were a senior in high school," his father said with a laugh. "You had your nose up some girl's skirt. You were lucky you even graduated."

"Tanner never said anything about this," he said more to himself than to his father and uncle.

Angus tipped his beer up, took a swallow, then turned his gaze on his son. "You can't blame yourself. Malcolm had no business hiring a kid to watch over his equipment. I'm just sorry you had to be the one to find your friend like that."

Jordan nodded, remembering the day he'd gone up to the construction site looking for Tanner. He'd been worried about him since it wasn't like Tanner to miss school.

He'd never forget parking and walking up the road to find the front door of the cabin open. He'd called Tanner's name and gotten no answer and yet, his friend's pickup had been sitting next to the cabin.

One glance and he'd seen that it was empty. He'd heard the creaking sound and at first thought it was a tree limb scraping against another limb.

It wasn't until he turned toward the fire pit where the party had been held the night of the vandalism that he saw the shadow. A breeze had stirred the pines, making the shadow flicker over the dead campfire. He'd called Tanner's name again, then with a sinking feeling he'd followed the creaking sound until he saw what was casting the long shadow over the fire ring.

He would never forget the sight of his best friend hanging from the tree limb.

Jordan took a drink of his beer, cleared his throat and said, "I never believed that Tanner killed himself. I knew he blamed himself for the vandalism because of the party up there that night, but now with Alex murdered… I have to find out what really happened."

"If I were you, I'd stay out of it," Angus said, looking worried. "Two of your friends are dead. Whatever's going on, you might be next."

LIZA HAD TO admit it. She was having fun. She and Dana had hit it off from the first time they'd met and Hilde was a whole lot of fun.

"Oh, you have to try this one," Hilde said as she pulled a black-and-white polka-dot dress from the huge pile she'd brought. "It's one of my favorites."

They'd been laughing and joking as Liza tried on one dress after another. Hilde had kidded Dana after exploring her closet and deeming it probably worse than Liza's.

"You cowgirls," Hilde said. "Jeans, jeans, jeans. Don't you ever just want to show off your legs?"

"No," Liza and Dana had said in unison.

The polka-dot dress was cute and it fit Liza perfectly. "Do you think it's *too* cute? Maybe it's not dressy enough," Liza asked.

"Come on, this is Montana, no one dresses up," Dana said.

Hilde rolled her eyes. "Sweetie, this is Big Sky and all the women will be dressed to the nines. The men will be wearing jeans, boots and Western sports jackets, but for these women, this is a chance to pull out all those expensive clothes, bags and high heels they're just dying to show off."

"Then I'm wearing this," Liza said, studying her reflection in the mirror. She loved the black-and-white polka-dot dress. "This is as dressy as this cowgirl is going to get."

Dana laughed. "Good for you."

As Liza changed back into her jeans, boots and uniform shirt, Dana said, "So have you seen my brother?"

She shook her head. "Not since earlier. I haven't had a chance to talk to him, either."

"He is still a suspect, right?" Hilde asked, sounding worried.

Liza realized that her two friends were worried about

her being taken in by Jordan. She had to smile, warmed by their concern.

"I hope I don't have to remind you that he was best friends with both Tanner and Alex and now they're both dead," Hilde said. "I grew up around Jordan. He always had a temper." She shot a look at Dana, who nodded, though with obvious regret.

"People change," Liza said, instantly regretting coming to Jordan's defense. She saw Hilde and Dana exchange a look. *"What?"*

"It's Stacy. I think *she's* changed," Dana said.

"You *hope* she's changed," Hilde corrected.

"Hud told me he was doing some checking into her past," Liza said. "I assume he didn't find anything."

"That's just it, he found nothing and that has him even more worried," Dana said. "Him and his marshal intuition."

Liza laughed. "Don't be joking around about our intuition." She'd been a green deputy six years ago, but Hud had taken her under his wing after seeing what he called an instinct for the job. Now he trusted her to handle this investigation and that meant everything to her.

The three women visited for a while longer, then Liza said she had to get moving. "The cocktail party and dinner is tonight. I've studied up on the players. Jordan had a list of those attending. Surprisingly, or maybe not, all eight of the Big Sky senior graduates will be up at Mountain Village tonight. Everyone but Alex and Tanner, that is." It was a small class twenty years ago. Although they attended high school down in Bozeman, they wanted their own reunion up here. Only in the past few years had Big Sky gotten its own high school.

"Just be careful," Dana said. "I know a few of those women." She pretended to shudder. "They're vicious."

"I don't think they're that bad," Hilde said. "I work out at Yogamotion. They're nice to me."

This time Dana and Liza exchanged a look. Hilde was petite, blonde and lithe. She would fit right in.

Dana reached for Liza's hand and squeezed it. "Just don't forget that one of them could be a killer."

JORDAN HAD SPENT the rest of the afternoon writing down everything he could remember about his senior year of high school, especially what might pertain to Tanner and Alex.

The trip down memory lane had exhausted him. When he glanced at his watch, he'd been shocked to see how late it was. He quickly showered and changed and drove over to pick up his date.

What surprised him was the frisson of excitement he felt as he rang Liza's bell. He realized with a start that he hadn't been on a real date in years. Since his divorce he'd stayed clear of women.

When he'd left the canyon, he'd shed the cowboy side of him like an old snakeskin. He'd wanted bright lights and big city. He'd wanted sophistication. He'd kicked the Montana ranch dust off his boots and hadn't looked back.

That was how he'd ended up married to Jill. He'd been flattered that a model would even give him a second look. She'd been thrilled that he came from Montana ranch stock, saying she was bored with New York City–type men.

What he hadn't realized was that Jill thought he had money. She'd thought the ranch was the size of Ted

Turner's apparently and couldn't wait to get her hands on the funds it would bring in once it sold.

He'd gotten caught up in trying to make her happy, even though she'd quit modeling the moment they were married and spent her days spending more money than he could make on Wall Street.

Now he could admit that he had become obsessed with keeping her. Although he hadn't acknowledged it to himself back then, he'd known that if he ran out of money, Jill would run out on him.

And she had—just as Dana had predicted. He hadn't wanted to hear it six years ago. Hell, he didn't like to think about it even now. The truth hurt. He'd fought back, of course, driving an even wider wedge between himself and his younger sister.

When Dana had discovered their mother's new will in that damned cookbook at the ranch house, Jill had realized there would be no ranch sale, no gold at the end of the rainbow, and she'd split. In truth, she'd already had some New York male model lined up long before that.

It had been some hard knocks, but he felt as if they had maybe knocked some sense into him. He saw things clearer than he had before. Mary Justice Cardwell had tried to instill values in her children. He'd rejected most of them, but they were still at his core, he thought as he rang Liza Turner's doorbell again.

When the door opened, he was taken completely off guard by the woman standing there. Liza took his breath away. She was wearing a black-and-white polka-dot dress that accentuated curves he'd had no idea were beneath her uniform. Her beautiful long curly hair had been pulled up, wisps of curls framing her face and she smelled heavenly.

"Wow, you look killer," he said when he caught his breath.

"So to speak," she said, sounding embarrassed as she quickly stuffed her gun into her purse. "My feet already hurt in these shoes."

He smiled at her. "You can kick them off the minute we hit the dance floor."

"Dance floor?" she asked, cocking an eyebrow.

"Didn't I mention I do one hell of a two-step?"

She took him in, her gaze pausing on his cowboy boots.

"Dana had a box of my clothes dropped off at the cabin," he said, feeling sheepish. It was so like Dana to be thoughtful. He'd found the boots as well as a couple of dress Western shirts and a Western-cut sports coat. He'd been surprised when everything still fit.

"You are a man of many surprises," she said, sounding almost as if she meant it.

He laughed. "You haven't seen anything yet." As he walked her to his rental SUV, he breathed in her scent, thinking he couldn't wait to get this woman in his arms on the dance floor.

DANA SUCKED ON her bleeding finger. Needlepoint wasn't for her, she decided after jabbing herself another time. She surveyed her stitches and cringed. As Stacy came into the bedroom, she tossed the needlepoint aside, glad for an interruption.

Earlier, Mary and Hank had come in and colored with her before their naps. She missed holding them on her lap, missed even more riding horses with them around the corral. All these beautiful fall days felt wasted lying in bed. But Hud had promised to take both kids out tomorrow.

As Stacy came over to the side of her bed, Dana saw that her sister had the cookbook open to their mother's double chocolate brownies.

"Is it all right if I make these?" Stacy asked.

They were Hud's favorite. That's why Mary Justice Cardwell had tucked her new will in her old, worn and faded cookbook next to the recipe. She'd wanted Dana not only to have the ranch—but the man she loved beside her.

"Sure. Hud would like that," Dana said, disappointed she couldn't even do something as simple as bake a pan of brownies for her husband.

"Mother used to make them for Dad, remember? Do you ever see him?"

"On occasion. Usually a holiday. He and Uncle Harlan keep pretty busy with their band." And their drinking, but she didn't say that.

Stacy nodded. "I might see them while I'm here. Maybe tomorrow if you don't mind me leaving for a little while in the morning?"

"Stacy, you don't need to ask. Of course you can go. Hud will be here."

"I suppose I know where I'll find Dad. Would you mind keeping Ella? I won't go until I put her down for her morning nap. I don't want to take her to a bar."

"I would be happy to watch her. You can bring her in here for her nap. She'll be fine while you're gone."

Stacy smiled, tears in her eyes, and gave Dana an impulsive though awkward hug. "I've missed you so much."

"I've missed you, too."

Her sister drew back, looking embarrassed, grabbed the cookbook and left. In the other room, Hud was playing fort with the kids. She could see a corner of the couch and chairs pulled into the middle of the room and covered with spare blankets.

Hud caught her eye. He smiled and shrugged as if to say, maybe she was right about her sister. Dana sure hoped so.

LIZA BRACED HERSELF as Jordan ushered her into the lodge at Mountain Village for the Friday-night dinner and dance. Tomorrow there would be a tour of Big Sky and a free afternoon, with the final picnic Sunday.

A room had been prepared for the reunion party that impressed her more than she wanted to admit. A DJ played music under a starry decor of silver and white. The lights had been turned low, forming pockets of darkness. Candles flickered at white-clothed tables arranged in a circle around the small shining dance floor.

A few couples were dancing. Most were visiting, either standing next to the bar or already seated at the cocktail tables.

"Hilde was right," Liza whispered. "I *am* underdressed." The women were dressed in fancy gowns and expensive accessories. The men wore jeans and boots and Western sports jackets, looking much like Jordan.

"You look beautiful, the prettiest woman here," Jordan said, putting his arm around her protectively.

She grinned over at him. "You really can be charming when you want to, Mr. Cardwell."

"Don't tell Hud," he said. "I've spent years cultivating his bad opinion of me. I'd hate to ruin it with just one night with you." He put his hand on her waist. "Let's dance." He drew her out on the dance floor and pulled her close. She began to move to the slow song, too aware of her dance partner and his warm hand on her back.

Jordan *was* full of surprises. He was light on his feet, more athletic than she'd thought and a wonderful dancer. He held her close, the two of them moving as one, and she lost herself in the music and him as she rested her cheek against his shoulder. He smelled wonderful and she felt safe and protected in his arms. The latter surprised her.

The night took on a magical feel and for the length of several Country-Western songs, she forgot why she and Jordan were here. She also forgot that he was a murder suspect.

When the song ended, she found herself looking at him as if seeing him for the first time. He appeared completely at home in his Western clothes. They suited him and she told him so.

He smiled at that. "I thought I'd dusted the cowboy dirt off me when I left here. My mother used to say this land and life were a part of me that I could never shed." He quickly changed the subject as if he hadn't meant to tell her those things. "Looks like everyone is here except for Tessa, Alex and Tanner. That's the nice thing about having a small graduating class. They're fairly easy to keep track of. Shall we get a drink?"

They'd done just that by the end of the next song when Shelby took the stage. She gave a short speech, updating anyone who didn't know about the members of the class, announced who had come the farthest, who had changed the most, who had the most kids.

"I thought we should have a few minutes of silence

for Alex," she said at the end. "Since he can't be with us tonight."

Liza spotted Tessa, who'd apparently just arrived. There was chatter about the murder around the tables, then everyone grew silent. It seemed to stretch on too long. Liza found herself looking around the room at the graduates.

She quickly picked out the main players Jordan had told her about. Shelby and her husband, contractor Wyatt Iverson; Tessa, who'd come alone; Whitney Fraser and husband and local business owner, Von; and Ashley Henderson and husband, Paul, had all congregated to one area of the room. Ashley and her husband and Whitney and hers appeared to be cut from the same cloth as Shelby and Wyatt. Brittany Peterson and husband Lee were visiting at a table of former students who were no longer Big Sky residents.

As Liza took them all in, she knew that what she was really looking for was a killer.

Wyatt Iverson was as handsome and put-together as his wife, Shelby. Liza waited until he went to the bar alone before she joined him.

"Wyatt Iverson? I don't think we've met. I'm Liza Turner—"

"Deputy marshal in charge of the Alex Winslow case," he said with a wide smile. "I know. I checked. I wanted to make sure someone capable was on the case. I heard great things about you."

"Thank you." She recalled a rumor going around that Wyatt was considering getting into national politics. Right now he served on a variety of boards as well as on the local commission. Wyatt was handsome and a smooth talker, a born politician and clearly a man with a driving ambition. He'd brought his father's business back from bankruptcy and made a name for himself, not to mention a whole lot of money apparently.

Shelby joined them, taking her husband's arm and announcing that dinner was being served in the dining room. "Everyone bring your drinks and follow me!" Ashley and Whitney fell into line and trailed after Shelby, just as Tessa did, but according to Jordan they'd been doing that for years.

To no one's surprise, Shelby had distributed place cards around a long table. Liza was surprised to see that she and Jordan were near the center, with Tessa and Brittany and her husband, Lee, at one end and Shelby's inner circle at the other.

She noticed that Tessa seemed surprised—and upset—when she found herself at the far end of the table. Clearly Tessa had done something Shelby hadn't liked. Either that or Shelby was sending her friend a message. If Shelby had anything to do with Alex's murder and Tessa knew about it, Liza feared that Tessa might get more than banished at the reunion dinner table. Whatever had Shelby upset with her could get Tessa killed just as it had Alex.

Chapter Nine

Jordan could have wrung Shelby's neck even before dinner was served. They'd all just sat down when Shelby insisted everyone go around the table and introduce their dates and spouses before dinner was served.

When it came Jordan's turn, he squeezed Liza's hand and said, "This is my date, Liza Turner."

"Oh, come on, Jordan," Shelby said. "Liza Turner is our local deputy marshal and the woman in charge of investigating Alex's murder." She smiled as she said it, but Jordan couldn't miss the hard glint in her eyes. "So, Deputy, tell us how the case is going."

"It's under investigation, that's all I can tell you," Liza said.

Shelby pretended to pout, making Jordan grit his teeth. "Oh, we were hoping as Alex's friends we could get inside information."

Jordan just bet she was. Fortunately, the staff served dinner and the conversations turned to other things.

"How have you been?" Brittany asked him. She was still as strikingly beautiful as she'd been in high school, but now there was a contentment about her.

"Good. You look happy," he said, glad for her.

"My life is as crazy as ever with three small ones

running around and…" She grinned. "Another one on the way. Surprise!"

"Congratulations," Jordan said, meaning it. She didn't seem in the least bit upset to be seated away from Shelby and her other classmates. Unlike Tessa, who hadn't said a word or hardly looked up since sitting down.

Everyone offered their congratulations to Brittany, including Shelby, who seemed to have her ears trained on their end of the table.

"How many does this make now?" she asked.

"Four, Shelby," Brittany said, smiling although Jordan could tell Shelby irritated her as much as she did him.

Shelby pretended shock. "I think you get the award for most children and also our Look Who's Pregnant! Award."

Jordan glanced over at Liza. He knew she was taking all of this in. Like him, he was sure she'd noticed the way Tessa had been acting since they'd sat down. Also, Tessa had been hitting the booze hard every time she could get the cocktail waitress's attention.

Jordan couldn't have been happier when dessert was finally served. Shelby had been running the dinner as if it was a board meeting. He noticed that, like Tessa, Shelby had been throwing down drinks. Just the sound of her voice irritated him. He was reminded why he hadn't wanted to come to his reunion.

"Jordan, what was the name of your wife, the one who was the model?" Shelby asked loudly from the other end of the table.

He didn't want to talk about his marriage or his divorce. But he knew Shelby wasn't going to let it go. "Jill

Ames. She was my *only* wife, Shelby," he said and felt Liza's calming hand on his thigh.

"Jill Ames is *gorgeous*. What were you thinking letting her get away?" Shelby said and laughed. She gave Liza a sympathetic look. "Jill Ames would be a hard act to follow."

"Shelby, you might want to back off on the drinks," Brittany said, throwing down her napkin as she shoved to her feet. "Your claws are coming out." She shot Jordan and Liza an apologetic look and excused herself before heading for the ladies' room. Shelby glared after her for a moment, then followed her.

Liza waited until Shelby disappeared down the hallway before she, too, excused herself. She was within ten feet of the ladies' room door when she heard their raised voices. She slowed, checked to make sure there was no one behind her, before she stepped to the door and eased it open a few inches. She could see the two reflected in the bathroom mirrors, but neither could see her.

"How dare you try to embarrass me," Shelby screeched into Brittany's face.

"Embarrass *you?* Seriously, Shelby?" Brittany started to turn away from her.

Shelby grabbed her arm. "Don't you turn your back on me."

"Touch me again and I'll deck you," Brittany said as she jerked free of the woman's hold. "I don't do yoga every day like you, but I do haul around three kids so I'm betting I'm a lot stronger and tougher than you are. I'm also not afraid of you anymore."

"Well, you should be."

"Are you threatening me?" Brittany demanded as

she advanced on her. "This isn't high school, Shelby. Your reign is over." She turned and went into a stall.

Shelby stood as if frozen on the spot, her face white with fury as Liza stepped into the ladies' room. Seeing the deputy marshal, Shelby quickly spun around and twisted the handle on the faucet, hiding her face as she washed her hands.

Liza went into the first stall. She heard Brittany flush, exit the next stall and go to the washbasin. Through the sound of running water, she heard Shelby hiss something.

"Whatever, Shelby." Brittany left, but a moment later someone else came in.

"Aren't you talking to me? What's going on?" Tessa whined, sounding like a child. "Are you mad at me? I don't understand. I haven't done *anything.*"

She was sure Shelby was probably trying to signal that they weren't alone, but Tessa was clearly upset and apparently not paying attention.

"I told you I wouldn't say anything. You know you can trust me. So why are you—"

"Tessa, this really isn't the place," Shelby snapped.

"But all evening you've—"

Liza had no choice but to flush. As she opened the stall door, both Tessa and Shelby glanced in her direction. "Ladies," she said as she moved to the sinks and turned on the water.

"I could use some fresh air," Shelby said. "Come outside with me for a minute." She smiled as she took Tessa's arm and practically dragged her out of the bathroom.

Liza washed her hands, dried them and then stepped out. She could see Shelby and Tessa on the large deck in what was obviously a heated discussion. She watched them for a moment, wishing she could hear their conversation, but having no way to do that went back to the table and Jordan.

"Everything okay?" he asked quietly.

She smiled at him. "Great."

"I love your dress," Brittany said.

Liza laughed. "That's right. You like polka dots. I remember your apron." Liza liked Brittany. She could see why Jordan had had a crush on her in high school. Probably still did.

With dinner over, everyone began to wander away from the table and back into the first room where the music was again playing.

Liza pulled Jordan aside and told him what she'd overheard.

"So basically you just wanted to let me know I was right about Tessa," Jordan said, grinning.

"Apparently, you can be right once in a while, yes." She smiled back at him, realizing he was flirting with her again and she didn't mind it.

A few moments later Shelby came back in from the deck. She put her game face on again and breezed by them, already dancing to the music before she reached the dance floor. But she didn't fool Liza. Shelby was trying hard to hide whatever was really going on with her and Tessa.

"I'm going to talk to Tessa," Liza said. "Save me a dance."

As Jordan left the dining room and joined the others, he spotted Shelby talking to her other two cohorts. Ashley and Whitney could have been sisters. They were both brunettes, both shapely, both pretty—at least from a distance. He knew his perception of them had been poisoned a long time ago.

He liked to think all of them had changed, himself included. But he could tell by the way Ashley and Whitney were listening to Shelby that they still followed her as blindly as they had in high school. It made him sad. Brittany had grown up, made a life for herself and seen through Shelby. But apparently Brittany was the only one who'd made the break from Shelby's control.

"Jordan, do you have a minute?"

He turned to find Paul Henderson, Ashley's husband. Paul had been two years ahead of them in school. "Sure," he said as Paul motioned to the empty lobby of the lodge.

"I hope I'm not speaking out of school here," Paul said. "But there's a rumor going around that Alex was asking about Tanner before he was…killed. I figured if you really were with him at the falls, then he must have talked to you."

"We didn't get a chance to talk," Jordan said, wondering if Paul had any information or if he was just fishing.

"Oh." He looked crestfallen.

"*You* talked to him?"

Paul nodded and met Jordan's gaze. "I wasn't sure if I should tell the deputy marshal."

"What did Alex tell you?"

He hesitated for a moment, then said, "Alex asked me if I remembered the party Tanner had that night at the cabin, the night the equipment was vandalized?"

Jordan nodded. He vaguely remembered the party. He'd drunk too much and, after his fight with Tessa, had left early with some girl from Bozeman who he couldn't even remember. "Were you there?"

"No. I was grounded from the past weekend. He was asking if I knew where Shelby was that night."

"Shelby?"

"He wanted to know if Ashley had been with her."

"And was she?"

"That's just it. I told Alex that I thought she was because she called a little after two in the morning. She'd been drinking. We argued and I hung up. The next day when I asked her where she'd been the night before, she swore she didn't go to the party. But Alex said something about some photos from the party that night that proved not only were Ashley and Whitney there, but Shelby and Tessa were, too."

"Why was he interested in photos of the party?" Jordan asked.

Paul shrugged. "That's just it. I can't imagine what some photographs of a high school kegger twenty years ago could have to do with anything. That's why I haven't said anything to the deputy marshal."

"Did you ask Ashley about them?"

"She still swears she wasn't at the party that night, but…" He looked away for a moment. "I'd like to see those photos. Alex seemed to think there was something in them that could explain why Tanner is dead."

"I'll mention it to the deputy marshal," Jordan said. "She might want to talk to you."

Paul looked relieved. "I didn't know if I should say anything, but I'm glad I did. Okay, back to the party huh?" He didn't look as if he was enjoying the reunion any more than Jordan had enjoyed dinner.

The only thing that kept Jordan from calling it quits was the thought of another dance with Liza.

TESSA STOOD AT the deck railing, her back to the lodge. She looked cold and miserable and from the redness around her eyes, she'd been crying.

Liza joined her at the railing. "Shelby's trying to bring you back under control, you know."

Tessa glanced over at her and let out a laugh. "I'd pretend I didn't know what you were talking about, but what would be the use?"

"Talk to me, Tessa. Tell me what Shelby is so terrified I'll find out?"

Tessa hugged herself and looked away. A breeze whispered in the nearby pines. Earlier it had been warm. Now though, the air had cooled. It carried the promise of winter. Closer, Liza could hear the muted music from inside the lodge. The party was resuming. She was betting that Shelby wouldn't leave Tessa out here long. If Liza didn't get the truth out of her quickly—

A door opened behind them. "Tessa?" Whitney called from the open doorway. "Shelby needs your help with the awards."

"I'll be right there," she said over her shoulder and started to turn toward the lodge.

"Tessa," Liza said, feeling her chance slipping through her fingers. She was genuinely afraid for Tessa. For some reason, the woman had been cut from the herd. Liza feared for the woman's life.

"Let me think about things. Maybe I'll stop by your office Monday."

Liza nodded. The one thing she'd learned was when to back off. "I can help you."

Tessa laughed at that and looked toward the lodge. "I'm not sure anyone can help me," she said and pushed off the railing to go back inside.

Liza bit down on her frustration. Tessa needed her best friend's approval. But surely she was tired of playing Shelby's game.

Telling herself this night hadn't been a total waste, Liza waited for a few moments before going back inside. The moment she saw Jordan, she thought, no, this night had definitely not been a waste.

He stood silhouetted in the doorway, reminding her that she'd come with the most handsome man at the party. Suspect or not, Jordan Cardwell was a pretty good date, she thought as he drew her into his arms and out on the dance floor.

Out of the corner of her eye she saw that Shelby had Tessa in the corner. Liza met Tessa's gaze for a moment before the woman shoved away from Shelby and dragged Wyatt Iverson out on the floor to dance with her.

"You might want to talk to Paul Henderson," Jordan said, as they were leaving the reunion party a few dances later. "Apparently, Alex asked him about the party at the cabin that night. Alex thought there were photographs taken at the party that might have something to do with Tanner's death."

"Photographs?" Liza asked. She'd settled into the SUV's passenger seat, still feeling the warmth of being in Jordan's arms on the dance floor. She'd had fun even though she hated to admit it since she was supposed to be finding a murderer.

"Paul wasn't at Tanner's kegger, but he seems to think Ashley might have gone and lied about it."

"And how does all of this lead to Alex's death?" she asked, wanting to hear Jordan's take on it.

"Tanner was staying in a cabin up on the mountain to keep an eye on Iverson Construction equipment," he said as he drove. "He throws a party, the equipment gets vandalized, he gets in trouble. Malcolm Iverson, who is on the edge of bankruptcy, believes his competitor Harris Lancaster is behind the vandalism in an attempt to take over his business. Malcolm goes gunning for him, shoots Harris accidentally and goes to prison for a couple of years. When he gets out, he drowns in a boating accident." He looked over at her. "These things have to be connected and if there really are photographs from Tanner's party, then maybe they tie it all together—and explain why Tanner is dead."

"Tanner sounds like such a sensible kid," Liza said. "Why would he throw a party at the cabin with the construction equipment nearby?"

"He swore he didn't. People just started showing up. So he went with it. But after the equipment was vandalized, he felt horrible about it." He shrugged as he drove down the mountain. "I know he blamed himself."

"Was Tanner drinking a lot that night?"

Jordan sighed. "I don't know. I got drunk and left with some girl."

"So if these photographs exist, then they might not just show who was there and with whom, the photographer might have captured the vandalism on film."

"That's what I was thinking, and if Ashley's father, Harris Lancaster, was behind it, he would have good reason not to want the photographs to surface and so would Ashley."

Liza thought of the suicide scene photos in Tanner's

file, the campfire ringed with rocks, the charred beer cans, all the tracks at the scene. "If Harris was questioned about the vandalism, there should be something down at the office in the file."

"Both Malcolm Iverson and Harris Lancaster are the kind of men who would have taken the law into their own hands," Jordan said. "And so are their sons. I doubt either of them reported anything."

"I think I should talk to Harris Lancaster," Liza said.

"Let me go along. Just to make sure you're safe. Truth is, Lancaster is the kind of man who won't take a female deputy seriously. No offense."

"Oh, none taken," she said sarcastically. "But you've done enough, thanks. So what do you have planned tomorrow?"

He'd grinned over at her. "Worried about me?"

"Tell me I don't have any reason to be."

"Look, I'm touched but—"

"It isn't personal, so save it," she said quickly. "I have one murder on my hands, maybe two. I don't need you adding another one for me to solve."

"Don't worry, Deputy. I have no intention of getting myself killed. I'll watch my back. You do the same."

She nodded. "I'm driving up to West Yellowstone to see Brick Savage. He was the investigating marshal on Tanner's death."

"I need to go see my sister. But maybe I'll see you later tomorrow? How about dinner?"

She shook her head. "I don't think that's a good idea."

"I get it. You're afraid that over dinner I might charm you into thinking I'm harmless, if you weren't careful."

"You aren't that charming and you're far from harmless."

He grinned at that. "I'm going to take that as a compliment."

"I was sure you would."

As he drove toward her condo, he said, "Seriously, watch your back tomorrow."

WHEN THEY REACHED Liza's condo, Jordan insisted on walking her to her door.

"This really isn't necessary," she said, shaking her head at him as she dug for her key. He saw the glint of her weapon in her purse along with her badge. For a while on the dance floor, he'd forgotten she was a deputy marshal. She was merely a beautiful woman in his arms.

"A gentleman always walks his date to the door."

"This isn't a date."

"Because I'm a suspect?"

She looked up from searching in her purse for her key. He'd noticed that she'd suddenly become ill at ease when he'd driven up in front of her condo. Now she froze as he moved closer until they were a breath apart.

"Do you really think I'm dangerous?" he asked.

Her laugh sounded nervous. "Absolutely."

"Well, date or not, I had fun with you," he whispered and kissed her gently. She still hadn't moved when he drew back to look into her beautiful green eyes.

He knew he should leave it at one quick kiss, turn and walk away, but there was something so alluring about her that he gripped her waist and pulled her to him. This time he kissed her like he'd wanted to since the day he'd seen her sitting astride her horse, watching him from the darkness of the trees. There'd been something mysterious and sensual about her even when he'd realized who she was.

Now she melted into him, her hands going to his shoulders, her lips parting, a soft moan escaping from deep within her.

He felt his own desire spark and catch flame. It had been so long since he'd felt like this, if he ever had before. Liza was slight in stature, but had curves in all the right places. There was something solid and real about her. He couldn't help thinking how different she was from his ex, Jill. Jill ate like a bird. If she'd consumed even a portion of the food Liza'd had tonight at the dinner, she'd be anxious to get inside the condo and throw it all up. He'd gotten so sick of her constant dieting and complaining about the way she looked.

Liza was so different from any woman he'd ever known. She knew who she was and what she wanted. She looked perfect as she was, felt perfect. He wanted to sweep her into his arms, take her inside and make love to her until daylight.

AT THE SOUND of a vehicle coming up the street, Liza pushed back from the kiss as if coming up for air. She was breathing hard, her heart pounding, desire making her blood run hot.

As a white SUV slowly drove past, she saw the woman behind the wheel and swore.

"Shelby," she said, mentally kicking herself for not only letting this happen but also wanting it to.

Jordan turned to watch the vehicle disappear down the street. "Sorry."

It was bad enough that a lot of people didn't think a woman could do this job. She'd only made it worse by letting someone like Shelby see her kissing Jordan Cardwell.

"I should never have gone to the reunion dinner with you," she said.

"You were working."

"That kiss wasn't work."

"No," he said and grinned at her.

"Go home," she said.

He raised both hands and took a step back. "You want to pick me up at the cabins or should I meet you tomorrow to—"

"I already told you. I can handle this without your help."

He stopped. "Liza, I'm not giving up until Alex's killer is caught."

"It's too dangerous."

He studied her for a moment. "Too dangerous for who?" he asked, stepping to her again. He cupped the side of her face with one of his large hands. She was surprised to feel the calluses. Taking his hand, she held it to the light.

"I thought you worked on Wall Street?" she asked, hating the suspicion she heard in her voice. Worse, that Jordan had heard it.

"I used to. I quit. I've been working construction for a few years now."

"Do you even live in New York City?"

He shook his head. "Why are you getting so upset?"

"Because I've run background checks on everyone involved in this case—except *you*."

"Because you know I didn't kill Alex."

"Do I?" She glared at him, although it was herself she was angry with.

He held up his hands again. "I'm sorry if one little kiss—"

"It wasn't one little kiss," she snapped and closed her eyes as she realized what she'd said. The kiss had shaken her. Worse, it had sparked a desire in her for this man, of all men.

"Run your background check. Do whatever it is you have to do," he said as he took a step away. "I have nothing to hide. But know this. That wasn't just some little kiss for me, either. If I had my way, I'd have you inside that condo and I'd be taking off your clothes right now. Good night, Deputy Marshal. I had a nice time. You make a nice date."

With that, he turned and walked to his vehicle while she stood trembling on the condo stoop thinking about what he'd said. Imagining the two of them tearing at each other's clothing. She knew that if he had taken her inside, they would have never made it to the bedroom.

As he drove away, she stood breathing in the cold night air, trying to still the aching need inside her. She'd always prided herself on her strength and determination. Nothing had kept her from realizing her goal to get where she was now. That had meant not letting a man either slow her down or stop her dead in her pursuit.

She wasn't going to let Jordan Cardwell ruin not just her reputation, but her credibility as a deputy marshal. The realization that she wanted him as much as he wanted her shocked her. No man had ever interested her enough for the problem to come up before. She reminded herself that Jordan was a suspect.

After a moment she dug into her purse until she found her key. With shaking fingers, she unlocked the door and stepped inside.

Even before she turned on the light, she knew something was terribly wrong. Someone had ransacked her condo.

She stood staring at the mess, trying to make sense of it. Why would someone do this? Her heart began to pound. This felt as if it was a warning.

Or had someone been looking for something and not finding it, just decided to tear the place up? Were they looking for the photographs Alex had been asking about?

Either way, she felt as if she'd gotten the message. Unfortunately, she'd never been good at heeding these kinds of warnings.

If anything, she was more determined than ever to solve this case and get Jordan Cardwell off her suspect list.

Chapter Ten

Saturday morning after cleaning up her condo, Liza drove up the canyon. It was one of those amazing Montana fall days. The sky was robin's-egg blue and not a cloud was in sight. The deciduous trees along the river glowed in bright blinding golds and deep reds next to the dark green of the pines.

At the heart of it all was the Gallatin River, running clear and beautiful, as it wound through the canyon and rocks. Harris Lancaster lived in a large modern home that looked as if it had been picked up in some big city and accidentally dropped here by the river.

His wife answered the door and pointed Liza toward a building a ways from the house. She followed a graveled path to the door and knocked.

Harris was a big burly brisk man with a loud deep voice and piercing gray eyes. Liza tried to imagine him in the very feminine furnishings of the house she'd glimpsed before his wife had closed the door.

His office looked like him, large and messy. The space was taken up by everything from dirty outdoor clothing and piles of papers and building plans to equipment parts and an old couch that Liza suspected he probably slept on more often than not. Given the pristine look of the house and Malcolm's wife, Liza doubted he was allowed to set foot inside it.

He cleared off an old wooden chair, motioned her into it and took a seat behind his cluttered desk. "So what's this about?" The office smelled of cigar smoke.

"I want to talk to you about Tanner Cole," Liza said.

"Who?"

"He worked for Malcolm Iverson twenty years ago when he was in high school."

He laughed. "*Seriously?* I can't remember who works for me right now, why would I remember who worked for Malcolm?"

"Tanner committed suicide twenty years ago after Malcolm Iverson's construction equipment was vandalized. It was just days before Malcolm shot you and went to prison."

He shook his head. "I try not to think about any of that."

"Tanner was in the same class as your daughter Ashley. He lived in a cabin near the construction site. Malcolm held Tanner responsible, but ultimately, he believed you were behind the vandalism that forced him into bankruptcy."

He scoffed at that. "Malcolm didn't know anything about running a business. He spent too much time in the bar. But I had nothing to do with vandalizing his equipment. He was just looking for someone to blame. Anyway, I heard the vandalism was kid stuff. You know, sugar in the gas tanks, broken and missing motor parts. Pure mischief. That's what happens when you get a bunch of drunk kids together."

"Or it was made to look like kids did it," she noted, but Harris Lancaster didn't seem to be listening.

"I do remember something about that Tanner boy now that you mention it. Ashley was real upset. We all were," he added. "Tanner's family has a ranch on the way to West Yellowstone. Too bad, but I don't see what any of that has to do with me."

"You benefited by Malcolm going broke."

He shrugged. "Maybe, at the time. But there was plenty of work to go around. His son and I are competitors, but we aren't shooting each other and we're both doing quite well."

He had a point. Maybe his problems with Malcolm and vice versa had nothing to do with Tanner's death. Maybe it had been guilt. Or maybe there were some photographs somewhere that told a different story.

JORDAN PULLED UP out in front of the house where he'd been raised. He sat for a moment just looking at the large two-story house. The other day when he'd come into town, he'd driven in from the other side of the ranch to make sure no one was at home before he'd come down to borrow a hat.

At least that had been his excuse. He'd wanted to wander around the house without anyone watching him. He knew his sister would think he was casing the joint, looking for valuables he could pawn or sell on eBay.

He and Dana had always butted heads, although he wished that wasn't the case. He'd always respected her. She worked harder than anyone he knew and made the rest of them feel like slackers.

Even after the good luck he'd had after Jill had left, he still felt like he could never measure up to Dana. Now as he opened his car door and climbed out, he half expected Dana to meet him on the porch. Possibly with a shotgun in her hands. Then he remembered that Hud had said she was pregnant with twins and having a hard time.

At the door, he knocked. It felt strange to knock at a door he'd run in and out of for years.

To his surprise, Stacy opened the door. He'd thought she was just passing through. But then again that would explain the beater car with the California plates he now saw parked off to the side. He hadn't even noticed it he'd been so busy looking at the house.

"Stacy," he said, unable to hide his surprise.

"Jordan?" She put a lot into that one word.

"It's all right. I didn't come by to cause trouble. I just wanted to see my sister. Sisters," he corrected. "And my niece and nephew."

"Nieces," she said and stepped back to let him come in.

"That's right. Hud said you have a baby?"

"Don't sound so surprised." Stacy studied him for a moment. "I'll see if Dana is up to having company."

"I'm not company. I'm *family*."

She lifted an eyebrow as if to say, "Since when?"

As if *she* should talk, he thought as she headed for the downstairs sunroom that had been their parents' bedroom, then their mother's and now apparently Dana's.

"Where are the kids?" he called after Stacy.

She shot him a warning look. "Down for their naps."

"Sorry," he whispered. He stood in the doorway, afraid to step in and feeling badly that it had come to this.

Stacy returned a moment later. She didn't look happy. "Dana isn't supposed to be upset."

"Thanks for the warning," he said and stepped across the living room to the doorway Stacy had just come from.

He stopped the moment he saw Dana. She looked beautiful, propped up against an array of pillows. Their gazes locked and he stepped the rest of the way into the room, closing the door behind him.

"Hey, sis," he said.

"Jordan." She began to cry.

With a lump in his throat at her reaction, he closed the distance and bent down to hug her awkwardly. "Are you all right?" he asked pulling back to look at her. "You look…beautiful."

"I thought you were going to say…big," she said laughing and crying as she wiped at her eyes. "It's the hormones," she said pointing at her tears. "I cry over everything."

"That explains it. For a minute there I thought you might have missed me," he said as he pulled up the chair next to the bed.

She stopped drying her tears to meet his gaze. "You seem…different."

He smiled. "Oh, I'm still that stubborn, temperamental brother you remember. But maybe some of the hard edges have gotten knocked off."

Dana nodded. "Maybe that's it. Hud told me why you were in town."

"I didn't think you wanted to see me or I would have come by sooner."

"You're my older brother."

"Exactly," he only half joked.

The bedroom door opened. Stacy stuck her head in.

"I think I'll run that errand I told you about yesterday. The kids are still down. Should I move Ella?"

"No, I'll have Jordan bring her in before he leaves."

Stacy looked to her brother as if she wasn't sure that was a good idea.

"I haven't dropped a baby all day," he said.

"And Hud should be back any minute," Dana said to reassure her sister.

Stacy mugged a face at him and closed the door. He listened to her leave. But it wasn't until they both couldn't hear her old beater car engine any longer before they spoke.

"I did a lot of soul searching after everything that happened," he said. "I'm sorry."

"Me too."

"I went up to the cemetery and saw Mom the first day I got here. I borrowed a hat. Nothing else," he added quickly.

"Jordan, this ranch is your home too."

"I know, sis," he said putting a hand on her arm. "Mom always thought I'd come back and want to help you ranch."

Dana chuckled at that. "She said Stacy and Clay were gone, but you…well, she said there was ranching in your blood."

"Yeah. So tell me what's going on with you."

She placed her hands over her huge stomach. "I'm on bed rest with these two for the last weeks. I'm going insane."

He laughed. "I can imagine. And Stacy is…?"

"She's been great. Mary and Hank adore her."

"Mary and Hank. I can't wait to meet them."

"You should come back for dinner tonight," Dana said.

He shook his head. "Not sure that's a good idea given the way your husband feels about me, not to mention everything else going on right now."

"I wish you would. At least once before you leave," Dana said, tearing up again.

"You and your hormones." He got up and hugged her again. Straightening to leave, he asked, "So where's this baby I'm supposed to bring you before I leave?"

At the sound of the front door opening, Dana said, "Sounds like Hud's home. You'll have to come back to meet Ella."

"I'll try. You take care of yourself and your babies." As he opened the door, he came face to face with his brother-in-law again. "I was just leaving and no, I didn't upset her."

Hud looked past him to Dana. "What is she crying about then?"

"It's just the hormones," Dana said.

Jordan shrugged. "Just the hormones."

As he left, he found himself looking toward the barn, remembering his childhood here. Amazing how the place looked so different from the way he remembered it the last time he was here. Had he really tried to force his sister into selling it, lock, stock and barrel?

He felt a wave of shame as he walked to his rental SUV and climbed inside.

"WHERE'S STACY?" HUD ASKED as he stuck his head in the bedroom door later.

Dana saw that he had Ella on one shoulder. She realized she'd fallen asleep after Jordan had left and had awakened a few moments ago when she'd heard the baby cry.

"She said she wanted to go see Angus," Dana said groggily as she pulled herself up a little in the bed. "She said she wouldn't be gone long." Glancing at the clock beside her bed, she was shocked to see what time it was. "She hasn't come back?"

Hud shook his head. "I just changed Ella. I was going to heat some formula for her." He sounded worried.

Past him, Dana could see that it was dark outside. She felt a flutter of apprehension. "Stacy should have been back by now. Here, I'll take the baby. Call my father. Maybe they got to visiting and she just lost track of time."

"The kids and I are making dinner." Hud handed her Ella. "They ordered beanie wienies."

"Sounds great." She could smell the bacon and onions sizzling in the skillet. But her gaze was on the baby in her arms. Ella smiled up at her and she felt her heart do a somersault. Stacy was just running late. She probably didn't remember how quickly it got dark this time of year in the canyon.

A few minutes later, Hud came into the bedroom. "I called your father. He hasn't seen Stacy."

She felt her heart drop, but hid her fear as the kids came running in excitedly chanting "beanie wienies."

Hud set up Mary and Hank's small table in the bedroom so they could all eat dinner with her. The beanie wienies were wonderful. They finished the meal off with some of the brownies Aunt Stacy had made.

"Is Auntie Stacy going to live with us?" Mary asked.

"No, she's just visiting," Dana told her daughter. There was still no sign of Stacy. No call. Dana found herself listening, praying for the sound of her old car coming up the road. But there was only silence. "I'm not sure how long your aunt can stay."

Hank looked over at Ella who was drooling and laughing as she tried to roll over on the other side of the bed. "She can't leave without her baby," he said. "Can she?"

She shot Hud a look. Could Stacy leave without her baby?

"I'm going to call Hilde and see if she can come over while I go look for Stacy," Hud said. "I called Liza but she's in West Yellowstone. Apparently, she went up there to talk to my father about the case she's working."

Dana nodded, seeing her own worry reflected in his face.

"I'll call you if I hear anything." Big Sky was relatively small. Stacy couldn't have gone far. Unless she'd changed her mind about seeing their father and gone into Bozeman for some reason. But she'd said she would be back before Ella woke up from her nap. What if something had happened to her sister?

Trying to rein in her fear, Dana told the kids to get a game for them all to play.

"Ella can't play, Mommy," Mary cried. "She'll eat the game pieces."

"No, Ella will just watch," she told her daughter as she fought the dread that Stacy hadn't changed at all.

In that case Dana hated to think what that might mean. That Stacy wouldn't be back? Or worse, she'd left her baby. If it was her baby.

Chapter Eleven

Jordan felt at loose ends after leaving his sister's. On impulse he drove as far as he could up the road to the construction site where he'd found Tanner that horrible morning twenty years before.

The road was now paved and led up to a massive home. He could tell from the looks of it that the owner wasn't around and probably didn't come up but for a few weeks in the winter and summer.

The house had been built on a cleared area high on the mountain where the construction equipment had been parked twenty years ago. The small log cabin where Tanner had lived was gone. So was the camp-fire ring. Nothing looked as it had except for the tree where he'd found Tanner hanging that spring day.

There was also no sign that this was the spot where his best friend had taken his life. No log stumps. No rope mark on the large old pine limb. Nothing left of the tragedy even on the breeze that moaned in the high boughs. Jordan doubted the place's owners knew about the death that had occurred within yards of their va-cation home.

He felt a sadness overwhelm him. "Why, Tanner? Why the hell did you do it?" he demanded as he looked up at the large limb where he'd found him. "Or did you?" He feared they would never know as he looked again at the dried-pine-needle-covered ground. Did he really think he was going to find answers up here?

Too antsy to go back to his cabin, he drove up the canyon. When he saw his father's truck parked outside The Corral, he swung in. He found his father and uncle sitting on their usual stools at the bar.

"Son? I thought you would have left by now," Angus Cardwell said. "Bob, get my son a beer."

Jordan noticed there were a few men at the end of the bar and several families at the tables in the dining area eating.

Angus slapped his son on the back as Jordan slid onto a stool next to him. The bar smelled of burgers and beer. Not a bad combination, he thought, figuring he understood why his old man had such an infatuation with bars.

"What have you been up to?" Uncle Harlan asked him.

"My twenty-year class reunion," he said, figuring that would suffice.

"You actually went to it?" his father said with a laugh.

"I went with the deputy marshal."

Both older men hooted. "That's my son," Angus said proudly.

Jordan had known that would be his father's reaction. It was why he'd said it. He was just glad Liza hadn't been around to hear it.

The draft beer was cold and went down easy. Heck, he might have a burger while he was at it. He settled in, listening to the watering hole banter, a television over the bar droning in the background.

"Your deputy figured out who killed that man at the falls?" his uncle asked him.

"Not yet, but she will," he said with confidence.

His father smiled over at him and gave him a wink. "That what's really keeping you in the canyon, ain't it?"

Jordan smiled and ordered burgers for the three of them.

Later when he drove back to Big Sky and stopped by the Marshal's Office, he was disappointed to learn that Liza hadn't returned from West Yellowstone. He thought about what his father had said about his reasons for staying around. If he was being honest with himself, Liza definitely played into it.

LIZA FOUND BRICK SAVAGE sitting on the deck of his Hebgen Lake home. She'd heard stories about him and, after he'd ignored her knocks at his front door, braced herself as she approached his deck.

"Mr. Savage?"

He looked up, his gaze like a piercing arrow as he took in her uniform first, then studied her face before saying, "Yes?"

"I'm Deputy Marshal Liza Turner out of the Big Sky office. I'd like a moment of your time."

"You have any identification?" His voice was gravelly but plenty strong.

She pulled her ID and climbed a couple of steps so he could see it.

He nodded, amusement in his gaze. "Deputy Marshal. Times really have changed. I heard my son left you in charge of the murder case."

"That's correct."

"Well, come on up here then," Brick said and pushed

himself up out of his chair. He was a big man, but she could see that he used to be a lot bigger in his younger days. There was a no-nonsense aura about him along with his reputation that made her a little nervous being in his company.

He shoved a chair toward her as she reached the deck and waited for her to sit before he pulled up a weather-grayed log stump and settled himself on it.

"I hate to take your chair," she said, wondering about a man who had only one chair on his deck. Apparently he didn't expect or get much company. Did that mean he didn't see much of Hud and family?

"So?" Brick said as if his time was valuable and she was wasting it.

"I want to ask you about Tanner Cole's death. He was a senior—"

"I know who he was. Found hanging from a tree up on the side of the mountain overlooking Big Sky twenty-odd years ago," Brick said. "What do you want to know?"

"Was it a suicide?"

He leveled his gaze at her. "Wasn't it ruled one?"

"At the time. Is it possible Tanner had help?"

"It's always possible. Was there any sign of a struggle like scratches or bruises? Not according to the coroner's report but if you did your homework, you'd already know that. As for footprints, there were a lot of them. He'd had a beer bash, kegger, whatever your generation calls it. He'd had that within a few days so there were all kinds of tracks at the scene."

She knew all this and wondered if she'd wasted her time driving all the way up here. Past him she could see the deep green of the lake, feel a cold breeze coming off the water. Clouds had already gathered over Lion's Head Mountain, one of the more recognizable ones seen from his deck. Add to that the sun had already gone down. As it was, it would be dark before she got back to Big Sky.

"I can tell you this, he used his own rope," Brick said.

She nodded. "What about Jordan Cardwell?"

"What about him?"

"You found him at the scene. Is there any chance—"

"He didn't kill his friend, if that's what you're asking."

"You're that sure?" she said, hearing the relief in her voice and suspecting he did too. She'd started to like Jordan, suspect or not. She knew it was a bad idea on so many levels, but there was something about him...

"What did you really come up here to ask me?" Brick demanded.

"I guess what I want is your gut reaction."

"My gut reaction isn't worth squat. Do I think he killed himself?" The former marshal shrugged. "Strangulation takes a while. Gives a man a lot of time to reconsider and change his mind, but with all his body weight on the rope, it's impossible to get your fingers under the rope and relieve the pressure."

She looked at him in surprise. "Are you telling me he—"

"Changed his mind and clawed at the rope?" He nodded.

"Why wasn't that in the coroner's report?"

"It's not uncommon. But also not something a family member ever wants to know about. I would imagine Rupert wanted to spare them any more pain."

Liza shook her head. "But couldn't it also mean that

Tanner Cole never meant to hang himself? That someone else put that rope around his neck?"

"And he didn't fight until that person kicked the log
out?" Brick asked. "Remember, there were no defensive wounds or marks on his body."

"Maybe he thought it was a joke."

The elderly former marshal studied her for a moment. "What would make you let someone put a noose
around your neck, joking or otherwise?"

That was the question, wasn't it?

"You think he killed himself," she said.

He shrugged. "Prove me wrong."

HUD SPENT A good two hours canvassing the area for his
sister-in-law before he put out the APB on her vehicle.
He checked with the main towing services first though,
telling himself her car could have broken down. All
kinds of things could have happened to detain her—
and maybe even keep her from calling.

But after those two hours he knew in his gut that
wasn't the case. Stacy had split.

At the office he did something he'd hoped he
wouldn't have to do. He began checking again for kidnappings of children matching Ella's description and
realized he needed to narrow his search. Since Stacy
was driving a car with California plates...

He realized he should have run her plates first. Feeling only a little guilty for having taken down her license
number when he'd first become suspicious of her, he
brought up his first surprise.

The car had been registered in La Jolla, California—
but not to Stacy by any of her former married names or
her maiden name of Cardwell.

The car was registered to Clay Cardwell—her brother.

He picked up the phone and called the family lawyer who was handling the dispersing of ranch profits to Dana's siblings.

"Rick, I hate to bother you, but I need to get a phone number and address for Dana's brother Clay. I understand he's living in La Jolla, California."

Rick cleared his voice. "Actually I was going to contact Dana, but hesitated when I heard she's on bed rest at the ranch pregnant with the twins."

News traveled fast, Hud thought. "What's up?" he asked, afraid he wasn't going to like it.

"Clay. He hasn't been cashing his checks. It's been going on for about six months. I just assumed he might be holding them for some reason. But the last one came back saying there was no one by that name and no forwarding address."

Hud swore under his breath. Six months. The same age as Ella. Although he couldn't imagine what the two things could have in common or why Clay hadn't cashed his checks or how it was that his older sister was driving a car registered to him.

"I think we need to find him," Hud said. "I'd just as soon Dana didn't know anything about this. Believe me, she has her hands full right now. One more thing though. Stacy. Did she give you a new address to send her checks?"

"No. She's moved around so much, I wait until I hear from her and usually send them general delivery."

"Well, could you do me a favor? If you hear from her, call me."

"I thought she was here in the canyon."

"She was, but right now she's missing and she left a small…package at the house."

IT WAS DARK by the time Liza drove past the Fir Ridge cemetery, climbed up over the Continental Divide and entered Gallatin Canyon.

This time of year there was little traffic along the two-lane road as it snaked through pines and over mountains along the edge of the river.

She kept thinking about what Brick Savage had told her. More to the point, the feeling she'd had when she'd left him. He'd challenged her to prove Tanner Cole had been murdered. No doubt because he knew it would be near impossible.

And yet if she was right and Alex's murder had something to do with Tanner's death, then the killer had shown his hand.

Pulling out her phone, she tried Hud's cell. In a lot of spots in the canyon there was no mobile phone service. To her surprise it began to ring.

"Marshal Savage," he snapped.

"Sorry, did I catch you at a bad time?" she asked through the hands-free speaker, wondering if he was in the middle of something with the kids.

"Liza. Good. I'm glad you called. Did you get my message?"

She hadn't. Fear gripped her. Surely there hadn't been another murder. Her thoughts instantly raced to Jordan and she felt her heart fall at the thought that he might—

"It's Stacy," he said. "She left the house earlier. No one has seen her since. She hasn't called. I've looked all over Big Sky. She left the baby at the house."

"What?" It took her moment to pull back from the thought of another murder. To pull back from the fear and dread that had had her thinking something had happened to Jordan. "Stacy wouldn't leave her baby, would she?"

"Knowing Stacy, I have a bad feeling the baby isn't even hers."

Liza was too shocked to speak for a moment. "You think she…stole it?"

"Something is wrong. I've suspected it from the get-go. Dana was hoping I was just being suspicious because it's my nature, but I'd been worried that something like this would happen. I didn't want Dana getting attached to that baby, but you know Dana, and Ella is adorable, if that is even her name."

"Oh, boss, I'm so sorry."

"So you spoke to my father?" Hud asked.

"He was the investigating officer at Tanner Cole's suicide."

"What did he tell you?"

"That it was Tanner's rope."

Hud let out a humorless laugh. "That sounds like Brick. Have you met him before?"

"Never had the honor. He must have been a treat as a father."

"You could say that." He sighed. "Look, Hilde's at the house. I'm going to make another circle through the area to look for Stacy before I go home."

"I'm about twenty minutes out. Do you want me to stop by?"

"If you don't mind. I know you're busy with this murder case…"

"No problem. I'll see you soon." She snapped the

phone shut, shocked by what he'd told her. She was so deep in thought that she hadn't noticed the lights of another vehicle coming up behind her.

She glanced in the mirror. One of the headlights was out on the approaching car. That struck her about the same time as she realized the driver was coming up too fast.

She'd been going the speed limit. By now the driver of the vehicle behind her would have been able to see the light bar on the top of her SUV. Only a fool would come racing up on a Marshal's Department patrol car— let alone pass it.

And yet as she watched, the driver of what appeared to be an old pickup swerved around her and roared up beside her.

Liza hit her lights and siren, thinking the driver must be drunk. She glanced over, saw only a dark figure behind the wheel wearing a black ski mask. Her heart jumped, but she didn't have time to react before the driver swerved into her. She heard the crunch of metal, felt the patrol SUV veer toward the ditch and the pines and beyond that, the river.

She slammed on the brakes, but was traveling too fast to avoid the truck crashing into her again. The force made the vehicle rock wildly as she fought to keep control. The tires screamed on the pavement as the SUV began to fishtail.

Liza felt the right side of the vehicle dip into the soft shoulder of the highway, pulling the SUV off the road. She couldn't hold it and felt her tires leave the pavement. A stand of trees blurred past and then there was nothing but darkness as she plunged over the edge of the road toward the dark green of the river.

Chapter Twelve

Hud was headed home when he heard the 911 call for an ambulance come over his radio. His heart began to race as he heard that the vehicle in the river was a Montana marshal's patrol SUV.

He threw on his siren and lights and took off up the canyon toward West Yellowstone. As he raced toward the accident, he called home, glad when Hilde answered the phone.

"Tell Dana I'm running a little late," he said to Hilde. "Don't act like anything is wrong." He heard Dana already asking what was going on. Hilde related the running a little late part.

"We're just fine," Hilde said.

"It sounds like there's been an accident up the canyon," he told her. "It's Liza. I don't know anything except that her car is in the river. I don't know how long I'm going to be."

"Don't worry about us."

"Is it my sister?" Dana demanded in the background.

"I heard that. Tell her I haven't found Stacy. I'll call when I have news. I just don't want Dana upset."

"Got it. I'll tell her."

He disconnected and increased his speed. Liza was

like family. How the hell did she end up in the river? She was a great driver.

As he came around a bend in the windy road, he saw her patrol SUV among the boulders in the Gallatin River. Some bypassers had stopped. Several of the men had flashlights and one of them had waded out to the patrol vehicle.

Hud parked, leaving his lights on to warn any oncoming traffic, then grabbing his own flashlight, jumped out and ran toward the river. As he dropped over the edge of the road to it, he recognized the man who was standing on the boulder beside Liza's wrecked vehicle.

"Jordan?" he called.

"Liza's conscious," he called back. "An ambulance is on the way. I'm staying with her until it gets here."

Hud would have liked to have gone to her as well, but he heard the sound of the ambulance siren and climbed back up the road to help with traffic control.

All the time, though, he found himself wondering how Jordan just happened to be on the scene.

"WHAT'S HAPPENED?" DANA demanded the moment Hilde hung up. "Don't," she said before Hilde could open her mouth. "You're a terrible liar and we both know it. Tell me."

"He hasn't found your sister."

She nodded. "But something else has happened."

"There's been an accident up the canyon. He needed to run up there."

Dana waited. "There's more."

"You're the one who should have gone into law enforcement, the interrogation part," Hilde said as she came and sat down on the edge of the bed. On the other side of Dana, baby Ella slept, looking like an angel. Hilde glanced at the baby, then took Dana's hand as if she knew it was only a matter of time before her friend got the truth out of her. "Hud didn't know anything about the accident except that Liza is somehow involved."

"Oh, no." Her heart dropped.

"Now don't get upset and have these babies because Hud will never forgive me," Hilde said quickly.

Dana shook her head. "I'm okay. But I want to know the minute you hear something. Are you sure you can stay?"

"Of course."

"You didn't have a date?"

Hilde laughed. "If only there were more Hudson Savages around. All of the men I meet, well…they're so not the kind of men I want to spend time with, even for the time it takes to have dinner."

"I *am* lucky." Dana looked over at Ella. "What if Hud is right and Ella isn't Stacy's baby?"

"Where would she have gotten Ella? You can't just get a baby off eBay."

"She could have *kidnapped* Ella. You know Stacy."

"I'm sure Hud checked for any kidnapped babies six months old with dimples, blond hair and green eyes," Hilde argued.

"Yes, green eyes. You might have noticed that all the Justices have dark brown eyes and dark hair, including Stacy."

"Maybe the father has green eyes and Stacy carries a green-eyed gene. You don't know that Ella isn't Stacy's."

"No," Dana admitted, but like Hud, she'd had a bad feeling since the moment Stacy had arrived. "I think

Stacy only came here because she's in trouble and it has something to do with that poor little baby."

"You think that's why she left Ella with you?"

Dana fingered the quilt edge where someone had stitched the name Katie. "I wish I knew."

JORDAN WOKE WITH a crick in his neck. He stared down at the green hospital scrubs he was wearing for a moment, confused where he was. It came back to him with a start. Last night his clothes had been soaking wet from his swim in the river. He'd been shivering uncontrollably, but had refused to leave the hospital until he knew Liza was going to be all right.

That's how he'd ended up in scrubs, he recalled now as he sat up in the chair beside Liza's bed and smiled at the woman propped up staring at him now.

"What are you still doing here?" she asked, smiling.

"I *was* sleeping." He stood up, stretched, then looked to see what she was having for breakfast. "You haven't eaten much," he said as he took a piece of toast from the nearly untouched tray.

"I'm not very hungry."

He was famished and realized he hadn't eaten since yesterday at noon. "How are your ribs?" he asked as he devoured the piece of toast.

"They're just bruised and only hurt when I breathe."

"Yep, but you're breathing. Be thankful for that."

Liza nodded and he saw that her left wrist was also wrapped. Apparently, it was just badly sprained, not broken. His big worry, though, had been that she'd suffered internal injuries.

Apparently not, though, since all she had was a bandage on her right temple, a bruised cheek and a scrape on her left cheek. She'd been lucky.

"So what did the doctor say?" he asked.

"That I'm going to live."

"Good."

She looked almost shy. "Thank you for last night."

He shrugged. "It wasn't anything. I just swam a raging river in October in Montana and clung onto a slippery boulder to be with you." He grinned. "I'm just glad you're all right." He'd been forced to leave the room last night while Hud had talked to her, but he'd overheard enough to more than concern him.

"You said last night that someone forced you off the road?" he asked now. "Do you remember anything about the vehicle?"

She narrowed her gaze at him and sighed. "Even if I knew who did it, I wouldn't tell you. I don't want to see you get killed."

He grinned. "Nice that you care—"

"I told you, I don't have time to find your killer, too."

"Why would anyone want to kill me? On second thought, scratch that. Other than my brother-in-law, why would anyone want me dead?"

"Hud doesn't want you dead."

"He just doesn't want me near my sister."

"Can you blame him?"

"No," he said with a sigh. "That's what makes it worse. I would be the same way if someone had treated my wife the way I've treated my sister." He looked away.

"Do you mean that?"

He grinned. "Do you question everything I tell you?"

"Yes."

He laughed and shook his head. "I've been more

honest with you than I have with anyone in a very long time. Hud doesn't want me near you, either." He met her gaze and saw something warm flash in her eyes.

"I talked to the investigating officer in Tanner's death yesterday before the accident," she said, clearly changing the subject. "He cleared you as a suspect, at least in Tanner's death."

"Did Brick Savage tell you what I did the day I found Tanner?"

"I would assume you were upset since it was your best friend."

"I broke down and bawled like a baby until Hud's old man kicked me in the behind and told me to act like a man. He said I was making myself look guilty as hell." He chuckled. "I took a swing at him and he decked me. Knocked me on my butt, but I got control of myself after that and he didn't arrest me for assaulting an officer of the law so I guess I respect him for that."

Liza shook her head. "Men. You are such a strange breed. I think it would have been stranger if you hadn't reacted the way you had."

He shrugged. "Tanner left a hole in my life. I've never had a closer friend since. Sometimes I swear I can hear his voice, especially when I do something stupid."

She smiled. "So he's still with you a lot."

"Yeah. You do know that when I say I hear him, I don't really *hear* him, right?"

"I get it."

"I didn't want you to think I hear voices. It's bad enough you still see me as a suspect."

She nodded slowly. "I mean what I said about wanting you to be safe. You need to keep a low profile."

"How can I do that when I have a reunion picnic to go to this afternoon?"

"You aren't seriously planning to go?"

"What? You don't think I can get another date?" he joked.

"What do I have to do to make you realize how dangerous this is?"

His expression sobered. "All I have to do is look at your face and think about where I found you last night."

"You could be next," she said quietly. "What time is the picnic?"

"The doctor isn't going to let you—"

"What time?" she demanded.

"One."

"I'll be there."

He grinned. "Good, I won't have to find another date." He wanted to argue that she needed to stay in bed. He couldn't stand the thought that she was now a target. Last night when he'd seen her car in the river— Just the thought made it hard for him to breathe even now.

He barely remembered throwing on the rental car's brakes, diving out and half falling down the bank to the river. All he could think about was getting to her. The moment he'd hit the icy water of the Gallatin, he'd almost been swept away. He'd had to swim to get to her, then climb onto a large slick boulder to reach the driver's-side door.

At first he'd thought she was dead. There was blood from the cut on her temple.

Impulsively, he reached for her hand now. It felt warm and soft and wonderfully alive. He squeezed her hand gently, then let it go.

"Unless you need a ride, I guess I'll see you at one on the mountain then," he said and turned to leave.

"Liza isn't going anywhere, especially with you," Hud snapped as he stepped into the hospital room. "I'll speak to *you* in the hall," he said to Jordan.

Liza shot him a questioning look. Jordan shrugged. He had no idea why his brother-in-law was angry with him but he was about to find out.

"Later," he said to Liza and stepped out in the hall to join Hud.

The marshal had blood in his eye by the time Jordan stepped out into the hall. "What were you doing at the accident last night? Were you following Liza?"

He held up his hands. "One question at a time. I had tried to call her. I knew she'd gone up to West Yellowstone to talk to your father. I got tired of waiting for her to return and drove up the canyon. I was worried about her."

"Worried about her?" Hud sighed. "And you just happened to find her?"

"The other driver who stopped can verify it."

"Did you pass another vehicle coming from the direction of the accident?"

"Several. A white van. A semi. An old red pickup."

"The red pickup. Did you happen to notice the driver?"

He shook his head. "I just glanced at the vehicles. I wasn't paying a lot of attention since I was looking for Liza's patrol SUV. You think the truck ran her off the road."

Hud didn't look happy to hear that Jordan knew about that. He ignored the statement and asked, "Where is Liza going to meet you later?"

"At the reunion picnic up on the mountain."

"Well, she's not going anywhere." Hud started to turn away, but swung back around and put a finger in Jordan's face. "I want you to stay away from her. I'm not sure what your game is—"

"There's *no* game. No angle. Liza is investigating Alex Winslow's murder. I've been helping her because I know the players and I think it is somehow tied in with Tanner's death."

"That better be all there is to it," Hud said and started to turn away again.

"What if that isn't all it is?" Jordan demanded, then could have kicked himself.

Hud turned slowly back to him. "Like I said, stay away from Liza." With that, he turned and pushed into his deputy's room.

"Tell me you weren't out in the hall threatening the man who saved me last night," Jordan heard Liza say, but didn't catch Hud's reply, which was just as well.

He collected his clothes at the nurse's station, changed and headed for the canyon and Big Sky. Now more than ever he wanted to get to the bottom of this. Someone had tried to kill Liza. He didn't doubt they would try again.

But what were they so afraid she was going to find out? He suddenly recalled something he'd overheard Hud say to his deputy marshal last night at the hospital. Something about her condo being ransacked. Someone thought she had something. The alleged photographs?

LIZA COCKED HER HEAD at her boss as he came around the end of her bed. "Well?" she asked.

He gave her a sheepish look. "You don't know Jordan like I do. He's…he's…"

"He's changed."

Hud shook his head. "I really doubt that he's changed any more than his sister Stacy."

"Talk about painting them all with the same brush," she said.

"Look, I don't want you getting involved with him."

Liza grinned. "I'm sorry, I must have misheard you. You weren't telling me who I can get involved with, were you, boss?"

"Damn it, Liza. You know how I feel about you."

She nodded. "I'm the most stubborn deputy you've ever had. I often take things in my own hands without any thought to my safety. I'm impulsive, emotional and driven and I'm too smart for my own good. Does that about cover it?"

"You're the best law officer I've ever worked with," Hud said seriously. "And a friend. And like a real sister to my wife. I just don't want to see you get hurt."

She smiled. "I can also take care of myself. And," she said before he could interrupt, "I can get involved with anyone I want."

He looked at his boots before looking at her again. "You're right."

"That's what I thought. Did you bring the information I asked for?" she asked, pointing to the manila envelope in his hand and no longer wanting to discuss Jordan.

Truthfully she didn't know how she felt about him— waking up to see him sleeping beside her hospital bed or being in his arms the other night on the dance floor.

"I brought it," Hud said with a sigh. "But I don't think you should be worrying about any of this right now. How are you feeling?"

"Fine," Liza said, reaching for the manila envelope and quickly opening it.

"There are Alex's phone calls over the past month as well as where he went after arriving at Big Sky."

Liza was busy leafing through it, more determined than ever to find out who'd killed him—and who'd tried to do the same to her the night before.

"Alex was in the middle of a contentious divorce?" she asked, looking up in surprise from the information he'd brought her. "He had a *wife?*" When she'd notified next of kin, she'd called his brother as per the card in his wallet.

"Her name is Crystal."

"A classmate?"

Hud nodded. "But not from Big Sky. She lived down in Bozeman."

"What was holding up the divorce?" Liza asked.

He shook his head and had to take a step back from the bed as Liza swung her legs over the side and stood up. *"What are you doing?"*

"I'm getting up. I told you, I'm fine. Just a little knock on the head and a few cuts and bruises and a sprained wrist, but it's my left wrist, so I'm fine. All I need is a vehicle."

He shook his head. "I can't allow—"

"You can't stop me. Someone tried to *kill* me. This has become personal. Not only that, you need to stay close to home," she said as she rummaged in the closet for her clothes. "No sign of Stacy yet?" He shook his head. "What about the baby?"

"The lab's running a DNA test. We should be able to tell if the baby is Stacy's by comparing Ella's DNA to Dana's. Liza, you're really not up to—"

"Could you see about my clothes?" she asked, realizing they weren't anywhere in the room. Her clothes had been wet and the nurses had probably taken them to dry them. "Stubborn, remember? One of the reasons I'm such a good law officer, your words not mine." She smiled widely although it hurt her face.

He studied her for a moment. "Clothes, right. Then get you a vehicle," he said, clearly giving up on trying to keep another woman in bed.

DANA WATCHED HILDE TRYING to change Ella's diaper until she couldn't take it anymore. "Give me that baby."

Hilde laughed. "You make it look so easy," she said, handing Ella to her.

Ella giggled and squirmed as Dana made short work of getting her into a diaper and a sleeper. Hud had come in so late, Hilde had stayed overnight and gotten someone to work for her this morning. He'd promised to be back soon.

"I'm just so glad Liza is all right," she said as she handed Ella back to Hilde. Through the open bedroom door she could see Mary and Hank playing with a plastic toy ranch set. She could hear them discussing whether or not they should buy more cows.

"Me, too," Hilde said. "Fortunately, Liza is strong."

"Hud's worried now that she and Jordan might be getting involved."

Hilde arched an eyebrow. "Really?"

"I have to admit when Jordan stopped by, he did seem different. But then again I said Stacy had changed, so what do I know? I can't believe we haven't heard anything from her. What if she never comes back?" Dana hadn't let herself think about that at first, but as the hours passed… "Did she leave anything else besides Ella and the baby's things?"

"I can check. She was staying in the room I slept in last night, right?"

"I would imagine Hud already checked it, but would you look? That should tell us if she was planning to leave the baby all along or if something happened and she can't get back."

Hilde jiggled Ella in her arms. "Watch her for a moment and I'll go take a look." She put the baby down next to Dana on the bed. Ella immediately got up on her hands and knees and rocked back and forth.

"She is going to be crawling in no time," Dana said with a smile. Stacy was going to miss it. But then maybe Stacy had missed most of Ella's firsts because this wasn't her baby.

Hilde returned a few minutes later.

"You found something," Dana said, excited and worried at the same time.

"You said she didn't have much, right?" Hilde asked. "Well, she left a small duffle on the other side of the bed. Not much in it. A couple of T-shirts, underwear, socks. I searched through it." She shook her head. "Then I noticed a jean jacket hanging on the back of the chair by the window. It's not yours, is it?"

"That's the one Stacy was wearing when she arrived."

"I found this in the pocket."

Dana let out a surprised groan as Hilde, using two fingers, pulled out a small caliber handgun.

ALEX WINSLOW'S WIFE, CRYSTAL, lived up on the hill overlooking Bozeman on what some called Snob Knob.

In the old days it had been called Beer Can Hill because that was where the kids used to go to drink and make out.

The house was pretty much what Liza had expected. It was huge. A contentious divorce usually meant one of three things. That the couple was fighting over the kids, the pets or the money. Since Alex and Crystal apparently had no children or pets, Liza guessed it was the money.

She parked the rental SUV Hud'd had delivered to the hospital and walked up to the massive front door. As she rang the bell, she could hear music playing inside. She rang the bell a second time before the door was opened by a petite dark-haired woman with wide blue eyes and a quizzical smile.

"Yes?" she asked.

Liza had forgotten her bandages, the eye that was turning black or that all the blood hadn't completely come out of her uniform shirt.

She'd felt there wasn't time to go all the way back to Big Sky to change. Her fear was that if she didn't solve this case soon, someone else was going to die.

"Crystal Winslow? I'm Deputy Marshal Liza Turner. I need to ask you a few questions in regard to your husband's death."

"*Estranged* husband," Crystal Winslow said, but opened the door wider. "I doubt I can be of help, but you're welcome to come in. Can I get you something?" She took in Liza's face again.

"Just answers."

Crystal led her into the formal living room. It had a great view of the city and valley beyond. In the distance, the Spanish Peaks gleamed from the last snow-fall high in the mountains.

"How long have you and Alex been estranged?"

"I don't see what that has to do—"

"Your *estranged* husband is dead. I believe whoever murdered him tried to do the same to me last night. I need to know why."

"Well, it has nothing to do with me." She sniffed, then said, "A month."

"Why?"

For a moment Crystal looked confused. "Why did I kick him out and demand a divorce? You work out of Big Sky, right? I would suggest you ask Shelby."

"Shelby Durran-Iverson?"

She nodded, and for the first time Liza saw true pain in the woman's expression—and fury. "I knew he was cheating. A woman can tell. But *Shelby?* I remember her from high school. People used to say she was the type who would eat her young."

"That could explain why she doesn't have any children," Liza said. She still felt a little lightheaded and knew this probably wasn't the best time to be interviewing anyone.

"Did Alex admit he was seeing Shelby?"

Crystal gave her an are-you-serious? look. "He swore up and down that his talking to her wasn't an affair, that he was trying to get her to tell the truth, something involving Tanner Cole."

"You remember Tanner?"

"He hung himself our senior year. I didn't really know him. He was a cowboy. I didn't date cowboys. No offense."

Liza wondered why that should offend her. Did she look that much like a cowgirl?

"I think your husband might have been telling you the truth. I believe he was looking into Tanner's death."

"Why would he do that?"

"I was hoping you could tell me since I suspect that's what got him killed."

"You don't know for sure that he wasn't having an affair with Shelby though, right?"

"No, I don't. But Alex mentioned to other people that he felt something was wrong about Tanner's suicide, as well. He didn't say anything to you?"

"No."

"Do you or your husband own any weapons?"

Crystal looked appalled. "You mean like a Saturday night special?"

"Or hunting rifles."

"No, I wouldn't have a gun in my house. My father was killed in a hunting accident. We have a state-of-the-art security system. We didn't need *guns.*"

Liza nodded, knowing what that would get Crystal if someone broke into the house. She could be dead before the police arrived. "Alex didn't have weapons, either?"

"No. I still can't believe this was why Alex was spending time with Shelby."

"Did she ever call here?"

Crystal mugged a face. "Shelby said it was just to talk to Alex about Big Sky's reunion plans. They wanted their own. Ours wasn't good enough for them."

Liza could see that Crystal Winslow had been weighted down with that chip on her shoulder for some time.

"But I overheard one of his conversations," she said

smugly. "Shelby was demanding something back, apparently something she'd given him. He saw me and said he didn't know what she was talking about. After he hung up, he said Shelby was looking for some photographs from their senior year. He said she was probably using them for something she was doing for the reunion."

"You didn't believe him?"

"I could hear Shelby screeching from where I was standing. She was livid about whatever it really was."

"Did he send her some photos from high school?"

"I told you, that was just a story he came up with. He had some photographs from high school. I kept the ones of me and gave him the rest."

"Where are those photos now?"

"I threw them out with Alex. I assume he took them to his apartment," she said.

"Do you have a key?"

"He left one with me, but I've never used it." She got up and walked out of the room, returning a moment later with a shiny new key and a piece of notepaper. "Here's the address."

Liza took it. "Was that the only Big Sky friend who contacted Alex?"

"Right after that was when Alex started driving up to Big Sky and I threw him out."

"What made you suspect he was seeing Shelby?" Liza asked.

For a moment, Crystal looked confused. "I told you—"

"Right, that a woman knows. But how did you know it was *Shelby?*"

"After Tanner broke up with her in high school, she made a play for Alex. He was dating Tessa Ryerson before that. The two of them got into it at school one day. That's when he and I started dating."

"Did he tell you what his argument with Shelby was about?"

She shrugged. "Eventually everyone has a falling-out with Shelby—except for her BFFs." She made a face, then listed off their names like a mantra. "Shelby, Tessa, Ashley, Whitney and Brittany."

Liza noted that Brittany was on the list. "When did Alex and Shelby have the falling-out?"

Crystal frowned. "It was around the time that Tanner committed suicide. After that Alex hadn't wanted anything to do with her. That is until recently."

Liza could tell that Crystal was having second thoughts about accusing her husband of infidelity.

"You said your father was killed in a hunting accident. Did you hunt?"

"No. Alex did and so did his friends," she said distractedly.

"What about Shelby?"

"She actually was a decent shot, I guess, although I suspected the only reason she and her friends hunted was to be where the boys were." Her expression turned to one of horror. "You don't think Shelby killed Alex, do you?"

Chapter Thirteen

Dana stared at the sleeping Ella as her husband updated her on Liza's condition. She'd had a scare, but she was going to be fine. In fact, she'd already checked herself out of the hospital and was working.

"You didn't try to stop her?" Dana demanded of her husband.

He gave her a look she knew too well.

"All right, what did you find out about Stacy?" she asked and braced herself for the worst.

"There is really nothing odd about her having Clay's car," she said when he finished filling her in. "Obviously they've been in contact."

"It wouldn't be odd if Clay had been cashing his checks for the last six months," Hud said. "Why would he be driving an old beater car if he had money?"

"Maybe it was a spare car he let Stacy have," she suggested.

Hud rolled his eyes. "It is the only car registered to your brother. Nice theory." He instantly seemed to regret his words. "I'm sorry. I'm not telling you these things to upset you. On the contrary, I know you'll worry more if I keep them from you."

"Which proves you're smarter than you look," she

said, annoyed that he was treating her as if she was breakable. "The babies are fine. I'm fine. You'd better not keep anything from me."

He smiled. "As I said…"

"So you can't find Clay or Stacy."

"No. But I've put an APB out on Stacy's car. It was the only thing I could do."

"Something's happened to her," Dana said. "She wouldn't leave Ella." When Hud said nothing, she shot him an impatient look. "You saw how she was with that baby. She loves her."

"Dana, we haven't seen your sister in six years. She doesn't write or call when she gets pregnant. She just shows up at the door with a baby, which she then leaves with us. Come on, even you have to admit, something is wrong with this."

She didn't want to admit it. Maybe more than anything, she didn't want to acknowledge that Stacy could have done something unforgiveable this time. Something that might land her in prison.

"What do we do now?" she asked her husband.

"I've held off going global with Ella's description, hoping Stacy would show back up. But Dana, I don't think I have any choice."

"You haven't heard anything on the DNA test you did on Ella and me?"

"I should be hearing at any time. But if the two of you aren't related, then I have to try to find out who this baby belongs to—no matter what happens to Stacy."

LIZA DROVE TO the apartment address Crystal Winslow had given her. She used the key to get into the studio apartment. As the door swung open, she caught her breath and pulled her weapon.

The apartment had been torn apart. Every conceivable hiding place had been searched, pillows and sofa bed sliced open, their stuffing spread across the room, books tossed to the floor along with clothing from the closet.

Liza listened, then cautiously stepped in. A small box of photographs had been dumped onto the floor and gone through from the looks of them. She checked the tiny kitchen and bath to make sure whoever had done this was gone before she holstered her weapon and squatted down to gingerly pick up one of the photographs.

It was a snapshot of Jordan Cardwell with two other handsome boys. All three were wearing ski clothing and looking cocky. She recognized a young Alex Winslow and assumed the other boy must be Tanner.

A curtain flapped loudly at an open window, making her start. Carefully, she glanced through the other photographs, assuming whatever the intruder had been looking for wasn't among these strewn on the floor.

It took her a moment though to realize what was missing from the pile of photos. There were none of Crystal. Nor any of Shelby or the rest of her group. That seemed odd that the women Alex had apparently been close to were missing from the old photographs. Nor were there any wedding pictures. Crystal had said she'd taken the ones of her. But who would have taken ones of Shelby and the rest of the young women he'd gone to school with in the canyon?

Rising, Liza called it in to the Bozeman Police Department, then waited until a uniformed officer arrived.

"I doubt you'll find any fingerprints, but given that Alex Winslow is a murder victim and he hasn't lived here long, I'm hoping whoever did this left us a clue," she told the officer. "I've contacted the crime lab in

Missoula. I just want to make sure no one else comes in here until they arrive."

As she was leaving, Liza saw an SUV cruise slowly by. She recognized Crystal Winslow behind the wheel before the woman sped off.

JORDAN HAD JUST reached the bottom of the gondola for the ride up the mountain to the reunion picnic, when he spotted Liza.

She wasn't moving with her usual speed, but there was a determined look in her eye that made him smile.

"What?" she said when she joined him.

"You. After what happened, you could have taken one day off."

"I'm going to a picnic," she said. "I'm not even wearing my uniform."

She looked great out of uniform. The turquoise top she wore had slits at the shoulders, the silky fabric exposing tanned, muscled arms as it moved in the breeze. She wore khaki capris and sandals. Her long ebony-dark hair had been pulled up in back with a clip so the ends cascaded down her back. For as banged up as she was, she looked beautiful.

"I'm betting though that you're carrying a gun," he said, eyeing the leather shoulder bag hanging off one shoulder.

"You better hope I am." She laughed, but stopped quickly as if she was still light-headed.

"Are you sure you're all right?" he whispered, stepping closer.

"Dandy."

Past her, he saw Whitney and Ashley. Neither looked in a celebratory mood. When they spotted the deputy marshal, they jumped apart as if talking to each other would make them look more guilty.

"This could be a fun picnic," he said under his breath.

A few moments later Brittany arrived with her husband and small brood. Jordan was taken back again at how happy and content she looked.

I want that, he thought as his gaze shifted to Liza.

As their gondola came around, they climbed in and made room for Whitney and Ashley, who'd come up behind them. Both women, though, motioned that they would take the next one.

"I'd love to know what they're hiding," Jordan said as he sat across from the deputy marshal. The gondola door closed then rocked as it began its ascent up the mountain. He had a view of the resort and the peaks from where he sat. And a view of Liza.

He could also see the gondola below them and the two women inside. They had their heads together. He wondered at the power Shelby still held over these women she'd lorded over in high school. Did anyone ever really get over high school?

"There's something I need to ask you," Liza said, drawing his attention back to her, which was no hardship. "How was it that you were the first person on the scene last night?"

He smiled, knowing that Hud was behind this. "I got worried about you and I wanted to see you. I drove up the canyon thinking I could talk you into having dinner with me. Another car had stopped before I got there. I was just the first to go into the river." He hated that she was suspicious of him, but then again he couldn't really blame her.

"Did you see the pickup that forced me off the road?"

He nodded. "But it was just an old pickup. I was looking for your patrol SUV so I really didn't pay any attention."

She nodded. "I'd already told you I wasn't having dinner with you."

He grinned. "I thought I could charm you into changing your mind." He hurried on before she could speak. "I know you already told me no, but I thought we could at least pick up something and take it back to my cabin or your condo."

"You just don't give up, do you?"

"Kind of like someone else I know," he said and smiled at her. "I didn't have any ulterior motives. I've given this a lot of thought. Somehow, I think it all goes back to that party Tanner had at the cabin that night and the vandalism."

"And the photographs?" she asked.

He nodded. "I wish I'd stayed around long enough that night to tell you who took them."

They were almost to the top of the gondola ride. Off to his left, he saw where the caterers had set up the food for the picnic.

The gondola rocked as it came to a stop and the door opened. Jordan quickly held the doors open while the deputy marshal climbed out, then he followed, recalling what he could of that night, which wasn't much.

LIZA HOPED THE PICNIC wouldn't be quite as bad as the dinner had been. Jordan got them a spot near Shelby and the gang on one of the portable picnic tables that had been brought up the mountain.

"*Whatever* happened to you?" Shelby exclaimed loud enough for everyone to hear when she saw Liza.

While everyone in the canyon would have heard about her accident, Liza smiled and said, "Tripped. Sometimes I am so clumsy."

Shelby laughed. "You really should be more careful." Then she went back to holding court at her table. The usual suspects were in attendance and Tessa had been allowed to join in.

Liza watched out of the corner of her eye. Shelby monopolized the conversation with overly cheerful banter. But it was as if a pall had fallen over her group that not even she could lift.

After they ate, some of the picnickers played games in the open area next to the ski lift. When Liza spotted Tessa heading for the portable toilets set up in the trees, she excused herself and followed.

Music drifted on the breeze. A cloudless blue sky hung over Lone Peak. It really was the perfect day for a picnic and she said as much to Tessa when she caught up with her.

"Deputy," Tessa said.

"Why don't you call me Liza."

The woman smiled. "So I forget that I'm talking to the *law?*"

"I'm here as Jordan Cardwell's date."

Tessa chuckled at that, then sobered. "What happened to you?"

"Someone tried to stop me from looking into Alex's and Tanner's deaths."

The woman let out a groan.

"I was hoping you would have contacted me to talk," Liza said. "I can see you're troubled."

"Troubled?" Tessa laughed as she glanced back toward the group gathered below them on the mountain.

Liza followed her gaze and saw Shelby watching them. "We should step around the other side."

Tessa didn't argue. As they moved out of Shelby's sight, Tessa stopped abruptly and reached into her shoulder bag. "Here," she said, thrusting an envelope at the deputy marshal. "Alex left it with me and told me not to show it to anyone. He said to just keep it and not look inside until I had to."

Liza saw that it was sealed. "You didn't look?"

Tessa shook her head quickly.

"What did he mean, 'until you had to'?"

"I have no idea. I don't know what's in there and I don't care. If anyone even found out I had it…"

"Why did he trust *you* with this?" Liza had to ask.

Tessa looked as if she wasn't going to answer, then seemed to figure there was no reason to lie anymore. "I was in love with him. I have been since high school. Shelby always told me he wasn't good enough for me." She began to cry, but quickly wiped her eyes at the sound of someone moving through the dried grass on the other side of the portable toilets.

Liza hurriedly stuffed the envelope into her own shoulder bag.

An instant later Shelby came around the end of the stalls. "Are they all occupied?" she asked, taking in the two of them, then glancing toward the restrooms.

"I just used that one," Liza improvised. She turned and started back down the hillside.

Behind her she heard Shelby ask Tessa, "What did she want?"

She didn't hear Tessa's answer, but she feared Shelby wouldn't believe anything her friend said anyway. Tessa was running scared and anyone could see it—especially Shelby, who had her own reasons for being afraid.

Liza thought about the manila envelope Alex had left in Tessa's safekeeping. What was inside it? The photographs that Shelby had been trying to get her hands on? Liza couldn't wait to find out.

HUD HAD PUT a rush on Ella's relational DNA test. He'd done it for Dana's sake. He saw that by the hour she was getting more attached to that baby. If he was right and Stacy had kidnapped it, then Dana's heart was going to be broken.

He was as anxious as she was to get the results. Meanwhile he needed to search for Stacy as he continued to watch for possible kidnappings on the law enforcement networks.

So far, he'd come up with nothing.

He found himself worrying not only about Stacy's disappearance, but also everything else that was going on. He'd done his best to stay out of Liza's hair. She could handle the murder case without him, he kept telling himself. Still, he'd been glad when Hilde had called and said she could come stay with Dana if he needed her to.

His phone rang as he paced in the living room. He'd never been good at waiting. He saw on caller ID that it was Shelby Durran-Iverson.

"Marshal Savage," he answered and listened while Shelby complained about Liza. It seemed she'd seen the deputy kissing Jordan. Hud swore silently. He had warned Liza about Jordan, but clearly she hadn't listened.

"Deputies get to have private lives," he told Shelby.

"Really? Even with the man who was with Alex

when he was murdered? I would think Jordan Cardwell is a suspect. Or at least should be."

It was taking all his self-control to keep from telling Shelby that she was more of a suspect than Jordan was.

"I'll look into it," he said.

"I should hope you'd do more than that. Isn't fraternizing with a suspect a violation that could call for at least a suspension—if not dismissal?"

"I said I would look into it." He hung up just as a car pulled up in front of the house. With a sigh of relief, he started to open the door to greet Hilde when he saw that it wasn't her car. Nor was it Stacy's.

When he saw who climbed out, he let out a curse. Before he could answer the door, his phone rang again. Figuring to get all the bad news over with quickly, he took the call from the lab as he heard footfalls on the porch and a tentative knock at the door.

"Hud, who is that at the door?" Dana called.

He listened to the lab tech give him the news, then thanked him and, disconnecting, stepped to her bedroom doorway.

"What is it?" she demanded. "Was that the lab on the phone?"

He nodded. "Ella *is* your niece."

Dana began to cry and laugh at the same time as she looked into Ella's beautiful face.

There was another knock at the door.

"Is that Stacy?" she asked, looking up, her eyes full of hope.

He shook his head. "I wish," he said and went to answer the door.

Chapter Fourteen

"Clay?" Dana said as her younger brother appeared in the bedroom doorway, Jordan at his heels.

"Hi," he said shyly. Clay had always been the quiet one, the one who ducked for cover when the rest of them were fighting. "Jordan told me you're pregnant with twins. Congratulations."

"Jordan?" she asked, shooting a look at her older brother. "Clay, what are you doing here?"

"I called Clay at the studio where I knew he was working," Jordan said.

"The studio let me use the company plane, so here I am," Clay said.

"Tell me what is going on. Why haven't you cashed your checks for the past six months and why does Stacy have your car?"

"Easy," Hud said as he stepped into the room. He gave both her brothers a warning look.

She didn't look at her husband. Her gaze was on her younger brother.

"I've been in Europe the past six months, then I changed apartments and forgot to put in a change of address," Clay said. "That's why I haven't cashed my checks. As for the car, I wasn't using it, so I told Stacy she could have it. I'm working for a movie studio in L.A. so I have a studio car that picks me up every morning."

"I'm glad things are going well for you," Dana said. "But you know what's going on with Stacy, don't you?"

"All I know is that she said she needed to get here to the ranch and could she borrow my car," Clay said. "So where is she?"

"That is the question," Hud said next to him. "She seems to have disappeared."

"Well, if you're worried because she has my car, it's no big deal."

"It's not the car that we're worried about," Dana said. "She left her baby here."

"Her *baby?*" Clay said. "Stacy has a baby?"

At the sound of another vehicle, Hud quickly left the room. Dana assumed it would be Hilde, but when he returned, he had Liza with him.

"You've met my brother Clay," Dana said.

Liza nodded. "Looks like you're having a family reunion."

"Doesn't it though," Hud said under his breath.

"Yes, all we need is Stacy," Dana said. "And a larger bedroom." She saw a look pass between the deputy and her husband. "I know that look. What's happened?"

"I just need to talk to the marshal for a few moments," Liza said. "But I'm going to need Jordan." He nodded and stepped out of the room with her and Hud, closing the door behind them.

"I can't stand being in this bed and not knowing what's going on," Dana said.

Clay was looking at the baby lying next to her. "Is that Stacy's?"

"Yes," Dana said with a sigh as Ella stirred awake.

At least Stacy hadn't kidnapped Ella. This little baby was Dana's niece. But where was Stacy? And did whatever Liza needed to talk to Hud and Jordan about have something to do with her sister or the murder?

"I THINK YOU'D better see these photographs," Liza said to Hud the moment the bedroom door closed behind him. "Tessa gave them to me. She said Alex had left them in her safekeeping."

"Alex *trusted* Tessa?" Jordan said. "He had to know how close she was to Shelby."

"Obviously Alex trusted her not to give the photos to Shelby," Hud said and gave Jordan a how-did-you-get-involved-in-this-discussion? look.

"Tessa and Alex had a history," Liza said and told them what Crystal Winslow had told her. "She thought Alex was having an affair with Shelby, but I think it might have been Tessa. The two of them were dating in high school when Shelby broke them up so Tessa could spy on Tanner, right, Jordan?" He nodded and she continued. "That's a bond that Alex and Tessa shared against Shelby. With Tessa's marriage over and Alex's apparently not going well, they reconnected."

Hud looked through the photos then reluctantly handed them to Jordan. "You know the people in the photos?" he asked his brother-in-law.

Jordan nodded. "So someone took photos of the party. This can't be enough to get Alex killed over."

She waited until Jordan had finished going through the photos before she took them back, sorted through them until she found the two she wanted, then produced a magnifying glass from her pocket. "Check this out."

They all moved over to the table as Liza put the large

magnifying glass over the first photograph. "You can clearly see Malcolm Iverson's construction equipment in the background. But look here." She pointed at a spot to the left of one of the large dump trucks.

Jordan let out a surprised, "Whoa. It's Shelby."

Liza moved the magnifying glass to the second photo and both men took a look.

"Shelby vandalized the equipment," Jordan said. He let out a low whistle and looked at Liza. "You can clearly see Shelby dressed in black, dumping sugar into one of the two-ton trucks' gas tanks. If these photographs would have come out back then, she could have gone to jail."

Liza nodded. "Shelby has every reason in the world not to want these photographs to ever see daylight. She's married to the man whose father she bankrupted by vandalizing his construction equipment. The rest is like knocking over dominos. She vandalizes the equipment, Malcolm Iverson blames Harris Lancaster and shoots him, Malcolm goes to prison, then gets out and mysteriously dies in a boating accident."

"She didn't pull this off alone," Jordan said.

"No," Liza agreed. "In these two photos you can see Whitney and Ashley are keeping everyone's attention on them at the campfire," she said as she showed them two other photographs of the girls pretending to strip to whatever music was playing.

"Where was Tessa?" Jordan asked.

"With Tanner in the woods," Liza said and sifted through the photos until she found one of Tanner and Tessa coming out of the woods together.

Jordan let out a low whistle. "Shelby thought of everything."

"She just didn't realize that someone was taking photographs of the party," Liza said.

"I wonder where the negatives are. Alex wasn't dumb enough to trust Tessa completely. So who has the negatives?"

"Jordan has a point," Liza said.

Hud looked at his brother-in-law. "You should have gone into law enforcement."

Jordan smiled. "I'm going to take that as a compliment."

"I'm sure Hud meant it as one," Liza said.

"If Alex had the goods on Shelby and was blackmailing her, then why ask around about photos that were already in his possession? Or hint that Tanner's death wasn't a suicide?" Hud asked.

"Maybe he just wanted to shake up those involved. Or shake them down. What I'd like to know is who took the photos," Jordan said.

She looked over at him. "I just assumed Alex did since he isn't in any of them. Was he at the party that night?"

Jordan shrugged. "He was earlier."

"So these could merely be copies of photographs taken at the party," Hud said. "Which means there could be more than one person shopping the photos. That is what you're getting at, right, Deputy? Blackmail? For the past twenty years?"

Liza shook her head. "At least Alex hasn't been blackmailing Shelby for twenty years that I can find. I got his bank records for the past two years faxed to me. He made his first deposits only four months ago. Nine thousand dollars each month. He must have known that anything over ten thousand dollars would be red flagged by the bank."

"Why wait twenty years if he was going to black-mail Shelby?" Hud asked.

"I suspect that when his wife threw him out—along with all his stuff including some old photographs from high school, he hadn't looked at them in years," Liza said. "When he did, he saw what we're seeing and, since he already had reason to hate Shelby over the Tessa deal, decided to blackmail her."

"And she killed him," Jordan said.

Hud sighed. "Can we prove it?"

"Not yet," Liza said as she sorted through the photographs. "But I overheard Shelby on the phone with a creditor saying the check was in the mail. I asked around. Yogamotion has been having trouble paying its bills the past few months, but Hilde says it is packed for every class and it isn't cheap to join."

"So have you talked to Shelby yet?" Hud asked.

She shook her head. "There's something else you need to see." She pointed to a figure in the shadows of the pines at the edge of the campfire in one of the photographs.

"Stacy?" Hud said after taking the photo from her and using the magnifying glass to bring his sister-in-law's face into focus. He groaned and looked at Jordan.

"She wasn't there when I left," he said, holding up his hands. "It never dawned on me that she might have been at the party. We never went to the same parties or hung with the same crowd, so I have no idea what she was doing there."

"This could explain why Stacy came back to the can-yon," Hud said with a curse.

"Maybe it is just bad timing on her part." Liza tapped the photo. "But Stacy knows who was taking the photographs. She's looking right at the person with the camera."

"Which means she also knew there were photographs taken of the party that night."

"HUD?"

"Dana, what is it?" he cried, hearing something in his wife's voice that scared him. He rushed to the bedroom door to find Clay holding Dana's hand. Ella was crying.

"Can you take Ella? She needs a bottle," Dana said.

He tried to calm down. "That's all?" Then he saw his wife grimace. "What was that?" he demanded as Liza volunteered to take the crying baby and get Ella a bottle. Jordan had moved to the side of Dana's bed.

"A twinge. I've been having them all day," Dana admitted.

"Why didn't you tell me?" he demanded.

"Because I didn't want to worry you." She cringed as she had another one, this one definitely stronger from her reaction.

"I'm calling the doctor," he said and started to turn from the crowded room.

Hud hadn't heard a car drive up let alone anyone else enter the house so he was surprised to turn and see Stacy standing in the doorway of Dana's bedroom.

Maybe more shocking was how bad she looked. Both eyes were black and the blood from a cut on her cheek had dried to a dark red. Her hair was matted to her head on one side with what Hud guessed was also blood.

Dana let out a startled cry when she saw her sister.

"I wasn't completely honest with you," Stacy said in a hoarse voice as she stumbled forward.

That's when Hud saw the man behind her, the one holding the gun.

"Just get the baby," the man ordered Stacy, jabbing her in the back with the barrel of the gun. "Then we won't be troubling you people any further."

Stacy moved toward the bassinet that had been brought in next to Dana's bed. She leaned over it, gripping the sides.

Hud saw the bruises on her neck and noticed the way she was favoring her left side as if her ribs hurt her. He looked at the man in the doorway still holding the gun on Stacy.

"What's this about?" he asked the man, trying to keep his tone calm while his heart was pounding. Dana was in labor. He needed to get her to the hospital. He didn't need whatever trouble Stacy was in right now.

"Didn't Stacy tell you? She made off with my kid."

"She's my baby, too, Virgil," Stacy said, still staring down into the crib.

Hud remembered that the crib was empty because Liza had taken the baby into the kitchen with her to get her a bottle.

"He took Ella away from me," Stacy said, crying.

"Her name isn't *Ella*," Virgil snapped. "I told you I was naming her after my mother. Her name is Katie, you stupid b—"

"He took her from me right after she was born and has been raising her with his girlfriend," Stacy said through her tears. "He would only let me come see her a few times."

"Because you'd make a crappy mother. Letting you

even see her was a mistake," the man spat. "Now get the damned baby and let's go."

Even the thought of this man taking Ella made Hud sick to his stomach. But he couldn't have any gunplay around Dana, especially since his own gun was locked up like it always was when he was home with the kids.

Dana still kept a shotgun by the kitchen back door though, high on the wall where the kids couldn't reach it, but handy for adults. He wondered if Liza had heard Stacy and the man come in, if she had any idea what was going on?

Stacy turned her head, her gaze locking with Hud's, as she pleaded for his help.

"Let me get the baby for you," Hud said and stepped to the bassinet.

LIZA HAD BEEN heating a bottle of formula for Ella when she heard the door open, then close softly. She listened, drawn by the faint sound of footfalls crossing the living room to Dana's door.

She peered around the corner in time to see the man with the gun. Her heart leaped to her throat. She was out of uniform, her weapon was in the car and she had a baby in one arm. She carefully opened the door of the microwave before it could ding and looked at Ella. The baby grinned at her and flapped her arms.

"I'm going to have to put you down. I need you to be really quiet," Liza whispered. She looked around for a place to put the baby and decided the rug in front of the sink was going to have to do. Carefully, she put down the baby. As she was rising, she saw the shotgun hanging high on the wall over the back door.

Knowing Dana, the shotgun would be loaded. All

she could do was pray that it was since she wouldn't have the first idea where to look for shells. She could hear Ella babbling on the rug behind her and trying to snake toward her.

Hurry. She reached up on tiptoes and eased the shotgun off its rack. Trying not to make a sound, she cracked the gun open. Two shells. She dearly loved Dana who knew there was nothing more worthless than an unloaded shotgun.

Ella was watching her expectantly as she crept to the kitchen doorway. She could see the man with the gun, but she could hear voices coming from Dana's bedroom. Normally, she was cool and calm. It was what made her a good cop. But so much was riding on what she did now, she felt the weight of it at heart level.

She had no idea what she would be walking into. No idea who the man was or why he was in this house with a gun. Moving along the edge of the room to keep the old hardwood floor from creaking, she headed for the bedroom doorway.

"Come on, hurry it up. Give me the baby," snapped a male voice she didn't recognize. "We don't have all day."

Liza was next to the doorway. She could see the man holding the gun. He had it pointed at Stacy who was standing next to Hud beside the empty bassinet. Hud had his hands inside the bassinet. He appeared to be rolling up Ella's quilt.

Taking a breath, she let it out slowly, the same way she did at the gun range just before she shot.

Then she moved quickly. She jammed the barrel of the shotgun into the man's side and in a clear, loud voice said, "Drop the gun or I will blow a hole in you the size of Montana."

The man froze for a moment, then slowly turned his head to look at her. When he saw her, he smiled. "Put down the shotgun before you hurt yourself, little lady."

"There's something I wasn't honest with you about either," Stacy said turning from the bassinet. "My brother-in-law is a marshal and that woman holding a shotgun is a deputy. She will kill you if you don't drop your gun."

"But I'll kill you first," he snarled and lifted the gun to take aim.

Liza moved in quickly, slamming the barrel hard into his ribs as Hud threw Stacy to the floor. Her momentum drove the man back and into the wall. She knocked the pistol from his hand, then cold-cocked him with the shotgun. As his eyes rolled back into his head, he slid down the wall to the floor.

Hud already had the man's gun and bent to frisk him, pulling out his wallet. "Dana, are you all right?" he asked over his shoulder. Liza could hear Stacy sobbing.

"I'm fine," Dana said.

The marshal rose. "I'll get my cuffs." He was back an instant later and had the man cuffed. Liza hadn't taken her eyes off their prisoner. She'd seen his hand twitch and knew he was coming around.

"Stacy, Ella is in the kitchen on the floor," Liza said over her shoulder.

"I'm not leaving without my baby," the man screamed at Stacy as she hurried past her and into the kitchen. "I'll kill you next time. I swear, I'm going to kill you."

Hud hauled him to his feet. "You aren't going anywhere but jail. You just threatened to kill my sister-in-law in front of a half dozen witnesses."

"I'll take him in," Liza said. "You take Dana to the hospital. I heard her say her water just broke." As she led him out of the house, Liza began to read him his rights.

Chapter Fifteen

After booking Virgil Browning, Liza was just in time to catch Shelby as she was coming out of Yogamotion. She had a large bag, the handles looped over one shoulder, and seemed to be in a hurry. As Liza had walked past Shelby's SUV, she'd noticed there were suitcases in the back.

"I'm sorry, we're closed, Deputy," Shelby said. "And I'm in a hurry."

"You might want to open back up. Unless you want to discuss why you were being blackmailed at your house with your husband present."

All the color washed from the woman's face. She leaned into the door as if needing it for support. "I don't—"

"Don't bother lying. Alex would have bled you dry since his wife was taking everything in the divorce, right? He needed money and he had you right where he wanted you. *Of course,* you had to kill him."

"I didn't kill Alex." When Liza said nothing, Shelby opened the door to Yogamotion and turned on the light as they both stepped back inside.

Liza saw the sign that had been taped to the door.

Closed Until Further Notice. Shelby was skipping town, sure as the devil.

"I swear I didn't kill him," she said as they went into her office and sat down. "Why would I kill him? I had no idea who was blackmailing me," Shelby cried.

Liza studied her face for a moment, trying to decide if she was telling the truth or lying through her teeth.

"So how was it you made the payment if you didn't know who was blackmailing you?"

"I sent ten thousand dollars in cash to J. Doe, general delivery in Bozeman each month."

"You were that afraid of the truth coming out?" Liza had to ask.

"How can you ask that?" Shelby cried. "It wasn't just the vandalism. Wyatt's father lost his business, went to prison and probably killed himself, all because of what I did." She was crying now, real tears.

"You had to know it would eventually come out."

She shook her head adamantly. "It would destroy my marriage, my reputation, I'd have to leave town. Wyatt has said if he ever found out who did that to his father, he'd kill them."

Liza felt a chill run the length of her spine. "Maybe he's already killed. Didn't he blame Tanner for what happened?"

She quit crying for a moment and wiped at her tears, frowning as she realized what Liza was saying. "Yes, he blamed Tanner, but he wouldn't..." The words died off. "Tanner killed *himself*."

"Did he? Was Wyatt jealous of your relationship with Tanner?" Liza saw the answer in the woman's expression. "Tanner was supposed to be watching the equipment, right?"

"No, Wyatt wouldn't…" She shook her head. "He's had to overcome so much."

"Does he know about the blackmail?"

"No, of course not."

But Liza could see the fear in the woman's eyes. "If he found out that you were being blackmailed and thought it was Alex Winslow behind it, what would your husband do?"

"He couldn't have found out," she said. "If he knew, he would have left me."

Liza thought about that for a moment. "What if you weren't the only one being blackmailed?"

Shelby's head came up. "What?"

"Has your husband been having similar financial problems to yours?" Liza asked.

"It's the economy," Shelby said. "It's not…"

"Because he's been paying a blackmailer just like you have?"

"Why would he do that?" Her eyes widened and Liza saw that, like her, Shelby could think of only one reason her husband might be paying a blackmailer.

"Oh, no, no." She began to wail, a high keening sound. "He wouldn't have hurt Tanner. Not Tanner." She rocked back and forth, hugging her stomach.

"I have to ask you," Liza said. "Were you ever pregnant with Tanner's baby?"

Her wailing didn't stop, but it slowed. She shook her head, before she dropped it into her hands. "I didn't want him to leave Big Sky after graduation. I thought that if he married me I could say I had a miscarriage. Or with luck, I could get pregnant quickly."

"Where is your husband?" Liza asked her.

"He's been out of town, but I expect him back tonight."

"That's why you were leaving. You're afraid your husband has found out."

Shelby didn't have to answer. The terror in her eyes said it all.

"I'd tell you not to leave town," Liza said, "but I'm afraid that advice could get you killed tonight."

Shelby's cell phone rang. She glanced at it. "I need to take this."

As Liza was walking away, she heard Shelby say, "I'm so sorry." She was crying, her last words garbled but still intelligible. "Really? Just give me a few minutes."

AFTER LEAVING THE RANCH, Jordan drove around aimlessly. His mind whirled with everything that had happened since his return to the canyon.

Foremost was Alex and Liza's blackmail theory. Alex had always resented the rich people who came and went at Big Sky—but especially those who built the huge houses they lived in only a few weeks each year.

So had Alex blackmailed Shelby for the money? Or for breaking him and Tessa up all those years ago?

But was that what had gotten him killed? As much as he disliked Shelby, he couldn't imagine her actually shooting Alex. True she used to hunt, maybe still did, and hadn't been a bad shot. And she was cold-blooded, no doubt about that.

It just felt as if there had to be more.

Both Hud and Liza had warned him to leave town and stay out of the investigation. He couldn't, even if he wanted to. Driving past Yogamotion, he saw that the lights were out. There was a note on the door. Getting out, he walked to the door. Closed Until Further Notice.

He pulled out his cell phone and tried Shelby's house. No answer. Then he got Crystal Winslow's number from information and waited for her to pick up.

"Hello?"

"Crystal, you probably don't remember me, I'm Jordan Cardwell."

"I remember you." Her voice sounded laced with ice.

"I need to ask you something about Alex. I heard he majored in engineering at Montana State University. Is that how he made his money?"

"He was a consultant. He worked for large construction projects like bridges and highways and some smaller ones that I am only now finding out about."

He heard something in her voice, a bitterness. "Smaller jobs?"

"Apparently, he was working for Shelby Iverson and had been for years. Her husband signed the checks, but I'm betting she was behind it. He must have thought I was so stupid. What could Iverson Construction need an engineer consultant for? They build houses."

"Crystal, how often did they hire Alex?"

"Every month for years."

"Twenty years?"

"All these years." She was crying. "That bitch has been…playing my husband like a puppet on the string."

More likely it was Alex playing her. So he had been blackmailing not Shelby, but Wyatt since Tanner's death and hiding it as work-related payments. No wonder Liza hadn't found it.

As he told Crystal how sorry he was and hung up, he wondered how Wyatt had been able to hide this from

Shelby all these years. With building going crazy at Big Sky until recently, maybe it hadn't been that much of a strain on Wyatt.

He would ask Wyatt when he saw him. Which would be soon, he thought as he parked in front of the Iverson mansion on the hill. The place looked deserted. As he started to get out a big black SUV came roaring up.

WYATT IVERSON LOOKED HARRIED and dirty as if he'd just been working at one of his construction sites. He had a cut on his cheek that the blood had only recently dried on and bruises as if he'd been in a fist fight. "If you're looking for Shelby, she's not here."

"Actually, I was looking for you," Jordan said, not caring what had happened to Wyatt Iverson or his wife. "Have a minute?"

"No, I just got home. I've been out of town."

"This won't take long," Jordan said, following him up the steps to the front door and pushing past him into the large marble foyer. "I just need to know how you killed Tanner Cole. I already suspect *why* you did it, misguided as it was." Through an open doorway he saw a large bedroom with women's clothing strewn all over the bed and floor. Shelby either had trouble finding something to wear tonight or she had hightailed it out of town.

"I really don't have time for this," Wyatt said behind him.

He got as far as the living room with its white furniture he would bet no one had ever sat on, before he turned to look into the other man's face. Wyatt was magazine-model handsome, a big, muscled man, but Jordan was sure he could take him in a fair fight.

Unfortunately, when he saw the gun in Wyatt Iverson's hand, he knew he wasn't going to get a chance to find out.

"You want to know how your friend died?" Wyatt demanded. "I told him that everything was going to be all right. That he shouldn't blame himself for my father's construction equipment being vandalized. He'd already had a few drinks by the time I got to the cabin." Wyatt stopped just inches from Jordan now.

"Tanner felt horrible about what had happened, blamed himself," he continued, a smirk on his face. "I suggested we have more drinks and bury the hatchet so to speak. By the time we went out by the fire pit, he was feeling no pain. I kept plying him with booze until he could barely stand up, then I bet him he couldn't balance on an upturned log. You should have seen his expression when I put the noose around his neck."

Jordan knew the worst thing he could do was go for the gun. Wyatt had the barrel aimed at his heart and, from the trapped look in the man's eyes, he would use it if provoked. But seeing that Wyatt Iverson felt no remorse for what he'd done and realizing the man was ready to kill again, Jordan lunged at the gun.

Wyatt was stronger than he looked and clearly he'd been expecting—probably hoping—Jordan would try something. The sound of the gunshot ricocheted through the expanse of the large living room, a deafening report that was followed by a piercing pain in Jordan's shoulder.

Wyatt twisted the gun from his fingers and backhanded him with the butt. Jordan saw stars and suddenly the room started spinning. The next thing he knew he was on the floor, looking up at the man. His shoulder hurt like hell, but the bullet appeared to have only grazed his skin.

"You lousy bastard." Jordan struggled to get up, but Wyatt kicked him hard in the stomach, then knelt down beside him, holding the gun to his head.

"Your friend knew he deserved it. I told him how my old man had let his insurance on the equipment lapse, how this would destroy my family and your friend Tanner nodded and closed his eyes and I kicked the log out."

"You *murdered* him," Jordan said between clenched teeth.

"He got what he deserved."

"He didn't deserve to die because of some vandalized equipment even if he had been responsible. Shelby set up Tanner that night—from the party to the vandalism—to get back at him. It was that old story of a woman scorned."

With a start Jordan saw that this wasn't news. Wyatt had known. "How long have you known that you killed the wrong person? Then you killed Alex to keep it your little family secret and end the blackmail?"

"*Alex?* I didn't kill Alex."

Jordan started to call the man a liar. But why would he lie at a time like this when he'd already confessed to one murder? With a jolt, Jordan realized that Wyatt was telling the truth. He didn't kill Alex. *Shelby.* No wonder she'd taken off. Not only would it now come out about her vandalizing the Iverson Construction equipment, but that she'd killed Alex to keep the photographs from going public.

"Where's your wife, Iverson?" Jordan asked through the pain as Wyatt jerked him to his feet and dragged him toward the front door with the gun to his head.

"Have you known all along it was her? No? Then you must be furious. Did you catch her packing to make her getaway?" Jordan had a thought. "Does she know that you killed Tanner?"

Wyatt made a sound that sent a chill up Jordan's spine.

He thought about the cut and bruise on Iverson's cheek, that harried look in his eye—and the dirt on him as if he'd been digging at one of his construction sites. "What did you do to her?" he demanded. "You wouldn't kill your own wife!"

"One more word and I'll kill you right there," the man said as he pulled him outside to the rental car. He reached inside and released the latch on the hatchback.

"You're going to kill me anyway. But you have to know you can't get away with this." He felt the shove toward the open back of the SUV just an instant before the blow to his head. Everything went dark. His last clear thought was of Tanner and what he must have felt the moment Wyatt kicked the log out from under his feet.

LIZA CALLED HUD'S cell on her way to the Iverson house.

"How is Dana?" she asked first.

"In labor. We're at the hospital and they are making her comfortable. They're talking C-section, but you know Dana. She's determined she's going to have these babies the natural way."

"Give her my best. Did you get a chance to ask Stacy about Tanner's party?" she asked as she drove toward the mountain and the Iverson house.

"She was pretty shaken up after what happened and I got busy, but she's standing right here. I'll let you talk to her since I have to get back to Dana." He handed off the phone.

A moment later a shaky-voiced Stacy said, "Hello?"

"I need to know about the party Tanner Cole had at the Iverson Construction site twenty years ago."

"What?"

"You were there. I've seen a photograph of you standing around the campfire. I need to know who shot the photos. Come on, Stacy, it wasn't that long after that that Tanner died. Don't tell me you don't remember."

"I remember," she said, sounding defensive. "I was just trying to understand why you would ask me who took the photos. I did. It was my camera."

"*Your* camera? Why were you taking photographs at the party?"

"Jordan. I wanted to get something on him," she said. "He was always telling on me to Mother."

Blackmail, great. Liza sighed. "If it was your camera, then how is it that there's a photo of you?"

Silence then. "Alex Winslow. He wanted to borrow the camera for a moment. I made him give it back—"

"By promising to get him copies," Liza finished.

"Yes, how did you—"

"Do you still have the negatives?"

"I doubt it. Unless they're stored in my things I left here at the ranch."

"Let me talk to Jordan," Liza said, feeling as if all the pieces of the puzzle were finally coming together.

"Jordan? He's not here. He asked me who took the photos, then he left, saying he'd come by the hospital later."

"Do you know where he went?" Liza asked, suddenly worried.

"He said something about blackmail and the other side of the coin."

Ahead, Liza saw the Iverson house come into view in her headlights. "If you see him, tell him to call my cell." She gave Stacy the number, then disconnected as she pulled into the wide paved drive.

Parking, she tried Jordan's cell phone number. It went straight to voice mail. She left a message for him to call her.

The Iverson house could only be described as a mansion. But then Wyatt Iverson was in the construction business. Of course his home would have to be magnificent.

Liza got out and walked up the steps to the wide veranda. She rang the doorbell, heard classical music play inside and was reminded of Crystal Winslow's house down in Bozeman. It wasn't anywhere as large or as grand.

Liza thought about an old Elvis Presley song about a house without love. Or honesty, she thought as she rang the bell again.

Getting no answer, she checked the five-car garage. There was a large ski boat, a trailer with four snowmobiles and the large black SUV, the same one Liza had seen Wyatt Iverson driving the night of the reunion dinner.

He'd returned home. So where was he? And where was Jordan? She tried his cell phone again. As before, it went straight to voice mail.

Something was wrong. She felt it in her bones. If Wyatt Iverson had returned, where else might he have gone? She recalled overhearing Shelby say what sounded like she was going to meet someone. Was she stupid enough to agree to see her husband? If so, where would they have gone if not their house?

Yogamotion was her first thought. But she'd seen Shelby hightail it out of there. Was it possible Wyatt had taken another vehicle? She thought about Jordan. What if he'd come up here as she suspected?

She didn't want to go down that particular trail of thought. Maybe Wyatt Iverson had gone by his construction office. Unlike his father, Wyatt kept all his equipment under lock and key at a site back up Moonlight Basin.

She hurried to her rental SUV and, climbing behind the wheel, started the engine and headed for Moonlight Basin. All her instincts told her to hurry.

Chapter Sixteen

Jordan came to in darkness. He blinked, instantly aware of the pain. His wrists were bound with duct tape behind him. More duct tape bound his ankles. A strip had been placed over his mouth. He lay in the back of the rented SUV. Outside the vehicle he heard a sound he recognized and sat up, his head swimming. Something warm and sticky ran down into his left eye. Blood.

Through the blood he looked out through an array of construction equipment. He couldn't see the piece of equipment that was making all the noise, but he could see a gravel pit behind the site and catch movement.

Now seemed an odd time to be digging in a gravel pit. Unless, he thought with a start, you wanted to bury something.

Jordan knew he was lucky to be alive. He'd been a damned fool going to Iverson's house unarmed. What had he hoped to accomplish? The answer was simple. He'd wanted to hear Wyatt Iverson admit to Tanner's murder. He'd also wanted to know how he'd done it.

So he'd accomplished what he'd set out to do—a suicidal mission that had been successful if one didn't take his current predicament into consideration.

Hurriedly, he began to work at the tape on his wrists.

There were few sharp edges in the back of the SUV. Nor could he get the door open thanks to child locks. In frustration at modern advances, he threw himself into the backseat and was headed for the front seat to unlock the doors, when he heard it.

The noise of the running equipment had dropped to a low purr.

Jordan felt around quickly for a sharp edge. He found it on the metal runner of the front passenger seat and began to work frantically at the tape. Whatever Wyatt Iverson had been up to, he'd stopped. Jordan had a bad feeling that he'd be coming for him any moment.

The tape gave way. He quickly peeled the strip from his mouth then reached down to free his ankles.

The back door of the SUV swung open and he was instantly blinded by the glaring beam of a heavy-duty flashlight.

"Get out," Iverson barked.

Jordan saw that the gun was in the man's other hand and the barrel was pointed at him. He freed his ankles and did as he was told. As he stepped out, he breathed in the cold night air. It made him shiver. Or it could have been the sudden knowledge of what Iverson planned to do with him.

Standing, he could see where the earth had been dug out in a long trench. There was already one vehicle at the bottom of the trench. He recognized Shelby's expensive SUV.

"Get behind the wheel," Iverson ordered, and holding the gun on him, climbed in behind him in the backseat.

Jordan could feel the cold hard metal of the gun barrel pressed against his neck.

"Start the car." Iverson tossed him the keys.

His hand was shaking as he inserted the key. The

engine turned right over even though he was wishing for a dead battery right then.

"Now drive through the gate to the back of the property. Try anything and I'll put a bullet into your brain and jump out."

Jordan drove through the gate and down the path that led to the gravel pit and ultimately the trench Iverson had dug for Shelby—and now him. He realized there was only one thing he could do. Iverson would have him stop at the high end of the trench. He would get out and send Jordan to his death—either before he buried him at the bottom of the trench or after.

He hit the child locks so Iverson couldn't get out and gunned the engine. He would take Iverson with him, one way or the other.

As the Iverson Construction site came into view, Liza noticed that the large metal gate hung open. She cut her headlights and slowly pulled to the side of the road.

It wasn't until she shut off her engine and got out that she heard the sound of a front-end loader running in the distance. Drawing her weapon, she moved through the darkness toward the sound.

She'd just cleared the fence and most of the equipment when she saw an old red pickup parked back between some other old trucks. She could see where the right side of it was all banged up. Some of the paint of the patrol SUV was still on the side. It was definitely the pickup that had run her off the road.

Ahead she heard a car start up. She could make out movement in the faint starlight. She hurried toward it, keeping to the shadows so she wasn't spotted.

But the car didn't come in her direction as she'd

thought it would. Instead, it went the other way. In its headlights she saw the gravel pit and finally the trench and the front-end loader idling nearby.

To her amazement the vehicle engine suddenly roared. The driver headed for the trench.

Liza ran through the darkness, her heart hammering, as the vehicle careened down the slope and into the narrow ditch. She reached the fence, rushed through the gate and across the flat area next to the gravel pit in time to see the lights of the vehicle disappear into the trench.

Her mind was racing. What in the—

The sound of metal meeting metal filled the night air. She came to a skidding stop at the edge of the trough and looked down to see two vehicles. Smoke rose from between their crumpled metal, the headlights of the second one dimmed by the dirt and gravel that had fallen down around it.

She waited a moment for the driver to get out, then realizing he must be trapped in there, the trench too narrow for him to open his door, she scrambled down into the deep gully, weapon ready.

As she neared the vehicle, she recognized it. The rental SUV Jordan had been driving. Her pulse began to pound. Jordan did crazy things sometimes, she thought, remembering how he'd swum out into the river to be with her while she waited for the ambulance to arrive.

But he wouldn't purposely drive into this trench, would he? Which begged the question, where was Wyatt Iverson?

"COME ON, BABIES," Dana said under her breath and pushed.

"That's it," her doctor said. "Almost there. Just one more push."

Dana closed her eyes. She could feel Hud gripping her hand. Her first twin was about to make his or her way into the world. She felt the contraction, hard and fast, and pushed.

"It's a boy!" A cheer came up at the end of the bed. She opened her eyes and looked into the mirror positioned over the bed as the doctor held up her baby.

A moment later she heard the small, high-pitched cry of her son and tried to relax as Hud whispered that they had a perfect baby boy.

Dr. Burr placed the baby in Dana's arms for a moment. She smiled down at the crinkled adorable face before the doctor handed the baby off to the nurses standing by. "One more now. Let's see how that one's doing."

Dana could hear the baby's strong heartbeat through the monitor. She watched the doctor's face as Dr. Burr felt her abdomen first, then reached inside. Dana knew even before the doctor said the second baby was breech.

"Not to worry. I'll try to turn the little darling," the doctor assured her. "Otherwise, sometimes we can pull him out by his feet. Let's just give it a few minutes. The second baby is generally born about fifteen minutes after the first."

Dana looked over at her son now in the bassinet where a nurse was cleaning him up. "He looks like you," she said to her husband and turned to smile up at him as another contraction hit.

LIZA REACHED THE BACK of the car. She could hear movement inside. "Jordan!" she called. A moment later the back hatch clicked open and began to rise. She stepped to the side, weapon leveled at the darkness inside the SUV, cursing herself for not having her flashlight. "Jordan?"

A moan came from inside, then more movement.

"Liza, he has a gun!" Jordan cried.

The shot buzzed past her ear like a mad hornet. She ducked back, feeling helpless as she heard the struggle in the car and could do little to help. Another shot. A louder moan.

"I'm coming out," Wyatt Iverson called from inside the SUV. "I'm not armed."

"I have him covered," Jordan yelled out. "But you can shoot him if you want to."

Liza leveled her weapon at the gaping dark hole at the back of the SUV. Wyatt Iverson appeared head-first. He fell out onto the ground. She saw that he was bleeding from a head wound and also from what appeared to be a gunshot to his thigh. She quickly read him his rights as she rolled him over and snapped a pair of handcuffs on him.

"Jordan, are you all right?" she called into the vehicle. She heard movement and felt a well of relief swamp her as he stumbled out through the back. "What is going on?"

"He planned to bury me in this trench," Jordan said. "I think Shelby is in the other car. I suspect he killed her before he put her down here."

Wyatt was heaving, his face buried in his shoulder as he cried.

"Can you watch him for a moment?" Liza asked, seeing that Jordan was holding a handgun—Wyatt's, she assumed.

She holstered her own weapon and climbed up over the top of the SUV to the next one. Dirt covered most of the vehicle except the very back. She wiped some of the dirt from the window and was startled to see a face pressed against the glass.

There was duct tape over Shelby's mouth. Her eyes were huge, her face white as a ghost's. Blood stained the front of her velour sweatshirt where she'd been shot in the chest at what appeared to be close range since the fabric was burned around the entry hole.

Liza pulled out her cell and hit 911. "We'll need an ambulance and the coroner." She gave the dispatcher directions, then climbed back over the top of Jordan's rental SUV to join him again.

Wyatt was still crying. Jordan, she noticed, was more banged up than she'd first realized. He was sitting on the SUV's bumper. He looked pale and was bleeding from a shoulder wound.

"Come on, let's get out of this trench before the sides cave in and kill us all," she said. "Are you sure you're all right?"

He grinned up at her. "Just fine, Deputy," he said, getting to his feet. "I sure was glad to see you."

As she pulled Wyatt to his feet and the three of them staggered up out of the hole, she smelled the pine trees, black against the night sky. The air felt colder as if winter wasn't far behind. She looked toward Lone Peak. The snow on the top gleamed in the darkness. Everything seemed so normal.

The rifle shot took them all by surprise. Wyatt suddenly slumped forward and fell face-first into the dirt. Jordan grabbed her and knocked her to the ground behind one of the huge tires of a dump truck as a second shot thudded into Wyatt's broad back.

Liza rolled and came up with her weapon. She scrambled over to Wyatt, checked for a pulse and finding none, swore as she scrambled back over to Jordan out of the line of fire. She could hear the sound of sirens in the distance. It was too dark to tell where the shot had come from.

But over the high-pitched whine of the sirens, she heard a vehicle start up close by. "Stay here," she ordered Jordan and took off running toward her SUV.

A SECOND SON was born seventeen minutes after the first. Dana began to cry when she saw him.

"Identical twin boys," Dr. Burr told her. "Congratulations."

Hud hugged her. "We really have to quit doing this," he whispered. "I can't take it."

She laughed through her tears. No one was more fearless than her husband, but she knew what he meant. Her heart had been in her throat, afraid something would go wrong. She couldn't bear the thought of losing her babies.

"You did good," the doctor said, squeezing her hand. "Do you have names picked out yet?"

Dana shook her head and looked to Hud. "I have a couple of ideas though."

He laughed. "I'm sure you do. I'd better call everyone."

"You mean Liza," she said. "You haven't heard from her?"

He checked his phone. "No."

She could tell he was worried.

"Jordan left without telling anyone where he was going, but everyone else is out in the hall waiting for the news."

"Go do whatever it is you have to do, Marshal," she said, smiling. "But let me know when you hear from Liza—and my brother."

He grinned at her. "It's going to be so nice to have you back on your feet."

LIZA REACHED HER patrol SUV just moments after seeing a set of headlights coming out of the pines in the distance. Jordan was hot on its heels. He leaped into the passenger seat as she started the engine. She hurriedly turned around and went after the killer.

The other vehicle was moving fast. She saw the headlights come around as the vehicle hit the narrow strip of pavement, the driver almost losing control.

Liza followed the other vehicle headed down the mountain. The road was treacherous with lots of switchbacks. She had to assume whoever had killed Wyatt knew the road. But the driver was also running scared.

She glanced over at Jordan. He needed medical attention. "You should have stayed back there to wait for the ambulance," she said as she managed to keep the vehicle in front of her in sight. "Call and tell the ambulance to wait in Meadow Village. The coroner might as well wait, too."

"See, you would have missed my company if I hadn't come along," he said. "And Wyatt wasn't great company when he was alive, let alone dead."

She shot him another look, worried that he might be hurt worse than she thought. "Did he say anything about why he killed Shelby?"

"We didn't get to talk much. He knew she vandalized his father's equipment. I don't think he took it well. He swore he didn't kill Alex. But he killed Tanner and Alex has been blackmailing Wyatt for years, writing it off as a business expense."

Liza suspected that whoever had killed Alex Winslow had just killed Wyatt Iverson as well, but why? Shelby was dead. So who had just shot Wyatt?

"All of this started because Shelby was going to force

Tanner into marriage, one way or the other," Jordan said. "When he broke up with her, she vandalized the construction equipment he was responsible for to get even with him. She hadn't given a damn whose equipment it was. Ironic it turned out to be her future father-in-law's. And look where the repercussions of that one malicious act have landed us all."

The vehicle ahead swung through a tight curve, fishtailed and for a moment Liza thought the driver would lose control and crash. She could make out a figure behind the wheel, but still couldn't tell who it was. All the SUVs looked similar.

Liza knew who wasn't behind the wheel of the car in front of her. Shelby was dead. So was Malcolm Iverson and his son Wyatt. Alex had found the photographs and gotten himself killed when he'd blackmailed Shelby— her husband. She'd been so sure that Wyatt had killed Alex because of it. Alex had somehow figured out that Wyatt had killed Tanner.

Now she suspected that the last piece of the puzzle was in that SUV ahead of her. Whoever had shot Wyatt Iverson must have shot Alex. But why? Was it possible Alex had been blackmailing someone else?

Ahead she caught a glimpse of the lights of Meadow Village. She was right behind the vehicle in front of her. The driver didn't stand a chance of getting away.

She thought about the photos and tried to remember if there was anything else in them. "That one photograph," she said more to herself than to Jordan. "Wasn't it of Tanner and Tessa coming out of the woods?"

"Like I said, Shelby thought of everything."

"Including making her best friend go into the woods with Tanner?"

Jordan let out a curse. "I never could understand why Tessa did what Shelby told her to. She said Shelby even talked her into marrying Danny Spring, when apparently she has always been in love with Alex."

Liza felt a chill race up her spine. "But Alex had these photographs. He would have seen Tessa coming out of the woods with Tanner."

"What are you saying?" Jordan asked.

"Alex would have known just how far Tessa would go to protect Shelby. So why give her the photographs for safekeeping?"

"That's what I said. Unless he *wanted* her to look at the photos. But once she did, why wouldn't she destroy them to protect Shelby?"

"Because she was through protecting Shelby," Liza said. "Shelby had finally done something that she couldn't forgive. Alex's estranged wife believed Alex was having an affair with *Shelby*. I suspect Tessa thought the same thing."

"That would have been the last straw for Tessa. She would have felt betrayed by all of them."

"You're saying if Tessa found out, it would have been the last straw."

Ahead the SUV fishtailed on one of the turns and Liza had to back off to keep from hitting it.

"Tessa. She's in that car, isn't she?" Jordan said. "She used to go out shooting for target practice before hunting season with Shelby and the rest of us. She always pretended to be a worse shot than Shelby, but I always suspected she was better and just didn't dare show it. She's been hiding her light under a bushel for years, as my mother used to say."

"Not anymore," Liza said as the vehicle ahead of

them went off the road on the last tight turn. It crashed down into the trees. Liza stood on the brakes. "Stay here or I'll arrest you!" she shouted to Jordan and jumped out.

With her weapon drawn she hurried to where the SUV had gone off. She hadn't gone far when she heard the shot.

Liza scrambled down into the trees, keeping out of the driver's sights until she finally reached the back of the vehicle. She saw that just as she'd suspected, Tessa was behind the wheel. There was a rifle next to her, the barrel pointed at her. She was bleeding heavily from the crash and the gunshot wound to her side, but she was still breathing.

Liza quickly called for the ambulance. "Just stay still," she told Tessa. "Help is on the way."

Tessa managed a smile. "There is no help for me. Is Wyatt dead?"

"Yes."

"And Shelby?"

"She's dead, too."

Tessa nodded. "Good. They all ruined my life."

"Why kill Alex, though?" Liza asked. "I thought you loved him?"

Tessa got a faraway look in her eyes. "Alex was the only man I ever really loved. I thought he loved me but he was only using me. He said he forgave me for the past, but he lied. He used me just like Shelby and Wyatt used me." She smiled sadly. "They all used me. But I showed them. I wasn't as good at playing their games, but I was always a better shot than any of them."

Epilogue

The hospital room was packed with well-wishers, flowers, balloons and stuffed animals. Dana looked around her and couldn't help the swell of emotion that bubbled up inside of her.

"It's the hormones," she said as she wiped her eyes.

Clay and Stacy had brought Hank and Mary to the hospital to see their new little brothers.

"Hank wants to name them after his horses," Stacy told her. "Mary wanted to name them after her dolls." Stacy looked stronger. Hud had promised her that Virgil would never bother her again. Apparently, there were numerous warrants out on him, including the fact that he'd broken his probation. So added to the latest charges, Virgil would be going back to prison for a very long time.

Dana watched her elderly ranch manager make his way through the crowd to her. Warren Fitzpatrick was as dried out as a stick of jerky and just as tough, but he knew more about cattle than any man she'd ever known. He'd also been there for her from the beginning. As far as she was concerned he was a permanent fixture on the Cardwell Ranch. She'd already promised him a spot in the family cemetery up on the hill.

He gave her a wink. "That's some cute little ones. I just had a peek at them down the hall. Goin' to make some fine ranchhands," he said with a chuckle. "I've got a couple of fine saddles picked out for them. Never too early for a man to have his own saddle."

She smiled up at him. It was the first time she'd ever seen a tear in his eye.

Her father arrived then with a giant teddy bear. "How's my baby girl?" he asked. She'd always been his baby girl—even now that she was the mother of four and only a few years from forty.

"I'm good," she said as she leaned up to hug him. He put the bear down and hugged her tighter than usual.

"I was worried about you," he whispered.

"I'm fine."

"Yes, you are," he said, smiling at her.

Then Uncle Harlan came in with the second giant teddy bear and her father grinned, knowing that she'd thought he'd forgotten she was having twins.

Her father-in-law called. Brick Savage had been sick for some time, but he promised to make the trip down from his cabin outside West Yellowstone to see his new grandsons soon.

"I think we should all leave and let her get some rest," Hilde said to the crowd of friends and family.

"I agree," Hud said. He looked exhausted and so did Liza, who'd stopped in earlier. It had been a shock to hear about the deaths up on the mountain and Tessa Ryerson Spring's involvement. Tessa had died before the ambulance got to her.

Jordan had stopped by earlier, his shoulder bandaged. Dana had hugged him for a long time after hearing what he'd been through. Both he and Liza were lucky to be alive.

Dana noticed that they had left together. She smiled to herself. There was nothing like seeing two people falling in love.

Now as everyone said their goodbyes with Stacy and Clay taking Hank and Mary home, she finally relaxed. Everything was turning out just fine. Stacy had her baby—and a job working for Hilde at Needles and Pins.

"I want to stay around, if that's all right," her sister had said. "I want Ella to know her cousins."

Dana couldn't have been happier. Clay, though, said he would be returning to Hollywood, but that he would come visit more often.

And Jordan, well, Liza was right. Jordan *had* changed. Love did that to a man, she thought, studying her own husband as he came back into the room pushing two bassinets.

"I thought you'd like to see your sons," he said. "Isn't it time you told me what names you've picked out? I know you, Dana. Or do you want me to guess?"

She merely smiled at him.

Hud laughed and shook his head. "You do realize what you're doing to these two innocent little boys by naming them after our fathers, don't you?"

Dana nodded. "I'm giving them a little bit of family history. It isn't just about the ranch. It's about the lives we've carved out here."

Hud looked into the bassinets. "Angus?" he asked as he picked up one of their sons. "And Brick?" He handed her both infants. "So when is the building going to start on the new house?" he asked as he climbed up in the bed beside her and the babies.

"What new house?"

"Jordan's. You know he's staying."

"Did he tell you that?" she asked, unable to keep the hope out of her voice.

Hud gave her a disbelieving look. "You know darned well he is. I wouldn't be surprised if you haven't already picked out a spot on the ranch for him and Liza to live."

"You're taking this pretty well," Dana noted.

He chuckled at that. "Your mother always said Jordan would be back. Stacy, though, I think even that would have surprised your mother."

Dana nodded. "Mom did know her children. She always knew that one day you and I would be together. Mary Justice Cardwell was one smart woman."

"So is her youngest daughter," he said and kissed her.

LIZA REINED IN HER HORSE and looked out over the canyon. The day was warm and dry, possibly one of the last before winter set in. A light breeze stirred the fallen aspen leaves and sighed through the pine boughs.

Jordan brought his horse up beside hers.

"It's beautiful, isn't it?" she said.

"Yes. Beautiful."

She heard something in his voice and looked over at him. He was grinning at her and not looking at the view at all.

"She is *very* beautiful."

"You know you can't charm me," she said, embarrassed. No one had ever told her she was beautiful before. Cute, maybe. Unusual, often. But not beautiful. It wasn't even the word that warmed her to the toes of her boots, though. It was the way he looked at her. He made her *feel* beautiful.

She thought of the scars she'd carried since high school. This case had brought back those awful years, worse, those awful feelings about herself. It had also brought Jordan back to the canyon, a surprise in so many ways.

"You think I'm trying to charm you?" He chuckled as he swung down from his horse.

Before she knew what was happening, he cupped her waist with his large hands and pulled her off her horse and into his arms.

"No, Miss Turner, quite the opposite," he said, his lips just a breath away from hers. "You're the one who's charmed me. All I think about is you. You're like no one I've ever known. I'm under your spell."

She shook her head and laughed softly.

"I'm serious, Liza. You have me thinking crazy thoughts."

"Is that right?"

"Oh, yeah. I've been thinking that I want to stay here and work the ranch with my sister. How crazy is that? Worse, right now, I'm thinking there is only one thing that could make this day more perfect."

She grinned at him. "I'm afraid to ask."

"I'm the one who is afraid to ask." He dropped to one knee. "Marry me and make an honest man out of me."

"Jordan—"

"I know this seems sudden. We should probably at least go on a real date where I'm not just another one of your suspects."

"Be serious."

"I am. I've fallen hopelessly in love with you. Say you at least like me a little." Jordan looked into her wide green eyes and thought he might drown in them. "Just a little?"

"I like you."

He grinned.

"A lot. But marriage?"

"Yes, marriage because I'm not letting you get away, Deputy, and I can't stand to spend another day away from you. I'd marry you right now, but we both know that my sister Dana isn't going to allow it. She's going to insist on a big wedding at the ranch. But that will give us time to go on a few dates. So what do you say?"

Liza's laugh was a joyous sound. "What can I say but yes."

He laughed and swung her up into his arms, spinning them both around. As he set her down, he kissed her, then he drew back to look into her lovely face. Their gazes locked. Electricity arced between them, hotter than any flame.

"I suppose we should wait until our wedding night," he said ruefully.

"Not a chance," Liza said, putting her arms around him. "I can think of no place more wonderful to make love to you the first time than up here on this mountain."

THE WEDDING OF JORDAN CARDWELL and Liza Turner was a glorious affair. Hud and Clay gave Liza away, and stood up with Jordan. Hilde and Dana were Liza's attendants. Hilde had made Liza's dress, a simple white sheath that made her feel like a princess.

The ceremony was short and sweet and held in the large house on the ranch. Stacy baked the wedding cake and the kids helped decorate it. There were balloons and flowers and music. Jordan's father and uncle came with their band to play old-fashioned Country-Western music for the affair.

Neighbors and friends stopped throughout the day to offer felicitations. Even Brick showed up to congratulate them on their wedding and Liza on solving the Tanner Cole case.

The murders and deaths had rocked the small community. Only a few people knew the story behind them and the twisted motives of those involved.

Fall and winter had come and gone. Jordan had been right about Dana insisting on a big wedding. It was spring now. The canyon was turning green from the tall grass on the ranch to the bright leaves on the aspen trees. Work had begun on a ranch house up in the hills from the main house for the two of them.

Liza had never been so happy. She had loved this family even before she fell in love with Jordan. Now she was a part of it. Raised as an orphan, she'd never known this kind of family. Or this kind of love.

Construction on their house on the ranch wasn't quite done, but would be soon. In the meantime, the two of them had been staying in Liza's condo and dating.

Jordan had insisted on a honeymoon. "Hawaii? Tahiti? Mexico? You name it," he'd said.

But Liza didn't want to leave Montana. "Surprise me," she'd said. "Wherever you take me will be perfect."

"How did I get so lucky?" he asked and kissed her as they left in a hail of birdseed.

She had no idea where they were going. She didn't care. With Jordan she knew it would always be an adventure.

* * * * *

YOU HAVE
JUST READ A
HARLEQUIN®
INTRIGUE®
BOOK

If you were **captivated** by the **gripping, page-turning romantic suspense,** be sure to look for all six Harlequin® Intrigue® books every month.

SPECIAL EXCERPT FROM

HQN™

Read on for a sneak preview of
Just His Luck *by B.J. Daniels.*

Another scream rose in her throat as the icy water rushed in around her. She fought to free herself, but the ropes that bound her wrists to the steering wheel held tight, chafing her skin until it tore and bled. Her throat was raw from screaming, while outside the car, the wind kicked up whitecaps on the pond. The waves lapped at the windows. Inside the car, water rose around her feet, before climbing up her legs to lap at her waist.

She pleaded for help as the water began to rise up to her chest. But anyone who might have helped her was back at the high school graduation party she'd just left. If only she'd stayed at the party. If only she hadn't burned so many bridges earlier tonight. If only…

As the water lapped against her throat, she screamed even though she knew no one was coming to her rescue. Certainly not the person standing on the shore watching.

The pond was outside of town, away from everything. She knew now that was why her killer had chosen it. Worse, no one would be looking for her, not after the way she'd behaved when she'd left the party.

"You're big on torturing people," her killer had said. "Not so much fun when the shoe is on the other foot, huh?"

More than half-drunk, the bitter taste of betrayal in her mouth, she'd wanted to beg for her life. But her pride wouldn't let her. As her hands were bound to the steering wheel, she tried to convince herself that the only reason this was happening was to scare her. No one would actually kill her. Not even someone she'd bullied at school.

She was Ariel Matheson. Everyone wanted to be her friend. Everyone wanted to be her, sexy spoiled rich girl. No one hated her enough to go through with this. Even when the car had been pushed into the pond, she told herself that her new baby blue SUV wouldn't sink. Or if it did, the water wouldn't be deep enough that she'd drown.

The dank water splashed into her face. Frantic, she tried to sit up higher, but the seat belt and the rope on her wrists held her down. The car lurched under her as it wallowed almost full of water on the rough surface of the pond. Waves washed over the windshield, obscuring the lights of Whitefish, Montana, as the SUV slowly began to sink and she felt the last few minutes of her life slipping away.

She spit out a mouthful and told herself that this wasn't happening. Things like this didn't happen to her. This was not the way her life would end. It couldn't be.

Panic made her suck in another mouthful of awful-tasting water. She tried to hold her breath as she told herself that she was destined for so much more. The girl most likely to end up with everything she wanted, it said in her yearbook.

Bubbles rose around her as the car filled to the headliner, forcing her to let out the breath she'd been holding. This was real. This wasn't just to scare her.

The last thing she saw before the SUV sank the rest of the way was her killer standing on the bank in the dark night, watching her die. Would anyone miss her? Mourn her? She'd made so many enemies. Would anyone even come looking for her in the days ahead? Her parents would think that she'd run away. Her friends…

Fury replaced her fear. They thought she was a bitch before? As water filled her lungs, she swore that if she had it to do over, she'd make them all pay.

Don't miss
Just His Luck *by B.J. Daniels,*
available September 2019 wherever
Harlequin® books and ebooks are sold.

www.Harlequin.com